THE BRITANNIA CONSPIRACY

PETER C. MIDDLETON

Let me ask you a question.

If in the heat of battle I gave you a weapon that destroyed only the wicked, would you fear to use it in case it destroyed you and not your adversaries?

If you'd hesitate, even for a moment, go home and carefully re-evaluate yourself and those you would call your enemies.

The Guardian, AD61

A Britannia Publication

BRITANNIA

Published by Britannia Publications, 2014
14 Crown Woods Way. London. SE9 2NN
www.britanniapublications.com

ISBN: 978-0-9928902-6-1

A CIP catalogue record for this book is available from The British Library.

Printed by CreateSpace, An Amazon.com Company

Cover design by: Ilian Georgiev
Ebookadvisor.net

To Debra, Gareth, Samuel, Emily and Lucinda.
My family, my life.

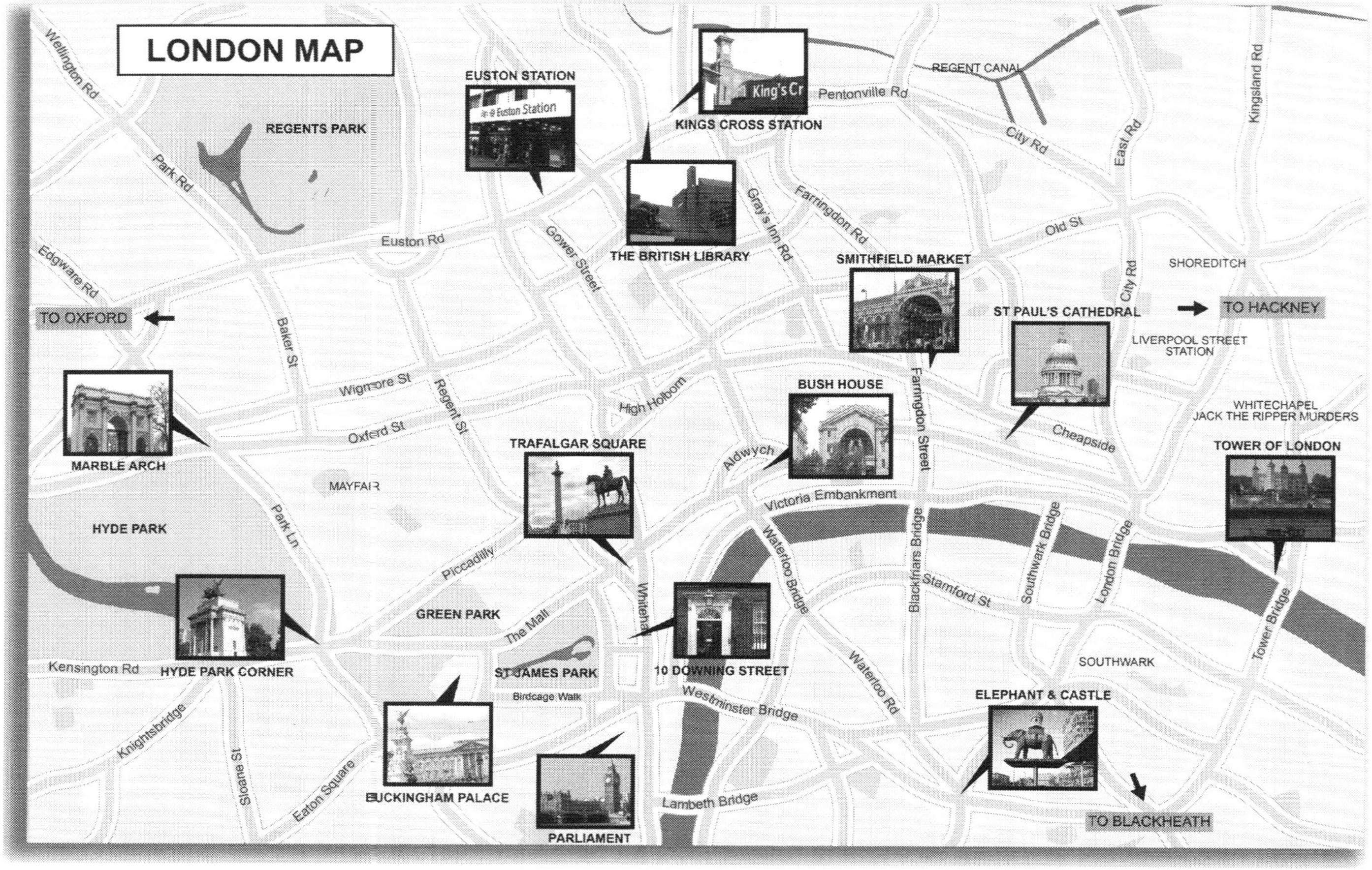
LONDON MAP
REGENTS PARK
EUSTON STATION
KINGS CROSS STATION
King's Cr
Pentonville Rd
REGENT CANAL
City Rd
East Rd
Kingsland Rd
Wellington Rd
Park Rd
Euston Rd
Gower Street
THE BRITISH LIBRARY
Gray's Inn Rd
Farringdon Rd
Old St
SHOREDITCH
Edgware Rd
TO OXFORD
Baker St
SMITHFIELD MARKET
ST PAUL'S CATHEDRAL
TO HACKNEY
LIVERPOOL STREET STATION
MARBLE ARCH
Wigmore St
Regent St
High Holborn
Oxford St
BUSH HOUSE
Farringdon Street
WHITECHAPEL
JACK THE RIPPER MURDERS
Cheapside
TOWER OF LONDON
MAYFAIR
TRAFALGAR SQUARE
Aldwych
Victoria Embankment
HYDE PARK
Park Ln
Piccadilly
Waterloo Bridge
Blackfriars Bridge
Southwark Bridge
London Bridge
Stamford St
GREEN PARK
The Mall
Whitehall
10 DOWNING STREET
Tower Bridge
Kensington Rd
HYDE PARK CORNER
ST JAMES PARK
Birdcage Walk
Westminster Bridge
Waterloo Rd
SOUTHWARK
ELEPHANT & CASTLE
Knightsbridge
Sloane St
Eaton Square
BUCKINGHAM PALACE
PARLIAMENT
Lambeth Bridge
TO BLACKHEATH

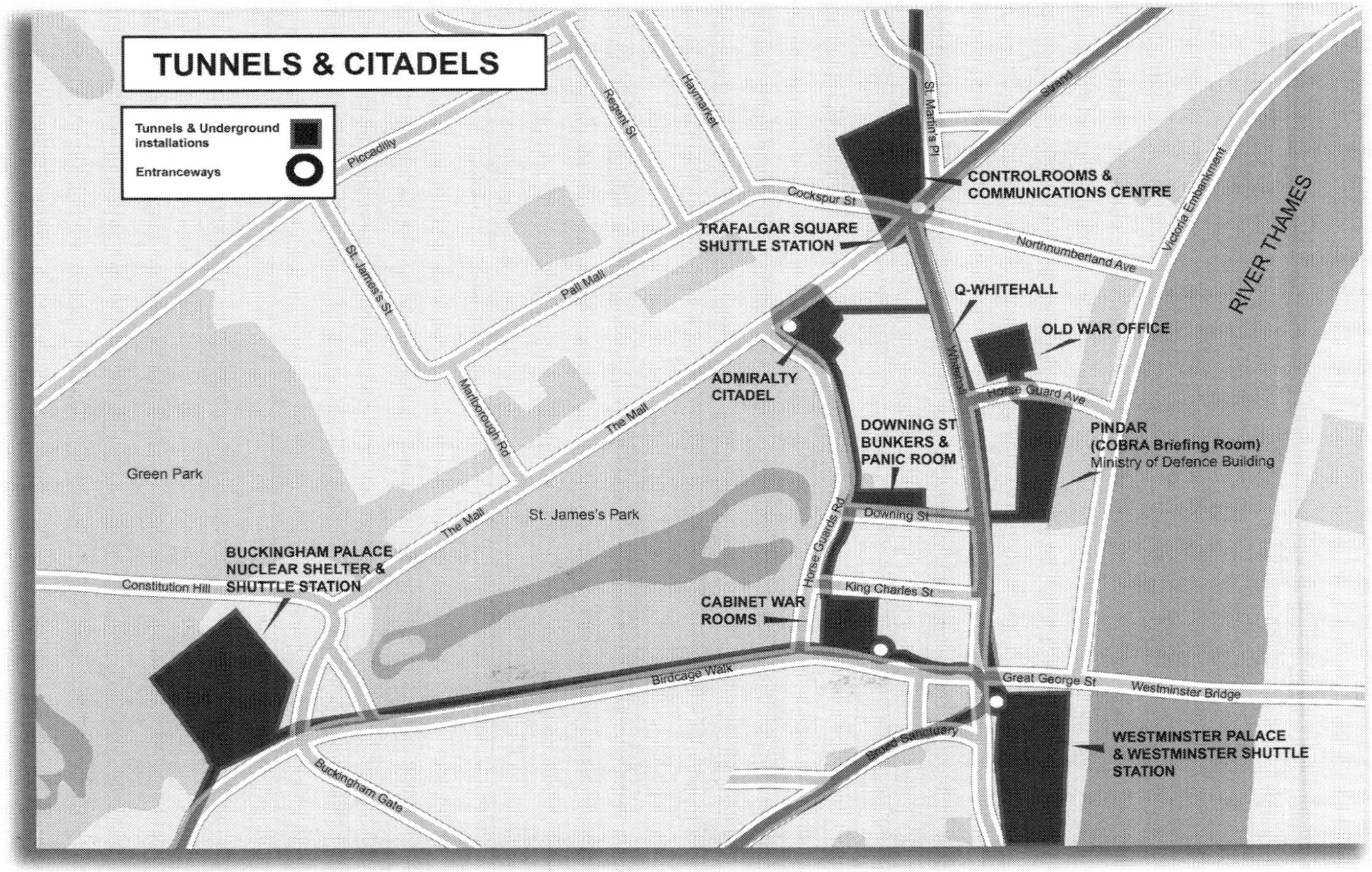
TUNNELS & CITADELS
Tunnels & Underground installations
Entranceways
Piccadilly
Regent St
Haymarket
St. Martin's Pl
Strand
CONTROLROOMS & COMMUNICATIONS CENTRE
Cockspur St
TRAFALGAR SQUARE SHUTTLE STATION
Northumberland Ave
Victoria Embankment
RIVER THAMES
St. James's St
Pall Mall
Q-WHITEHALL
OLD WAR OFFICE
Whitehall
Horse Guard Ave
ADMIRALTY CITADEL
Marlborough Rd
The Mall
DOWNING ST BUNKERS & PANIC ROOM
PINDAR
(COBRA Briefing Room)
Ministry of Defence Building
Green Park
St. James's Park
Downing St
BUCKINGHAM PALACE NUCLEAR SHELTER & SHUTTLE STATION
Horse Guards Rd
Constitution Hill
King Charles St
CABINET WAR ROOMS
Birdcage Walk
Great George St
Westminster Bridge
Broad Sanctuary
WESTMINSTER PALACE & WESTMINSTER SHUTTLE STATION
Buckingham Gate

Preface

Present Day. You may think that you know the history of Britain, but actually you don't. You know a version of history manufactured to protect you from the truth, but now that the dead are marching through your streets I may as well tell you everything, especially as today may well be the last day of your life.

I know the truth. I know the real history, because I have been here to observe it, ever since I was appointed as Guardian of this island over 2,000 years ago. I have lived through your wars and plagues, through reformation, exploration and revolution. I have met most of your kings and queens, your heroes and villains and I've played no small part in protecting this nation against those who would invade or destroy it.

I have witnessed the constant struggle between good and evil, which has been waged on these shores, and have done all I could to protect you from knowing what lies beneath us and what lurks in the shadows of the night. Whenever evil has surfaced I have fought, with a select few, to drive it back to hell before it shattered your peaceful, ignorant lives.

Today, however, I can no longer hide you from the truth, evil has arrived on a scale we thought unimaginable and for now it cannot be controlled or contained.

You are scared right now, more frightened than you have ever been before, I understand that. The horrors that you thought only existed in legend or fiction are now forcing their way into your homes. The streets are full of the dead and dying and worse is to come…

You can try to hide, but they will find you. You can get into your car and try to leave the city, but by now they will have blockaded the main arterial roads and all of the backstreets are impassable. However far you travel, it will not be far enough, unless we can find a way to destroy them.

Your reality has been torn apart, and the challenges you have faced before, however big, have in the last few hours proven to be insignificant.

If you survive you will be changed forever, you will cling to your God and one another like never before. You will forget the differences in politics, race and religion that have so unnecessarily divided you, and you will at last be united by a common enemy that is now all too real, all too terrifying.

So if you are alive tomorrow, the very thing that is trying to destroy you may ironically have saved you.

But first we have to get through today…

In these pages, dear reader, I will tell you the truth, so at least, if you die today, you will not die in ignorance.

The Guardian

Chapter 1

5.00am. The first to leave London were the rats.

It's rumoured that wherever you stand in the capital, they're never more than three feet away. No one really believed that, until they began to rise.

Hundreds of thousands of the diseased rodents poured out of the sewers, the drains, the underground stations and cellars. Thousands more emerged from the embankments and streamed across the muddy shores of the River Thames until their numbers became so great they were forced to take flight in the river itself.

Rats were usually fearless, content to live under our feet feeding on our leftovers, which kept them fat and thriving. Not even the cats scared them anymore; after all, they outnumbered them one thousand to one!

But today was different; today they all felt a common fear that was so intense their survival instinct drove them from the City. In their hurry to escape they clawed over one another and ran blindly under the wheels of London's early morning commuter traffic.

As the cars, taxis and buses began to pour in, the rats were pouring out. Vehicles began to pull over and their drivers stared with awe, as the black tarmac became a sea of writhing fur.

No one was brave enough to leave their vehicles; even the die-hard London cabbies began to sense the fear arising within them, the very same fear that had caused this rodent exodus.

The next to flee were the dogs. Most had been aroused from their sleep as the ice-cold fingers of fear clawed through their coats. They began to bark loudly to alert their masters but their loyalty ended there, and they ran to escape the oncoming doom, leaving their providers to fend for themselves.

Larger dogs that could not find an exit from their homes bloodied themselves running at windows and doors until they broke free or collapsed from exhaustion.

Smaller breeds that were hopelessly trapped, began to cower close to their masters whimpering continuously, begging for help.

The cats came next, the domestic and feral running side by side. Despite the roads being full of old, injured and dead rodents, easy prey in better times, the cats just kept running with only one thought on their mind; to escape the horror that was coming.

The mighty stags in Richmond Park rose from their sleep, looked momentarily towards the City then turned and bolted, calling for the herd to follow them. They charged through the gates, ignoring the cattle grids that served to keep them in the park.

The quickest deer were maimed as their feet fell into the gaps between the metal bars and their legs and ankles snapped from the forward momentum on their run and from the animals pushing from behind. As they fell they became the platform over which the rest of the herd trampled forward, cracking bone and tearing flesh as they passed in a frenzied panic to escape.

Chapter 2

6.00am. The Dean of St Paul's entered the cathedral through a small entrance to the left of the Great West door and walked briskly along the nave, taking in the breathtaking view of this magnificent stone edifice. As always he was the first to arrive. When he reached the south transept he began to ascend the 530 steps that led to the summit of the cathedral's iconic dome, second only in size to St. Peter's Basilica in Rome.

It was something he did at this time every morning since the death of his wife. It has to be said that climbing these stairs at his age was a struggle, but it just had to be done.

There were, of course, the health benefits. While many of his fellow clergymen had expanding waistlines and failing hearts, he was trim and remarkably fit - but that was not his main motivation.

The Dean believed that every upward step brought him that little bit closer to the woman who had taught him how to love and be loved. This was his daily pilgrimage, thirty minutes alone with his wife, and the rest of the day to tend to his flock.

After 259 steps he reached the whispering gallery, which ran around the dome's interior. It gained its name because a whisper made on one side of the gallery will travel along the walls and be heard by someone on the opposite side, some 42 metres away.

Here, the Dean began to quietly sing. He knew he had a terrible voice, but he thought the acoustic properties of the inner dome actually, made him sound quite heavenly! While most people sang in the shower, the Dean enjoyed singing here. He was often tempted to try something other than a hymn, maybe the Beatles or even Meat Loaf, but he could not bring himself to do so in God's house.

He then walked around this gallery to the opposite doorway and climbed another 119 steps up a narrow, circular stone staircase, never once taking advantage of the benches that provided rest for the weary on every landing. When he reached the top he unlocked and pushed open a large wooden door emerging out onto the Stone Gallery, a narrow balcony, which ran above the colonnade at the

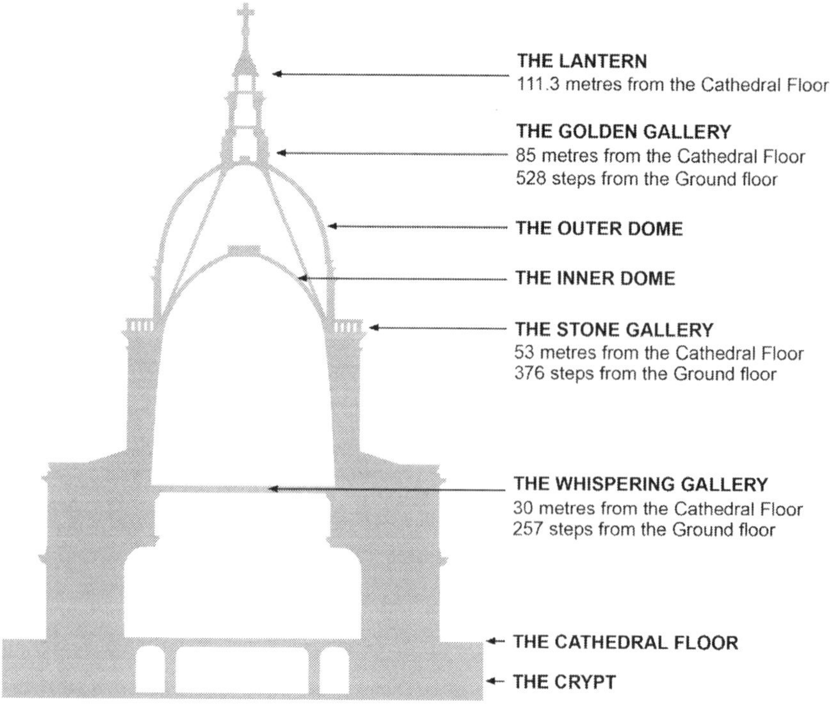

dome's base.

The cold morning air made him shiver. It was the middle of August and the weather forecasters had predicted a glorious sunny morning, but the skies were strangely overcast and there was an unnatural, eerie silence pervading the air. It was as if London had failed to wake and the birds were refusing to sing their dawn chorus. Something was wrong, very wrong.

He ran up a few more steps and hastily unlocked the door that took him into the space between the inner dome, seen from the floor of the cathedral and the much larger outer dome that had dominated the London landscape for the last 300 years. Once inside, he ran up the tall, twisting metal staircase, emerging breathlessly onto the even narrower Golden Gallery. This balcony encircles the huge stone lantern that sits majestically at the very top of the dome. The view of London from here is usually magnificent, especially during the summer, but today it was dark and foreboding.

From here the clouds seemed even darker than before and they seemed to be frantically swirling above him rather than passing gracefully across the sky.

As his eyes grew accustomed to the light he saw that it was not clouds at all, but a dense flock of birds that continually circled the dome growing rapidly in number. Then suddenly, they flew off to the west like a great dragon that had been driven from its lair.

He glanced northward toward Smithfield Market, his heart pounding in his chest. Suddenly the fear began to rise until it almost choked him.

He imagined that it might be because he was staring at a site of butchery. After all this was the home of the world famous meat market where livestock had been slaughtered over hundreds of years in underground tunnels and then brought up to be sold as fresh cuts of meat to London's butchers and restaurants.

Smithfield was also the scene of many public executions over the years including William "Braveheart" Wallace, who led the war for Scottish independence in 1305 and Wat Tyler the leader of the 1381 peasant's revolt. It was also the site of the burning of many Protestant reformers in the 16th century, to whom the Dean owed a great debt.

He had looked upon Smithfield's many times but he had never felt the dread that he experienced today. It was as if something was beginning to stir deep beneath the market floor.

His eyes were then drawn to the east from where he saw dark clouds spreading and spiraling across the sky as if the hand of evil was being extended towards him to take away his very soul. He felt incredibly alone. It was a sensation he had never felt before, because of his faith in God, and even when his wife Martha had died he knew there was someone by his side.

A terrifying thought then occurred to him: Was he feeling alone because God was no longer there to watch over him? Had God turned his gaze from mankind for the first time since we murdered his son, and if so why had he forsaken us? He wondered whether this could possibly be true. When the earth began to tremor he had no doubt...

As the church bells across London's East End began to sway in their stone towers chiming simultaneously in a deafening cacophony, he thought it an appropriate soundtrack to the doom that was approaching. Then, in the distance, to his abject horror he saw a flash of blinding light and the walls of the Tower of London began to crumble and fall.

Chapter 3

6.00am. John Brody had been an assistant harbour master on the River Thames for over twenty years, amongst other things. Although he claimed to be in his early forties, his face was ruddy and weathered and his hair and stubble had turned prematurely white earning him the nickname of 'Captain Birdseye' amongst his colleagues.

His employer was the Port of London Authority and it was his job to keep commercial and leisure users safe on his river which he knew better than the back of his hand. He was also charged with looking out for environmental threats such as illegal waste disposal. After all the Thames already had to cope with 39 million cubic tons of raw sewage legally dumped into the river each year! He was also looking for other threats to London, men and women who thrived on terror.

He captained a brand new catamaran called the "Kew" which had been brought to patrol the river during the 2012 Olympic games at a cost of over £500,000. He had proudly piloted the craft during the river pageant that marked the Queens Diamond Jubilee. He considered that to be the highlight of his, up to now, reasonably uneventful career, even though it had been freezing cold and pouring down with rain then.

As he pulled away from Greenwich Pier for a routine early morning inspection of the river between the Millennium Dome and Waterloo Bridge, he immediately noticed the silence. Even at this early hour he expected to hear the constant cry of gulls, especially at low tide, but they were nowhere to be seen.

His 13.5 metre launch was powered by two 200bhp John Deere marine diesel engines and was quite capable of reaching speeds in excess of 20 knots, but with an 8 knot speed limit on the river. John hoped for an emergency as it was the only time he was permitted to travel at full throttle. He would not be disappointed.

6.00am. Stan had been a Yeoman Warder at the Tower of London for many years; at 54 he was the oldest of the famous Beefeaters, and only one week from retirement. He knew that he was little more than a tourist attraction, but he didn't care; he was an old soldier, quite literally, having served 22 years in the Army, and he was pleased to serve his country in any way he could.

He was barracked in the Tower itself with the other Beefeaters, up to 30 serving soldiers and a small security team. Between them they had the responsibility of guarding the Tower and, most importantly, the Crown Jewels.

His shift started at 5am and it would be his job to carry out an inspection of the grounds before unlocking the great gates and welcoming the thousands of tourists who visited every day.

His jolly countenance was well known, and he was loved by everyone who worked there.

On this particular morning however, he didn't feel so jolly, in fact when he had kissed his wife goodbye, as he had done every morning for the last 31 years, he gave her an exceptionally warm hug and, with tears in his eyes, he told her how much he loved her. Sylvia was quite taken aback, as Stan rarely exhibited such emotion. She was also more than a little concerned.

As he waved goodbye he somehow knew he would never see her again and the thought terrified him. He wanted to stay with her and make the most of whatever time they had left together but duty called, and for a soldier, duty came first.

As he walked into the courtyard he was shaken out of his darkest thoughts by the panicked shouts of one of his colleagues on the other side.

"They've gone… they've all gone."

"What are you on about, Jimmy?"

"The bloody ravens. They've all gone. Every single one of them"

Stan had never seen his friend quite so distressed. Then he suddenly understood why there was so much anguish in the raven keepers voice. "You don't believe the legend do you?" asked Stan. "That when the ravens fly away the Tower will crumble and the monarchy will fall."

"Course not, it's a load of crap!" Jimmy shouted unconvincingly, "Don't tell me you believe all that superstitious bullsh--."

Before he could finish his sentence, a huge explosion behind him finished his life. Stan stared in disbelief as his friend was blown apart in front of his eyes.

The shockwave lifted Stan off his feet and threw him to the ground as the imposing White Tower, the oldest structure in the castle with its signature four turrets, began to fall before him. He got to his feet and ran as fast as he could in his heavy ceremonial Tudor coat. He had travelled only a couple of metres when a tumbling piece of masonry, that had been previously undisturbed since the reign of William the Conqueror, crushed his skull.

Chapter 4

6.00am. Sam Callaghan had risen early and sped into London in his pride and joy, an e-type Jag lovingly restored to mint condition with golden metallic paintwork and low-profile tyres.

It had been bought at a Pinewood Studios auction in the late sixties, by his father, an avid James Bond fan. It was about to be used in *Goldfinger* but was replaced at the last minute with the DB5 when Aston Martin outbid Jaguar with a lucrative sponsorship deal, that the producers couldn't refuse.

Sam had rescued it from gathering dust in his father's garage and returned it to its former glory. This unique vehicle had been given several modifications courtesy of Pinewood's special effects and stunt teams. The bulletproof windows were genuine and the frame was reinforced with roll bars. The boot still contained a small oil tank designed to release its content on the road and slow down any pursuers and a compressed air tank that was to be used to flip the car at the end of a dramatic car chase, just as they had done with the chariots in *Ben Hur*.

It was totally impractical to have all this junk in the trunk, which on an e-type is tiny anyway, but Sam felt that the car had never had a chance to show what it could do and removing it would be almost sacrilegious, like removing a woman's womb before she'd had a chance to bear children.

As he had to commute from Chelmsford to London every morning, he always left his flat at 5am. This ensured that he would miss the rush hour traffic and the ridiculous congestion charge. It also meant he was guaranteed a car parking space and an hour in the gym before starting work.

Sam loved his job. Ever since he was 6 years old and started watching James Bond films with his dad, he had wanted to work for British intelligence. He would spend hours playing spy games with his friends and before he went to bed he loved to recreate James Bond poses in front of a full-length mirror in his bedroom.

At 12 years old, to the horror of his mother, his dad brought him an air pistol and a box of paper targets. He would practice every evening when he got home from school until he could hit the bull's eye from a holster draw every single time. He even practiced his night shooting from his bedroom window by firing at any fox, cat or badger that had been unfortunate enough to wander into his back garden.

At 14, he started his own conspiracy theory blog called "Believe No 1". Although most people interpreted the title as "Believe no-one" Sam was actually referring to himself as "Number One", a sure indication of his complete lack of humility.

It was this blog that first brought him to the attention of MI5, not just because he had used many keywords that had triggered the agencies' web crawlers, but also because his assessments were just too damn accurate for their liking. In particular, his suppositions surrounding the death of Princess Diana made them feel extremely uncomfortable.

At 16, he was excelling at school, getting twelve A-stars for his GCSEs without even trying. He was also excelling with the ladies especially as he had memorised every one of James Bond's chat-up lines and used them frequently. They were, of course, exceptionally cheesy but when delivered with an uncanny impression of the relevant actor, they proved to be irresistible.

Sam also benefitted from his looks, which his friends told

him resembled the love child of Brad Pitt and David Beckham.

At 18, despite the many distractions that stopped him revising, he managed to get 'A' grades for all five A-levels and was accepted into Oxford University. There he studied Classical Archaeology and Ancient History under Professor Alexander Ackerman. Sam and Ackerman quickly became good friends; he even started dating the professor's 19-year-old daughter Lucinda!

By now his blog had over three million followers, mostly avid conspiracy theorists, but also key members of MI5, MI6, GCHQ, the CIA and almost every intelligence agency in the world.

When he wrote a scathing exposé of the United States operations in the Middle East, the CIA demanded he be stopped. Thankfully for Sam, the Director of MI5 was extremely impressed with his writing and shared his distrust of their so-called allies. Therefore instead of Sam suffering an unfortunate accident - like Dr. David Kelly's. He was instead recruited into MI5 and made to sign the Official Secrets Act. This meant no more blogging and no more social media of any kind.

Sam's plan had worked perfectly and his hours of meticulous research and the liberal use of trigger words in his blog had paid massive dividends.

He was allowed to finish his degree and on July 12th, 2014 he was enrolled on the Intelligence Officer Development Program bypassing the highly competitive and time-consuming selection process.

As he drove west along the Victoria Embankment on the north bank of the Thames, he thought about Lucinda. He always thought about Lucinda, the girl he loved and tragically lost while still at university.

He was reminiscing about their last night together when his thoughts were interrupted by a sea of rats, which started to appear on the road in front of him.

At first there were just a few, then their numbers grew and grew until a sea of writhing rodents completely surrounded the car, making it difficult to drive as he crushed them beneath his wheels.

Then he heard a distant explosion behind him and within seconds, his car suddenly pulled violently to the left and then to the right. As he struggled to gain control of his vehicle, the buildings around him began to shudder. His first thought was that they must have missed some important intelligence on a terrorist attack; his final thought was what he should do to avoid the hotel that was collapsing before him.

Chapter 5

6.05am. John had never seen anything so sickening even though he had pulled many bodies from the river, some of which had surfaced after days of bloating and rotting on the riverbed.

Suicides were almost an everyday occurrence on the Thames, as the desperate took their last leap from one of London's twelve public bridges, and London gangs often used the river to dispose of their victims, often dismembered and deposited in black rubbish bags.

He had even had the distressing task of pulling students' bodies from the water when the "pleasure" boat, Marchioness, collided with the dredger, Bowbelle, killing fifty-one in the summer of '89. John had seen it all, but nothing had prepared him for the scene unfolding around him.

He had just passed under the expanse of Tower Bridge when he saw millions of rats pouring from Traitors' Gate, the river entrance to the Tower of London. They ran across the muddy flats and into the river, frantically swimming for survival. His eyes were then drawn to the walkway above where he saw a huge man dressed as a Roman centurion staring malevolently right at him.

Even at a distance he could see the evil in the centurion's

eyes, which stared at him without blinking. As the boat passed nearer he could see why – his eyelids had been savagely removed.

John was so mesmerized by the man's appearance that he momentarily lost all sense of his surroundings.

The centurion then removed his helmet and the full horror of the apparition was revealed. His skull was split into two, revealing pulsating brain matter and a huge gash that divided his brow, passing to the right of his nose and ending at his mouth revealing the bone and teeth of his upper jaw.

Sensing the fear, the centurion began a sinister laugh that froze John's soul, until it was drowned out by a deafening explosion.

A huge ball of flame appeared within the Tower walls, which were pushed out toward him and tumbled into the river. A great wave then suddenly rose before John, knocking him off his feet and carrying his vessel at well over 20 knots away from the Tower toward London Bridge.

6.05am. The Dean of St.Paul's held onto the ornate metal railing of the Golden Gallery, as the entire dome began to shake. He knew he would not have time to run back round to the doorway before the narrow gallery on which he stood crumbled and fell, but he was not ready to die.

He looked down at the curvature of the dome below him. He would need to slide thirty metres across its surface before he reached the Stone Gallery below, but that too was beginning to break away. He also concluded that such a descent was impossible anyway, he would reach such a velocity before the dome curved into the gallery that he would go flying off the edge, and he was pretty certain that God would not be there to catch him.

The only way out was up....

6.05am. Sam's only option was the river, if he stayed on the road he would be buried alive. "Well, here goes!" He swung his Jag to the left while accelerating at full speed towards the river wall. If he hit it head on it was certain death; the only option was the flip tank, which he desperately hoped actually worked.

Just feet from the wall he pressed a button on the steering column and the cylinder in his boot rapidly released its compressed air lifting the rear of the car and somersaulting him into the air and over the wall.

As he flew towards the river he felt completely vindicated for not removing the Pinewood modifications, but his smugness left him as soon as the car hit the water and the extra weight in his trunk pulled the car quickly under the surface...

6.08am. The Dean knew a great deal about the structure of his cathedral. Even though the 800-ton huge stone lantern above him seemed to be resting on the outer dome, it was not. Christopher Wren had built two domes one within the other and it was the inner dome supported by the cathedral's immense stone superstructure that bore the lanterns weight. He was sure that, even if the outer dome and galleries fell away, the lantern would remain in place, so he hastily tied his robes around his waist and began to climb.

The building continued to shake wildly and the gallery completely crumbled away beneath him, cascading down the smooth surface of the lead dome and flying off into the gardens below. The ornate metal railings tumbled away leaving gaping holes in the dome's roof. He did his best to continue his climb, desperately grasping at the ridges between each massive stone that comprised the lantern's base. He momentarily lost his grip and as he swung on one arm the mobile phone in his pocket began to ring. Perfect timing!

He reached for it with his free hand, but as he removed it,

it slipped from his hand and fell, smashing on the dome below. He swore, and then rebuked himself as he climbed inside the lantern, and collapsed on the floor.

The shaking soon subsided. He was alive, but he was trapped up there and that wasn't good. He was pretty sure he knew why the Tower had fallen and he had to tell Sir Gareth, his friend and director of GCHQ. The Government needed to know where they should go for help and what needed to be done before their nation was utterly destroyed…

Chapter 6

6.08am. The *Kew* raced under London Bridge without hitting any of the stone supports, more by luck than judgment.

As the catamaran headed onward, on the crest of the mini tsunami, toward the next bridge, Blackfriars, the river continued to rise and John lost all control of his vessel. For several terrifying moments he was sure he was going to be slammed into the roof of the bridge as he passed underneath, but fortunately, he cleared it with literally centimetres to spare.

Buildings were now collapsing along both sides of the river and it was breaching its banks. Then, from the north bank, what looked to be an e-type Jaguar, flew over the wall into the river in front of him.

Sam wound down the driver's side window and allowed the filthy water to pour in. He then unbuckled his seat belt and, just before he was completely submerged, took a deep breath from the remaining air pocket and prepared to swim through the opening. Unfortunately, a shockwave from the explosion suddenly hit the car pushing it onto its side blocking his exit. He quickly turned and headed for the window on the passenger side. The car was now being constantly hit by debris being propelled along the river floor.

Every summer, he and his father had competed with one another in the swimming pools of their holiday villas to see who could hold their breath the longest. As Sam's lungs developed, he began to consistently beat his father but his record was only three minutes and one of those had already passed.

He frantically wound down the passenger side window and with a kick of his legs he propelled himself out of the car. He was instantly caught in the current and propelled forward making it difficult for him to find any upward momentum. To make matters worse, he was being constantly hit by hundreds of years of accumulated waste, which was being dislodged from the riverbed.

To his horror, all he could see as he neared the surface were rats, their tiny feet thrashing wildly as they fought to stay afloat.

He knew that if he tried to surface among them they would tear him to pieces in their panicked state. They would use him as a floating island and with incisors, quite capable of biting through brick and lead, they would make swift work of his Beckham cheeks and Sam Pitt chin.

Even if he were to survive them gnawing at his head and hands, a single gulp of the river, now full of rat excrement, would be seriously damaging to his health. Still if the option was certain death by drowning, he'd take his chance with the rats.

Chapter 7

6.08am. The Dean knew he had to get off the dome or he would just become a helpless spectator to the terrifying events that were about to unfold in the capital.

He watched the giant wave move down the Thames, pushing boats into the bridges and embankments, as it built up momentum.

The water flowed over onto the streets, rushing into nearby buildings and down the stairs and escalators that led into the underground system.

Commuters and staff at the Embankment Station were washed down the escalators, into the walkway tunnels and then onto the platforms and tracks.

The staff had had no time to cut the electricity so the water was instantly charged with 640 volts of murderous energy that electrocuted everyone unfortunate enough to be caught up in the maelstrom. The water then rushed through the network, engulfing oncoming trains and drowning or frying the occupants.

The Dean heard the screams even from his lofty prison. He had to get back down to the door through which he had emerged onto the Golden Gallery a few minutes earlier, but the walkway had now totally collapsed.

He would have to descend directly above the door, kick it

open with his dangling feet and swing inside. For a man in his fifties this was going to be a real test of his strength and agility, but with lives at stake, he had to try. With only a moment's hesitation he began to lower himself from the stone lantern and blindly tried to find a foothold for his feet. If he lost his grip on the descent it would be certain death, but he had no choice.

6.10am. As Sam spun around in the churning waters, he pulled his suit jacket over his head and pulled his sleeves down over his hands - the cloth would offer little protection to the rats' dagger-like teeth, but it was all he had. He then pushed upward towards the surface and probable death.

Suddenly the twin fuselages of a catamaran passed over him, the propellers passing each side of his head. The wake of the craft pushed the rats aside just as Sam broke the surface. Sam, seeing the craft in front of him, swam towards it as fast as he could, as the sea of rats began to, again, converge on him.

Just as his strength was failing him, a man with grey hair and a short grey beard appeared at the back of the catamaran and threw him a life ring; he tried to grab it but it slipped from his grasp and he started to fall behind.

John quickly pulled the life ring back into the ship and threw it again as hard as he could. He knew that if the young man failed to grab it this time he would be dead. The ring landed just behind Sam and as he spun round in the churning water, it came towards him. This time he managed to hang on, with the rats now just feet away.

John dragged him in as quickly as he could, his arms straining with the exertion. He could see the rats approaching, keen to find a way out of the raging river. They began to cling to Sam's clothing with tooth and claw, in their desperation to survive.

As John hauled him onto the landing deck he kicked at the rats. Although a few found their way on the boat, most were returned to the water. Thankfully, none had had time to bite into Sam's flesh and he lay exhausted on the deck.

When the wave began to slow and eventually die away, John again took control of his vessel, relieved it was still in one piece.

After a few minutes, Sam got onto his feet and stumbled into the cabin; John smelt his presence long before he saw him. "What the hell's going on?" John asked.

"I have no idea," said Sam. "There was a massive explosion behind me, somewhere in the East End I think. The buildings started collapsing on top of me, so I drove into the river. Thank God you came along or I'd either have drowned or been savaged by those disgusting rats!"

"The explosion was at the Tower of London." Said John, "It blew up in front of my face..."

He wasn't going to mention the centurion, he wasn't even sure he hadn't imagined it, after all, there is no way that a guy with his head split open like that could possibly be alive. Maybe, it was just a make up job, but it looked so real!

"You're kidding me, someone's blown up the Tower!" exclaimed Sam, "I have to get to my office, and quickly!"

"Where's your office?"

"Further down the river. The south side of Vauxhall Bridge"

"The MI5 building. You're a secret agent aren't you?"

"No." he lied.

"Yes you are. I'm not a bloody idiot, who else would drive a flying, freaking car."

"It was just a film prop from a James Bond movie," Sam said truthfully.

"Yeah right, and I am in command of the *Starship Enterprise*! Look you don't have to admit anything; I know how cagey you guys are. I'll get you there as soon as I can, but first, get out of those filthy clothes. I've gotta tell you, you smell pretty bad."

"Thanks mate!"

"Just saying how it is, that's all. There's a shower below and I have a dress uniform in the wardrobe. It'll be a bit loose round your waist, but at least you'll be half presentable."

"I appreciate that. Sorry, I didn't get your name?"

"John, John Brody."

"I'm Sam Callaghan. Just want you to know how grateful I am. You're a hero John!"

"Shut up and get your stinking body off my deck!"

"Yes sir!" Sam saluted the harbour master and disappeared below deck.

6.15am. The Dean was finding his descent precarious, to say the least. He was reaching out with his right hand for a gap between the stones where the mortar had broken away. He was hoping that this handhold would allow him to position himself directly above the door, so he could then lower his body and kick it open.

The problem was that it was just out of his reach; he would have to let go with his left hand in order for him to catch hold with his right, so for one brief moment he would have no support at all. If he didn't swing over with the correct momentum and get an immediate grip, he was finished. He closed his eyes, said a quick prayer, opened them and flung himself to his right.

Unfortunately, even though his fingers made the handhold they were not strong enough to hold him. As he started to fall towards the large green dome beneath, he swore again, this time loudly, and then wished he hadn't. It was not the best word to use when you're about to meet your maker!

6.20am. Sam emerged from below the deck of the *Kew* dressed in John's white dress uniform. John had been right, it was a little baggy around the waist, but a black leather belt successfully held the trousers in place.

Sam once more thanked John for saving his life and made him promise to recover his submerged car, agreeing to cover the costs, whatever they amounted to. Sam couldn't let his father's memorial rust away under the Thames.

It was probably the thought of his late father that caused Sam to give John an extremely affectionate hug as he disembarked at Victoria Embankment and ran to the MI5 building.

As he had lost all identification, it seemed to take forever to get past the security detail, who were naturally on high alert. When he eventually entered his office, the place was in a complete frenzy.

The intelligence community had thought of every possible threat to London and developed detailed contingency plans for every eventuality, but not in their wildest dreams had they imagined that anyone would have the audacity to blow up the Tower of London.

6.20am. The Dean had been wrong on one count: God was there to catch him. He fell from the lantern and landed on the top of the dome. The sudden jar caused his back to spasm as his vertebrae were momentarily compressed. He slid forward, unable to halt his forward momentum and rolled rapidly down the dome's curvature towards the edge.

He was battered and bruised on his downward journey and he closed his eyes preparing himself for certain death, but instead of flying off the edge into a 85-metre free fall to the ground below, his cassock caught on the guttering. Almost as soon as he took off into the air he was pulled back onto the Stone Gallery below and deposited head first onto what was left of the walkway floor. As the material tore apart, his head hit the concrete floor with some force and he instantly blacked out.

Chapter 8

7.00am. The Prime Minister called a COBRA crisis meeting in the government's emergency briefing room, hidden within a secret bunker, deep below the Ministry of Defence building at Whitehall.

The acronym C.O.B.R.A. used to stand for the Cabinet Office Briefing Room A, but they no longer met at the Cabinet Office, and the term was now more synonymous with the crisis meeting itself, rather than the location at which it was held.

Some of the most senior representatives of the British Intelligence Service, Police Force and Defense were all present, along with several members of the Cabinet. They were all getting updates on their phones and tablets from their investigators who had already made it to the Tower.

They wanted to make sure they were fully briefed before the Prime Minister arrived and started asking awkward questions. The Home Secretary who would normally be at this meeting was taking an early holiday in the Bahamas, which would undoubtedly have to be cut short.

A large LED video screen that filled the west wall of the Briefing Room was taking direct feeds from local surveillance cameras and from the main news channels that already had their helicopters circling over what remained of

London's greatest fortress.

Police cars, fire engines, military vehicles and the black Land Rovers of the intelligence services now surrounded the site. The fire brigades' search and rescue teams were carefully digging through the rubble and wreckage, looking for survivors, while police officers were checking for secondary devices, interviewing potential witnesses and cordoning off the entire area.

When the Prime Minister entered the room, everyone stopped speaking and stood in unison.

The PM got straight to the point. He was livid. "Right gentlemen, I want to know what the hell has happened here and who is responsible?"

No one in the room seemed eager to speak, and the one person who had the answers, wanted to find out how much the others knew before he revealed his hand.

General Dan Radford, the portly chief of Defense Intelligence was the first to speak.

"Well, we can rule out an earthquake, Prime Minister. Seismograph readings indicate a sizeable underground explosion directly beneath the Tower. It was one hell of a blast too, equivalent to over 2,000 kg of TNT and measuring 3.0 on the Richter scale, pretty similar to the Oklahoma City bomb in '95. The other devastation we've witnessed across the City was caused by shockwaves passing along the Thames and through the sewage and utility tunnels and the London Underground."

The PM had been told by his press advisors to show immediate concern about the people caught up in the explosion and he also needed some stats for his upcoming press conference. "How many casualties?"

Sir Vince Jones, commissioner of the Metropolitan Police Service, responded first.

"Too early to say, Prime Minister, but thanks to the early hour of the morning, there were no tourists in the vicinity and very few commuters. Most of the dead and badly injured were those working or living in the vicinity of the Tower, and the Underground network."

Andrew Smith, director general of MI5 stood. It was time for him to take control of proceedings.

"We're pretty certain the explosives were subterranean, probably placed in one of the tunnels directly underneath the tower. The White Tower, itself, seems to have been ground zero."

The PM flinched "My god that's where we keep the Crown Jewels. Were they taken?"

"No, Prime Minister, our agents have already confirmed that all of the Jewels are accounted for."

"So was it a terrorist attack?"

"At this stage, it seems to be the most likely scenario. They have succeeded in reducing the Tower of London, the symbol of British power and fortitude for almost a thousand years, to a pile of rubble. They've caused severe flooding from Greenwich to the Embankment and they have decimated the Underground system from Docklands to the City. So, London's businesses will be hit again, right on the heels of the worst recession in our history. Stock market trading will be suspended and you can expect severe damage to our economy, unless you can put a positive spin on this whole sorry affair."

"So what spin are you proposing Andrew? Do you want me to announce at my press conference that we thought it was time to demolish the Tower of London and build something a bit more contemporary?"

Director Smith wasn't used to being ridiculed by anyone, let alone the PM. "No, that's not what I meant. I am saying that we have to place blame somewhere and show the world that we have the situation under control."

"But we don't have the situation under control, do we? Answer me this, Andrew: How the hell did terrorists get into the tunnels under the Tower of London to plant a massive bomb without being detected by your security forces and why on earth were you unable to gain any intelligence that could have helped us to defend against this attack? That is your job isn't it?"

Before Director Smith could answer, the director of

GCHQ, Sir Gareth Fraser came to his rescue. He raised his hand as he stood in an effort to calm down the proceedings.

“I actually don't think it was terrorists Prime Minister. In some ways I wish it was, because what I suspect has happened this morning could be far more devastating.”

The Prime Minister was taken aback. “What could possibly be worse than a terrorist attack and the potential collapse of our economy, after my government has worked so hard to get this country back onto its feet?”

“What could be worse? I’ll tell you. It’s possible that in the next few hours every citizen of your country will either be dead or wish they were! We may well be about to witness events that are more frightening than your darkest imaginings, horrors that are beyond your comprehension or control.”

“What are you talking about Gareth?” said the PM rather nervously.

“Prime Minister, you are, I know, a religious man, who believes in God and is familiar with the concept of evil. Up to now you have probably imagined the worse kind of evil to be the dictators, the architects of genocide, the terrorists, the murderers, the child abusers and all those who seem to be devoid of any conscience or morality. But true evil is not confined to the thoughts or actions of any man; true evil is a terrifying power that, when unleashed, can bring plagues, pestilence, famine, war and death on a global scale."

Director Smith couldn't believe what he was hearing. "What a load of bloody nonsense, this is terrorism pure and simple!"

The PM wanted to know more. "Let him finish Andrew. You've had your say, let him have his."

The Prime Minister was actually far more knowledgeable on this topic than he let on. He was pleased, however, that it was Sir Gareth and not him who was putting forward this irrational possibility. After all, it was essential that he maintained his credibility and deniability if these unbelievable assumptions proved to be wrong.

"The tunnels under the tower contained a huge vault

which we believed, until today, to be impenetrable. The vault contained certain relics and artefacts that we took from the Nazis after Hitler's death in '45. Artefacts that, in my opinion should have been immediately destroyed."

"And now you're going to tell me that they've been taken from right under our noses?"

"Yes, Prime Minister, they've all disappeared."

"And you believe that they pose a danger of some kind?"

"Some of them certainly do! They're known as the 'Devil's Teeth', placed on earth, according to legend, so that men would have the means to eventually destroy themselves. They're relics from ancient civilizations, believed to harness unimaginable, destructive powers."

Director Smith interrupted again. "What a load of ridiculous speculation. Can we please dispense with this supernatural nonsense and get on with finding these damned terrorists!"

Everyone ignored his outburst. They found it hard to accept what Sir Gareth was saying but they had benefitted from trusting his wisdom and instincts on more than one occasion, and they wanted him to continue.

"Hitler sought these relics to further his lust for power. His ambition was to be the emperor of the world. But first he had to bring it to its knees.

"He sent his men all over the globe to find these evil relics and also to collect certain religious artefacts that were meant to hold the power of God, such as the Ark of the Covenant, the Holy Grail and the Spear of Destiny. Thankfully, few were found and most of those he did secure, proved to be nothing more than fakes or harmless religious tokens.

"Among the relics he did find, however, was the Pentalpha, a ring that, according to apocryphal writings, was given to King Solomon by the Archangel Michael so he could bind and command demons and spirits to assist him in the building of his great temple. Another find was the Amulet of Ankhef, otherwise known as the Amulet of Death, which they stole from the Cairo museum. The amulet is said to have the power to raise and control the dead. Among the religious relics he acquired was the Holy Lance, or Spear of Destiny, which was supposedly used to pierce Christ's side during the crucifixion."

Director Smith spoke again trying desperately to reassert himself. "If what you say is true why didn't Hitler use these supernatural weapons against us?"

"I'll tell you Andrew. The relics fall into two categories, 'religious relics' that can only be used by those who are righteous, and 'occult relics', which are used by those who are evil. Ironically, Hitler believed himself to be on a righteous crusade, so he tried to use the holy relics, which he'd stolen from churches and monasteries across Europe. Thankfully they were powerless in his hands and may even have contributed to his downfall.

If, however, he'd recognised that he was actually extremely evil and chosen any of the occult relics, we could well be speaking German right now!"

"So what makes you think that these artefacts genuinely pose a threat, Gareth? Surely there's a very high possibility that this is just mumbo jumbo," said the PM.

"To be honest Prime Minister I have no definitive proof of their power, however, it's widely believed that one of the Devils Teeth was used to trigger the Tunguska event in Siberia in 1908, an explosion that was estimated to be 1,000 times more powerful than the atomic bomb dropped on Hiroshima!

"It's mentioned all over the Internet, and no one has any other credible explanation for what happened.

"Many also believe that one of the occult relics was used to release the Black Death, which killed almost a third of the UK population in 1348, and the Great Plague that decimated London in 1665.

"That was just rats!" stated Smith extremely exasperated by the nonsense he was hearing.

"But who or what infected the rats in the first place!" responded Sir Gareth.

"Look, I know this is all really hard to believe, but I can tell you that over the years, I have held these objects in my hands and it was always a terrifying experience! Have you ever been in a room at night and suddenly you're filled with an irrational fear that puts a chill in your heart, and you just feel that something very evil is present?"

Several of the men nodded. "Well that's how I felt when I was in the presence of one of those relics. I was genuinely frightened, the evil is palpable and I found it hard to even breathe!"

"It's just your wild imagination, Sir Gareth. There's no such thing as evil objects, just evil people," said Smith dismissively.

"Then let's take a look at the religious relics. I don't need to tell you about the destructive power unleashed by the Ark of the Covenant against the enemies of Israel. That's well documented in the Bible."

"I don't believe in the Bible." said Smith.

"Well I do!" said the PM. "Please carry on, Gareth."

"If you are looking for more tangible evidence Andrew, there are many historical documents that testify to the power of the Holy Lance that pierced Christ's side. Charlemagne, the Holy Emperor of Rome, was given the spear by the Pope, and when he carried it into battle he had convincing victories against great Saxon and Muslim armies. He even succeeded in the conquest of Jerusalem, against absolutely overwhelming odds.

"In the early 900s Henry I of Germany, exchanged an entire city for the lance because of its purported power and when he died it was passed on to his son Otto I, who used it to achieve a decisive victory against Hungarian invaders in AD 955."

"Otto III also accredited many miraculous victories to the divine power of the spear. It seemed that any army that carried it, was effectively invincible. That's why both pagan and Christian leaders have gone to great lengths to obtain it, and why Hitler started a world war to obtain it!"

The committee members were still sceptical but remained silent.

"Now let's talk about today. Over the last few hours every

animal that lived in this city has left, even the rats. It's a well-known fact that animals have a sixth sense and can predict the onset of earthquakes and other great disasters. Around 40 years ago, Chinese officials evacuated the city of Haicheng based on the unusual behaviour in animals. Hours later they were hit by a 7.3 magnitude earthquake.

"Before a huge tsunami hit India and Sri Lanka it was reported that dogs refused to walk on the beach, elephants ran for higher ground, and flamingos fled their low-lying breeding areas.

"Today, something has caused the mass migration of every animal from this city. Look at the footage on the monitors again for heaven's sake, these creatures were scared out of their minds! They knew that something dreadful was coming.

"Mark my words, a great evil is at our doorstep, and we have to find a way to stop it before, Prime Minister, you no longer have a country to govern."

Chapter 9

8.00am. Paul, Aaron and Conran sat in Castle park in Colchester sniffing glue. They'd bunked off school for the fourth time that week and it was only Thursday. Some say that sniffing glue destroys brain cells, and these three had very few to spare between them.

Paul was ticked off. "Did you see all that crap in the news this morning, those Arab, towel-headed, freaks blowing up the Tower of London? Dad said it was treason and they'd be hung if they got caught. I'd love to see that! I bet it'd be all over YouTube just like when they hanged that Saddam guy."

"They won't catch 'em," said Aaron, the skinniest of the bunch. "They never caught those terrorists that flew the planes into the Twin Towers, did they? And they killed thousands of people."

Paul laughed. Aaron's stupidity was a constant source of amusement. "Of course they never got caught, the planes blew up with the terrorists on board!"

"Oh yeah!" said Aaron sheepishly. He hadn't thought of that.

"You're such an idiot Aaron!" Conran shouted. He was built like a bull, and with a ring in his large flat nose, he looked like one as well. When he was having a fix he always shouted, as if he wanted the whole world to know that he was the biggest and toughest guy in town.

Bethany, a young mother, sat on a park bench watching her three-year-old son playing happily in the nearby playground; she had also been keeping a close eye on the three hooded teenagers. It was clear to her that they were trouble and representative of the new generation of Essex boys who had received no discipline at home or at school and thought of no one but themselves.

She was determined that Noah would grow up differently even if it meant moving away to a better neighbourhood.

Conran's outburst annoyed her, and her disapproval showed on her face.

Unfortunately he was looking in her direction.

"What are you looking at?" he asked menacingly.

Bethany decided not to answer him and turned back to her son, hoping he would leave it at that.

"I said, what are you looking at?" His voice was getting even louder; he didn't like to be ignored. Little Noah was startled and started to cry.

Bethany continued to ignore the teenager; she got up from the wooden bench and started to walk towards her distressed son.

"Don't you dare disrespect me!" he screamed as he took out his pocketknife. He was going to teach this woman a lesson.

When she saw the knife her first instinct was to run, but she couldn't leave her son behind and she would never get over to him in time. She did the only thing she could think of: she screamed at the top of her voice.

Conran was, however, not deterred. While his friends begged him to stop and get out of the park before the coppers came, he pressed forward, his knife arm extended, his intent clearly etched across his face.

Bethany continued screaming unable to move and her son started screaming too. Dog walkers and joggers turned towards the commotion and when they saw what was about to happen many began to run to her aid, but they were too far away. There was no way to stop the inevitable. Aaron and Paul decided it was time to leave so they deserted their friend and legged it.

Conran was just four steps away. I'm gonna slash that bitch's face, he thought, but suddenly he could no longer move his right leg. He thought he must have caught it in a tree root but when he looked down he discovered, in the last minute of his life, that he wasn't the toughest guy in the park that day. Around his ankle was a boney hand reaching out from the ground and it was gripping him like a vice.

As he tried to get free, the pressure increased until his bones began to crack and he cried out in agony and blind fear. To his left another hand emerged followed by a long skeletal arm that shook off dirt and dried parched skin as it reached for his thigh. Then from the ground directly before him, there emerged a skull.

The hands pulled at his body, and a Roman soldier rose from the ground, still wearing the armour that he had died in. The hand on Conran's ankle moved upward and grabbed his arm. Conran dropped his knife and tried again to get away but he could not move.

Bethany grabbed her son and turned him away from the carnage as the soldier gave Conran a full embrace and bit deep into his neck, feasting upon the blood that pumped from his carotid artery. As the soldier fed on Conran's face, new muscle began to grow on the Roman's skeletal limbs and across his back, buttocks and chest. Organs and eyes began to form and fresh skin spread across his entire body.

He threw Conran's limp, lifeless body to the floor then reached into the ground to retrieve the weapons that he had not wielded for nearly two thousand years.

He turned abruptly to face the crowd that had come to save Bethany and roared with such ferocity that the ground began to shake, as did everyone within hearing range. Dirt mounds suddenly grew and exploded throughout the park as more dead Romans emerged from their graves. The crowd fled, running in every direction, desperate to find a safe passage to freedom. Most never made it, they were captured and consumed by the growing army who killed at will to satisfy a need for human blood.

Bethany sat silently in the bough of a large oak tree, holding her son tightly in her arms, shielding his eyes with her chest and his ears with her hands. She felt his tiny body shake uncontrollably and she knew that he would be damaged forever.

Chapter 10

8.00am. Smithfield Market had been quiet all morning. The usual flood of meat buyers had become just a trickle as news spread of the explosion and the subsequent events that had brought London to its knees. The wholesale butchers began loading their unsold slabs of meat back into their refrigerated lorries cursing the terrorists that had already substantially reduced their business revenues.

The traders cursed and yelled, taking out their frustration on anyone who crossed their paths. A fight broke out as one butcher accused another of stealing one of their regular customers, and a traffic warden who had dared to put a ticket on one of the illegally parked vans was quickly surrounded and summarily abused.

The truth was that everyone felt uneasy and a little frightened. Their city had experienced a devastating attack and everyone sensed that it was only the beginning.

The tunnels underneath the market had lain empty for over a century when they were used as the slaughterhouses for the livestock brought to the market. Now they were mostly sealed.

When the noises began to echo up from these subterranean passageways, the market traders and the few remaining customers were immediately spooked.

It sounded like there was a gathering army down there, metal being scrapped across walls, wood splintering, stone breaking, leather soles running across the floors, and low guttural sounds as if orders were being issued by commanders who could barely speak.

The footsteps soon gathered in number, at first they were disjointed but slowly they began to synchronise and gain a sustained rhythm that caused the floor of the market to vibrate and the stalls to collapse.

The large grates all across the vast market floor began to lift and were thrown aside as a resurrected Roman legion began to emerge looking for blood. Across Smithfield and Farringdon there were several huge Roman burial sites, which were also now giving up their dead.

The stallholders ran for the nearest exits but found them barred by more soldiers who had been emerging from beneath roads, pavements, parks, gardens, cemeteries, office buildings and homes. In minutes everyone were slaughtered in a bloody massacre that surpassed any in Smithfield's grim history.

Chapter 11

8.00am. St Albans was once a thriving Roman community. A few burial urns had recently been discovered in the area south of Abbey Church, around St. Stephens Hill and King Harry Park, but no one knew the scale of the Roman cemetery until the day the dead rose.

Archaeologists had been working on a small excavation near the park for the last few years. Professor Duggery, who was overseeing the dig, arrived early that morning because they'd made an incredible discovery that needed to be prepared for a much-anticipated press conference that very afternoon.

Since he was a child at St. Columbus College, less than a mile away, he was fascinated by local history and he was determined to separate fact from legend by, quite literally, digging up the truth.

Earlier that month he'd unearthed the skeleton of a middle-aged, perfectly proportioned Roman general whom, he was sure, was none other than Claudius Germanicus, a nephew of the Emperor Nero. The dagger found at his waist bore the family emblem together with the symbol of his exalted rank.

It was believed that Claudius had been murdered by one of his own tribunes, one Liberius Aurelius, who had been made to witness the barbaric execution of his wife, a beautiful red-headed Briton called Helena, and his young son, Flavius.

Duggery had uncovered the body in a sandstone sarcophagus together with several clay jars containing beans, lentils and flour as well as two casks of wine. It was all obviously intended to feed him on his long journey to the Underworld.

What excited the archaeologist most of all was the roman sword, known as a 'gladius', that had been plunged into the general's back all the way to the hilt and never removed - an eternal witness to the betrayal that had ended his life.

Interestingly, the general's head had been separated from his body and Duggery was keen to establish whether this had happened at the time of his death or later as part of the Roman burial ritual. There was also no sign of his helmet or robes, which would normally have been buried with him.

He leaned into the sarcophagus and lifted the skull so he could take a closer look. Normally the lower jaw would separate from the rest of the skull as soon as the muscles had rotten away but in this specimen, it was still attached. He held the back of the skull with his left hand and with his right he tried to manipulate the jaw to work out what was holding it together. He pulled it down slightly and noticed that on one of the molars at the rear of the upper jaw was a perfect example of one of the earliest gold shell crowns.

He opened the jaw further and reached inside to see whether the crown might come loose. Suddenly the jaw snapped shut completely severing Duggery's thumb and forefinger. He screamed in pain and then in horror as his blood seemed to react with the skull causing its flesh to return and its eyes to form in the empty sockets. He dropped the skull in disgust and immediately the rest of the body started to move, the skeletal hands grasping the skull and replacing it on top of its spinal column.

As Duggery backed away, the general rose from the sarcophagus and in one swift movement pulled the sword from his back and spun round to cut through the archaeologist's neck. It then reached down and lifted Duggery's head, hungrily drinking the blood from the exposed neck in an attempt to quench an unbearable thirst.

As his flesh and muscle returned he looked out across the park where his army was beginning to rise and assemble. He walked among them inspecting and organising, even embracing long lost friends. Twenty minutes later three legions, comprising of over 1500 legionaries stood in perfect formation with centurions and tribunes at their head awaiting their orders.

At the general's signal they began to move as one, out of the park and north up St. Stephens Hill to the town centre, in search of blood. Police cars had already been called to the site and they cautiously followed with blue lights flashing and sirens blaring to warn the public of approaching death.

One of the officers, against orders, drove at full speed into the back of the column but the car had no impact on these zombies and crumbled on impact. The Romans then turned and dived through the windscreen, tearing apart the driver and his partner.

The rest of the cars kept their distance, even when the killing started in earnest the police stayed in their vehicles frightened and powerless, reporting what they were seeing on police radios and mobile phones and recording what they could on their traffic cameras for live transmission to their county commander. He in turn relayed details to the commissioner in the COBRA briefing room.

As unsuspecting housewives searched through Sainsbury's refrigerated meat cabinets in search of the plumpest, tastiest joints, the legionnaires did the same on the streets of St Albans, satisfying two millennia of hunger by gorging themselves on early morning shoppers. They entered every store sometimes through the doors but mostly through the windows.

Jordan was a precocious twenty-year-old looking for a new dress for her 21st birthday party. Her first stop of the morning was Ocean Lane, her favourite store on St. Albans High Street. She had taken three dresses into the changing room knowing that the store policy was just two at a time.

As soon as she pulled the curtains closed she tightly folded up her favourite dress and put it in her handbag, then she tried on the other two deciding which she would steal the following week.

When she had made her choice she put them both back on their hangers and prepared to leave. The sound of breaking glass startled her; the screams that followed and the sounds of breaking bones and tearing flesh made her cower at the back of the cubicle staring at the curtain and willing it not to open. She promised God she'd never steal again. She promised she would give back everything she had ever taken, if only He would not let that curtain open.

Unfortunately, God knew she was lying, except on one count; she would certainly never steal again.

An armed response vehicle arrived at the scene with a team of six strategic firearm officers who quickly positioned themselves on the roof of the 15th-century clock tower, from where they had a clear view of the High Street. After wasting hundreds of rounds trying to kill Roman soldiers, who were technically already dead, they decided it was time to leave. The sergeant was concerned that they were starting to draw attention to themselves. Unfortunately, he was right; the general had already dispatched several of his men to the tower.

The hardened police officers saw them coming and immediately weighed up their options. They made an immediate request for air support but they were told that the police helicopters were all on the ground at Lippits Hill in Essex. If they took off immediately it would take at least eight minutes to get there, and that was too damn long.

There was no way they could defeat them in hand-to-hand combat. The officers had seen the Roman's strength as they ripped their victims limb by limb. They tried shattering the legs of the approaching zombies with high velocity bullets, but they just bounced off their bones without even slowing their advance.

Some of the Romans had now entered the building and their footsteps could be heard running up the stone steps. The police marksmen barricaded the doorway as best they could but they knew it wouldn't hold for long. They had to go over the edge but they only had two abseil ropes between the six of them.

Having established that there were no hostiles waiting at the foot the west face of the tower, they lowered the ropes and secured them to the iron railings. Their sergeant knew, however, that there was only time to get one, maybe two, of his men down each rope. As he looked from one man to the next, he couldn't decide who to save or who should stay and die with him.

"I need volunteers to stay and fight with me," he said, "the rest of you get down those ropes."

No one would leave their comrades behind. Without exception, every man stepped forward and took up position by the entranceway. The sergeant looked at the resolve on each man's face and a simple nod communicated their mutual respect and their final farewell. The ropes were never used; it was all over in less than a minute.

The police surrounding the area heard everything on their radios. Some watched the last stand of the armed response team through high-powered binoculars. Many of the observers openly wept, overwhelmed by the bravery of their comrades and the way they had died. Their inspector wasted no time in relaying what had happened directly to Westminster.

"Call in the army sir, let's send those abominations back to hell!"

Chapter 12

8.00am. The rescue teams at the Tower of London were confused. Their ultrasonic equipment was showing many bodies moving beneath the rubble but the thermal imaging cameras were showing no signs of life at all. What's more, they were told that there were no more than thirty men patrolling the Tower at that time of the explosion, but they were picking up signatures of more than a hundred.

At first they put it down to faulty equipment and they kept on digging, mainly by hand, afraid that heavy machinery would endanger the lives of those who were buried beneath tons of fallen masonry.

Bradley Bodfield was one of the first firefighters on the scene and he had immediately volunteered to take part in the rescue, despite the fact that there was a high probability of further explosions.

He had already managed to free a Beefeater called Stan but the old man's head had been severely crushed and he doubted the man had long to live. He had just been taken away with his distressed wife by ambulance to Guys' Hospital on the other side of the river.

Now Bradley was sensing movement directly below him and he felt a surge of excitement that he might be able to rescue someone else. He used all his strength to lift and move aside rock after rock while speaking words of reassurance to the person below.

"You'll be alright mate, just hang on, I'll have you out in a minute or two. Can you hear me? Can you speak?"

All he got in return was a grunt and he assumed that the victim must have severe damage to his chest or neck. He continued to dig, more frantically than ever, now he could actually see movement below him. He leaned forward and peered between the rocks just as a boney hand pushed through and grabbed him by the throat, tearing out his larynx.

Across the courtyard the rubble began to move and one by one, the Roman soldiers emerged, rushing at the nearest rescuers before they had a chance to escape. Tens became hundreds and hundreds became thousands as the entire area swarmed with dead legionaries. Every policeman, medic, firefighter, security guard and soldier were slaughtered in minutes despite courageous attempts to fend off their attackers. The whole scene was captured by the TV crews in the helicopters above and broadcast across the world to a terrified public.

Those who had just woken up and turned on their TVs thought they were watching some new zombie movie and were angry that the BBC would broadcast such carnage when many kids had not even left for school.

Those who had kept abreast of the news started locking their windows and doors. Some started praying, some called to check on their loved ones and some headed for their medicine cabinets to end their lives.

8.30am. When they had finished their massacre of mostly innocents in St. Albans the legionaries reassembled in King Harry Park where two large black lorries were waiting. Mercenaries dressed in black except for red lightning bolts embroidered on their shirts pulled open the rear doors and began to warily hand over armaments to each and every

Roman soldier. In just 33 minutes they were all fully armed and prepared for the 26-mile march to Central London.

9.00am. News helicopters circled the skies of Hertfordshire and Essex following the relentless march of the Roman legions as they converged upon London. Line upon line of grotesque corpses in various stages of regeneration pressed forward. Some wore rusted armour and tattered tunics, others who'd recently been rearmed looked like they'd just emerged from the set of *Gladiator*.

Most wore helmets with protective cheek plates and a flair at the back to protect the neck. Some helmets were crested with a red horsehair plume, others were crested with a blade or spikes. In their left hands they held shields bearing Jupiter's thunderbolt in a bronze relief over a red leather covering. In their right hands they held either sword or javelin and on their left hip they bore their traditional daggers. Some wore shoes; most didn't.

Cars pulled over to let them pass as they travelled along the A1 and A13 at an unnatural speed. Vehicles that had been abandoned were cast aside as if made from balsa wood. For now the killing had stopped, but they were on a mission and their target was Central London.

The news helicopters were told by the police and military to return to their bases or they would lose their precious press licenses but they ignored the warnings. Soon army helicopters arrived, supported by heavily armed drones.

The news reporters got excited believing they were about to film some real action but when the first missiles passed inches above their rotor blades, they knew it was time to exit the proceedings.

10.00am. The legions were gathering in Hyde Park, column upon column, from Marble Arch in the north to Hyde Park Corner in the south. The military estimated that there were around 100,000 Roman soldiers.

The legionaries had also surrounded Buckingham Palace, Whitehall, the Houses of Parliament and 10 Downing Street. Only metropolitan police with riot gears, tazers and truncheons stood between them and the country's leaders they were assigned to protect.

As Liberius watched general Claudius marching at the head the Legions that were arriving from St Albans, he felt a pang of guilt for the first time in 2,000 years. This walking corpse had once been a great Roman leader who had served his country well, only to die at the hands of his own tribune.

Liberius regretted killing him, but the general had mocked him after the death of his family, telling him that his wife and son had deserved to die and their fate was sealed the day he had chosen to take a worthless Briton as a bride.

In a fit of rage Liberius had killed Claudius with his own sword and removed his head. Now the shell of this once great man was leading a Roman legion once more, but he no longer had a soul of his own, he was completely under Liberius's control.

Quickly, Liberius pushed these thoughts from his mind. He could not allow sentimentality to weaken his resolve. Today, he would have his revenge, even if it meant killing other great leaders, like Claudius, in the process.

10.00am. When the Dean regained consciousness he sensed his world had changed for the worse. The evil was now all-pervasive. It surrounded him and drowned him. He looked at his watch, and saw that he'd been unconscious for over three hours. He was so annoyed with himself. It was time that he could ill afford to lose. He had to get moving, but there was something he had to do first.

He got on his knees and thanked God for preserving his life so miraculously, then, he asked for forgiveness for his momentary loss of faith and begged for the strength to do what had to be done.

He was sure he had been preserved because of the knowledge he held, knowledge that was essential to defeat the rising evil. He just had to get hold of Sir Gareth or Ackerman and tell them what had to be done. If that failed, he had to do the unthinkable himself.

When he had finished his prayer, he opened his eyes to the sound of screams. He leaned forward and looked over the edge of the balcony to the streets below - his worst fears were confirmed. As far as he could see the dead were walking and the living were dying. The reanimated corpses of Roman soldiers were attacking anyone who came near to the cathedral.

He got to his feet even though he could barely stand. The only way out was down through the cathedral and he wondered what horrors might be waiting for him in the corridors below. After all he was certain they would be searching the cathedral and he knew they had come for him.

Chapter 13

10.00am. The Prime Minister watched the broadcasts with horror. They were surrounded, and even though the COBRA briefing room was meant to be impenetrable, they couldn't stay holed up there forever.

What worried him the most, however, were the legionaries that had surrounded the gated entrance to Downing Street. That's where his wife and children were, and they had very little protection at all.

Sir Gareth turned to Director Smith with a look that said "I told you so."

The PM pulled himself away from the television monitors and addressed the COBRA committee, his face drained of blood.

"Sir Gareth, how do we stop them?"

"Someone is using the Amulet of the Dead to resurrect these Roman armies and control them. We have to find out who that is and where they are, then we can destroy the amulet. It won't be easy though. The Americans detonated high explosives right next to it in '49 and it remained completely intact. If we are going to destroy it we need to consult the Dean."

"Who's the Dean?" asked Director Smith.

"The Dean of St Paul's. He has dedicated his life to the

study of relics such as these. If anyone knows how to destroy them he will."

"Then why wasn't he allowed to destroy them years ago, before we got ourselves into this mess?" the Prime Minister demanded.

General Radford glared at Sir Gareth trying to intimidate him into silence, but it had no effect whatsoever.

"The sacred, religious relics with no known power were mostly returned to Vienna and Rome, from where they'd been stolen. The occult artifacts were all to be destroyed soon after the war but the army demanded that they should be preserved in the interest of national security and they have had charge over them ever since. That's why they were interred beneath the Crown Jewels, which are also in the Army's care."

The Prime Minister turned to General Radford. "Is this true?"

"Yes it is, but the decision was made long before I took charge and I assure you we had reviewed the situation and were planning to destroy them once and for all."

Sure you were! Thought Sir Gareth.

"Where do we find the Dean?" asked the PM.

"That's the problem I called him over an hour ago and his mobile phone was dead. I have sent agents over to the cathedral to find him. They should be there about now."

"But isn't the area around St Paul's teeming with these Roman monsters?"

"Yes, it is, but don't worry Prime Minister, the Dean is a very resourceful man. I belie---"

He was cut short by an interruption to the broadcasts being piped into the COBRA briefing room. On the feeds from every station appeared a grotesquely deformed man whose face seems to be split in two. He was wearing the helmet and robes of a Roman general.

"My name is Liberius. I was once tribune in the Second Augusta Legion of the Roman army stationed here in Britain nearly 2,000 year ago, but now I have returned to claim the title of emperor. I have summoned my fallen comrades from the dead to fulfill a mission assigned to us in 61AD, which was to conquer Britain.

Your country has taken everything I loved from me, and I will now return the favour. I call upon your Prime Minister to surrender the sovereignty, wealth, land and properties of your nation to the Roman Empire, which I now govern. If he does so you will all become my subjects and your lives will be spared. If he refuses, we will kill every citizen until your country is on its knees. I have already given you a small taste of what my men are capable of, but you have not yet seen the full extent of my destructive powers."

"You have until midnight to surrender. After that deadline, the killing will begin again, and we will start with the Prime Minister's own family." The PM visibly flinched.

"Let me finish with a severe warning, that any attempt to destroy us will be met with a merciless response!"

The broadcast ended and the Prime Minister collapsed into his chair, the weight of responsibility suddenly too heavy to bear.

Chapter 14

10.05am. The Dean slowly descended the cathedral's staircase listening intently for any movement below. His head was still throbbing from the concussion and his back was killing him from the fall. He could hear footsteps echoing up the stairwell, the sound of maybe four or five men continually moving from one place to the next, they were definitely searching for him.

The Dean dared not even breathe but knew he had to continue his descent and try to escape undetected.

If they started to climb these steps there was no escape, he would be trapped and would have to do the one thing that he had been trying to avoid all morning: throw himself off the dome. He would have the unenviable choice to jump either from the Whispering Gallery onto the cathedral floor, or from what was left of the Stone Gallery into the gardens beneath. That would be a much longer fall, but at least he would not have to be mopped up from the cathedral's marble floor.

With every downward step the Dean made, the sounds below grew louder. Now he imagined there to be ten or more of the Romans in his cathedral moving through the nave, quire, aisles and transepts. So much for evil not being able to stand on hallowed ground!

As he tentatively emerged onto the whispering gallery, he knew that even the slightest sound would reverberate around the inside of the dome and alert those below.

He edged around the balcony slowly, pressing his extremely painful back tightly against the walls, hoping that he wouldn't be seen by the enemy below. It would take him two or three minutes to edge his way round to the next descending staircase and all this time he would be in plain sight.

Every second seemed like a minute, but thankfully the soldiers were so engrossed in their search below that they did not look up. The Dean reached the second staircase and again started to descend. Despite the cool temperature in the cathedral he began to sweat due to the pain that he was suffering, which seemed to grow in intensity as each minute passed, along with the fear.

St. Paul's Cathedral Floor Plan

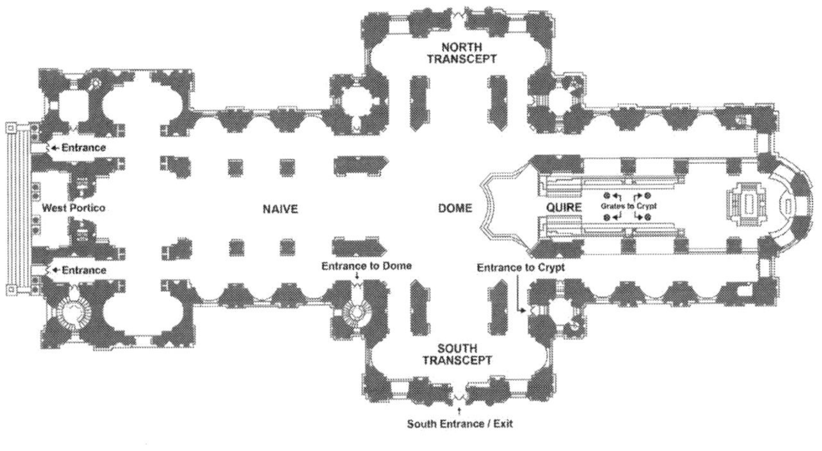

When he reached the bottom of the stairwell he froze as he heard the sound of approaching feet. He tucked himself behind the open door, pressed himself against the wall and held his breath. A soldier charged through the doorway and ran immediately up the stairs. The Dean was about to venture out from his hiding place when he heard more approaching steps. He hid again and another soldier passed, and then another. He could hear the footsteps above echoing ominously as they reached the whispering gallery.

A fourth soulless soldier entered the doorway but this time it stopped and remained perfectly still. The Dean was not sure if it had sensed his presence or was just contemplating whether it really wanted to make the climb. It then began to turn towards him and he was certain that he was about to be discovered but the soldier just exited the door and ran back into the cathedral.

He knew that it was pointless making a dash for the nearest exit as it was over 100 yards away and he would have to cross the south transept or naive where there was nowhere to hide or take cover. He wished for a moment that there had been some confession boxes to hide in, even though he was strongly opposed to such instant absolution.

His best route, he decided was to head for the quire and hide in the pews, crawling beneath them until he was just feet from the east door. Then he would have to make his dash and hope that there were no legionaries waiting for him outside. With the odds stacked against him he decided that he should leave a message for those that might come looking for him. He had no paper or pens, paint or pencils. But he still had his keys fastened to his belt.

He thought about scratching a message into the stairway door or one of the pews, if he got that far, but the sound would alert his pursuers and it may not be noticed when they came to find him, as he was sure they would. Instead he pushed the point of the key deep into his palm and with the blood that flowed from his hand he drew a large symbol and a single word on the wall to the right of the stairway door.

Unfortunately for the Dean, the smell of fresh blood immediately permeated the air and reached the nostrils of all the Roman soldiers inside the cathedral. They all turned simultaneously in the direction of the Dean. He barely had time to offer his soul to Christ before they descended upon him.

10.20am. The secret service agents who had been sent to bring the Dean to Westminster arrived six minutes later. The cathedral was deserted and there was no sign of the Dean except for an odd symbol smeared on the wall. It looked like the head of a trident with each spike ending in an arrowhead, and below it was the word "Ackerman".

They had taken photographs from every angle and just texted those to their boss at GCHQ when they heard the sound of footsteps coming from the apse in the east end of the cathedral, three other Roman soldiers emerged into the south transept and ran towards them, and two more ran from the dome stairwell and joined in the chase.

The agents headed back to the main entrance, through the heavy oak doors and down the steps to the waiting black Land Rover Discovery. One of the agents lost his footing and fell heavily from the fifth step.

Unfortunately there was no time to go back for him. The Romans were upon him in seconds, tearing at him with clawed hands and teeth. The remaining agents grabbed their weapons from the vehicle and emptied the MP5s and Glocks into the Roman soldiers, but their bullets just bounced off of armour and bone. They did however succeed in putting their colleague out of his suffering.

10.25am. Sir Gareth left the COBRA briefing room when he saw he had received a text from his agents at St Paul's. When he read their message, his hand began to shake visibly and his eyes moistened.

The Dean was one of his closest friends and a true confidant. The world was a safer place with him in it, and it seemed he was gone, just when he was needed most. He then saw that there were images attached to the text and he quickly opened the first.

He immediately recognized the symbol and the name.

"Ackerman" was a professor of some standing at Oxford University, specializing in ancient and occult history, who had proven to be an invaluable resource in the past when they had come across the unexplained.

He had thought of Ackerman when the crisis had begun but approaching him now would be a difficult task. Ackerman had refused to speak to any representative of the government, including him, for several years, ever since his adopted daughter, Lucinda, was killed in a government operation under tragic circumstances.

Having received this message, however, it was clear that the Dean offered no viable alternative, their only real hope lay with the professor.

Thankfully Sir Gareth had a contingency plan. He knew there was one person that Ackerman still trusted, a promising young agent at MI5 called Sam Callaghan who had studied under the professor at Oxford and even dated Ackerman's daughter, until the 'accident'.

He called the MI5 offices directly, bypassing their director. He'd enough of Andrew Smith and his irritating skepticism and he was not going to give him the chance to question or veto his plans. If Ackerman could not be persuaded to cooperate, there would probably be no other way to stop Liberius.

Well there was *one* other option, but Sir Gareth could never allow that to happen. Although it would undoubtedly destroy Liberius and his army, others might die too, including him. He felt he would stand a better chance of survival battling single-handedly against the Roman army!

Sir Gareth returned to the briefing room to tell the committee what they needed to know, and keep from them what they didn't.

Chapter 15

10.25am. MI5 had been given the responsibility to find out who was behind the bombing and why Roman soldiers, who had been dead for nearly two thousand years, had rampaged through St Albans, Colchester and London and were now gathering in Hyde Park. News had also reached them of Liberius's ultimatum and they knew that time was running out.

Sam stared in disbelief at the images coming into the office from news channels, surveillance cameras and satellites. He was desperately trying to formulate a plan when he was summoned into the supervisor's office.

"Where the hell have you been and why are you dressed like a dick?" was the greeting he received from Mark Blunt, head of 'A' Branch where he'd been stationed ever since he completed his induction and training.

"It's too long a story to bore you with boss," said Sam, a little too disrespectfully.

Mark let it pass. "Sam you need to get over to Oxford University immediately. There's a fully-fuelled helicopter waiting on the roof. Don't ask me why, but the request has come personally from Sir Gareth Fraser, head of GCHQ. That's it. Get lost."

"Blunt by name, blunt by nature," thought Sam as he ran

to the lift and ascended rapidly to the roof. He was scared, but intrigued. Why on earth would the director of GCHQ be sending him to Oxford? Sure, he had studied Roman and British history there as part of his Ancient History degree but what good was that knowledge when battling the supernatural? Then it hit him. Of course, they want me to speak with Ackerman!

When he reached the roof, there was indeed a helicopter waiting. He ducked as he ran forward, as at 6 feet and 3 inches tall there was a good chance of him being scalped by the rotors. An agent gave him a warm coat and a helmet equipped with communication equipment and bundled him aboard. Before he had even fastened his seat harness the helicopter was rising into the sky.

He felt a sudden anger rise within him when he saw Agent Philips sitting opposite him. They had history, and Sam wondered for one brief minute if he could get away with throwing him out of the helicopter. This was going to be a longer journey than he first thought.

As they flew across North London he could see that public disorder was already beginning to manifest itself in the streets. London's criminal element and mindless youths were making the most of the total lack of any police presence. They were breaking into stores and looting all across the capital. Sam suspected that they would not live long enough to enjoy their spoils unless Ackerman had some answers.

Chapter 16

10.25am. "Gentlemen," said the Prime Minister, putting down the phone, "I have just received confirmation that the Royal Family are currently at Balmoral Castle where they will remain until this crisis is over. My family has been moved to the panic room below 10 Downing Street, and they are currently under the protection of the most trusted and experienced members of the Diplomatic Protection Group. Our friends the Americans have offered us military aid, which we politely, but firmly, refused, as I am absolutely confident that we can handle this crisis ourselves. General Radford, I believe you wish to outline a plan of attack."

"Yes, Prime Minister," said Radford. "Our men are now in place to launch an all-out attack on the Roman soldiers at Hyde Park. We have tanks, missile launchers, attack helicopters, drones with incendiary bombs and about ten thousand men. Just give the word and we'll show those creatures the huge advances that have been made in warfare over the last two millennia. They won't know what hit them. This will be the biggest mass cremation since they burned the plague victims. I assure you there will be nothing left but ash, and your re-election will be guaranteed!"

"What about the residents and hotel guests along Park Lane?" said the Prime Minister, liking what he was hearing.

"There will be casualties, of course, but it will be acceptable collateral damage considering the potential threat to this nation if they start to attack."

"And the Roman soldiers outside Downing Street and Parliament?" asked the Prime Minister, still concerned about the welfare of his family. He was sure they would be safe in the bunker but he was concerned that Liberius might have more high explosives.

"We have troops standing by in Whitehall with flame throwers that can project over 100 metres. The Romans will be incinerated in a matter of seconds. Do not be concerned, Prime Minister, your family will be perfectly safe. As soon as you give the order, we will attack all primary targets simultaneously and eradicate this threat forever."

"You're sure that this will work?"

"As sure as I can be."

"OK let's get on with it, you have my permission to proceed."

"Wait!" Sir Gareth's voice shook everyone in the room. That one word was both a command and a plea. "If you attack them now it will be a catastrophic mistake. You cannot kill these creatures with conventional weapons - they have no lives to take. They are controlled by Liberius and inhabited by either demons or an extension of his own dark soul. All you'll succeed in doing is evoking a devastating backlash that will endanger every British life, starting with your own wife and children. I know this man, he is devoid of any morality!" Sir Gareth suddenly realized he had said too much.

"You know this man?"

"I do." he admitted.

"And you tell us only now?" piped in Director Smith. He smelt blood and it was time for some payback.

"I know of him *only* by reputation. He's a cold blooded killer with an insatiable hatred for this country," replied Sir Gareth.

"I can't believe what I am hearing," Smith yelled in mock outrage. "Are you telling us that you've always been aware of this psychopath and you didn't think it was important to share this information with this committee?"

"Oh come on, let's get this into perspective Andrew. All of you hold secrets that this committee is entirely unaware of. It comes with your office: tough decisions you've made in the interests of national security, the provision of arms to murderous regimes, undercover operations within allied governments, the assassination of world leaders, and worst of all covering for the White House as they murdered thousands of their own people in the pursuit of oil and a foothold in the Middle East!"

The committee looked at each other uncomfortably.

"All of us are also in the possession of truths, that if revealed to the general public, would cause outrage, hysteria, paranoia, anarchy, suicide and God knows what else. We keep our secrets to protect this government and the citizens we serve. Yes, Liberius has been *my* secret, but let's face it, if I'd told you before today that a 2,000 year old Roman soldier was posing a serious threat to national security you would have rushed me off to the nearest asylum! Liberius is certifiably insane, bent on the destruction of this country, and he has obviously been planning this attack for decades. He would not leave his entire army exposed like this if he thought, for one moment, that your missiles and bombs could destroy them. I don't understand the power that has been unleashed from the amulet, that is enabling these corpses to rise from the dead, but I am certain that we will only defeat them if we find a relic that wields an equal or greater power. Prime Minister, you have to give us time to interview Professor Ackerman *before* you order this attack."

General Radford rose to his feet. "No Prime Minister, you have to be decisive and act now. The people are frightened; civil unrest has already begun. What you do in the next hour will define your leadership. You cannot afford to be seen as weak or indecisive - we have to strike immediately!"

"And what do the rest of you think?" asked the PM.

Smith was the first to express his views. He was not going

to side with Sir Gareth even if he believed the crap he was spouting. “I agree with the General. Attack now, while we can!”

Sir Vince Jones, the Met Police Commissioner, was never a cautious man. “Destroy them before the country descends into complete chaos.”

The remaining members all voted for military action - it was the only option they really understood.

"I'm sorry Gareth, I have no choice. Send in the troops Radford, let's end this."

"Then you will have to live with the consequences!" Sir Gareth stood and left the room. They were not going to listen to him and they would have to pay a heavy price. He decided to leave them to their folly, when their plan backfired they would have to listen to him, meanwhile, he needed a moment to mourn the loss of one of his dearest friends.

Chapter 17

10.25am. It was cold and dark in the crypt below St Paul's Cathedral where the Dean lay on a tomb nine feet above the floor. He had been there for two hours unable to move while the Romans continued their search of the cathedral. He had bandaged his injured hand with what was left of his torn cassock and had held tightly onto his wrist to stop the further flow of blood. His back and head was still killing him but at least he was alive!

When the Romans had attacked, he had thrown himself under the pews in the quire as planned and as he scrambled underneath them, towards the rear entrance, he'd noticed the grate in the marble floor. Thankfully it was unsecured and he was able to move it aside and throw himself into the crypt below.

Unfortunately, he did not have time to replace it and a few seconds later he heard at least three of the Roman soldiers jump down behind him.

The crypt of St Paul's contains the tombs of such dignitaries as Lord Nelson, the Duke of Wellington and the cathedral's architect Sir Christopher Wren. Although it was impossible to make them out in the pitch black, the Dean knew his way around and headed straight for the duke's burial chamber quietly climbing up onto the brown granite sarcophagus where he now lay perfectly still.

He had been certain that the object that lay deep beneath this particular tomb would keep the Romans at bay and so far he had been proved right.

He had heard the arrival of the agents and their hasty departure but he had remained silent not wishing to give away his position, especially as there had been a Roman soldier standing within metres of the tomb.

For the last two hours since the agents had left, the Romans had searched for him in vain. Thankfully the duke's tomb was so large that even when they looked up, as they often did, they were unable to see him and, as he suspected, they were not willing to set foot on, or near, the sarcophagus. They sensed the immense power emanating from the object that lay deep beneath, a power that might be unleashed upon them if they were to venture too close.

Time, however, was running out, and the Dean had to get out of the cathedral. He wrapped his keys in the blood-soaked cloth, which he'd used to bind his injured hand, and threw it in the direction of the stairwell, where they fell with an almighty clatter. He was not sure if the Romans would respond to the sound or just follow the smell of blood, but either way he hoped that the ruse would get them away from the Duke's tomb.

To his relief it worked. He heard the Romans sprint up the stairwell back to the ground floor of the cathedral.

Cautiously he climbed down from the tomb, and slowly walked up the stairwell. When he reached the ground floor he could see that the Romans were running toward the main entrance in the west wing, so he quickly headed toward the fire exit in the south transept and ran out into the gardens and to freedom. With no visible traffic on the streets he headed south to the river. Maybe there would be a vessel there that could take him to Westminster.

He needed to make sure that Sir Gareth had received his message and made peace with Ackerman; if not, he would have to do something quite terrible to stop this unholy army - something that could result in the extermination of millions. He would have to summon the Angels of Death.

Chapter 18

11.00am. Jessica Pickering's alarm went off at exactly 11am as it did every Monday morning. Her first lecture was at 12.30pm and so she took full advantage of the opportunity to lie-in after another weekend of partying with her student friends at the prestigious Oxford University.

Even without make-up, Jessica was stunningly beautiful, tall, elegant and athletic. Her long brown hair was tied, as always, in a pony tail at the back of her head revealing high cheekbones, full lips and striking brown eyes with a slight orange tint that made her look slightly feline.

Jessica was just 19 years old and was in her second year of a Classical History degree. She had an excellent secondary school education at the prestigious Roedeans boarding school in Sussex, at the expense of her wealthy parents.

She excelled at everything: getting top grades in all of her GCSEs, becoming head girl, and captain of her school's hockey and netball teams. She also played hockey for her county and would probably have made Team GB had she had sufficient interest, but her first love was history. She especially enjoyed studying the lives of those special women who had risen above their male counterparts and made a significant impact in the shaping of the world.

She was also immensely ambitious and was determined

that she too would make a significant contribution to the planet, so that her name would also be written of in the annals of history.

What she would do to achieve this status was unclear to her until she was accepted into Oxford and met Professor Ackerman.

She idolized him because he believed in her and had taken her under his wing after just a few weeks at the University. There was no physical attraction. She couldn't deny that he was handsome, but she preferred men her own age.

Ackerman had told her, on more than one occasion, that he knew the perfect man for her, and the more she learned about Sam Callaghan, the more she believed he could be right.

Under Ackerman's expert tuition she had not only gotten a better understanding of Classical History than she ever thought possible, but he had taught her to use her talents to reach her full potential. She now had a clear idea of what she was capable of and what she needed to do in order to reach her lofty goals.

She walked over to her vintage, portable, black and white television and turned it on to find out what was happening in the world. She could never have imagined what she was about to witness. For the next thirty minutes, she sat spellbound and horrified as the latest reports came in from across the country. Once the shock had begun to subside, another feeling grew inside her. This, perhaps, was the day she would discover what she was truly capable of.

Chapter 19

11.15am. The helicopter continued its journey west. As they neared Oxford, Agent Philips opened his mouth for the first time to give Sam the brief he had been expecting.

"We need you to talk to Ackerman and convince him to help us."

Sam was about to reach for his throat and it took every ounce of his self-control to resist the temptation. Agent Philips, was the MI5 agent responsible for anything unexplained, the British equivalent to Agent Fox Mulder from *The X files*. The difference was that his only incentive to find the 'truth out there' was to kill it and bury it before the human race discovered that they were not alone.

"I don't think he'll need convincing," said Sam. "He'll be fully aware of what's happening and he won't just sit by and watch this Liberius follow through on his threats."

"We know that Callaghan, but we need to make sure we are all working from the same page. If he knows how to destroy these Roman zombies, it's important that the Prime Minister gets the credit. Ackerman is a maverick and we can't have him embarrass the Government again."

"You are referring, of course, to his outburst when you killed Lucinda."

"That was unfortunate."

Ackerman's adopted daughter Lucinda also worked for MI5. She had volunteered to bring in a man who had killed his family and several of his colleagues.

He wasn't evil, and he didn't want to harm anyone, but an accident at a military research facility had turned his body into some kind of living anti-matter that instantly imploded anyone he touched.

Lucinda knew that the government wanted him dead, and their nasty secret covered up, but she was determined to bring him in alive.

"Do we have to go through this again? She was in the line of fire, and refused to move. I was ordered to pass a shot through her chest and into the heart of the killer. As I said, it was unfortunate."

Sam's anger exploded in his chest and he started to unbuckle his safety restraints.

"If you'd have waited just a minute or two, she would have lived and you might have had a chance to debrief a man with extraordinary powers."

"There's no room on this planet for men like him."

"So you executed him and branded him a serial killer when his only crime was to possess a power that he could not control!"

Sam was now rising to his feet.

"Sit down you idiot. I was following orders!"

"You killed them in cold blood!" Sam lunged for him just as the helicopter made a sudden turn, and he went crashing to the floor. Philips drew his Glock and pointed it at Sam's face while placing his boot on the younger agent's throat.

"We've had this debate many times before Callaghan. You need to let this go! Your girlfriend is dead. It's time to move on."

"She is dead because of you!"

"Yes, I could have ignored those orders, but I honestly believed that it was better for one person to die than hundreds more to be put at risk! I hate that I killed her, and I have to live with that every day of my life, but I did what I had to do and if I was in the same position again I would still pull the trigger!"

Sam calmed down a little. This was the first time that Philips had expressed any remorse and it seemed almost genuine. Philips put away his Glock and allowed Sam to stand and return to his seat.

"Let's concentrate on the task in hand. We've just received these photographs." He passed his mobile phone to Sam. "They were taken an hour ago at St Paul's Cathedral. The Dean there drew that with his own blood just before he disappeared. We think it might be important. We want you to show it to Ackerman and see if he knows what it means."

Sam recognized the trident immediately; he had seen it one evening while studying late at the university. He had entered Ackerman's study without knocking, as he had often done, many times, in the past, and he was surprised to see Lucinda there. She had told him that she was going out with some friends that night.

Ackerman was showing her the trident and talking excitedly, but when Sam entered the room he abruptly stopped the conversation. Quickly, yet carefully, he placed the weapon on his desk, and escorted Sam back into the corridor.

He then earnestly asked Sam to forget what he had seen and to never talk of it again.

"What do you think it is?" Philips asked.

"It looks like some kind of trident, I guess."

"Do you recognize it? It is kind of distinctive."

"No, I have never seen it before," lied Sam.

"Well we think it may be the weapon that can stop these zombies, but we have no idea who has it or where it's located. Still, we may not need it."

"Why?"

"Because, I understand, we're just about to blow them all to kingdom come!"

Jessica made herself a cup of coffee and took a quick shower.

She looked at her watch. She was running out of time. As she got quickly dressed her thoughts went to Isabella, her closest friend and study partner. She had taken the day off to visit her mother in London. Today of all days!

She tried her mobile but got no answer, but that was not unusual for Isabella, whose phone was never charged! Jessica left a voice message asking her to call back immediately.

Isabella was in the same year as Jessica and they had become friends after just a month or two at Oxford University. Since that time they'd been pretty much inseparable.

They were in all of the same classes and most of the same clubs. They were both feminists, and they were also the center of attention when it came to boys.

The only times when they had a falling-out were normally centered around Ackerman. Isabella was clearly jealous of the time Jessica and he spent together, and the private tuition Jessica had been receiving.

It had come to head a few weeks ago. Jessica and Ackerman were talking in his study when the professor received an alert on his phone. He was extremely security conscious and had recently fitted a motion detector with a built-in camera in the corridor above his study door. The alert was to tell him that someone was lurking there. Ackerman showed the camera feed to Jessica who was horrified to see that it was Isabella, clearly spying on them.

Jessica pulled open the door and Isabella almost fell into the study. Her friend went straight onto the offensive, and accused Jessica and Ackerman of having an affair.

Jessica was mortally embarrassed and told Isabella in no uncertain terms to mind her own business and get out of her life.

Their relationship suffered for days, with hardly a word spoken, but one evening Isabella arrived on her doorstep and sincerely apologized, sweetening the deal with a tin of her homemade brownies, Jessica's favourites. They had hugged and made up and there had been no more mention of the incident, but Jessica felt a distance that hadn't been there before.

Jessica hoped desperately that Isabella was safe in London, but having seen the carnage that was happening there she feared that she might never see her friend again.

Chapter 20

11.30am. The COBRA briefing room had direct video feeds from the helicopters, drones, tanks and even the helmets of the frontline troops. Everything that happened would be broadcast from every possible angle, giving them a front row seat for the coming battle.

The room suddenly lit up as huge explosions could be seen on the monitors; missiles were raining down on the park from every direction. They were streaming in from the skies and from the tanks and missile launchers on the ground. The noise was deafening as one explosion followed another in quick succession.

The entire spectacle was watched by the guests and staff in the towering five-star hotels that lined Park Lane, on the east side of Hyde Park. The Hilton, The Dorchester, The Four Seasons, The Marriott and The Inter-Continental all offered superb views of the proceedings.

The guests cheered enthusiastically when the first missiles hit believing they were watching the destruction of the most frightening army ever to walk the earth. They soon dived for cover though as the blasts began to shatter windows and push shards of lethal glass into their luxury hotel rooms. Those who were slow to react were cut down where they stood. Acceptable collateral damage.

The onslaught lasted twelve minutes and when it was finished the entire park was full of fire and smoke. Visibility was just a few feet and the infantry stood by waiting to see what, if anything, was left of the walking corpses.

As the smoke began to disperse they moved slowly forward. The Prime Minister and his team held their breath as they watched the scene unfold and heard the chatter from the military radios.

The first communications from the ground forces began to filter through.

"This is Charlie Echo 4-503. We are advancing now into the park from Speakers' Corner. It's impossible to give you a visual yet, but as far as we can tell there's no sign of movement, no sign of life."

The committee cheered and began to shake one another's hands.

For the next few seconds there was silence, then…

"We are now approximately 200 metres into the park, advancing slowly as the ground has been torn apart by the explosions, but we are yet to encounter any hostiles. It's all quiet here."

The hugs continued. The Prime Minister was jubilant. The general was right: this great victory would assure him another term in the May elections.

"Wait! Something just ran across my field of vision, did anyone else see that?"

The celebrating stopped.

"Negative sergeant, it all seems clear to us."

Another dark shape seemed to pass to the left of the sergeant, barely visible in the heavy smoke; surely it had to be one of his own men?

"Has anyone broken rank?"

"That's another negative sergeant, we are all right here behind you."

"What the hell!" Suddenly the dark shapes began to increase in number, passing to his right and left. They were being outflanked.

"Company retreat, get out of the park now, that's an

order!"

The command came too late - they were completely surrounded. The loud speakers in the briefing room came alive with the sound of death. Grown men screamed and cursed as they were hacked to death by assailants they could hardly see. Then there were a few bursts of machine gun fire, more cries, and then silence.

For a minute or two each of the men in the briefing room buried their heads in their hands and contemplated the consequences of what had just transpired. Then there was another voice, dark, angry, full of hate.

"You disappoint me Prime Minister!"

11.30am. The Dean was frantic. He'd seen military jets and drones fly overhead and he'd heard huge explosions and the sound of heavy ordnance, but he knew that they would never kill such evil with conventional weapons.

He was just yards from the Millennium Bridge now but the creatures were everywhere, searching for him.

He was pinned down and, for now, escape seemed impossible. If they saw him he would be dead for sure, but with time running out he just might have to put his faith in God and run for it.

But if he were to die, he doubted that there was anyone else that would do what was necessary to save Britain - unless they'd managed to get to Ackerman.

Chapter 21

11.45am. Sam's helicopter flew over Oxford towards the university buildings where he had spent three very eventful years of his life.

The Faculty of Classics is the largest and oldest in the world. For over 900 years they have educated students in ancient history, Latin, Greek and classical architecture, admitting only 150 undergraduates a year. Sam had considered himself immensely fortunate to have been one of them, especially under the expert tutorage of Alexander Ackerman.

The faculty is based at Balliol College in the centre of Oxford. Previous students had been as diverse as John Wycliffe, who inspired the first translations of the Bible from Latin to English, building the faith of millions, to Richard Hawkins the renowned biologist and atheist whose book *The God Delusion* had robbed people of their faith in equal numbers.

As they landed in the college quadrangle Sam thought about his first meeting with Ackerman. He was tall, dark and enigmatic with long, black hair parted at the centre and falling onto broad shoulders. He had friendly blue eyes that seemed unnaturally bright, a long slender nose, and a square jaw.

Sam imagined him to be in his late thirties because he had few wrinkles and not a single grey hair, but his immense knowledge of British history belied a man of that age. He not only knew every significant event since the Bronze Age, he also spoke of them in such vivid detail that Sam could almost believed that Ackerman had witnessed them for himself.

Their friendship began to develop after Ackerman had delivered a fascinating lecture on "The Alternative History of Britain" which outlined his belief that the island has always been a battleground for the forces of good and evil.

Sam had asked him why he spent so much time studying the occult and he had simply said, "We cannot combat that which we do not understand."

This answer had intrigued Sam, and as a result they had spent hours together during his time at Balliol as Ackerman opened up his mind to a world that Sam never knew existed.

He had chosen not to believe everything Ackerman told him mainly because, if true, it would be terrifying. The events of this morning however had made him completely reassess his initial scepticism.

Ackerman was also a master of ninjutsu, an ancient Japanese martial art with many varied disciplines which included: free running, disguise, escape, concealment, pyrotechnics, medicine, unarmed combat, and combat with stick, spear, sword and staff. Sam became a disciplined student recognising the immense value of these skills in his chosen career. He became a black belt after just 18 months.

Ackerman was not the first "ninja" professor in Balliol's rich history.

The Ackerman family had practiced the art for generations and had been faculty members on and off since the fourteenth century. Their involvement with the college had become legendary, but often for the wrong reasons.

The Ackermans were considered to be brilliant academics but habitual philanderers. For example his great-great-grandfather Charles Joseph Ackerman joined the faculty in 1895 and went missing twenty years later during the early months of the First World War along with one of his students, a beautiful 20-year-old blonde called Catherine Huxley. At the time, it was a sensational scandal as she was the daughter of British nobility.

His grandfather, Edward Archibald, had joined the faculty in the late twenties and then resigned in 1941, supposedly to enlist in the RAF. It was widely believed, however, that he too had formed an inappropriate relationship with one of his most promising students and they had decided to elope, a rumour that gained credence when it was discovered that there was no record of any Edward Archibald Ackerman ever joining the Royal Air Force. Neither were ever seen or heard of again.

Despite the reputation of his predecessors Alexander was welcomed into the faculty in 2001, although he had to assure the Vice Chancellor that he and his family would not bring any further embarrassment to the university.

Ackerman had kept his promise and maintained a reasonably low profile until he adopted an 18-month-old, baby girl called Lucinda Fletcher. A former student had made the request for him to look after her daughter in a hand-written will that she had hastily scrawled before committing suicide. The headline in The Times read, "Oxford Professor adopts Miracle Baby."

The "miracle baby" referred to the fact that Lucinda had been terminally ill with leukaemia until the day of her mother's suicide and then she had a complete overnight remission.

Everyone assumed that Ackerman must have been the father, so he agreed to a DNA test to ally the university's concerns, which to their relief came back negative.

He doted on his new daughter and she benefitted greatly from his love, dedication and wisdom. She sailed through school and university and then went to work for the secret service despite Ackerman's protestations. Less than two years later she was dead.

Sam had met Lucinda at the end of his first term, when she returned to spend Christmas with her father. He warmed to her immediately and was keen to learn as much as he could from her about her career at MI5. There was little that she was able to share with him but she encouraged him to pursue his dream, "Who knows," she'd said, "we might even get to work together some day."

Over the next two years Sam and Lucinda became inseparable, as far as his studies and her work would allow. Ackerman even encouraged the relationship, as he was extremely impressed by Sam's intellect, drive and devotion to his daughter. It wasn't long before they were planning their future together.

Sam decided that he would propose after his graduation ceremony and spent days trying to find a ring worthy of her, that he could afford to buy with his meager student grant. He barely ate for a month so he could get the required funds together.

Sam was to learn of Lucinda's death on the same day that he'd finally found the perfect ring. Two agents interrupted one of Ackerman's afternoon lectures and asked to speak with him outside.

The shouts of despair and anger that echoed around the corridors touched the hearts of every student, but none more so than Sam, who knew immediately that it had something to do with Lucinda.

He ran out of the auditorium and found Ackerman on his knees, his face rippled with tears. The agents had already left. Obviously they'd come to deliver the news without any words of comfort. On seeing Sam, the professor stood and embraced him tightly, uttering the two words that would confirm his greatest fear and completely shatter his life: "She's gone."

In the days that followed it proved impossible to get any real answers from MI5 other than the formal statement that "she had died a hero while protecting the interests of her country."

Sam was convinced that Ackerman knew of the circumstances that surrounded Lucinda's death, but he steadfastly refused to discuss the matter. Sam's suspicions were confirmed when Ackerman wrote a scathing open letter that was published in an early edition of the Sunday Times. In it he declared that Lucinda "had been sacrificed on the altar of ignorance by a government that preferred to destroy the unexplainable rather than seek any form of understanding." The letter was removed from later editions and never appeared on the Internet. What made matters much worse was the fact that there was, mysteriously, no body to identify. Ackerman and Sam had found this completely unacceptable, but were told it was a matter of national security. So, at her funeral they buried an empty casket, and both men had felt that emptiness every since.

After the funeral, Sam was angry that Ackerman had clammed up, just when he needed and deserved answers. He decided not to attend his own graduation and instead took a stroll down to Folly Bridge and then along the Isis to Iffley Lock, as he had done on many a Sunday afternoon with Lucinda.

When he reached the lock he stopped to throw the engagement ring into the river and solemnly watched it sink into the murky waters along with all his dreams of a future with the woman he loved.

After graduation, Ackerman took a year's compassionate leave away from the university, and everything and everyone that reminded him of Lucinda. No one knows where he went or what he did and he refused to take calls even from Sam.

Sam started the Intelligence Officer Development Program at MI5 and set new records in almost every test he took, whether academic, strategic or physical. The martial arts training that he had received from Ackerman together with the unrelenting anger he felt after Lucinda's death made him a formidable opponent in all combat situations. He remained undefeated throughout training and even floored his instructors on more than one occasion, much to the delight and amusement of the other recruits.

As he was given more and more freedom he dug deeper and deeper into the events surrounding Lucinda's death until he finally learned the truth. His first confrontation with

Agent Philips, and the violence that followed, nearly cost him his job. In fact, it would have been one of the shortest intelligence careers in British history if it had not been for the intervention of Sir Gareth Fraser, as a personal favour to Ackerman. It was the only time the two of them had spoken since Lucinda's death.

As Sam climbed from the helicopter, Agent Philips grabbed him by the arm.

"I think it's in everyone's best interest if Ackerman doesn't know I'm here."

Sam pulled his arm free, without responding, and walked towards the lecture theatre.

He was certain he would never love anyone again the way he had loved Lucinda, but within minutes of entering the classroom he found out that he was mistaken.

Chapter 22

11.45am. The face of Liberius appeared on all of the briefing room monitors. He was filming himself using the camera on the helmet of one the recently deceased troops. Whether the head was still in that helmet was unclear until Liberius shook it free and filmed it rolling on the ground at his feet.

"Messy business war, isn't it?" he said mockingly. "I warned you Prime Minister that any attack on me or my men would result in a merciless reprisal. You played your hand and lost, and now I will play mine. I take it that you have a feed into your office from Downing Street? I'm afraid the flamethrowers you deployed there were quite useless. Those huge, clumsy fuel tanks that your troops wore on their backs made perfect targets for my snipers. It took just one bullet to ignite each canister and incinerate the soldier carrying it. Oh yes, I have snipers too, an army of mercenaries, providing us with a little ground support. They planted the bombs for me at The Tower and, I am delighted to report, they have now done the same beneath your home.

"There are just far too many tunnels under your city and I know them all. After all with a face like this I've been forced to live in them for much of the last two thousand years, even built some myself actually!" There was the noise of a mobile ringing in the background. "Please excuse me for just a moment Prime Minister, I think that might be some of my mercenaries on the phone now."

The broadcast broke off.

"Get my family out of there and quickly," the Prime Minister ordered General Radford. "And get the bomb disposal guys down into those tunnels"

"It'll be suicide sir, they'll never find and disarm those bombs before they're detonated".

"It's an order Radford!"

The general erupted. "Don't you think you've sent enough men to their deaths today!"

Before the Prime Minister could answer Liberius was back on their monitors, "Now where was I, oh yes, the bombs under Downing Street. I am quite sure that they will be able to penetrate the panic room that currently houses your family - after all we blew apart your so-called 'impenetrable' vault at the Tower quite easily, enabling me to reclaim this powerful little amulet."

He showed the relic to the camera. For most in the committee this was the first sight of one. It was oblong in shape and carved from hematite, a mineral formed from oxidized iron, that takes its name from the Greek word *haima*, meaning *blood*. It was such a dark red that it was almost black and on all sides it bore Egyptian hieroglyphics and occult symbols. It was tied around his neck with rope and it had a curved indent on the topside, where it was originally used to support the head of the dead pharaoh Ankhef.

"I know how it feels to watch your family die, as I was made to do so myself, so I will at least give you a chance to say your goodbyes, a privilege that I was never given. You have thirty seconds, Prime Minister."

The Prime Minister looked pleadingly at his general.

"I'm sorry sir, there just isn't enough time."

The PM tried to remain calm. "Liberius, I apologise for underestimating you. We should never have launched that attack. Please spare my family and I will do what I can to meet your demands."

"You have no intention whatsoever of meeting my demands, I am aware of that. At least, not until enough of your people have died. You have twenty seconds left, you're wasting precious time."

The Prime Minister broke down "I'm begging you Liberius, please, please don't kill my family!"

"Sir, it's your wife," Director Smith passed the satellite phone to the Prime Minister. The panic room had been receiving the entire Liberius broadcast.

A crackle then a desperate voice, "Duncan, you have to do something! You can't just stand by and let him murder us! Give him whatever he wants and do it now - your children are here for heaven's sake and they're terrified! Duncan, please don't let us die! Talk to me!"

The Prime Minister could clearly hear the sobs of his two children in the background. His voice cracked, "I love you and the kids so much. Cathy, I am so sorry!"

"No David, I don't want to do---" The blast shook the war rooms knocking men, cabinets, tables, tablets and computers to the floor. The feed from the entrance to Downing Street showed a burst of white light, then nothing but static.

A news helicopter above the explosion, which had ignored the flight exclusion zone, was hit by the blast and burst into flames. There would be no need to revoke their press license. The adjacent Cabinet Office was badly damaged and the Cenotaph in Whitehall, which had honoured Britain's war dead for nearly 100 years, crumbled and fell. Around it lay the fresh bodies of service men who were on their way to the scene, including the Metropolitan Police's crack bomb disposal team, the EXPOS.

When the smoke cleared, Downing Street was just a large crater. Another monument to Britain's power and former supremacy had been utterly destroyed.

"You had your warning Prime Minister, and you ignored it. Now another warning. I am bringing the deadline forward to 9pm this evening. If you have not surrendered this country to me by then, the killing will start again and this time it will not end."

Liberius once more began his maniacal laugh.

"Turn that damn monitor off!" demanded the Prime Minister in tears.

11.45am. The Roman soldiers that had been strategically placed near all of London's airports began tearing down the wire fences and flooding onto the runways preventing flights from leaving or landing. Others stood guard at each of the mainline train stations, even though there was no one to drive the trains.

All of the main arterial roads out of London's West End and City were blocked by Roman soldiers and abandoned, or crashed, vehicles. The only way out was through the back streets, but they were congested with thousands of Londoners desperate to leave the capital and crowds of youths who were ransacking the abandoned shops and homes.

London was in turmoil, yet amid the atmosphere of frenzied fear, the rational and brave began to gather in groups, in market squares and in community buildings. They were all called together on Twitter, Facebook and other forms of social media.

Jews, Muslims, Christians and outright atheists sat or stood together trying to understand what was happening and plan their resistance. They were frightened but resolute. If they couldn't rely on anyone else to save them, they would make a stand themselves. A decision was made that everyone would gather on Blackheath Common later that afternoon and then march together on Hyde Park before the latest deadline. Better to die fighting than wait in fear.

Chapter 23

11.46am. John had taken the Kew up the Thames as far as Hammersmith to see the extent of the flooding and to try to assess what was going on.

He was navigating his way back up the river, passed the Houses of Parliament, when he spotted a company of Roman soldiers marching down the embankment from Westminster towards Waterloo Bridge.

The British Army with the help of the Metropolitan Police had set up roadblocks with tanks and other armoured vehicles on each of the bridges to stop them entering the highly populated areas of South London, but John doubted that the roadblocks would last long if the Romans decided to attack.

This was of great concern to him, as his family lived in one of the high-rise blocks of flats at Elephant and Castle, one of London's oldest and largest council estates. His priority was to get home, as soon as he could, and protect his family.

Suddenly there was a flash of white light over the cityscape on his port side, followed by a loud explosion that violently shook the buildings along the north bank, dislodging tiles from roofs, cracking numerous windows and activating the alarms of the cars parked out on the streets. It seemed to John that the blast had come from the Whitehall area - maybe the Cabinet office or Downing Street.

A few minutes later came the sounds of multiple sirens and suddenly a large black van, with red thunderbolt transfers on the side, swung onto the Victoria Embankment from Horse Guards Avenue with the screech of tyres and the smell of burning rubber.

It was travelling at high speed and being pursued by six police cars. The Roman soldiers parted to let the black van through and then they turned, closed ranks and pointed spears and swords in the direction of the oncoming police cars.

The police cars could not slow down in time and drove headlong into the Romans who threw their weapons and themselves through the windscreens of the first three cars, which quickly came to a halt as the drivers were torn to pieces.

The remaining three cars ploughed into the stationary vehicles and those drivers too were immediately savaged.

John turned to look at the escaping van. Its driver side window was open and the driver was glancing back with a sneer at the carnage behind him, slapping the door in delight.

Anger rose within John and he quickly grabbed one of the flare guns from a box on the forward side of the Kew's wheelhouse. He tracked the van for a few seconds to gauge its speed, and then he fired the flare, aiming a few feet in front of the van's windscreen.

His aim was perfect and the flair sailed through the van window and exploded in the driver's face, instantly blinding him and dissolving his nose, cheeks and ears. The van veered towards the river, hit the wall at about 120 mph and exploded.

Unfortunately, the blast blew a large hole in the river wall sending large slabs of masonry across the Thames towards John's ship. He had no time to do anything but dive to the deck as the flying debris smashed into his cabin.

Thankfully the hull was undamaged and as he got back onto his feet, a huge cheer and round of applause erupted from the soldiers at the barricade on Waterloo Bridge. John took a bow; strike one in the war against the Romans had gone to Captain Birdseye!

Chapter 24

12.25pm. London's street gangs gathered in London Fields, Hackney just across from the Blackstone Estate. Crews and urban collectives who would on any other day gladly knife or shoot one another, stood side by side. They had brought with them, as instructed, every weapon at their disposal, which they brazenly carried or hung from their trouser belts, holsters or jackets. It was an impressive arsenal consisting of pistols, semi-automatics, shotguns, knives of various lengths, swords, meat cleavers, and even grenades. London gangs have no problem getting guns. They claim they get them from the government who supply them with arms in the hope that they will kill one another.

The gathering had been called by the LFB, one of the biggest and most notorious, gangs in North London. It was the first time they had invited rival gangs into their 'hood but they had to do something before the Romans took over their city and started to interfere with their operations.

Word had spread quickly and over the last two hours 88 gangs had arrived with more on their way. This was, however, only a small percentage of London's street gangs - Hackney alone had over 30 - but many were too busy taking advantage of the lack of police by looting, mugging, raping and the occasional murder. Others were just too suspicious of the LFB's motives, to set foot in their area.

As Jerome Lawrence, leader of the LFB, looked out over the gathering of some 6,000 youths, he felt a mixture of pride and fear.

While most adults were fleeing the city, they had all chosen to stay and fight. They were survivors; most had lost friends and family in relentless street battles over the last decade, sometimes simply for slipping into the wrong postcode.

Jerome was aware, however, that the gangs were also highly unruly, volatile and extremely violent. They had come heavily armed, so if they chose not to listen, he could have brought the biggest gang war in history right to his own doorstep.

He raised his hands to calm the crowd and spoke with as much authority as he could muster. Any sign of weakness and the precarious truce would fall apart in seconds.

"Safe bedrin, tings is bad, we can't be owned by no Roman rude boys. We have ta kill 'em, it's bate man."

"Hey Jerome, who made you top boy?"

"Yeah man, why you in charge?"

"There's no killin' these tings, you don't know jack, Jerome!"

Murmuring began throughout the crowd, then, there was shouting.

Jerome raised his arms and his voice, "Hush bluds and listen!"

"We ain't your bluds!"

A shot rang out from somewhere in the middle of the crowd and Jerome fell to the ground. The LFB pulled out their guns immediately and started firing in the general direction of the shooter. As nobody really knew who had fired, everyone panicked and just as Jerome had feared, they turned on one other.

The sound of guns and automatic weapons could be heard all over the borough. Many gang members fled but most stayed to fight.

Twenty minutes later, when the Junction Boys and

Tooting Tamils eventually arrived in Hackney, only 421 of the 6,000 gangsters were still standing and most of those were injured in some way. There was no police to intervene and no medics to help the injured. If the government has supplied them with guns to kill each other, today they had certainly achieved their objective.

Eventually the youths who could still walk left the park, carrying the injured and the spoils of war. The fields were stained red with blood and littered with discarded shotgun cartridges, bullet casings and corpses.

One of the LFB found Jerome lying amidst the carnage. He had gunshot wounds to his leg and chest and he was coughing up a froth of blood. "Look what you've done, Jerome. These boys are dead 'cause of you."

He raised his gun and shot Jerome in the head. It was time for someone else to lead the LFB.

12.25pm. Over recent years much of South East London, in particular New Cross and Deptford, had seen a huge rise in Pentecostal churches. Ministers had taken over offices, cinemas, bingo halls and even whole industrial estate units to cope with the demand for highly charged church services where congregations could witness and benefit from the 'Gifts of the Spirit'.

These ministers are mostly well dressed, drove nice cars and were supported extremely well by the offerings of their devout followers. At an average service you could expect to see several healings, some speaking in tongues, and the casting out of spirits. The congregations had complete faith in their ministers as conduits of these marvelous manifestations and that is why they had insisted on an emergency meeting at *The Church of the Holy Light* on the Old Kent Road.

When everyone was seated the more vocal members of the assembled congregation stood and asked their ministers to get over to Hyde Park and cast out the demons.

The ministers unanimously praised the congregation for their faith, but respectfully explained that such a task could not be done except after much fasting and prayer.

"Then yoos better get fastin' and prayin' on your ways over there, you hear!" shouted one very frightened worshipper.

"'Specially if want any more off'rins from us!" shouted another.

A large Jamaican woman then stood and walked towards the podium, pointing at the ministers. "You say you is the Lord's servant on earth. So you go jump in those fancy cars of yours, which incidentally we is payin' for, and do His will. Go save our poor wretched souls from those murderous devils!"

"Hallelujah!" the congregation shouted in unison.

The ministers could see that any further objections were futile, the congregation had spoken, and there was nothing they could do to dissuade them. They have used every trick in the book to convince these people of their spiritual powers and now the chickens had come home to roost. They nervously got to their feet and were ushered out of the assembly hall and into their cars. Hundreds gathered in the street to see them off, crying, waving, praying and praising. Some even got in their own cars and followed, wanting to witness good triumphing over evil.

As the ministers drove away one of them turned round to his associates and said, "What the hell we gonna do now!"

Chapter 25

12.27pm. Ackerman had arrived at the lecture theatre in the early hours to prepare his presentation on "Exploration, Exploitation and Enlightenment". He, therefore, had no idea about the incredible events that were systematically destroying the country he loved. His lecture was to start in three minutes and he was surprised that there was no sign of his students.

Suddenly the door flew open and in walked Jessica, who looked harassed.

"Hi Jessica," he said. "It looks like you may be my only student today, where is everyone?"

Jessica began to update the professor on all of the morning's news. As she did so, others began to arrive. They were understandably frightened and desperately hoped that Ackerman could give them some answers and reassurance.

They were all surprised that Ackerman seemed to be unfazed by these events, even when they mentioned the resurrected Roman armies.

"What's your assessment Jessica?" he asked once everyone had taken their seats.

"My guess is that somebody has used an ancient relic such as the Amulet of Ankhef, or some demonic spell to raise the dead. As they have summoned an army consisting entirely of

Roman soldiers I would say we should be looking for some Italian, power hungry male with the delusion of becoming the next emperor of Rome. His intention is clearly to conquer Britain and finish off what they couldn't achieve at the height of the Roman Empire."

"I would say that you have given us an excellent summation, Jessica." He then looked to the back of the lecture theatre. "What do you think, Sam?"

All eyes turned to see the young man who had recently entered the room, still dressed in John's white Port Authority uniform.

"Remarkable, she's remarkable," he said quite spellbound. It was clear to everyone that he was not just talking about Jessica's synopsis.

He suddenly regained his composure. "Professor we have to speak alone, it is a matter of national security."

"Would you mind if Jessica joined us? She's very knowledgeable in Roman and occult history. I think you might find her input invaluable".

Sam's nod of approval came as no surprise to anyone, and Ackerman dismissed the rest of the class, advising them that they should go back to their families until this was all over, unless, of course, they were living in London.

When the students had left, Sam embraced Ackerman. "It's good to see you professor, it's been a while."

"Good to see you too Sam. This is Jessica, probably the most promising student I have ever had, including you."

"Good to know." Sam offered Jessica his hand. "I'm Sam Callaghan I used to---"

Jessica shook his hand and smiled, "I know who you are. The professor has told me all about you."

"I suppose the government sent you to ask for my help," said Ackerman.

"You would be right."

"Well my first inclination would be to send you back with this board rubber up your backside. But under the circumstances I think we'd better talk. Tell me all you know."

Sam told Ackerman everything, ending with: "Liberius has delivered an ultimatum. He wants us to surrender by 9pm, passing the sovereignty of our nation and all its wealth, properties and territories to the Empire of Rome and recognising him as our supreme ruler and emperor. If we fail to meet this deadline his army will kill relentlessly until we surrender."

"Sounds like a charmer!" said Jessica.

"The PM decided to launch a military attack late this morning, which failed. Just before I walked in here I was told Liberius had destroyed Downing Street in retaliation, killing the Prime Minister's wife and children in the process."

"My god!" For the first time Jessica looked noticeably shocked.

"There has also been another significant casualty, I'm afraid the Dean of St Paul's is missing, presumed dead. I believe you knew him well."

Ackerman looked visibly shaken. "I did. We worked together more than once when evil tried to poke its head out of hell's gates. He'll be missed."

"He left you a message before he died," Sam showed the professor the pictures on his mobile phone.

"That trident, you have it don't you?"

"Not exactly."

"But you know where to find it?"

"I do."

"What's so special about it Alexander, do you think this weapon could somehow destroy those Romans?"

"Well it certainly has in the past, but that's a long story. In fact there is much to explain Sam, but first I need to ask you a question. Is Agent Philips with you?"

Sam smiled, knowing exactly where this was heading. "He told me to tell you that he wasn't."

"That's all I needed to know. Give me a few minutes Sam; I just need to pay our mutual friend a quick visit. When I get back I'll tell you everything you need to know. Get to know Jessica while I'm gone!"

He cracked his knuckles and left the room.

Chapter 26

12.45pm. John was just approaching the Millennium Footbridge when he saw a priest running across, frantically waving at him. He slowed down the *Kew* and was shocked to see that the man was climbing over the safety rails as if he was about to jump into the river. He grabbed his loud hailer.

"Could you please climb back down onto the bridge? If you jump or fall into this river from that height there's a very high possibility that you will die!"

The priest was shouting back but John could not make out what he was saying. He assumed that he was not of sound mind; perhaps his faith had taken a battering when the dead Romans started marching through the streets.

"Please sir, return to the safety of the walkway!" he shouted.

John looked along the length of the bridge and then suddenly understood what was happening: approaching from the opposite direction were four badly decomposed Roman soldiers. Two other Romans had followed him onto the bridge. The minister was trapped.

A chill ran down John's back, not just because the minister was in mortal danger, but also because some of the soldiers were coming from south of the river not a mile from where he lived. They must have crossed the river before the barricades had been put in place or they were rising from their graves over there as well.

Suddenly the priest jumped into the river about 100 yards in front of his boat and disappeared under the surface, then, one of the soldiers jumped in after him. John grabbed the life ring for the second time that morning and looked earnestly into the murky river, waiting for the man to resurface.

He knew, however, that there was a good chance that the fast flowing tides and eddies would keep the priest under and pull him along the riverbed until he drowned.

He was also concerned that the Roman soldier was beneath him but he was pretty sure that its heavy armour would anchor it to the river floor some five metres below his boat.

After a full minute John was sure that the priest must be dead. Then suddenly just off the starboard side he broke the surface gasping for air. John threw him the life ring and dragged him to the side of the boat. He reached out for the minister's hands and noticed that one of them was badly damaged causing him to cry out in pain. As he tried to pull the minister aboard, John was surprised that it was taking him so much effort. Then he noticed the boney hand wrapped around the minister's ankle.

Chapter 27

12.45pm. As Sir Gareth returned to the briefing room he saw the Prime Minister staring at the video screens, his hand covering his mouth, his shoulders moving up and down as he sobbed uncontrollably.

He intended to say "I told you so" but when he saw the state of the man he decided it was best to hold his tongue.

He knew it has been a difficult decision for the Prime Minister and the man had paid dearly for his refusal to follow Sir Gareth's counsel.

His thoughts went back to a time, just over a decade earlier, when a previous Prime Minister *had* listened to him when he warned about another powerful relic that had been tracked down in Iraq.

For centuries men had speculated as to the whereabouts of the Ark of the Covenant, considered to be the most powerful of all holy relics. The Bible revealed that the Israelite armies that carried the Ark were not just invincible, but the Ark itself could strike down opposing armies and entire cities without the need for the Israelites to fight.

British Intelligence had discovered, from an ancient Aramaic manuscript, dug up in Syria, that the Babylonians had, in fact, stolen the Ark when they captured Jerusalem, and destroyed Solomon's temple in 587 BC.

The document recorded that the Ark had been taken back to Babylon, which was now called Iraq, and hidden beneath King Nebuchadnezzar's imperial palace, just 53 miles south of Baghdad.

Somehow Saddam Hussein heard about the treasure, probably due to a spy in British Intelligence, and he ordered an immediate excavation of the site between the Tigris and Euphrates Rivers, dedicating hundreds of his men to the task.

When Sir Gareth's spies heard about the excavation, he immediately told the Prime Minister of the potential danger if Saddam Hussein was to get his hands on the Ark and he urged the PM to invade Iraq immediately, before it was discovered. The chances were that Ark would be powerless in the hands of an evil dictator like Saddam, but Sir Gareth could not take the risk.

The Prime Minister at that time was a devout Christian who understood the implications, and immediately told the world that Saddam had a weapon of mass destruction. When he made this revelation and called for an invasion he had, in fact, *not* lied. The Ark *was* capable of mass destruction, should the bible accounts be believed.

After the invasion, the weapons inspectors of the allied forces looked, in vain, for chemical, nuclear or biological weapons. The secret service, however, with the assistance of Ackerman and the Dean took over the excavation of Babylonia and after seven months of digging they discovered the Ark.

Ackerman had told Sir Gareth how frightening the discovery had been. The Ark had vibrated as if it were carrying an enormous electrical charge and as they approached it, every hair rose on their bodies and every movement required great effort, as if they were walking into a sand storm.

The Dean instructed his men not to touch the artefact directly under any circumstances, reminding them of the fate of the Israelites who had reached out to steady the Ark many millennia before.

During the first night after its discovery, they found out who the mole was in British Intelligence. His dead body lay beside the Ark along with four officers from Saddam's Republican Guard. They had fourth degree burns all over their bodies and their final expression of abject fear was captured on their charred faces. The traitor, Doug Rainer, had been in charge of the security team at the site, and he'd clearly tried to take the Ark from under their noses.

The following day the artefact was, very respectfully and very carefully, crated up using cranes and pulleys, and then secretly transported back to the UK on a C-130 Hercules which transported it to RAF Northolt just 6 miles north of Heathrow.

From there it was taken in an unmarked van to St Paul's Cathedral, which was conveniently closed due to a major £40m renovation project. There it was interred deep beneath the tomb of the Duke of Wellington in the cathedral's crypt, where it had remained under the ever-watchful eye of the Dean.

The, then Prime Minister had shouldered the blame for the so-called "unwarranted" attack on Iraq ever since, but he was prepared to be labelled a war criminal, knowing that letting the Ark fall into the hands of Saddam would have been unthinkable.

When Sir Gareth heard that the Dean was missing he had feared that Liberius had taken the Ark, but his men had reported that the crypt floor was undisturbed.

Sir Gareth had considered recovering the Ark himself, that morning, and using it against Liberius, but the risks were too great. He was frankly not sure of the consequences of releasing such power on British soil and he could not risk it getting into the Roman's evil hands. Besides, if the Dean felt it appropriate he would have drawn the Ark, not a trident, with his blood.

General Radford was standing at the far corner of the room, video conferencing with the brigadier who was stationed at Hyde Park. Radford was doing his best to avoid eye contact with anyone in the room.

Andrew Smith looked at Sir Gareth and exhaled heavily before speaking.

"OK, we tried it our way and failed. What now?"

"Your agent Sam Callaghan is interviewing Professor Ackerman, who, I'm told, is now cooperating fully after seriously assaulting another of your agents, Brian Philips."

"Who the hell authorized their involvement?"

"I did!"

Before Director Smith could react, Commissioner Vince Jones intervened. "We do have some positive news Sir Gareth. A van was spotted carrying Liberius's mercenaries away from the Downing Street explosion.

It was chased down by some of our patrol cars and was destroyed, killing everyone on board. We're not sure if this was the only mercenary force at Liberius's disposal, but at least we've nailed the scum who killed the PM's family. Unfortunately, we lost several good men in the pursuit."

"Well at least we've made *some* progress. Congratulations commissioner" Sir Gareth was already aware that the van was destroyed by a civilian, but he did not want to alienate anyone else.

He turned back to Director Smith. "What progress have your teams at MI5 made?"

"Well apparently some of my agents have been sent, without my knowledge, to Oxford," he reported testily. "The rest are researching every source possible to find a way to wipe out the Roman army before Liberius lets them loose on the general population. They have even resorted to reading blogs on how to kill zombies for God's sake, and the only idea that they've come up with so far is to encase them in quick drying cement!"

Sir Gareth was not impressed. "They've dug themselves out of deep graves buried under two millennia of this city's foundations, I don't think cement will prove to be much of an obstacle."

"Then what do we do?" asked the commissioner genuinely frightened.

"We get our Prime Minister to pull himself together so he

can address and calm the people. We wait for the report back from Callaghan and we capture one of those Roman zombies and see if our scientists can find a way to immobilize it."

12.47pm. John looked on in horror as the Roman soldier clawed its way over the Dean's body into his ship. It had discarded its heavy armour and weapons and stood there unarmed, dripping water, mud and rotten flesh. It stared malevolently at John as he quickly dragged the Dean out of the water.

The two men stood side by side and out of breath, anticipating the creature's attack. John quickly weighed up his options. As the creature moved slowly towards them they backed up to the bow of the ship. John desperately ran through every instrument and piece of equipment in his cabin, trying to think of something that might save their lives.

He had heard that the army had failed to destroy the soldiers with incendiary bombs so his remaining flare would be of no use whatsoever. Then he looked at the soldier's exposed rib cage. Although the creature was strong, without its armour it weighed next to nothing. Maybe he could find a way to throw it off the ship without a fight.

As they got level with the cabin John yelled to the Dean to hang on to something. The Dean reached for the mooring rope as John dived into the cabin, putting one engine full throttle in reverse and the other forward.

With the engines going full speed in opposite directions the catamaran abruptly began to spin. As it hit its own wash, the boat suddenly tipped and the creature lost its balance and fell back into the river. The Dean held on for dear life and just managed to stay in the boat.

As John straightened the vessel, the Dean clawed his way into the cabin and drew John's attention back up to the Millennium Bridge.

The remaining soldiers were poised to jump aboard as

they passed beneath. John recognised the danger immediately and as they started to jump he accelerated again to the full 20 knots. The soldiers fell harmlessly into the river behind them.

Chapter 28

12.50pm. Ackerman returned to the lecture theatre with a huge grin across his face. His hair and clothes were now considerably tousled, his knuckles were grazed and there was a small cut in his lower lip.

Sam laughed. Jessica was startled. "Are you OK Professor? Did you fall over or something?"

"You could say that Jessica," said Ackerman, "now back to work".

"Do I need to call a medic?" Sam asked.

"No I'm fine!"

"I'm not talking about you Alexander!"

"Oh no, Agent Philips is being attended to by the pilot. Apparently he has had first aid training."

"Will he report the incident?"

"No, he doesn't like Agent Philips either! Now where were we? Oh yes, the trident. I'm afraid this is going to sound like a history lesson, but I'll jazz it up and make it as exciting as I can."

"Just as if you were actually there?" Sam said.

"Yes, naturally. That's the only way to really appreciate history. Now you've heard of Boudicca of course, or Boadicea as she is sometimes called?"

"Of course I remember that lecture. She was an incredible

woman," said Sam. Jessica looked at him approvingly. It was rare even in the 21st century for men to have any great appreciation of woman like Boudicca.

"She was, but she was even more incredible than you think. I must confess that in that lecture I didn't tell you everything Sam, no, not by a long chalk. The account I gave then was mainly that of the Roman historian, Publius Cornelius Tacitus. He had tried to piece the events together from accounts given by the occupying Roman leaders when they returned, but those accounts were, of course, rather biased and there were things that they did not wish to repeat and frankly could not understand.

"The real story of Boudicca is known only to a very select few. As a professor of this university I have access to certain manuscripts and ancient documents that generally remain under lock and key. Some were, until quite recently, largely believed to be lost but were found at recent excavations near Looe, in Cornwall, and in St Albans.

"From these manuscripts I was able to piece together the true story of the Iceni Queen which up until now, I haven't repeated to another living soul, even you Sam, simply because it would not have been believed. After this morning's events, however, I think the world might be ready to listen!

"Jessica, how about a cup of tea before I start?"

"Can I get one for you too Sam?" Jessica asked with a warm smile. When Sam politely declined she reluctantly left for the kitchen.

"In AD 61, as you know, Imperial Rome was ruled over by the insane Emperor Nero, and was at the height of its power. Its influence stretched from the Urals in the east to this mysterious island in the west known then by its inhabitants as Albonium. When the Romans arrived they renamed it Britannia after one of the first tribes they encountered here.

"The Romans shared an uneasy peace here with the Celtic tribes, many of whom had allied themselves to the Romans. One such tribe was the Iceni, who occupied an area that encompassed much of Norfolk and the north of Suffolk."

Jessica returned with tea and biscuits for the professor and a bottle of water for Sam, which he gratefully accepted. The professor dipped a biscuit in his tea and took a bite.

"Delicious, thank you Jessica. I think she'll make someone a perfect wife, Sam."

"I am sure she would," said Sam with a smile. Jessica reddened and looked at the floor.

Ackerman winked at Sam and continued. "Their leader, King Prasutagus, was on good terms with the Romans right up until his death. In his will, he had even named his two daughters, and the Emperor Nero as co-heirs in the hope of preserving his kingdom."

Sam was beginning to get impatient. "Alexander, I know all this, tell me something I don't know! We have just eight hours left before Liberius carries out his threat and the killing begins!"

"Patience Sam. I am just getting to Liberius. He was there you know, nearly 2,000 years ago…"

Chapter 29

AD 61. As Boudicca, stood with her daughters, before her husband's burning funeral pyre, she'd every reason to believe that the Romans would continue to respect the rights and freedom of her people. But she was wrong...

A few days later Boudicca sat outside her tent with her closest friend Alvena, an outspoken, beautiful red-head who had never married, as she was considered too feisty by the men of the tribe and was completely devoted to the service of the queen. She'd been appointed as a maid to Boudicca when she was just sixteen and had never left her side since.

They watched as Boudicca's daughters – Siorra, 14 and Isolda, 15 - practiced their swordsmanship by fighting one another with wooden swords. The girls were both incredibly strong for their age and showed great skill as warriors.

"They've been at it for hours," Boudicca observed. "You'd think they'd have grown tired of it by now."

Alvena laughed. "Not those two. They're too much like their mother."

"I was never so warlike."

"And yet there is not a single man in this tribe who would willingly face you in hand-to-hand combat. Many a time your late husband was heard to wish that you were half as proficient with a darning needle as you were with a sword!"

The sound of approaching hooves drew the women's attention. A small detachment of Roman soldiers was approaching from the south.

"This cannot bode well," said Alvena.

Boudicca tried to stay calm. "I dare say it's just a delegation from General Claudius sent to offer his condolences on the loss of my husband."

The soldiers pulled up in front of Boudicca. Their leader immediately spoke. "I am Liberius, tribune in the Roman army. I am looking for Boudicca, Queen of the Iceni."

"I am she."

Liberius held up a scroll. "On behalf of His Imperial Majesty Nero Caesar Augustus Germanicus, General Claudius sends his greetings."

One of the soldiers dismounted, took the scroll from the tribune and offered it to Boudicca who warily took it from him.

"And what's this?" she asked.

"It is," said Liberius, "a very rough estimate of the legacy left by King Prasutagus to his Imperial Majesty. General Claudius requests – no, demands - that all gold, jewelry, coins and other goods belonging to Nero be amassed in one place and made ready for collection three days hence. You are also to assist his representatives in mapping out the estates that now belong to the emperor."

"Nero is only a co-heir to my husband's wealth. Half belongs to my daughters."

"That is not the case Boudicca. Roman law does not recognise the rights of women to inherit property when there is a male heir. This kingdom, in its entirety, now belongs to Nero. We will be back in three days to begin collecting what is his."

Then in an uncharacteristic friendliness for a Roman officer he whispered, "I am sorry Boudicca, but you have no choice."

As the Romans rode off, Boudicca angrily shouted her defiance at them. "Nero gets nothing! Do you hear? Nothing! This is Iceni land. It belongs to us – not to Rome. I will defy you, *this* is my choice."

"That doesn't sound like the Liberius who's doing his best to destroy this country Alexander," said Sam.

"At that time, Liberius was a *good* man. He had already been stationed here for eight years and had married a Briton, a beautiful Celt seamstress, called Helena who had given him a son, called Flavius, whom he dearly loved.

"As you will hear, it was the death of his family that changed him forever, but we have not gotten there yet. Do you mind if I continue? Uninterrupted!"

Chapter 30

AD 61. With the soldiers gone, Boudicca's anger showed little sign of abating. "Rally the clans! I want every warlord in the kingdom at my tent by nightfall."

"You intend to fight?" asked Alvena, somewhat concerned. "Against Rome?"

"What would you have me do? Surrender my daughters' birthright to that fat pig, Nero?"

"Of course not. But there must be some other way."

"Sweet Alvena, you know there is none. Right now, more than at any time in my life, I need to know that you are with me."

"Of course I am, my queen. If you fight, I fight beside you."

Three days later, Boudicca looked on in trepidation as a vast Roman army advanced upon her tribal settlement, shaking the barren, windswept moorlands of Norfolk with their relentless march.

Boudicca had made blood sacrifices to her gods, and her priests had promised her certain victory, but as she beheld line upon line of well-disciplined, well-armed Roman soldiers, she began to experience doubt.

She turned to Alvena, who, true to her word remained at her side. "I did not think there would be quite so many of them."

"It matters not; one Iceni warrior could match any ten Romans. The day will be ours, Boudicca, for we have the gods on our side."

Mounting her chariot, Boudicca drew her sword and raised it high. Her drummers began to pound steadily on their deer skin drums, slowly increasing the tempo and volume...

"Death or glory!" shouted Boudicca.

A mighty cheer rose up from her army behind her. With Boudicca at their head, they charged at the approaching Romans.

The Iceni fought with a ferocity that the Romans had not expected. Boudicca herself slew many a legionary that stood in her path. Even when her horses were slain, she leapt from her chariot and continued to fight on foot, wielding her sword with as much skill and strength as any man on the field that day.

Covered in blood and surrounded by the dead and dying, she fought on with Alvena and her eldest daughter, Isolda, by her side, even as the remains of her army fled to the hills.

When she eventually realised that all was lost, Boudicca determined not just to die in battle, but to die in glory.

Seeing General Claudius mounted triumphantly at the rear of his army she ran forward with all the speed she could muster, sweeping aside his guards with her sword as she passed. She eventually reached the general's mighty stallion, but before she could pull him to the ground the great animal turned and reared up before her trampling her into the ground. Her vision blurred then failed and the sounds of battle faded from her ears.

Alvena saw what had happened through the corner of her eye. She pulled her sword from the stomach of her most recent kill and rushed to Boudicca's aid, but before she could reach her, Alvena's path was blocked by the tall, muscular frame of Liberius.

Before she could even raise her sword, he was swinging his towards her head. She knew that she would have no time to avoid the blow so she closed her eyes to accept death. Just before the sword made contact, however, Liberius twisted it by ninety degrees so she was struck with the flat of his blade rather that its edge. She fell unconscious into the mud. Liberius had never killed a woman or child before, and he was not about to start now.

An hour later Boudicca awoke into a nightmare, her head throbbed, her clothes were torn, and her hair was partly shorn. She was tied to a wooden post at the heart of her settlement and her ribs, arms and legs were racked with an almost unbearable pain.

The Romans had rounded up as many of her subjects as they could find to witness her final humiliation.

The soldiers stood in a circle around Boudicca, ready to suppress any dissent from the crowd.

Claudius stood before her and watched with a cruel smile as one of his men threw a bucket of water into her face.

"What manner of a people, are you," he asked the crowd, "that you let your women fight for you? You are no better than animals!"

He turned to Boudicca and spoke with a mixture of respect and disgust. "Look at you! No woman should or *could* fight as you have done this day and no mother, with a shred of decency, would lead her own daughter into battle.

"For too long, we Romans have treated you as our equals. This has been a very grave mistake on our part, and it stops right now! You and your people are now subjects of Rome. Our law is your law. Your land is our land. Do you understand, woman?"

Boudicca raised her head and spat at the general. "We are Iceni! We are subject to no-one."

Claudius shrugged off her defiance. "You will acknowledge the emperor's ownership of all Iceni lands and property!"

"I will not!"

"Very well. Then you leave me no choice."

At a signal from Claudius, a Roman soldier tore at Boudicca's remaining clothing, baring her naked back.

Boudicca's daughters, who were being restrained by Roman soldiers, all cried out in despair begging them not to hurt her further. Alvena turned to Liberius who was restraining her. "You must not allow this. She has already been humiliated in defeat. Do not punish her further!"

"What did she expect when she dared to defy the emperor of Rome?" Liberius whispered. "I warned her, now there is nothing more I can do for her."

Claudius stepped back and gave another signal. A Roman soldier built like an ox advanced with a leather whip into which was bound many small pieces of sharp stone. "Begin."

"Liberius please!" Alvena cried in abject despair as the first blows tore away the flesh from Boudicca's back.

"I am sorry, I cannot intervene."

Boudicca's daughters cried uncontrollably and Alvena looked at Liberius in disgust.

Despite the searing pain the queen of the Iceni did not cry out or beg for mercy. Every stroke, instead of breaking her will, served to increase her thirst for vengeance. She stared at Claudius blinking only momentarily as each stroke fell.

When the torture finally ended Boudicca was barely conscious and was bleeding profusely, but still she looked straight into the general's merciless eyes.

Another bucket of water was thrown at her and he again stepped forward. "Now do you concede that all your husband owned belongs to Rome?"

Boudicca glared at him defiantly. But only managed to respond in a whisper, "Never!"

He shrugged. "Very well. You shall have one more lesson. Then perhaps you'll change you mind."

Claudius clicked his fingers. "Bring me her daughters!"

Isolda and Siorra were dragged before their mother, screaming, and thrown roughly to the ground. Alvena struggled in vain to release herself from Liberius's grip but he held her fast and pleaded with her to remain still. "If you run to their aid they will cut you down!"

"I don't care," replied Alvena.

"I do!"

In an act intended to break Boudicca's will, she was made to watch as her daughters were savagely and repeatedly raped.

"Liberius, how can you let this happen? The gods will not allow this act to go unpunished. For the sake of us all, you must make them stop"

"I cannot defy Claudius. I am his tribune. It will be treason to speak out against him."

"Then find a way before you lose your soul."

The horror was too much for Boudicca; her screams of fury and despair echoed throughout the moorlands and chilled all who heard it.

In her outrage Boudicca made a solemn vow, then and there, that she would have her revenge and rid her country of these merciless oppressors.

When the ordeal was over, the girls lay still and sobbing on the ground.

Claudius again addressed the queen. "I give you one last chance, Boudicca. Profess before your people the supreme authority of Rome, or you will watch your daughters die."

"We would all rather die than live under Roman rule. Do what you will, Claudius, and to hell with you and your precious Nero!"

Claudius turns to his soldiers. "Find three trees. Let's crucify this bitch and her daughters and burn their settlement to the ground. I am tired of trying to reason with animals."

"Liberius please!" begged Alvena.

He released her and respectfully took the general's arm whispering quietly in his ear. "My lord, may I speak privately with you?"

Claudius's first instinct was to pull away and tell Liberius not to interfere, but he had come to respect his tribune and felt he should listen to what he had to say.

"What is it, Liberius? Have you conceived of a more appropriate death for these women?"

"Forgive my impertinence, my Lord, but I would strongly advise against killing Boudicca or her daughters. If you do so you will transform them into martyrs and the Celtic tribes will rebel against you. I am sure that it would serve Nero's purposes, and please him greatly, should you show that Rome can temper justice with mercy."

"But she defied me!"

"And now she has paid the price, her daughters are ruined, her army has been decimated and her people will now desert her. She is finished."

Claudius thought for a while and then said, "You speak wisely, Liberius." He walked back and addressed the assembled crowd.

"People of the Iceni, you have shown yourselves to be brave but foolish. Foolish to follow this woman who would have you die to satisfy her pride. She will be the ruin of you if you let her. Therefore, I offer you this one concession. You have one month to persuade your fallen queen to give up her lands and entitlements. If you fail you will leave me no choice, I will slaughter each and every one of you and erase all trace of the Iceni from this Earth."

He climbed upon his horse and held a finger in the air. "One month to decide if you want to live or die."

With that he turned his horse and rode away.

Liberius glanced at Alvena, who gave him a nod of gratitude. He too mounted his horse and followed his general. The rest of the Roman army followed behind.

1.15pm. Jessica was in tears. Sam was almost speechless. "So Liberius saved their lives?"

"Yes he did, and in doing so, risked his own."

"I still can't believe we are talking about the same man. There must have been many Romans called Liberius stationed in Britain at that time."

"I am sure there was, but this is definitely the same Liberius. If you would stop interrupting me you'll find out why I am so sure. Get me a fresh cup of tea please Jessica, this one has gotten a little cold."

Jessica wiped her eyes and stood, "Okay professor, but wait until I am back before you continue the story."

"Don't worry child, I will."

As she left the room for the second time Ackerman put his hand on Sam's shoulder. "She reminds you of Lucinda doesn't she?"

"She does, Professor."

"Me too. I think you should consider asking her out."

"But Professor..."

"But nothing. It has been three years since we lost Lucinda. It's time to move on. Jessica has almost become a daughter to me over this last year, and I think she likes you too!"

When Jessica returned holding a fresh pot of tea the two men abruptly stopped their conversation and stared at her.

She looked confused. "What?"

"Oh nothing," said the professor. "I was just saying what lovely tea you make! Now where was I?"

1.15pm. Isabella ran along Upper Street in Islington, amidst rioting, looting and general mayhem. Someone just in front of her threw a brick through the window of a Ryman Stationers and ran inside after kicking out the remaining glass. He was soon followed by six other opportunists. Seconds later, they emerged with Kindles, smart phones and a variety of electronic tablets.

Isabella stood shaking her head in disgust. As she turned away she saw a man standing outside St Mary's Church encouraging those that seemed genuinely distressed to come inside for shelter.

She was crossing the road towards him, when a large

white man with a crew cut, bikers t-shirt, leather waistcoat and Nazi tattoos grabbed her arm. "Come with me, love," he said, steering her towards the church gardens. The expression on his face told her immediately what he was about to do.

She tensed, then, swung round towards him, punching him hard in the throat. He let go immediately, fighting desperately to breathe. She then kicked him hard between the legs and then spun round to deliver another kick in his rear. He crumpled to the floor and she stamped on his neck. The crowd around her temporarily put down their stolen goods and began to clap. Isabella gave them a stately bow then ran into the Town Hall.

No one realized the man was dead until blood began to seep from his mouth, but even then, nobody really cared there were far greater things to worry about, like their own survival.

Chapter 31

1.20pm. The Pentecostal ministers arrived at Hyde Park Corner followed by their entourage of worshippers. They got out of their cars, straightened out their suits and walked up to the huge, wrought iron gates.

They peered through the railings and saw police and British soldiers gathered around the perimeter. In the middle of the park stood the huge army of Roman soldiers, lined up in their respective cohorts, standing perfectly still but surveying the onlookers with their eyes – well those that had them.

Parading between the lines of soldiers was a tall, disfigured man, on a black steed who was wearing the armour of a Roman general, the cloak of an emperor and the face of a monster.

He sensed the arrival of the ministers, even at a distance, and he turned to beckon them over. They looked at each other, each thinking the same thing: There is no way I am going into that park. Then they looked behind them. The crowd had swelled and there were now at least fifty or sixty of their congregations egging them on.

"Git into that park," the Jamaican woman shouted and moved toward them as if she was going to push them through the gates. They instantly knew that there was no escaping their duty.

They pushed aside the gates and rather nervously walked into the park where they were immediately approached by a young army officer. "I'm afraid I can't let you in here, gentleman, it's far too dangerous!" he said firmly but kindly.

"Oh I'm so sorry to hear that, we'll be leaving then," said a very relieved minister and he immediately turned back with the others following.

Their path was blocked immediately, by the large Jamaican woman, who stood there in her bright floral dress, with both hands on her hips, and a very disapproving look on her face.

"Where d'you think you're going?" she asked.

"I'm afraid they won't let us into the park, Vera."

"Did you tell 'em that yous are ministers and you're going to use the power of God to send those ugly creatures back into the eternal flames of Hell!"

"Well not exactly!"

"Are yous mice or men!" she shouted as she barged past them and approached the officer.

"Do you believe in Jesus?" she asked.

"Not exactly," he said taken aback by her question.

"Not exactly! How can you 'not exactly" believe in Jesus, you either does or you don't, plain and simple!"

"Then I guess I don't. He may have existed but I don't believe he's a God or anything like that."

She turned to the congregation. "He don't believe!" Some put their hands over their mouths, some gasped and others shook their heads in disapproval.

"Well look sir," she continued. "I 'preciate that this is unorthodox and probably difficult for yous to understand, but these here men are ministers of God and they have the power to destroy these monsters here and now. So let 'em pass!"

"I'm sorry lady I can't do that," said the officer.

Vera was furious. "So you are going to stand between these creatures and God, are you? You, who couldn't kill these beasts with all your fancy weapons, are goin' to stand in the way of these apostles of Jesus Christ!"

"I guess that's about the measure of it, lady."

"Then I have no choice!" She pounced on the officer, knocking him onto the floor and then sat on top of him.

"Well what are you boys looking at?" she said to the ministers. "Git your butts in that park, now!"

The ministers reluctantly moved forward. All this time Liberius had been riding in their direction laughing at Vera's antics.

"Can I help you?" he asked.

One of the ministers held up a cross, which was visibly shaking in his hand. The others followed suit.

"We command you by the power of the Almighty to return to hell and take these creatures with you!"

"You dare command *me*!" he screamed with a voice so loud that the ministers trembled.

As Liberius charged towards them the ministers turned to run, but before they could get out of the park Liberius had removed their heads, right in front of their horrified congregation. Some cried out, others fainted but most ran for their cars.

Vera, who had rolled off the officer as the horse passed by, got herself back onto her feet, and when she saw the headless bodies lying before her she screamed at the top of her voice startling the tribune's horse. It raised its front legs high into the air and threw Liberius onto the ground. The few remaining members of the congregation quickly overcame their shock and cheered loudly as Vera ran out of the park as fast as her pounds would allow, and closed the gate behind her.

"I think we're going to need some new ministers!" she announced as they all got into their cars.

Liberius stood and looked derisively at the onlookers and then at the departing congregation.

"Make the most of your petty victories," he shouted. "At nine o'clock tonight the killing will begin and I will personally ensure that you will be among the first to taste of death!"

Chapter 32

AD 61. Alvena rushed forward to untie Boudicca who was trying to find the words to comfort her daughters who lay sobbing in the mud. The queen's strength had completely failed her so Alvena carried her into her tent and laid her on her bed. Her daughters were brought in and laid beside her.

Boudicca could hardly move her savaged body but managed to put her arms around her distraught daughters and they all cried together. Alvena lovingly washed each of them and applied balm and herbs to their wounds.

"If Claudius thinks we are broken, we'll make him think again." said a still defiant Boudicca. "The evil that Rome wrought upon us this day will be paid for in blood over and over again." She kissed her daughters and told them to sleep.

"You must rest too," Alvena advised her.

Boudicca shook her head and unsteadily got to her feet.

"Where on earth are you going?"

"To address my people. Right now they are in need of leadership. The last words they heard was the general's poison now they need to hear from their queen!"

Boudicca asked the men outside her tent to gather her people together - the old, the young and even the wounded. When all were assembled, she addressed them.

"Until the death of my husband, we had no quarrel with

Rome, nor Rome with us. We were Rome's friends and allies. And how has Rome repaid our loyalty? With greed, treachery and degradation!

"They want to take from you all that you have – your lands, your homes, and your freedom. Are you prepared to live as slaves and cowards, suffering one indignity after another, or will you fight for the lands that have been entrusted to you, even to sacrifice your lives, if necessary?"

Immediately Alvena stepped forward raising her sword. "I was born free and I will die free, whether it be at home or on the battlefield. I will fight with you until my last breath is taken!"

A wounded man stepped forward. "I was a loyal subject of the king and am now a loyal subject to you, his queen. Where you lead, I shall follow, even if it is to my death."

"And I!" cried several more stepping out from the surrounding crowd, but then there was a long and awkward silence.

"No one else?" asked the Queen.

One of Boudicca's captains stepped forward holding his bloodstained battle sword by his side. "I would fight with you my queen, as I have done many times before, if there was even a whisper of a hope. But you have seen what the Romans are capable of. If we fight, death is certain. You must surrender as they have asked or we will all perish."

Boudicca surveyed the crowd to see if others shared his opinion. It was confirmed when few would meet her eye.

Despite the pain, she straightened her body and her voice rose with her anger. "You can live as slaves and cowards if you want, but I will not. I will fight to the death for my people and my country." She was about to turn away in disgust and return to her tent when she heard a familiar voice behind her.

"As will I," declared Isolda, stepping out of the tent supporting Siorra beside her. "The Romans may have stolen our virtue, but not our spirits. We'll stand by our mother, as she has stood by us and we'll fight by her side until every soldier at Nero's command trembles at the very mention of her name."

A sturdy washerwoman called Genofeva then stepped forward and turned to face the crowd. She began by spitting on the ground before her. "When I married, I put away my sword and armed myself with a cooking pot. Now, it seems to me, it's time to let the men do the cooking while we take out our sword and fight once more!" The women in the crowd shouted in support.

"If our men have become snivelling cowards and will not fight, then we will just have to fight for them! Who is with me?"

Almost every woman in the crowd stepped forward, even those holding babies and small children, and they stood shoulder to shoulder with their queen.

"Do I believe my eyes?" demanded Alvena. "Is this to be a war waged only by women?"

"No it is not! We will all fight together." The queen's captain laid his sword at Boudicca's feet and knelt before her ashamed. "I am sorry my queen, my courage failed me."

Then one by one the remaining men stepped forward, touched and humiliated by the courage of the queen's teenage daughters and their own wives and mothers.

"Death to the Romans!" Boudicca cried, fighting desperately to stay on her feet.

"Death to the Romans!" shouted her people as Alvena stepped forward to support her queen before she fell to the ground.

"Well maybe we can return to our cooking pots after all!" said Genofeva winking at her queen.

1.20pm. Jessica was impressed. "Now *that's* what I call Girl Power! I've read about Boudicca many times but I had no idea how amazingly resilient she was."

Suddenly Jessica's phone began to ring. She answered it immediately. It was Isabella.

"Isabella, where the hell have you been? I've been worried

sick about you!" The conversation continued for several minutes and she turned off her phone.

"Isabella is in Islington. She's in a church with hundreds of local residents. They're planning on barricading themselves in until the danger has passed. I told her it was a waste of time, so she's going back to her mother's flat. I assured her that I'd come and find her when I get to London. That is where we'll be heading, isn't it Professor?"

"Yes, Jessica it is. As soon as we're finished here."

Sam was getting more than a little agitated. He knew that the 9pm deadline was absolute and unless they struck at Liberius before then, many more people would die. He did *not* want to have to live with those deaths on his conscious, because he hadn't completed his mission on time!

He knew, however, that there was no way to hurry Ackerman. This was not a history lesson but a detailed briefing and the professor was going to make sure that Sam fully understood his target, and the weapon, before Ackerman would let him loose. Sam had often suspected that his mentor was more than a history professor and now he was sure.

He remembered the way Ackerman had held the trident that night in his study and the animated way he was describing it to Lucinda. It was clearly extremely precious to him, so it was no wonder he wanted Sam to have the same appreciation of it that he had before he allowed Sam to take it.

He also sensed that Ackerman, for some reason, had already decided that Jessica should go with him to collect the trident; if that was the case it was understandable that he would want to ensure she was in safe hands, especially after Lucinda.

Then he had another thought: maybe he had decided that only Jessica should touch the trident and he was just there to provide transport and muscle. The thought agitated him.

"Your narrative is all very touching professor, but what about the trident?" asked Sam "When are you going to explain where that fits into your *history* lesson?"

"I was just getting to that!" Ackerman said sternly. He knew that Sam just wanted to get on with his mission. He still obviously possessed that hot-headedness that had disqualified him from being a useful asset to the professor in the past. When you are dealing with the occult it had to be a thoughtful, patient and disciplined approach. If he had used Sam while he was studying at the university he would have, most definitely, run into trouble very quickly, losing his life and possibly his soul.

This time, however, Ackerman had no choice but to use him, he hoped that in the short time they had together he would be able to adequately prepare Sam for what had to be done.

He loved Sam and Jessica like his own children and he was going to make damn sure they had the knowledge necessary to got through this seemingly impossible mission.

"Professor?" said Sam trying to arouse him from his thoughts. "With respect, I think you need to pick up the pace. We are seriously running out of time!"

Chapter 33

1.20pm. "We're running out of time!" the Dean exclaimed after John told him what he'd witnessed. He immediately asked to use the harbour master's phone.

A soon as John had handed him his mobile, the Dean called Sir Gareth, who filled him in on the remaining detail, after expressing his joy that his friend was still alive.

The Dean then tried to call Ackerman, and was frustrated that his phone went straight to voice mail. Sir Gareth had told him about the young MI5 agent who had gone to meet with the professor, but he was concerned that they might not be able to get the trident in time, and even if they did, would there be anyone qualified to use it?

There was too much uncertainty, and time was not on their side. He decided regretfully that he had no choice but to pursue the last resort, but he knew he couldn't do it alone.

"John, I'm going to need your help again."

"What do you have in mind?"

"As far as I know, there are only two ways to stop this apocalypse: one way, involves the use of a holy relic which I cannot get my hands on at the moment, the other, relies on two men, you and me, doing something extremely dangerous, that has not been done for literally thousands of years."

"OK. I'm intrigued. What do we have to do?"

"I think you're going to find this a little difficult to get your head around."

"Try me!"

"Alright, but you have to remain open minded"

"Get on with it!"

The Dean swallowed, looked John right in the eye and began his explanation. "The creatures that you've seen today are being controlled by an evil power, older perhaps than this planet, a power that can't be destroyed by any conventional weapons. There's only one way to combat it, and that is with a power that is just as old, and just as destructive. That power is held in a holy trident, that you and me could never find in time, and by two individuals who are not quite human?"

"Could you please be a little bit more specific?"

"If you insist. We are about to summon the Angels of Death, or the Destroying Angels, as some call them."

"The Angels of Death! You've got to be kidding me?"

"No, I am deadly serious!"

"Are we talking about the same angels that killed the firstborn in Egypt, destroyed all of the inhabitants of Sodom and Gomorrah and killed 185,000 Assyrians who were about to attack Jerusalem?"

"Yes John, the same, and therein lies the problem. If we do manage to summon them, they will certainly have the power to kill Liberius and his entire army, but they may also decide to strike down every wicked person in this city while they're here"

"And how exactly would you define 'wicked'?"

"Well that's a hard one. I suppose anyone that has knowingly hurt someone else."

"Then you'd better give me five minutes before we start, actually make that ten! You Protestants do take confessions, don't you?"

John needn't have worried, although it was true he had killed many men in his lifetime, it had always been for his country. In fact, John had always lived by the motto 'Live simply that others might simply live'. He lived with his family in a modest three-bedroom flat in Elephant and Castle, gave ten percent of his income to charity and was constantly bringing home waifs and strays, much to the frustration of his wife. For the mission that lay ahead, John would be a perfect soldier.

Chapter 34

1.20pm. General Dan Radford knew that capturing a Roman soldier with the strength of twenty grizzly bears was not going to be easy. In fact, he would much prefer to try capturing the bears.

He reviewed the plans again with his brigadier and an elite SAS team as they set off in a military helicopter towards Blackfriars Bridge, where an unarmed Roman had been seen climbing from the River Thames.

They had on board a titanium cage provided by Director Smith, which the intelligence service had constructed just in case they ever encountered a creature from this earth or another that they might need to contain. That day had come.

All they needed to do was to get the Roman into the cage! They had mulled over many plans, none of which seemed very promising. In the end Corporal Jennings from the SAS team had reluctantly presented a possible solution, knowing it would most likely cost him his life.

Firstly, they located the isolated Roman soldier running along Newgate Street, presumably on his way to a rendezvous with the others at Hyde Park. They then lowered the titanium cage onto the street about 500 yards ahead of him, close to the Prince Albert Memorial, along with the eight members of the SAS team. Seven were tied, by long ropes, to the helicopter above, the eighth, Corporal Jennings, was not. His feet were planted firmly on the ground and he was bleeding with a self-inflicted wound to his left arm.

When the Roman came in sight they opened fire. Past experience had taught them that these creatures ran towards danger rather than away from it, and this was something they planned to take full advantage of. As soon as the first shots were fired the Roman started to sprint towards them, head and hands stretched forward, his jaw wide ready to bite into human flesh.

When it picked up the scent of fresh human blood it honed in on Corporal Jennings like a great white shark. When it was just fifty yards away, the helicopter rose taking with it seven of the SAS men. The Corporal, however, was left to stand his ground in front of the doorway to the titanium cage. He continued firing, wondering if he had the agility to dodge the charging Roman or whether this would be his last day on earth.

He thought of the great bullfighters who made their livelihoods doing exactly what he was about to attempt. There was always a first time for them too and they had all survived - well most anyway.

He judged that from the speed the Roman had reached, it would be impossible for it to change direction, once it was about three metres from the cage. This would give the corporal a mere fraction of a second to get out of its way.

He bent his knees in anticipation and prepared to jump. His comrades all looked down from the air willing him to succeed. When the Roman was just 10 metres away he threw his MP5 to the floor and counted down the remaining distance in his head 9 metres, 8, 7, 6, 5, 4, 3…

He dived to his right, the Roman slammed into the back of the cage and the door automatically shut behind him. Corporal Jennings rose to his feet to the cheers of his mates above and shouted "Olé!"

1.30pm. "Why do you need my help when you have so many

connections in the government?" John asked the Dean, when he had finished his lengthy confession. "You could probably get a lift in a helicopter with a few SAS officers to assist you."

"That would involve me telling them what I was planning, and they're hardly going to sanction their own deaths," replied the Dean. "You have no idea what our government has been involved in over the years. I imagine that they will certainly be at the very top of the Destroying Angel's hit list."

"Surely they could repent too," suggested John.

"Believe me, there wouldn't be time!" said the Dean with no hint of a smile.

"So how are we going to do this?"

"In a nutshell: we have to get to the British Library without getting eaten; gain access to the vaults, without setting off the alarms and getting trapped inside; find the Syriac Apocryphal Manuscripts, in particular the Apocalypse of Abraham; utter the prayer for the summoning of angels, which is in the pure Aramaic language by the way; and then, when the angels arrive, we have to persuade them to kill Liberius and his army and leave the rest of us alone."

"That's your plan?"

"Yep, that's the plan. Are you in?"

"Hang on Dean, aren't these manuscripts on the Internet somewhere?"

"No they're not. When the monks from the monastery of Deir al'Syriani in Egypt handed over the manuscripts to British historians in the 1840s they made them promise to keep certain portions *sealed*. These were instructions given to the prophets for their eyes only. I only knew of its existence because last time I was at the Library with Ackerman, we noticed in the index of these sealed portions an entry called 'The Summoning of Samael'. As you can imagine we were curious, and temporarily unsealed it."

"And Samael is one of the Destroying Angels?"

"He is."

"And has this ever been done before?"

"I don't believe so."

"So our chances of success are--?"
"Negligible."
"I was afraid you were going to say that!"

2.00pm. The experimentation started as soon as the creature arrived at the government's high security, science laboratories in Ruislip, just northwest of London. Everything was being transmitted directly to the COBRA briefing room where Sir Gareth had a direct communications link with the technicians.

The staff there were extremely apprehensive about getting anywhere near the creature but fortunately it seemed surprisingly docile, as if it was asleep on its feet. Its one fully formed eye, however, followed all movement around the room, missing nothing.

They started off trying to test its senses. The roving eye proved that it could see but the creature seemed not to be startled by any loud noises in the room - either it was deaf, or it was choosing to ignore them. It also seemed to be impervious to pain despite being shot, burnt, lasered and electrocuted.

Next, they experimented with the regeneration process. They took a litre of blood from one of the lab assistants, and threw it at the creature, in the areas of his body where there was just bone or very little flesh. Immediately those areas began to regenerate. Organic material began to grow, forming organs, blood vessels, muscle and finally flesh.

"Throw some into its face," ordered Sir Gareth and the lab technicians complied.

Instantly the face began to form: nose, ears, hair, mouth and lips and finally the remaining eye. Everyone took an intake of breath, as the creature now exactly resembled the lab technician who had donated the blood.

"Just as I thought," said Sir Gareth. "These creatures are using the DNA in the blood cells to regenerate their bodies, in effect creating a clone of the donor. We should warn everyone to look out for any strange behaviour from any staff that has arrived at work since the Romans appeared or been absent for any period of time since the occupation.

"Has anyone heard one of these creatures speak?" Everyone shook their heads.

"Well that doesn't mean they can't, and, theoretically, since they have the same lungs, larynx, tongue and lips as their donor they would probably sound very similar."

"I think it's unlikely that they will be able to access the donor's memories but we don't know yet *what* they are capable of. If this evil power, that's possessing them, can replicate DNA, who's to say it can't steal the thoughts and memories of the donor once the brain is formed.

"Even if they can't speak, I'm concerned that Liberius may use cloned creatures to get close to key targets, so we should all be on the alert. It is possible that one of these creatures is loose in the room with you right now."

All of the lab technicians looked at one another, Sir Gareth's words had created instant paranoia.

"OK let's now concentrate on trying to kill or immobilize the creature. Try everything at your disposal: acids, toxins, viruses, extremes of temperature, hell, even crucifixes, holy water, stakes and silver bullets! There's a lot of truth hidden in legend you know. If you have any success whatsoever, I need to know immediately. Is that clear?"

"That's clear, sir," answered the senior technician.

Chapter 35

2.30pm. The Prime Minister was being prepared for the press conference. It was essential that, despite his terrible loss, he delivered a speech that would reassure the people and send a message to the world that he was in total control of the situation.

When his PR team found out that the Army had successfully captured one of the Roman soldiers they were determined to have it displayed in a cage beside the Prime Minister as he spoke. They insisted that it would communicate a powerful message that the government was in the process of capturing the enemy and the PM would be seen as a national hero, maybe even a saviour of his people.

Everyone else in the Cabinet thought it would be a bad idea, especially Sir Gareth who wanted the creature to undergo further tests especially as, so far, their attempts to destroy the creature had all proven to be completely ineffective, and time was running out.

Despite Sir Gareth's protestations, the Prime Minister remained insistent and the cage containing the Roman was placed in the Queen Elizabeth II Conference Centre in Westminster where the press conference was to be held.

Journalists arrived in their hundreds and, after having their credentials checked, they were ushered into the main auditorium. Many gasped when they saw for themselves the grotesque, living carcass in the cage.

The effects of the experimentation was clear for all to see, as parts of its body showed signs of horrific burns, bruising and bullet holes. His face was badly disfigured and now unrecognizable, and one of its eyes had been completely removed for further analysis. Yet it simply stood there, fierce and tall, staring at the crowd with a visible hatred, through its remaining eye.

It wore only a leather tunic revealing long skeletal arms and legs covered only in strands of muscle and pieces of flesh. It then started pointing at certain journalists, as if selecting them for future consumption so that it could regenerate its wounded body.

Everyone was a little frightened but tried to hide the fact with upbeat banter about, what was undoubtedly, the news event of the century.

At exactly 3pm, the Prime Minister made his entrance and the creature's attention was drawn to him immediately. The PM was clearly uncomfortable but had no problem meeting its eye. He was hurting deeply due to the loss of his family and his reputation, and he was extremely angry. His absolute contempt for the creature was clearly evident. Eventually he turned away, walked up to the microphone and cleared his throat.

"All of you are aware of the loss I have suffered today, that all of us have suffered. We have seen our monuments destroyed and our people mercilessly murdered in our streets.

"We find ourselves confronted by an enemy that we do not understand, an enemy that is both frightening and powerful. But rest assured we will never, ever comply with their demands and we will soon eradicate them from the face of this earth!"

The crowd applauded.

The Prime Minister pointed accusingly at the titanium cage. "As you can see, we have already captured one of these hideous creatures---"

Suddenly the Roman let out an unearthly scream that had everyone present, including the Prime Minister, covering their ears to stop the pain. Then it spoke, not with the voice of the lab technician it had cloned, but with the deep, resonating, malignant voice of Liberius.

"Do you really think I'd let you capture one of my servants unless it was to my advantage? I want to thank you Prime Minister for inviting death to your press conference!"

The creature grabbed two adjacent bars of the cage and pulled them in opposite directions. The titanium bars gave way as if they were made of lead and before the PM could react, or his bodyguards intervene, it leapt onto the podium and bit deep into the Prime Minister's neck. It feasted upon him until his face had been completely devoured and then it threw his lifeless body to the ground.

The creature then took his place at the podium, his face already taking the form of the recently departed Prime Minister. This time he spoke with the Prime Minister's voice. "I'm afraid your Prime Minister will not be standing at the next general election. In fact, he won't be standing ever again."

The creature laughed cruelly then jumped from the stage into the auditorium, running through the masses of terrified reporters, ripping at them with its boney claws as it passed, and chasing them out into Parliament Square.

The cameramen and reporters that had remained outside the conference centre were not aware of what had just transpired and began filming what seemed to be a deranged Prime Minister attacking and eating his electorate, and those images were transmitted immediately all over the world.

3.05pm. Liberius stared at the video feed and smiled. His careful planning was paying off. In less than twelve hours the British Empire was collapsing for the entire world to see. Images of a crazed Prime Minister, mass rioting and lootings, the Tower and Downing Street in ruins, an empty City and an abandoned stock exchange were being shown continuously on almost every channel.

It hadn't all gone his way, of course. He had lost many of his mercenaries, but that didn't bother him - he would have killed them anyway when this was all over. He despised each of them because they were willing to do anything for money, even turn against their own people, something no Roman soldier would ever consider.

World leaders were already refusing to allow any planes or shipping that had left the UK to enter their air space or waters.

The United States was considering even more drastic measures to ensure that the infestation of monsters in Britain would not spread to their nation. US President Miles Cluney had contacted the Deputy Prime Minister, immediately the press conference was over, ominously given her an ultimatum to get her house in order. Britain was isolated and its end seemed to be in sight.

3.10pm. Sam put down his mobile phone. His face was ashen. "The good news is that the Dean has turned up alive, but the grave news is that the Prime Minister has been killed. He was attacked and murdered at a press conference this afternoon, by a Roman soldier that the Army had captured and put on display."

He then went on to describe the events in detail ending with the subsequent devastating news broadcasts.

"Liberius is making us look very stupid and world leaders have started to condemn us. Who knows what will happen if they consider his army to be a global threat!

"The COBRA committee are now pretty certain that Liberius will launch an all out attack at 9pm, just as he threatened, unless we surrender. He's even gathering reinforcements."

"What reinforcements?" asked Jessica. She could see that the situation was spiralling out of control and she desperately hoped that she really did have the qualities that Ackerman had seen in her, qualities that she would need if she was to fulfill her full potential.

"Traffic and surveillance cameras have picked up more dead soldiers rising from Roman burial sites all over the country," continued Sam "There is also another legion emerging from buildings around Kings Cross Station," answered Sam.

"The site of one of Boudicca's greatest victories. There are many Romans buried there! I thought that might happen," said Ackerman, "you'll find out why very soon, if I can continue my story…"

Chapter 36

AD 61. In the weeks that followed the Roman attack, Boudicca began to amass a great army of men, women and children from across her kingdom. She also forged alliances with other Celtic tribes who'd suffered similar humiliations at the hands of the Romans.

She used her commanders to provide as much combat training as they could, and she sent scouts all over the country to spy on the Roman forces.

When she received word that the Roman governor had taken several legions to control a Druid uprising in north Wales, she knew there would never be a better time to strike.

Her first target was Colchester, or Camulodium, as it was then called, which was the Roman capital of Britain. She learned that it had been left relatively undefended so she decided to leave for battle the following morning.

That night proved to be long and sleepless for Boudicca. She knew her army was inexperienced and victory was far from certain. Her greatest fear was that she might be leading them to their deaths as she had almost done before.

Sitting alone in her tent, she prayed to the gods of her ancestors and begged them to help her drive the Romans from Britain.

Thankfully, one God was listening.

At this point I would like to take over this tale because this part of the story is only mine to tell. I want to you to know where the trident came from and why I agreed to give up everything to become its Guardian.

It all began in 13AD. I was sitting on the pebbled beach at Looe in Cornwall, close to the harbour wall, as I did every morning.

I was 32 years old and a widower. A year earlier I'd lost my wife and son. They'd sailed out to sea in a small fishing boat because I had been too ill to work, and we couldn't afford to lose a day's catch. It wasn't the first time they'd stood in for me because of my failing health, but it was to be their last.

Very soon after they had left the harbour, a huge storm came in from the south. When the wind rose and the rain began lashing against our humble shelter, I feared the worst. I wrapped myself in a deerskin cloak and ran down to the coast, ignoring the fever that had plagued me for the previous two days.

I stood there in the storm shouting their names until I lost my voice and the darkness of night descended. I lit some torches and planted them on the beach as a beacon to guide them home and then I sat waiting for their return throughout the night. The next day I was joined by my friends and most of the village. Those with boats cast out to sea to search for my family, or what might remain of our old fishing boat; the others stayed to comfort me.

The search was in vain, my family never returned and their bodies were never found.

So every morning at dawn, before setting sail, I would sit on the beach and wait, hoping against all hope that, one day, they would return. Then, in the evening when I had delivered my catch, I would once more begin my vigil until the sun set and I retired wearily to what used to be a home.

On this particular morning I noticed a trading ship moored about a mile out to sea. It was not unusual to see them here. Looe was known for its tin mining and traders would travel great distances to come and collect our ore. By the shape of the ship I guessed it had come from somewhere in Asia. I was to learn later that it had come from Israel.

While gazing at the ship, I noticed a small rowing boat leaving the vessel. It travelled to the shore and came to rest just yards from where I was sitting.

It was being rowed by an older man, probably in his fifties, and in the bow was a boy, who was barely in his teens. The child sat tall and straight and stared right at me. He had the kindest eyes and the warmest smile I'd ever seen.

He jumped effortlessly from the boat then reached inside to retrieve a large cloth sack. Judging by the effort required to lift it, I was sure that his burden was extremely heavy, so I stood and ran to the boy's aid, while the older man dragged the boat onto the shore.

The boy thanked me and asked my name. Then he told me his. He introduced his companion as Joseph, and told me that they had sailed from a place called Arimathea, a small port town in Judea.

I was intrigued to know why someone so young had travelled such a distance when he should be at home with his father and mother. The boy explained that his life had been in danger for some time, because the king of their country had ordered his death. His father, a carpenter who occasionally did repairs on the boat they had sailed in, had begged Joseph to take his son far away, where the king couldn't find him, and the tin trader had willingly agreed to do so.

I've known young boys to exaggerate the truth, so I had later asked the same question of Joseph, who confirmed everything the boy had said. "Why," I asked, "Would a king want to murder an innocent child?"

"Because he is no ordinary child," was the only reply that Joseph would give.

Joseph and the boy stayed at Looe for several days. They

would be gone by day, travelling to Glastonbury and other nearby towns, and in the evening they would return to the harbour where the boy would captivate the fishermen and their families with incredible tales of his birth and travels.

He would also tell us stories that made us feel, well, like we wanted to be better and make something more of our lives. Every night the crowd would grow as others came from neighbouring villages, where his fame had begun to spread.

One evening after his audience had dispersed to their homes, he asked me to sit and talk with him for a while, which I was glad to do. In the days that he was with us I had forgotten my daily vigil and was somehow whole again, even without my wife and son.

"Could you do something for me?" he asked.

"Of course master," I replied. I had began calling him master as we would any young boy, but over the days that I had sat at his feet the word took on a new meaning. Even though he was just thirteen years old I now considered him to be my Master and I was ready to do whatever he was to ask of me.

"When I first arrived you helped me by bringing a cloth sack out of my boat. Do you remember?"

"Yes, I do." I replied.

"Well I have it with me now." He pointed behind him and I leaned over and retrieved it for him once again. He then proceeded to unwrap the bundle and I was immediately overcome by the beauty and craftsmanship of the treasures that lay before me.

First, he showed me a helmet unlike anything I had seen before. It was made of silver, with pouncing lions carved into each side. On top of the helmet was a narrow blade or crest, which started at the very back and curved round to the front, ending in a sharp point that could be used to cleave an enemy's skull. There was a grated mask, housed in a channel at the base of the crest, that could be pulled down to protect the wearer's eyes, nose and jaw.

"This," he said, "is the Helmet of Solomon, worn by the

king himself when he sat in judgment over his people. It can endow its wearer with the wisdom of a God and the ability to see into the future, but only if it is for a righteous purpose."

He then extracted a shield, perfectly round and made of a dark solid wood that I was not familiar with. It was edged with a band of silver bearing etchings of vine leaves and, at its centre, was a silver spike protruding maybe three or four inches. Further bands of silver had been laid across the shield's surface creating a cross and then narrower bands divided each quarter.

"This is the Shield of David. It was given to him by King Saul when he was made commander over his armies, and taken from him after he sent Uriah, the husband of Bethsheba, to his death. The shield will give its bearer immortality and incredible strength."

Finally, he removed a trident. The shaft of which was made of wood but at the base, and at intervals of six or so inches, it was decorated with rings of silver. The fork itself was also made of silver, with arrowheads on the end of each spike.

He looked intently into my eyes. "This is the Jerusalem Trident, fashioned from the staff of Moses and possessing all of its power. It can divide land or sea, break down walls and strike down any enemy; man, beast or demon."

He paused briefly as if deciding whether to reveal more. He then nodded his head as if to signify that he had been given approval and then said, "As well as taking life, the trident can also give life, but at a very high price. The trident can be used to transfer its bearer's lifeforce to anyone who has recently perished, or is on the verge of death. Once their lifeforce has gone. The bearer dies. They sacrifice their life to save another. There is no greater love than this."

In my mind's eye I could see those who had born the trident before. I saw them fight valiantly in the defense of freedom and then I saw them give their lives to save another. As the boy continued to speak, I began to weep.

"Although I will now leave your island, I will not leave it

unprotected. If ever Britain is under attack I want you to find someone worthy to bear these arms, but it can never be you! I know your heart and you would sacrifice yourself to save the first mortally injured person you come across, especially if it were a woman or child. Then I would no longer have a Guardian to look after these precious relics." He stood and laid his hand on my arm, then he looked into my eyes and asked, "Will you accept this mission? Will you be my Guardian?"

I could not refuse. "Of course I will Master," I said, "but how will I know who to give these treasures to?"

"Look for those who fill their heads with wisdom, their lives with service and their hearts with love." he replied.

"I will my Lord."

"One more thing," he continued. "You will have to continue in this role until I return and that may not be for some time. Are you prepared to stay upon this earth while your friends and family grow old and die?"

"My family are already dead and my friends all think I'm crazy to have grieved for so long. I have not been good company since my family died."

The boy smiled sympathetically and said, "Do not worry about your family, they are at peace." He then embraced me and I felt the love he had for me, a feeling that has lived in my heart every day since. In that moment my weary body was instantly renewed.

"Close your eyes," he instructed and I obeyed. I then felt another embrace, long, warm and familiar and I knew it to be that of my wife. Then I felt another, the embrace of my son, holding me ever so tightly around my waist as he had always done, not wanting to let me go.

I cried openly and when the embraces had ended I heard the words, "Open your eyes, Guardian". When I did I was alone but my family were no longer lost to me.

Chapter 37

AD 61. As Boudicca lay awake tormented by doubt, she was suddenly aware that she was not alone. A stranger had entered her tent. She sprang from her bed, sword in hand. "Hold and identify yourself!"

The Guardian stood before her. "I am the Guardian. I'm here to help you, Your Majesty, and as you can see, I am unarmed."

The Guardian approached Boudicca. She raised her sword so it pointed at his throat. "Stop, or I will strike you down."

The Guardian was not deterred. He reached out with his free hand and brushed aside the mud-encrusted hair from Boudicca's face and smiling gently said, "You should know, that you can do me no physical harm. Please sit. We must complete our business in as short a time as possible."

Boudicca felt compelled to obey. She sat and watched with curiosity as the Guardian unwrapped his bundle and laid its contents at her feet.

"I have carried this burden for many years and many miles," said the Guardian. "Long ago, I was tasked with finding someone worthy to carry these artefacts into battle. Now I believe I have. You have been chosen, Boudicca."

"Chosen for what?" she asked

"To protect this nation. To defend this realm."

He showed her each of the relics in turn revealing their powers, just as they had been described to him. Boudicca sat quiet and incredulous, but she felt sure that this man had been sent from the gods. When he showed her the trident he made certain she understood the implications of using it to raise the dead.

"Boudicca you do understand, don't you, that if you ever use this trident to save a life, it will be at the expense of your own?"

"I understand, my lord and I am prepared to do so, if it is necessary."

"That is good, but try to resist the urge until you have driven the Romans back to Rome!"

"I will indeed try, my lord"

"Fine. Now, these relics can only be used for a cause that is just. If you attempt to use them for evil or for your own gain, they will lose their power and I will track you down and take them back. Do you understand?"

"I do my lord, but why have you chosen me? I am imperfect in so many ways."

"We are all imperfect Boudicca and it was not perfection that qualified you. I was looking for someone with the courage to do what is right, even at the expense of their life, someone willing to stand up for the downtrodden, and put the needs of others before themselves. I have watched you in battle, I stood in the crowd as you were flogged and forced to watch the degradation of your daughters. I marvelled at your courage and your determination not to surrender to the Romans, when most would have relented. I stood in the shadows as you emerged from your tent, bruised and bleeding, to address your people, when you could hardly stand. I felt the love and respect they had for you. You are the one Boudicca, I have no doubt."

"Then I will accept these treasures and use them to protect my people and I will drive these barbaric Romans from this land!"

"Then place your hand upon this shield and swear that

you will guard these relics with your life and wield them only for the protection of this land and its people."

She did as she was asked, "I so swear."

"Then take up these arms. From this time forth, you shall bear the name of the land that you have sworn to protect. You will be the first Britannia: Trident Bearer and Defender of the Realm!"

Without questioning the stranger further, Boudicca placed the helmet on her head, the shield in her left hand and the trident in her right. Her wounds instantly healed and her strength returned. She felt more powerful and more capable than she ever had before.

Then her ears began to ring with the sound of battle. The room faded from view and was replaced with a vision of Camulodium burning to the ground and her armies celebrating a great victory.

As the vision cleared, she was disappointed to discover that her visitor had left before she could even offer her thanks. She spent the rest of the night in a deep, untroubled sleep. When morning came, she prepared for battle and left her tent bearing the arms she had been given.

Then she climbed aboard her chariot and presented herself to her army, which had already assembled and was ready to march. When they saw her they marveled. Her daughters and Alvena, who stood behind her, were astonished to see that the deep gashes on her back had been miraculously healed.

"People of Britain, I see that you stare in wonder at the arms I now bear. These have not been fashioned by mere mortals. They were brought to me in the night as a gift from the gods. While I carry these into battle we cannot be defeated. Now is the day of our destiny. Now we begin the liberation of our people!"

To deafening cheers from her followers, Boudicca turned her chariot around and began the journey to Camulodium. Her army followed, talking excitedly about the morning's events. Without exception, they believed that they were invincible.

Chapter 38

AD 61. Although the three-day march upon Camulodium was arduous, Boudicca's army did not flag or waiver. Spirits and morale remained high.

At each settlement they passed, many joined her forces. By the time they reached the outskirts of the city her army numbered close to a hundred thousand.

Her troops were keen to attack. A desire for vengeance burned in all their hearts. A mile from the city, she issued the command to halt.

"Now," she said to Alvena, "we shall discover whether the Guardian spoke the truth."

She dismounted from her chariot and raised the trident high above her head. Her army fell silent as they felt the winds rise, the grounds stir and dark clouds gathering as if a mighty storm was about to be unleashed upon the land.

"This then is my vengeance!" she screamed and with that, she thrust the trident into the ground.

The Earth responded.

First there was a distant rumble. Then the ground began to tremble and tear apart.

Boudicca's warriors were at first alarmed. It seemed to them that the ground beneath their feet was about to swallow them up but the power of the trident was not so aimless. A fissure opened up before Boudicca that travelled like a bolt of lightning, towards Camulodium, swallowing everything that stood in its path.

When it reached the city walls, there was an earsplitting sound of tearing rock. The walls simply exploded and great clouds of dust rose into the air. When the dust had settled, they were no more than rubble. The great Roman temple that stood looking over the town also crumbled and many of the timber homes burst into flames. The screams and cries of the terrified occupants were carried on the wind back to Boudicca's army who cheered as one.

The Celts then bore down on the city with Boudicca's chariot at their head.

As they approached, they were met by a rain of arrows that bounced off Boudicca and her shield as if they were just raindrops.

As she leapt from her chariot, a dozen Roman soldiers immediately surrounded her. She spun around wielding her trident with a skill she did not know she possessed, effortlessly cutting through Roman armour and flesh. The men died long before they were close enough to strike her with their swords.

All around her, her troops slaughtered with relish. Those who'd witnessed the atrocities brought down upon Boudicca and her daughters took out their hatred and thirst for vengeance on every Roman they encountered.

With more luck than skill, a Roman sword found its mark and sliced into Boudicca's arm. Moments later, the soldier lay dying and she watched with awe as the huge gash in her arm healed miraculously within seconds.

The battle lasted scarcely more than three hours. When it was done, every Roman soldier in Camulodium lay dead or dying and every dwelling place was in flames.

"Gather together every Briton that lives here, tend to the injured and ensure they are fed. They will be a welcome addition to our army and they can fight by our side as we wipe from this country every trace of this Roman disease!"

3.20pm. Sam just wanted Ackerman to give him the one piece of invaluable information that he had come for. "Where's that trident now, Professor?"

"I'm coming to that, but please be patient. There is more you have to know."

If this trident really did exist and really did have that power, he wanted to retrieve it and use it immediately.

Many questions passed through his mind, however. Where would he find the Guardian and could he really still be alive after all these years? Even if he was to find him, would the Guardian give him the relics and was he worthy to wield them? What should he do if the Guardian refused, should he take them by force? Did the Guardian even still have them? Why had Liberius suddenly transformed from a man of principle to the crazed, merciless tyrant that was slaughtering hundreds of innocent people? And why was he still alive nearly 2,000 years later? The professor was right; there *was* more he had to know.

"Please carry on, Alexander" Sam said eagerly.

"Jessica, more tea!" said Ackerman.

3.20pm. Unknown to the three of them, a black armoured personnel vehicle was driving through the streets of Oxford. It was being driven by one of Liberius's mercenaries, and another sat in the passenger seat. In the back of the truck were ten, skeletal, heavily armed Roman soldiers who were hungry for human blood.

"How long before we reach Balliol College?" asked the driver.

"I would say about six or seven minutes," said his navigator.

"I wish Liberius had sent us alone. We could easily take out the professor and Callaghan without those freaks in the back. To be honest, they scare the crap out of me!"

"Well at least we're on their side."

"At the moment we are, but are you really going to stand by when they start slaughtering people we know, like our families and friends? Liberius isn't stupid, he knows our loyalty will only go so far, even with the millions he's paying us."

"He could kill my mother if he wanted, as long as he kept up with the payments."

"You're heartless, Cole!" he shook his head in disgust. "When we get to the university, I'll go in and locate the targets, while you release the monsters, okay?"

"How come I'm the one that always has to deal with the monsters?"

"Because you have a lot in common – they're heartless too!"

Meanwhile, inside the university and quite oblivious to the approaching danger, Ackerman continued his story…

Chapter 39

AD 61. That night, the Celts camped on the plain outside the smouldering remains of Camulodium. They feasted on Roman food and got drunk on Roman wine.

Boudicca joined the celebrations but refused to drink alcohol or accept the toasts that were offered in her name. She insisted that they gave thanks only to the gods who had given them the means to ensure their victory.

As soon as she could, without causing offense, she left to join Alvena, her commanders and her daughters to make plans for the next battle of her brutal campaign.

As morning dawned and Boudicca walked through the camp, few of her soldiers were awake.

She found an oak tree, beneath which she prayed and gave thanks for her victory. When she placed the Helmet of Solomon on her head, she immediately saw the fortified, stone walls of London, or Londinium as it was then called, and it was clear that few had been left to its defence. Better still, many were already fleeing from the city. As she removed the helmet she ran back to the camp and announced that they would leave at dawn.

The following day, as Boudicca and her army approached the east wall of the city, near the banks of the River Thames, her scouts reported that stories of her conquest of

Camulodium had already reached the town.

The Romans had been told that Boudicca wielded the power of the gods and commanded an invincible army and her gaze alone could turn men to stone!

The scouts also reported that the Roman Governor Suetonius had arrived with his cavalry the previous night but had left soon afterwards when he saw how depleted his forces were. He had taken with him the Romans of position and rank and left the others to their fate despite their pleadings and prayers.

When the few remaining soldiers beheld Boudicca and her hordes, their courage failed them and they offered little resistance. Before dusk, London was in flames and its Roman inhabitants had been hanged, gutted or crucified.

Boudicca allowed her army just a few days to enjoy the spoils of their victory and then prepared to march again. Her next target was to be St Albans, known then as Verulamium, the third largest Roman town in Britannia.

3.25pm. Sam began to make the connections. "So the Romans are rising from the towns that Boudicca destroyed. Liberius is amassing the armies that she defeated two thousand years ago, giving them a chance to avenge their defeat."

"I agree that these are the armies that Boudicca defeated, but I don't think these creatures have any memory of their deaths. They are just empty carcasses possessed by whatever evil Liberius has managed to conjure. He is in total control of them all. This is just about him, and his unquenchable thirst for power and revenge."

"So if we managed to kill him, they'd all die, right?" asked John.

"Possibly, but we can't kill him, as you'll find out shortly. He is now immortal so we have, instead, to destroy the very source of the evil, the relic that he stole from the Tower this morning."

"And only the trident can do that?"

"The trident, the Ark of the Covenant, and there is one last resort."

"I thought the Ark was lost? If we have it, why don't we use it?"

"It's far too dangerous, and we have no idea how to control its power. It's also very particular about who handles it!"

"And what is this *last resort*?" asked Sam.

"To summon the most deadly creatures on this planet, the Angels of Death." Replied Ackerman.

"And do we do that?"

"We don't. It's far too risky. In addition to destroying Liberius and his army, the Angels would strike down anyone they considered wicked, which could possibly be millions. They would continue their slaughter until they were stopped by God himself!"

Sam was getting extremely anxious, "Who knows how to summon these angels?"

"Only the Dean and I. As far as I am aware."

"And would he do it?"

"Like I said, it was always our plan of last resort should such an evil arise."

"Then we have to speak with him now and make absolutely sure we have exhausted all possibilities, before doing something so…so unthinkable."

"The Dean wouldn't do it without consulting me first. Now let me finish my story."

"Hang on, how do you know he hasn't tried to call you? Where's your mobile?"

"In my study. I never bring it to lectures, as you know."

"Do you remember his number?" asked Sam.

"Of course I do."

Ackerman reluctantly gave Sam the Dean's number, but every time Sam called the line failed. Then he tried to call the cathedral. There was no answer there either.

"Should I call my office?"

"You can," replied Ackerman. "But if you tell anyone related to this government why you want to get hold of him, they'll probably have the Dean shot on sight!"

"What about Sir Gareth? He's a friend of the Dean too, isn't he?"

"He is indeed but he too will certainly not want the angels released. You will still be putting the Dean in danger and I can't allow that."

"Then I'll have to lie to them."

"Are you sure that lying is wise under the circumstances? What if the Angels are released?"

"Believe me Alexander, that would be the least of my sins!"

Sam called his office and was put through to Director Smith. Before he could give a report Smith started to rant.

"Callaghan, what the hell are you doing in Oxford!"

"Following orders. Blunt sent me!"

"So why was I not informed?"

"No idea, sir. Maybe the order came from someone in higher authority."

Smith was outraged. "How dare you talk to me like that!"

Sam concluded he was wasting his time and ended the call. Seconds later his phone was ringing and it was, not surprisingly, Andrew Smith. He ignored it.

"That could cost you your job Sam!" said Jessica, who had arrived back with another pot of tea.

"I don't care. There are much bigger things to worry about right now. I need to try to get hold of Sir Gareth." Sam dialled his number and he answered immediately.

"It's Agent Callaghan Sir."

"I know who you are Callaghan, I have been waiting for your report." Sam could hear the loud protestations of Andrew Smith in the background. He then heard Sir Gareth telling Smith to leave the room, in no uncertain terms.

"Sorry about the language then, Callaghan." Sir Gareth said.

Sam couldn't help but smile. "That's quite alright Sir, I need to ask you a favour."

"And what would that be?" asked Sir Gareth.

"I need to speak to the Dean of St Paul's, could that be

arranged?"

"I'm not sure, apparently he dropped his phone from the dome of the cathedral this morning and the only contact we've had from him was when he borrowed a phone from a harbour master on the River Thames."

"Not Captain Birdseye?" Sam asked incredulously.

"Are you mocking me Callaghan?"

"No, not at all, it's a nickname, his real name is Captain John Brody."

"Yes, that's the man. How do you know him?"

"He pulled me out of the Thames this morning."

"That's some coincidence," said Sir Gareth mocking surprise. He knew exactly who John Brody was and why he was on the river.

"It is indeed. Do you still have John Brody's number?"

"Yes, it's still on my phone, but why do you want to speak to the Dean?"

"We need his help to find the trident."

"How are you getting on with Ackerman?"

"Just fine. Hopefully he'll lead me to the trident very soon." he said, not actually sure if he was telling the truth.

Sam took John Brody's number and was about to dial it when he heard the distinctive sound of a rifle shot coming from the courtyard.

Chapter 40

3.30pm. Sam looked out of the window and saw that a black Mastiff armoured personnel vehicle had pulled up about 200 yards from the helicopter. A man in black combat fatigues was lying on the floor next to the open driver's door; evidently he'd been shot by Agent Philips. A second man, also dressed in black, was attempting to open the rear door of their vehicle.

"We have company, we need to get out of here." Sam grabbed Jessica by the arm and pulled her toward the lecture theatre door. Ackerman followed.

Another shot rang out.

They worked their way through the corridors until they got to Ackerman's study. Just as they entered, Sam's phone rang again. It was Agent Philips.

"We're being attacked!"

"I know. I heard the shots," said Sam abruptly.

"I've killed two hostiles so far. No thanks to Ackerman!"

"What do you mean?"

"Well, it's hard to line up a kill when your eye is practically swollen shut!"

"You deserved it!"

"Yes, I probably did. Anyway this is my assessment: I killed the second hostile as he was trying to unlock the doors at the rear of their vehicle. I managed a clear shot through the head so he didn't complete the task. You can guess what's in there right?"

"Yes, I can."

"OK well they're pissed and trying to smash their way out. The vehicle is bulging all over the place. I reckon we have about a minute or two to get this chopper off the ground before they get over here and tear it to pieces. You're on your way right?"

"We were just picking up some weapons from the professor's office." Ackerman had grabbed his mobile and a small rucksack that he put on his back. He was now passing them the swords they had used when practicing ninjutsu.

"No time Callaghan. Get out here now!"

"We're on our way!" Sam put his phone in his pocket. "Why have you given a sword to Jessica?" he asked the professor.

"Because she's a damn fine martial artist!"

"Don't tell me, the best student you have ever had, including me!"

"That's about it!"

They ran out into the courtyard just as the Roman soldiers were emerging from the Mastiff. The helicopter's huge rotor blades were already spinning and Philips had ditched his sniper rifle in favour of a Heckler & Koch 40mm grenade machine gun. He was firing grenades at a rate of about 40 rounds a minute, directly at the Roman soldiers. It wasn't killing them but it was certainly slowing them down.

Sam, Jessica and Ackerman were sprinting to the helicopter but it was unlikely that they would get there before the Romans.

"It looks like we'll have to fight," shouted Ackerman above the sound of the rotor blades. "Remember your training, they're much stronger than you and no matter how many times you strike them they will not go down. You'll have to use your speed and agility to keep out of their way and attempt to use the impetus of their blows against them. If they strike you, you're dead. If they manage to grab you,

you're dead. You have to out manoeuvre them. Our only hope is to fend them off long enough to get onboard that helicopter."

The grenades from the machine gun were kicking up dirt and stone all over the place. So when Sam, Jessica and the professor came close, Agent Philips had to stop firing. The Roman soldiers spotted their arrival and immediately recognized the face of Ackerman, the man they were programmed to kill. As one, the Romans charged towards him drawing their swords as they ran and raising the weapons high above their heads.

The trio saw their opportunity. As soon as the Romans were within striking distance they dived to the floor and rolled between them, striking at the Romans' legs with their swords as they went. The Romans tried to strike their adversaries but by the time they brought down their swords, they had struck nothing but dirt.

The soldiers learned quickly from their mistake. They turned and charged again, this time with their swords held out in front of them and their ranks closed. The trio ran towards them but before they clashed, they simultaneously leapt into the air, somersaulting over the Romans. As they did so they struck three of the Romans on the back of their heads, knocking off their helmets.

The soldiers regrouped. This time they dropped their shields and grabbed their knives from their belts. With their swords in their right hand held at their waists and their knives in their left hands, held above their heads, they began surrounding the trio and prowling around them.

Agent Philips had seen enough, He jumped from the helicopter and sprinted away from the fight.

Sam saw him run and exchanged glances with Ackerman. Agent Philips was indeed the coward they always suspected him to be.

The Romans approached them cautiously. Sam pulled Jessica close to him. If he died saving her life it would be worth it. The Romans began wielding their weapons around at great speed, like human threshing machines. Sam pulled

Jessica in closer. When she looked at him he expected to see fear in her eyes but there was just resignation. This time there really was no way out!

Suddenly a shout came from the other side of the courtyard.

"Over here boys!" Agent Philips stood facing them. He was holding a commando knife in his right hand and with one swift stroke he cut through the flesh on his left arm from his elbow down to his wrist.

As soon as the blood began to flow, the Romans stopped and turned in unison towards the agent. Then they dropped their knives and swords and ran towards him, jaws agape and fingers extended like claws, the primordial evil within them drooling at the smell of fresh human blood.

The trio ran for the helicopter and jumped aboard as it rose from the ground.

Philips yelled as certain death approached, "I told you this morning Sam, that sometimes one life is worth sacrificing to save the many. This is my redemption! By the way, there's something you need to know about Lucin--." Sam turned Jessica's face away from the helicopter's open doorway and maintained eye contact with her as the Romans began to tear Agent Philips apart.

Ackerman picked up the rifle and shot Philips through the head, ending his suffering. He had dreamed of taking this shot many times since Lucinda died, but now that he had, all he felt was regret. Regret that he had not really taken the time to understand the man or his motives, regret that he had viciously attacked him that very morning and regret that he had doubted him when he had run from the helicopter minutes before. He resolved that, if they lived through this crisis, Agent Brian Philips would be remembered by him, and the entire nation, as a hero who had given his life for his colleagues and his country, and not, as the killer of his daughter. He took off his rucksack and strapped himself into his seat.

Chapter 41

3.30pm. John and the Dean moored the Kew at Blackfriars Bridge and went to have a chat with the colonel who was in charge of the blockade there.

"The way you stopped those mercenaries was pretty impressive," remarked the colonel. "We were a little embarrassed that we didn't get them first!"

"It was a lucky shot!" replied John modestly.

"Still we owe you one. What can we do for you?"

"We need to get to the British Library as quickly as possible. Can you drive us there in one of your vehicles?"

"Yes, I am sure we can do that for you. Any particular reason you need to go there?"

John and the Dean looked at one another. "We are just looking for ways to destroy these Roman soldiers," said the Dean. "I think there might be some answers in some of the old manuscripts that are held there."

"Do the staff there, know that you're coming?" asked the colonel.

"Yes, everything has been arranged," lied the Dean, making a mental note to repent before the angels arrived.

"Alright then." He turned to his troops and issued orders. "Sergeant Briggs, I need you to drive our friends here to the British Library. You know where that is right?"

"Yes sir, I can leave right away. Jump aboard gentlemen." He opened the door of a Saxon 'battle-taxi', a lightly armoured, ten-man vehicle that could only travel at up to 60mph, but it was extremely robust and built to withstand roadside bombs.

"You'd better take some of our men with you as well, just in case you run into any trouble."

"Wiggins and Bradbury," he shouted, "I want you to tag along, and take the blood bags."

"Blood bags?" enquired the Dean.

"Yes, every unit has just been issued with them. It seems that the creatures are obsessed with the stuff. If we want to create a diversion we just throw a blood bag as far away as we can and then shoot at it. When these dumb monsters smell the stuff they immediately charge in that direction, even if they are in the middle of a fight.

"It was the idea of the SAS corporal who captured one of the creatures earlier today. He volunteered to be the bait and stood, with a bleeding hand, in front of a titanium cage. He realized afterwards that a bucket of blood in the back of the cage would have had the same effect!"

"We live and learn!" said John.

"Well let's get on our way gentlemen, it seems that the future of this country may rest in your hands."

"Before we go," said the Dean, "I don't suppose you have any spare clothes do you? I am rather wet after having jumped into the river earlier."

"I'm afraid not, but take my combat jacket, it will at least keep you warm."

The Dean and John thanked him and climbed aboard the battle-taxi. Private Wiggins closed the door behind them and then climbed into the turret to man the machine gun. Sergeant Briggs and Private Bradbury jumped in the front.

"I hope you like rock music" said Briggs. "This vehicle is powered by it!"

As soon as he turned on the engine the anthem began. They proceeded at full speed up Farringdon Road, with all three soldiers nodding their heads to the soundtrack of

"Highway to Hell". It wasn't long before John was doing the same thing, and to his surprise, even the Dean started to sing along and play air guitar. Spirits were high, for a moment at least they were able to forget the enormity of the task before them. They were all singing at full volume and nodding their heads to the incessant beat, as they took what should have been, a short journey to the British Library.

3.35pm. Ackerman put down the rifle and looked at Sam who had a comforting arm around Jessica. Despite what had just occurred he allowed himself a smile. They looked like a couple already; maybe some good would come of this. "Right, let's get back to my story."

"Just a minute sir, where are we heading?" asked the pilot.

"I need you to take us to Kings Cross Station."

"Are you sure? I understand that the place is crawling with Roman soldiers."

"Yes, I'm sure, and I'm about to explain why. Can you put some headphones on or something as this is rather confidential?"

"Of course, sir." The Pilot complied without question.

"Now, where was I?"

"Boudicca had just destroyed London."

"Oh yes..."

Chapter 42

AD 61. Claudius was at the Roman fortress of Glevum near Colchester when he heard about the attacks on Camulodium and Londinium. He was furious and immediately sent for Liberius.

"Hail Nero!" Liberius exclaimed as he entered. Claudius didn't bother saluting back and spoke in icy tones. "What have you done, Liberius? What have you done?"

"I, my lord? I do not understand." He did, however, know exactly what Claudius was referring to.

"First, Camulodium, and now Londinium. Tens of thousands of Roman citizens and soldiers dead, our temples destroyed and our villas burned to the ground, and all by a mere woman. A woman I could have so easily killed months ago."

Claudius stabbed an accusing finger at Liberius's chest. "It was you who said she should be spared! You who said I should show mercy. How is it possible that you could have been so spectacularly wrong? If I hadn't listened to you, I would be heading for Rome right now with a ship full of gold to lay at the emperor's feet. Now I'll be lucky to ever see Rome again!"

Liberius bowed his head. He was certain that Claudius would have him put to death and used as the scapegoat for the humiliation Boudicca's victories had brought upon Rome. They had held control of Britain by keeping its tribes divided; now they were uniting together under Boudicca's leadership, which was of enormous concern.

"Let me tell you this, Liberius," the governor continued. "However bad my fate is, I shall see to it that yours is a hundred – no, a thousand times worse."

Liberius thought quickly how he could redeem himself.

"The battle," said Liberius, "is not yet lost. Boudicca took us by surprise when we were at our weakest. That advantage is now lost to her. We can, and will, defeat her and her army. I will see to it myself!"

For a moment Claudius was placated - the death of Boudicca would certainly save his skin.

"She marches now on Verulamium. I believe you have family there?"

"My wife, Helena, and my son, Flavius."

"I have given orders that no one is to leave the city under pain of death so if your family is to live, Boudicca and her army must be defeated and destroyed. The defence of Verulamium is in your hands Liberius. You will ride there immediately with the cavalry of the Ninth Legion and either die there with your family or return here with Boudicca's head. You do understand, don't you Liberius, that if you do not kill Boudicca, I cannot permit you to stay alive."

"I do understand sir. Hail Nero!" replied Liberius and he turned to leave.

"For the glory of Rome!" shouted Claudius after him.

As Liberius and the Ninth Legion rode towards Verulamium, Boudicca's army was making slow progress. They'd been joined by entire families of Britons who'd fled the ruins of Camulodium and Londinium. These families included the elderly and infirm as well as suckling mothers and small children. Their journey was made worse by a cold Arctic wind and driving rain.

Boudicca was not concerned, as she looked back over the hundreds of thousands that followed her she felt that Britain was at last uniting against it's enemies. It would not be long before the Romans would be defeated and driven from their shores.

"Quite a following you have there," exclaimed Alvena. "Who would have thought that the Iceni would come back from defeat to bring the Romans to their knees. I would not be surprised if they are talking of you in Rome itself. I dare say you have Nero quaking in his boots!"

"If he has not heard of me he soon will. After Verulamium we will send word to the Tribes in the North and West and we will gather at York to deliver the final and decisive blow. I cannot wait to march upon Claudius and all his fine legions and give them a taste of the trident's power!"

"We should let the people rest before we reach Verulamium. Lets pitch our tents and march on at sunrise."

"You are right, dear Alvena, bid them rest. If we leave at dawn we will be outside the gates of Verulamium by nightfall and victorious by midnight."

Chapter 43

AD 61. Liberius was weary. They had been riding at speed for four hours in torrential rain but he dare not stop with his family's lives at risk. He believed he loved them more than any man possibly could. He had fallen in love with Helena the first time he had seen her. He had been stationed at Verulamium for less than a month when he saw her drawing water from the town well. As she passed him he caught her eye and she gave him an approving smile. He immediately offered to carry her bucket and walk her home, an invitation that she readily accepted.

Her parents were totally against the relationship, but they soon discovered that Liberius was unlike other Romans. He was almost apologetic about their presence in Britain and he was always courteous and polite. Most importantly he treated their daughter like a princess, showering her with gifts and tokens of love. Eventually they conceded that there were no other suitors, even amongst the Britons, that would treat her as well and if Rome was to remain in Britain it would serve them well to have Liberius as a son-in-law.

They were married the following spring and by winter Helena had given birth to a son, which they called Flavius. Liberius's happiness was now complete. Leaving them on long campaigns across the barren British countryside broke his heart and all he could ever think of was returning into Helena's arms.

When Liberius and his legion entered Brasenose Forest, just east of Oxford, it was dusk. The trees stretched for miles to the North and South so there was no option but to ride through it and he could not wait until daybreak, by then it could well be too late.

As they rode between the trees their way was illuminated by constant flashes of white lightning, each, followed immediately by the deafening roar of thunder. A firebolt hit a tree just a few yards to his left and it split and fell, seconds later another struck one of the legionaries' horses to his left, the horse immediately dropped to ground crushing the leg of its rider who was then trampled by the horse following closely behind.

Lightning bolts began to fall all around them and the cavalry broke their disciplined formation and rode for their lives. Liberius felt as if the gods were using them for target practice. This was a bad omen.

The next firebolt hit a tree, almost in his path, which erupted into flames. Liberius's horse stopped abruptly and reared its front legs throwing him to the forest floor where he was impaled through the shoulder by a twisted bough. He could not extract himself and his legion rode past desperate to escape the forest and oblivious to their tribune's plight. As his vision began to fade he thought he saw a young woman emerge from the trees running to his aid, then there was darkness.

He woke abruptly to find himself in a wooden shelter; he was in great pain and could hardly move. He could hear a woman's voice uttering a strange incantation. He turned his head from left to right but could see no one, then a woman's face began to appear in view, dark and drawn but beautiful, and his vision once more faded into blackness.

He opened his eyes again and it was daylight. The sun was streaming through the gaps in the crude roof, constructed with twigs bound with twine. The room was full of the skulls of animals and men. Herbs hung drying from the roof and the hide of a stag hung across the doorway. He tried to move and was surprised that the severe pain, he'd felt the previous night, had completely gone. He rose from the bearskin bed upon which he had been lying with little effort and stood tall and straight. He manipulated his shoulder and it moved freely. He saw his armour lying on the floor and bent over to retrieve it, he put on his breastplate and was just in the process of donning his helmet when the stag's hide parted and his host entered the room.

She was tall and slim. Her hair, jet black and unkempt, cascaded down to her waist. She wore a long grey dress that seemed to have been mended on more than one occasion, and around her waist was a leather belt from which hung a twisted dagger with a bone handle upon which were many strange engravings. Her face was dirty and partly obscured by her wild hair but that did not hide her beauty. Her skin was a dusky brown, which emphasized the whites of her eyes and surprisingly healthy teeth. The eyes were emphasized further, by a thin line of black that surrounded them, and despite her disheveled appearance, she had the appearance of an Egyptian queen. Her arms were long and thin but her muscles were clearly defined. She was carrying his sword and began to advance towards him. He stepped back fearing she would strike but she offered him the hilt and he took it from her.

"My name is Rionna." she announced smiling.

"I am Liberius, tribune of Rome"

"Were you leaving?" she asked.

"Yes I was. My family are in danger and I must ride to their aid."

"I am afraid you cannot go, you're still recovering from your wounds. If you ride now you may die." Her voice was soft and compassionate.

"I must take that risk, I have lost a night already and must join my legion in Verulamium. Tomorrow, Boudicca, queen of the Iceni and her vengeful army will attack the town and I fear that my wife and son will be slain."

"You have lost more than a night my Lord you slept two

nights and a day while my magic healed your wound."

Liberius was frantic. "Two nights and a day! All is lost! Please let me pass. I have to leave right now!"

The woman's voice deepened and rose in volume, tinged with malice. "I have given you back your life, you ungrateful wretch, you must stay with me and repay my kindness!"

"I am truly grateful for all you have done for me, but my loyalty is to Rome and the one's I love".

"You will stay and love me!"

"I cannot!" He grabbed his tunic and shield and pushed her aside so that he could leave her dwelling. To his relief his horse was tethered to a nearby tree. As he ran towards it the woman emerged in fury. She pointed at him and for the first time he noticed that her nails were long and her hands wrinkled. He looked into her eyes and she seemed to have aged a century.

"If you leave now I will place a curse upon your head!"

"Do your worst witch!" He shouted in defiance as he mounted his horse.

"Very well!" she screamed. Both of her hands were now outstretched towards him and her face was distorted with rage.

"I curse you that you shall never die, but the wounds you receive will never heal, and the pain thereof will never cease. Your suffering will drive you to insanity and there will be no relief unless you return to me and pledge to be with me forever."

Liberius ignored her ranting and rode away. He did not believe in witchcraft, but her words still chilled his soul.

Rionna was indeed a witch. She'd been raised in Egypt by the Heka, a dark, wicked race with a long and mysterious past, who were credited with extraordinary powers. It was they who had overseen the construction of the great pyramids, and had been the sorcerers who mimicked the miracles of Moses in Pharaoh's palace: such as the transformation of wooden rods into living snakes and the turning of rivers to blood. Eventually, the Pharoah realized that the Heka had become too powerful and influential and there was evil intent behind everything they'd done, so he had them cast out of Egypt. Most of the Heka settled in Eastern Europe and Asia but Rionna found her way to England, where for centuries she'd lived alone. This day, however, she'd met the man that would dispel her loneliness, and she vowed to pursue him to the ends of the earth, because for a Heka witch, love was a lifelong obsession.

As Liberius rode from the forest the witch's limbs began to distort, her spine extended and curved, her face stretched into a snout, her teeth yellowed and sharpened and her black hair sprouted from every pore of her body. Her dress was unable to contain her beastly form and tore from her body as she fell forward onto her hands. In seconds, the transformation was complete and the huge, black she-wolf bounded off in the direction of the fleeing tribune.

Chapter 44

3.40pm. The battle-taxi stormed onto Farringdon Street now rocking to the Led Zeppelin classic *"Whole Lotta Love"*. As they crossed the first junction, Briggs abruptly bought the vehicle to a halt. A column of Romans had suddenly emerged from a passageway just ahead of them, on their left, and spread across the entire width of the road. They were less than a shoulder width apart so there was no way through. Then a black armoured Mastiff pulled up behind the legionaries and two mercenaries, each with automatic weapons, emerged taking up positions each side of their vehicle.

"I think we should just drive through them," shouted Sergeant Briggs over the music.

"You'd be wasting your time," shouted John. "I saw three police cars drive into these creatures earlier and they didn't move an inch."

Private Wiggins let rip with the machine gun and although the shells dented the monsters' shields and armour, they had no effect on the Romans themselves; the mercenaries took cover from the heavy ordnance behind the Mastiff.

Sergeant Briggs decided it was time to leave and spun his vehicle around to head back for the bridge but as soon as they turned they saw that another column of soldiers had emerged behind them blocking their retreat. Then both columns started advancing.

"If they reach our vehicle they'll pull it apart," shouted the Dean.

"Why don't we just throw one of the blood bags across the street, shoot a hole in it and drive past them when they are distracted?" shouted Private Bradbury convinced he had the solution.

"There's too many of them," said Briggs turning down the music. "We may lose one or two from the end of the column but not enough to escape. They'll immediately sense the blood but they'll realize there is simply not enough to go round. Would you join a queue for lunch if there was only one biscuit on the table?"

"Then we need to give them more of a feast," said John exiting the vehicle.

"Where are you going, John. Are you crazy?" said the Dean.

"Sergeant Briggs, hand me a couple of those blood bags. Quickly!" yelled John. The columns of Roman soldiers were now less than 10 metres away.

"Wiggins we'll have one chance at this so I'm hoping you know how to use that gun of yours. I am going to throw these bags above the Mastiff. Before they fall to the ground you need to blow them apart. Can you do it?"

"No problem sir!"

John threw the first blood bag high above the armoured vehicle. Wiggins fired the machine gun, but the blood bag fell intact of the Mastiff's roof. The Romans were now just 4 yards from John.

"Wiggins you miss this time and we're all dead!" John shouted.

"No pressure then!" responded Private Wiggins.

As John threw the remaining blood bag into the air one of the Romans grabbed his trailing wrist and pulled him backward. John felt like he had been caught in a vice and cried out in pain.

The Dean prayed as he watched the blood bag, as if in slow motion; pass over the Mastiff's roof. Once again, the machine gun began to roar, but this time the bag exploded, showering the mercenaries behind the vehicle with a litre of fresh A positive blood.

The Roman holding John was about to bite into his arm when it picked up the scent and looked towards the source. To John's relief it released its iron like grip.

The two mercenaries realized their predicament as the Romans all suddenly turned in their direction. One mercenary tried to flee, and the other locked himself in their vehicle, as both columns broke formation and ran towards them.

Sergeant Briggs waited for John to get back on board and then accelerated passed the Mastiff, just as it was having its doors ripped open. They then passed the running mercenary as he was overtaken by the remaining blood thirsty Romans.

As they broke free onto the open road Briggs cranked up the music.

"Captain Birdseye" shouted the Dean, "You are fast becoming a legend!"

Meanwhile, in a helicopter well above the Berkshire countryside, Ackerman continued his story…

Chapter 45

AD 61. When Liberius was still ten miles from Verulamium he could see that the town was in flames, his boots dug deep into his steed as he urged it to run faster. He could barely see through the tears that filled his eyes as he imagined what fate his family may have already suffered at the hands of Boudicca and her rebel army.

A few miles on he began to see soldiers, even those from his own legion passing him in the opposite direction. He yelled at them to follow him, but they either did not hear or pretended not to. As he approached the town walls he could see that there was still fighting in the streets, pockets of resistance making a last stand against certain death. Hope rose in his chest. Perhaps his family had not yet been discovered. He raced through the streets to his home.

Alvena saw the Roman Tribune riding through the streets and she ran to follow him, Boudicca saw Alvena leave her side and joined in the chase. They saw the Roman jump from his horse and enter a wooden home in the middle of the town. Alvena thought he was somewhat familiar but had not yet seen his face. As she ran into the house with her sword raised and ready to strike, she saw the tribune kneeling at the far end of the room clutching a small boy. She advanced and raised her sword, determined to kill the Roman officer but as he turned toward her, she immediately recognized Liberius. Remembering how he had saved Boudicca and her daughters and spared her life on the battlefield, she refrained from taking the fatal blow, but as she lowered her sword a slight red-headed woman emerged from behind the door through which Alvena had entered, and plunged a long knife deep into her back.

Liberius's shouted to his wife to stop but it was too late, she twisted the blade further and Alvena collapsed to the ground just as Boudicca and several of her men arrived.

Liberius's wife was first to react and leapt through an open window into the street, some of Boudicca's men raced after her, the rest apprehended Liberius and his son. Liberius offered no resistance through fear for his son's safety.

"Boudicca take my life in any way you see fit, but please spare my wife and son, Helena was just trying to save her family. She's a Briton like you. Please show her mercy, spare them just as I had Claudius spare your life and the lives of your daughters."

Liberius's words had fallen on deaf ears. Boudicca was staring at the fallen Alvena and her face was distorted in anger and pain.

"Bind Liberius and his son and find his bitch wife." She turned to the Tribune. "Today you will die but first you will be made to watch as I slaughter your treacherous wife and half-breed son!"

She then turned to her men. "I have had enough of Britons who harbour and mix with Roman filth. Kill every inhabitant of this town. Burn them, hang them, behead them or crucify them. Raise every dwelling to the ground. Send a clear message to our people that the price of collaboration is death!"

Two of Boudicca's men ran into the small dwelling dragging Liberius's wife. "She's a sneaky one, we lost sight of her completely then some of our men found her tied up under a cart. She claims that she has killed no one and has been bound for over an hour, lying cow, she must have tied the knots herself!"

Helena raised her head and saw Liberius and her son being bound, "Liberius you came! I knew you would try to save us!"

Liberius was puzzled he had spoken to his wife just a few minutes earlier and now she was acting as if they were meeting for the first time. Then he looked at the knife in Alvena's back and all became clear. It was the same dagger that was on the witch's belt.

Somehow she had beaten him to Verulamium and taken his wife's form. Now Helena was condemned to die for the witch's action and the truth would never be believed. He cursed the witch who had cursed him and wished that he had never crossed her path.

The murder, rape and destruction of Verulamium went on deep into the night. Liberius was kept at a separate location from his wife and son, and it wasn't hard for The Guardian to find him and slip past the tired guards.

"Liberius," The Guardian whispered. "We have to speak."

"Who are you and what are you doing here?" Liberius asked.

"I am a friend. I am called The Guardian and I need an account of what has happened here this day. Afterwards I will do all I can to have you and your family set free."

"Do you swear Guardian?"

"I so swear."

"Very well then." Liberius told him all of the events of the last few days and was surprised to know that The Guardian was already aware of much that had transpired.

At first Liberius thought to hold back on his encounter with the witch but for some reason he felt he could trust this man and wanted him to know the truth, that Helena was innocent of the crime for which she was charged.

He was surprised to learn that The Guardian knew of the shape shifting witch and even identified her as Rionna, who had been a thorn in his side for many a year.

When Liberius told The Guardian that Boudicca had ordered the execution of every Briton in Verulamium he appeared deeply troubled. He thanked Liberius for his honesty and said that he would immediately visit Boudicca and appeal to her for mercy.

"She will not listen to you Guardian, she is convinced that Helena killed her friend and her mind has been bent by grief."

"I will do what I can Liberius, I know that you do not deserve to die this night and neither does your family."

"I care not for myself Guardian, now that Verulamium has fallen I am an outcast anyway. If I return to my Commander I will be executed on sight, but please save my family."

The Guardian quietly entered Boudicca's tent as she stood issuing orders to her men. She had learned that the Romans were already gathering a huge army of many legions to try and defeat her, and she wanted to strike while the morale of her men was high. When her men had left The Guardian emerged from the shadows. Boudicca sensed his presence. "Why are you here Guardian?" she asked.

"To reclaim the relics", he responded, "You have broken your oath and slaughtered your own people."

"Do not lecture me or ask anything of me. I am Boudicca Queen of the Iceni and I will soon unite Britain and reign over this entire Kingdom."

"You will not. You have betrayed my trust in you and I must find another to take your place."

"Be careful what you say, your words are treason!"

"My words are truth!" he exclaimed with such power that Boudicca was taken aback. "Give me the relics now!"

Boudicca regained her composure and reached for the trident, fully intending to strike the Guardian dead, but the weapon seemed strangely heavy in her hand and she found it difficult to wield. The Guardian easily stepped out of her way.

"Give them back, they are useless to you now."

"I will not!" she screamed and called for her guards. "Arrest this man, bind him and throw him in with the Roman. Then prepare the woman Helena and her son for execution."

Helena and Flavius struggled and screamed for mercy as they were each tied to a large wooden wheel taken from a captured Roman chariot.

Liberius and the Guardian were tied to the same tree and a Briton, larger even than Liberius, held his head so that he was forced to watch the executions. When Liberius refused to open his eyes, his eyelids where pulled forward and sliced through and a strip of cloth torn from his cloak was used to stem the flow of blood.

"For treachery, treason and the murder of my beloved Alvena", Boudicca screamed. "These Britons are condemned to death and you Liberius will watch them burn!"

Boudicca's men then threw hot buckets of tar over Liberius's screaming family and the wooden wheels were raised onto their rims. At Boudicca's command they used flaming torches to ignite the tar and pushed the burning chariot wheels down the hill towards the remains of Verulamium.

The night was filled with the screams of Liberius's wife and son as the wheels disappeared into the distance and the equally disturbing sound of a mind and soul breaking apart as Liberius cursed Boudicca and vowed to utterly destroy her and the land in which he stood.

3.55pm. "So that is why Liberius is hell bent on destroying us," observed Sam.

"That was the beginning of his downfall certainly." replied Ackerman, "Watching his family being so brutally executed by a woman to whom he had once shown mercy, shattered any morality that he once had, from that point on all lives were worthless and expendable, including his own."

Chapter 46

AD 61. After the executions, Liberius and the Guardian were left tied together in the middle of Boudicca's camp, she wanted them to spend the night contemplating the horror of the execution before they were both hung at the break of dawn. Being hung was going to be nothing more than an inconvenience as they were both immortal but the idea of dangling at the end of a rope for hours, maybe even days was not pleasant and if the witch's curse was to be believed Liberius would not be spared the pain.

A mist had gathered during the night and visibility was low. Their guards kept them within view, which meant moving closer and closer to their captors as the mist increased.

The Guardian had been expecting abuse from Liberius for being unable to keep his promise and save his family, but the Roman remained quiet, except for an occasional guttural mutter and several attempts to break free of his bindings.

At around 4am, as The Guardian fought to stay awake, he was brought to full alert by a large black shape moving just inside the curtain of mist. It looked like a wolf but it was three or four times their natural size. The guards had obviously not seen the beast as they were loudly discussing their material and physical conquests after the previous day's battle. When they finally noticed it emerge, it was too late. The beast dived at the first guard gripping his head in its jaws and tearing it from his shoulders. The other guard began to run, but the wolf reached him in two strides pushing him to the ground and biting into the back of his skull.

The beast then turned to the captives and snarled at them. The Guardian felt himself tremble wondering how the immortal thing would work if he was torn to bits. Liberius just stared into the beast's eyes willing it to kill him. It then started to circle behind them and The Guardian closed his eyes waiting for it to strike. Instead he felt his bonds being cut. He turned to face the monster but in its stead stood the witch Rionna.

When Liberius saw her he fought against his bindings desperate to get free so he could grab her by the neck and squeeze it until her face turned purple and her bones cracked, but the bindings held firm. The Guardian just stared at her in disbelief.

"Well gentleman" said Rionna, "I guess I owe you an apology."

"An apology!" screamed Liberius, "you have caused the death of my wife and son - what you owe me is your life!"

"I didn't mean for her to die, I just wanted to replace her for a while and see what it would be like to be your wife. Then that Alvena stormed in I had no choice but to kill her. She was about to cleave your head in two which would be a very undesirable look, especially for an immortal."

"And I am supposed to thank you after you have destroyed my family and my life?"

"No, of course not, I just wanted to explain that's all."

"So you're the one who tied up my wife and left her to die!"

"No I am the one that tied up your wife and left her where she would be safe until the battle was over. I got her out of harm's way because I knew I could get to her before you did. I was just coming back to save Flavius when you arrived, bringing the Iceni with you. My intentions were always to save your family, you must believe me."

"Ok then, release me and let me give you a big hug!" sneered Liberius.

"The Guardian will release you after I am gone. Liberius, I know that right now you want me dead but hopefully one day you will understand that I was trying to help. Once more I am sorry Liberius." She began to change back into the beast.

"Then remove my curse!" shouted Liberius as she turned to leave.

"Only you can remove the curse, I will be waiting for you my love, although I suspect it may be for some time."

With that she disappeared into the mist.

"Do you believe her Guardian?" Liberius asked.

"Not a word," said The Guardian as he untied him.

"So The Guardian let him go?" asked Sam.

"He had to, at that point Liberius had done nothing wrong," replied Ackerman.

"I bet he regrets it now," said Jessica.

"Yes I am sure he does," said Ackerman.

Chapter 47

4.00pm. The battle-taxi pulled up outside the British Library playing Sabbath's 'Paranoid' and John and the Dean got out, followed by the soldiers.

"Thanks for getting us here in one piece." said the Dean.

"Well we wouldn't have managed it without John here." said the Sergeant patting John on the back. John smiled awkwardly not liking praise.

"Well I guess this is where we part company." said the Dean hopefully. He didn't want them around when he broke in and summoned the Angels of Death.

"Well if you're sure. I hope you find what you're looking for."

The soldiers shook hands with John and the Dean and then got back into their battle-taxi. The rock music slowly faded as they drove off into the distance, and it was replaced with an eerie silence.

As soon as they were sure the soldiers were completely out of sight, the Dean started climbing the high metal gates. Meanwhile John calmly walked through the turnstiles beside them.

The Dean looked down at him rather embarrassed, "The turnstiles should be locked when there is no security guard here, I guess they must have left in a hurry."

"Or someone got here before us." said John. "Who else knows about the manuscript?"

"I guess anyone who has read the index to the sealed portions, but as far as I know only the professor and I unsealed them."

"You mean everyone else obeyed the Monks wishes, Call yourself a priest!"

"Well if I hadn't peaked we wouldn't know what was in it would we? Now help me down from this blasted gate."

John raised his eyebrows and gave the Dean a disapproving look, a little surprised by his language then he helped him onto the ground. "Where to now?"

"Well we'll never get through the main entrance, of course, but last time we were here the professor and I attached a little device to that window up there." He pointed to a window on the second floor, next to the fire escape. "All I have to do is push the window slightly inward and the catch will open."

"Ok then get on with it!" said John. The Dean began to climb the fire escape. When he had got to the first floor John began to laugh.

"What's so funny Birdseye?" asked the Dean.

"I think you tore more than your cassock when you were sliding down that dome. You certainly are a 'holey' man," He laughed again at his own very poor joke.

"Oh my heavens!" said the Dean, "Avert your eyes at once! Better still you climb up here and let me attend to my modesty."

John and the Dean swapped places. John climbed up the ladder while the Dean started to tie what remained of his cassock strategically about his loins.

When John reached the second floor he surveyed the courtyard in front of the Library to ensure they were alone. He soon discovered they weren't.

"Hang on Dean, I think I've found you a change of clothes." He pointed to the area behind the security hut. The Dean walked over and saw the lifeless body of the Library's security guard.

Chapter 48

4.05pm. Ackerman suddenly remembered that he had picked up his mobile when they went to his study. He removed it from his jacket pocket and noticed immediately that there were two voicemail messages. He dialed 901 and listened. The first was from Sir Gareth filling him in on the day's events and asking him to bury the hatchet and give him a call. There was nothing new to be learned there.

The second message was from the Dean. It was a message he had hoped not to hear.

He immediately tried to return the call but it went straight to Voicemail. He could see that the incoming call had not come from the Dean's own mobile so he tried that number too. To his frustration the call failed.

"We have a problem." Ackerman told Sam and Jessica. "One of the messages was from the Dean, he's on his way to the British Library. He said he was going to summon the Angels of Death if I didn't get back to him in the next three hours."

"When did he call you?" Sam asked.

Ackerman checked the list of incoming calls, "He called at 1.25pm, two and a half hours ago!"

"Then call him back immediately!" said Sam a little panicked.

"I tried. The number he called on goes straight to voicemail and the Dean's own mobile doesn't seem to be working at all."

"What's the number of the phone he called you on?" asked Sam. Ackerman gave him the number and Sam compared it to the one Sir Gareth had given him earlier. His supposition was correct. The mobile numbers were the same. The phone belonged to Captain Birdseye. "It's John's number, the guy who pulled me out of the river, they must have gone to the Library together. We have to go there and stop them!"

"The British Library is only a few hundred yards from Kings Cross Station. When we get there, you two can get the trident while I find the Dean."

"So the trident is at Kings Cross Station? What the hell is it doing there?"

"Let me finish my story," said Ackerman. Jessica smiled knowingly.

4.05pm. Director Andrew Smith paced up and down the war room. Everything was going wrong and he had totally lost control of the situation. Since the Press Conference fiasco Sir Gareth was more unbearable than ever. Andrew once thought of him as his staunchest ally, but now Sir Gareth was undermining him at every turn and issuing commands to his own staff without his knowledge. Even his junior agent, Sam Callaghan, was ignoring his calls. He felt powerless for the first time since he was made director of MI5 and he didn't like that feeling at all.

What's more, he now had to answer to a woman. "You would have thought we'd have learned from the Thatcher fiasco!" he muttered under his breath.

"What was that?" the Deputy Prime Minister asked. They'd gotten her into the COBRA briefing room through the tunnels from Westminster Palace without a hitch.

"Nothing," he responded, "I was just mouthing my frustrations to myself."

Andrew had no time for the Deputy PM. In his opinion, the country went downhill last time a woman was in charge and he wasn't prepared to let that happen again. Right now the country needed strong leadership and he believed that Karen Shaw was no leader. What had she said when the US President had called making threats? Not 'we have everything under control, get out of my face and let me govern my country' but a weak 'Please give us more time Miles while we try to figure out what to do'.

"Before you figure anything out Karen, we'll have American nukes up our backsides," he muttered to himself.

"What was that?" Shaw asked.

"I was just saying that we ought to find out if General Radford and his team had come up with any other military solutions. Maybe we should consider some low-yield nukes."

"We will not use nuclear missiles in this country while I am Prime Minister!"

"With respect Karen, you're not the Prime Minister, and if we don't stop Liberius in the next few hours you never will be!"

Most of the other committee members turned away so that she wouldn't see the smiles on their faces. But their levity was short lived for they all knew that Andrew was right: if they didn't come up with an answer fast, there was no future for any of them. No future at all.

Not everyone shared the chauvinistic views of Andrew Smith - Sir Gareth seethed at his words. He couldn't abide Smith's blatant disrespect for Karen Shaw. He thought it incredibly ironic that the director's life and, in fact, the nation's, would very likely rest in the hands of a woman, but not this one…

Sir Gareth also had other concerns. Sam had told him he'd needed the Dean's help to get the trident, but why? He was certain that Ackerman was aware of its whereabouts. He also didn't understand why the Dean and John had failed to check in for over an hour. They were fully aware that he had to be kept up to date, so why hadn't they called? Something was definitely wrong. He found it inconceivable that his closest friends would have gone off the grid. Either they were dead or doing something that they knew he wouldn't approve of.

He tried to call John back, but his phone was still on voicemail. He called Sam, then Ackerman, but no one answered. Unbeknown to Sir Gareth, neither had heard their phones ring above the sound of the helicopter's rotor blades.

Sir Gareth thought the worst: Liberius had either captured or killed them. He prayed that he was wrong.

His deliberations were interrupted by another call from Liberius, this time he was asking for Karen Shaw. She took the phone and put it on loudspeaker so that the committee could hear every word.

"Hello Karen, I guess you owe me for opening up a job vacancy for you."

"I owe you nothing you murderous pig!"

That's the spirit, thought Sir Gareth.

"Now, now Karen. I would be careful how you address me if I were you. After all I will soon be your emperor."

"I would sooner die than let that happen."

"Very well, that will be arranged. By the way, I just wanted to remind you that you have less than five hours to surrender and be warned, my army is growing in number, and they are hungry for blood. I'm having to hold them back at the moment. They're pulling at the leash like a pack of rabid dogs so to be honest, even after your surrender, I'll still need to provide them with some sustenance. And as you requested Karen, I'll start with you. Anyone else in that room want to be on the menu?"

No one answered.

"No, I thought not! Anyway, have to go now and raise a few more Romans from the dead. See you soon Karen. But not for long!" The line went dead.

Karen slumped back into her chair, stress and fear written across her face.

"Well gentlemen, what are our options?"

Before Sir Gareth could answer, a text appeared on his phone. It was from Ackerman but he did not recognize the number. It read: *Meet me at the British Library as soon as you can. Tell no one".*

He asked Karen Shaw if he could be excused for an hour. He assured her that what he had to do might be crucial in the battle against Liberius and trusting him, she let him go.

Andrew Smith watched suspiciously as he left the room. Why had he not told them exactly where he was going?

Sir Gareth immediately descended into the tunnels and made his way through the long corridor to Q-Whitehall. He typed in an 8-digit security code and undertook a retina scan. He was successfully identified and his face appeared on a small screen beside the keypad. The lock clicked and he was able to push open the large steel door.

He walked hastily though their top-secret state-of-the-art communications facility, briefly acknowledging those he passed.

He then passed through another secure door that led to the old Trafalgar Square tube station, that had long since closed. It was now a key terminal on the Government's huge, private transportation network that branched out under London's streets linking together all of their key facilities.

He mused that it was far more reliable than the London Underground that had to move millions of commuters around the capital every day. This was partly due to the fact that it had cost a damn sight more, but mainly because it did not rely on train drivers under the control of an extremely belligerent union leader.

He crossed the platform and boarded one of the government's self-drive shuttle trains with the intention of heading north towards Kings Cross to meet up with Ackerman, but as he peered into the darkness he could make out movement on the tracks ahead.

When he turned on the shuttle's headlights he saw two mercenaries and a Roman soldier running in his direction. Behind them were ten more Romans.

They had infiltrated the Government's tunnel system. This was bad news indeed.

It was right then that he wished the million-pound shuttles could travel in reverse.

Chapter 49

AD 61. Boudicca was beside herself with anger when she found out that Liberius and the Guardian had escaped. She would have instantly executed the guards were they not already dead.

She still bore her relics but she felt strangely powerless. Her helmet had given her no visions, just a headache, and the trident was at least five times heavier than she ever remembered it to be. Maybe the shield, at least, would still offer her some protection.

She returned to her tent and called for her captains, her scouts and her daughters. With maps laid across the table the scouts showed her the positions of the Roman legions and with the captains they planned their battle tactics.

Despite her concerns about the sudden ineffectiveness of the relics she knew that her army now outnumbered the gathering Romans at least ten to one. There was no way that she would lose this fight and after she slaughtered these legions, removing the remaining Romans would be a relatively simple task.

She was so confident that she told her men to have their families meet them at Watling Street, just 50 miles north west of Verulamium to witness her greatest victory, which would turn the tide firmly against the Roman invaders.

Meanwhile Seutonius, who was the Roman Governor, and General Claudius had brought together the 14th Germina Legion, the 20th Valeria Victrix and any available auxiliaries they could muster. In all, they managed to gather around 10,000 men.

In contrast, Boudicca's army now stood at 230,000 and more were joining by the hour. She stood on her chariot and addressed the masses.

"We now have the opportunity to tear the heart out of the Roman army and end this brutal occupation. We will march upon the Roman vermin and dispatch them from this land and from this earth once and for all! I will, at last, fully avenge my battered body, our lost freedom and the abused chastity of my daughters. Let your hearts rejoice and be exceedingly glad. Let the earth break forth in singing for today this land will see its greatest victory!"

The Britons began their march to Watling Street singing and chanting and beating their swords and spears against their shields as they had often seen the Romans do.

Suetonius and Claudius awaited the arrival of the Britons. They knew that they would be heavily outnumbered so they chose a narrow field of battle so Boudicca could only put forth an equal number of troops to the Romans at any given time. They had also amassed catapults, javelin throwers and archers to greet the approaching hordes.

When the Romans were in sight the men looked to Boudicca to strike the first blow with the power of her trident, surely this would immediately break the spirits of the Roman army as it had three times before. They were astonished when she instead just rushed headlong into battle with her daughters, each in their own chariots by her side.

The men quickly shook off their surprise and charged after her. They were immediately met by a shower of javelins and arrows, followed by fireballs flung from the Roman catapults, which killed many as they ran. Then the Romans began to advance in a wedge formation with their swords and spears to the ready.

The Britons were not expecting such heavy resistance and despite Boudicca's cries to advance, they began to retreat. Their escape, however, were impeded by their own families who had positioned their wagons on the edge of the battlefield.

They had no choice but to turn back into the fight to try to keep the Romans from their loved ones, and so the slaughter began.

For hours the battle raged on. Boudicca refused to accept defeat and continued to fight while her daughters battled by her side. She had discarded the trident somewhere on the battlefield in favour of her sword and was caught in a ferocious battle with two Roman centurions.

After killing one, she blocked the blow of the other with her shield, and then out of the corner of her eye, she caught sight of a man that instantly chilled her blood. Liberius was entering the fray close to her youngest daughter Siorra who was sitting astride a Roman soldier, cutting his throat.

Liberius caught Boudicca's eye and smiled cruelly as he plunged his sword deep into Siorra's back. As he withdrew his weapon covered in her blood, she fell forward onto the soldier she had just killed.

Boudicca quickly dispatched the remaining centurion and rushed after Liberius. He watched her advance with relish, desperate to remove her head. She advanced with her sword held high. Liberius knew that the longer reach of his arm and sword would allow him to gut her before she could strike; at best she would cut off his arm, but it would be worth it.

As he lunged forward however, a hand grasped his ankle and he lost his balance. As he fell forward he caught a glimpse of Siorra, whose last act had caused his downfall. His world turned black as Boudicca's sword cut through the top of his head.

"So Siorra died saving her mother's life," said Sam "I guess Liberius got his revenge after all, but at the cost of the world's worst hair-cut!"

"Let him finish Sam, that's not how this ends." Jessica did not appreciate Sam's frivolity; she knew what was to come.

Ackerman continued…

Chapter 50

AD 61. Boudicca carried Siorra's body from the battlefield. Blood was seeping profusely from her wound and from her mouth. The Queen knew that her daughter was dying, as did Isolda, who had rushed to join them as soon as she was able. All three women wept.

Boudicca's heart was full of regret. She had been given the opportunity to liberate her country with a gift from the gods and she had let her lust for revenge cause her to abandon the cause that she had so valiantly believed in. Now, her army was defeated, her daughter was dying and the Romans had prevailed.

She laid Siorra on the ground and prayed over her, begging the gods to let her daughter live. Her prayers became louder and more anguished, rising above the sobs of Isolda. She was oblivious to the figure entering the clearing, with a weapon by his side.

Isolda's warrior heart pushed aside her sorrow and she stood to face the visitor, determined to strike down anyone bold enough to intrude on their grief. She was immediately disarmed by the gentle, sympathetic smile of the Guardian.

"I have come to bring you the opportunity of salvation Boudicca," he said. "For you and for your daughter. God has heard your prayers and gives you one last chance to redeem yourself. Here is the trident that you left on the battlefield." The Guardian passed it to Boudicca. "You know what you must do!"

"What does he mean?" asked Isolda.

"Hush my child, come embrace me."

Isolda knelt by her mother and held her as tight as she possibly could. She did not understand what was happening, but she knew that this was the last time she would embrace the woman who had given her life.

Boudicca kissed her cheek then pushed her aside and leant forward to embrace the dying Siorra, who was now too weak to lift her arms or even open her eyes. "I love you both so very much. Please forgive your mother for her foolishness. I was blinded by rage at the death of Alvena and I did some terrible things. I no longer deserve to live, but at least I can die with honour. Isolda, please look after your sister when I am gone."

Without giving her daughters the opportunity to respond she raised the trident and, without hesitation, placed its three golden prongs on Siorra's chest. Immediately, Boudicca felt her life force flow from her, just as the Guardian had told her it would. Siorra's eyes suddenly opened and she quickly raised her arms to catch the body of her mother as she slumped forward upon her.

The great warrior queen of the Iceni was dead.

When the battle of Watling Street was over, almost 80,000 Britons lay dead or mortally injured. Those that survived the war and escaped the subsequent executions, heard from Boudicca's daughters about her selfless, heroic death.

They took turns in carrying her body to Battle Bridge, the site of her great victory against the Roman stronghold at Londinium. Here they buried her in a chamber, which they had constructed deep beneath the ground. Alongside her they placed the relics that they had once believed came from the gods, and which they now blamed for her death and defeat.

As they sealed the tomb, they prayed that it would never be discovered so their queen could lie undisturbed, and the relics would never be recovered.

The Guardian looked on and wept.

In 383AD, after another 320 years of battling with the brave and resolute Britons, the last Romans troops were withdrawn and Britain was again free. Historians agree that it was the heroic acts of Boudicca that united the tribes against their invaders and gave them the courage to eventually drive them from their shores.

4.10pm. Sam now wanted the specifics. "Where exactly is Battle Bridge?" he asked.

"The site has been built upon many times over the last two thousand years. The tomb now lies directly beneath platforms 9 and 10 of Kings Cross Station," replied Ackerman. "That is where you and Jessica are heading."

"Do you think the relics are still there?" asked Sam.

"It's a distinct possibility," said Ackerman.

"But how do we find the tomb? There is probably thousands of tons of concrete above it now."

"As soon as the Iceni left Battle Bridge the Guardian began building a tunnel through to the tomb so that he could access the relics whenever they were needed. When the underground was built at Kings Cross in 1863, the Guardian dug through to link one of their tunnels with his," explained Ackerman.

"And do you know where that tunnel is?"

"Yes we do." replied Jessica.

Sam turned to her in surprise, then back to Ackerman as he continued.

"As you are aware after Lucinda's tragic death I took some leave, during which time I busied myself searching for Boudicca's tomb. Four months ago I found it and we have been excavating it ever since." Sam listened but there was something in Ackerman's eyes and at the back of Sam's mind that made him question what he was being told. Still, he would soon find out if the professor was telling him the truth.

"So Jessica have you been to the tomb before?"

"I have. When we arrive at the station I will lead you there."

"This is all so bizarre," retorted Sam a little hurt. "Why didn't you tell me any of this when I was at the university? We were close; I would have thought that you would have confided in me. We could have discovered the tomb together."

"It was not the right time for you Sam. You were a little too headstrong back then. The knowledge would have put you in danger."

"Did Lucinda know?" asked Sam. Ackerman was silent.

"I asked you if Lucinda knew." Then he remembered. He had seen the professor show Lucinda the trident many months before her death. He had confided in his daughter but had been unwilling to involve Sam.

He was about to confront the professor when the pilot shouted, "We've arrived at Kings Cross Station, but look below, this place is crawling with Roman Soldiers and more of those black, armoured vehicles. Where the hell do you expect me to land this thing?"

Chapter 51

4.10pm. John pushed slightly at the second floor window and he immediately heard a click. He was then able to pull the window towards him until it was fully open. He waited a few seconds to see if an alarm would be triggered, but there was nothing.

The Dean felt bad taking clothes from a dead man but the security officer wasn't going to need them anymore. He left the shirt as it was covered in the man's blood that flowed from a single bullet wound in his chest, but he took the trousers and shoes, which thankfully seemed to be a perfect fit. He also took a pistol from the man's holster. He then searched the security hut for more weapons but found nothing except for more ammunition for the pistol, which he stuffed into his pockets.

He then clambered up the fire escape and followed John through the open window.

"I think Liberius's mercenaries are here, but no Romans," said the Dean, "otherwise the security officer would have been badly mutilated. I took the guard's gun but I have no idea how to use it."

"Give it to me," said John, "I've fired a few of these in my time!"

"I thought you told me that you'd worked on the river all your life," said the Dean questioningly as he handed over the gun and ammunition.

"I have, but that's just my day job."

"And the rest of the time?"

"I work for Military Intelligence, Naval Division. And I have trained with the SBS."

The Dean was impressed. "So have you always been patrolling the Thames?"

"Yep, for over ten years now. Everyone at the Port Authority knows me only as a Harbour Master. Actually since I am putting my cards on the table, you should be aware that I know Sir Gareth too. I have done some undercover work for him from time to time when undesirables have made the mistake of trafficking on my river. That's probably why he asked you to pass on his personal thanks for pulling you earlier."

"Small world."

"Indeed."

The two moved quietly through the building, making their way down the staircases into the basement. John had taken the lead and scoured every room and every landing carefully like a professional soldier.

They saw no sign of the mercenaries, but this didn't surprise the Dean. He was certain that, if they knew why he was there, they would wait until the manuscript was retrieved before they struck. He was certain that if Liberius was aware of the manuscript he would want to destroy it, along with the Dean.

When they reached the basement, the Dean directed John to the archive room where the vault was located.

"They're probably down there waiting for us," whispered John.

"I am sure you are right, but they'll wait until we are in the vault before they strike."

"Unless I get them first. Wait here!" With that John charged into the room, rolling across the floor.

Chapter 52

4.10pm. Ackerman looked down from the helicopter. Kings Cross Station was surrounded by at least 100 Roman soldiers and four black Mastiff vehicles were parked in the area, two at the station's main entrance and one on each of the side streets.

"I think it would be best if you drop Sam and Jessica at Euston Underground station," Ackerman instructed the pilot. He turned to Sam.

"You'll have to make your way from there by foot, along the tube tunnels. I can't guarantee that you'll be alone down there but it'll be safer than landing at Kings Cross."

The helicopter turned west and travelled the short distance to Euston; thankfully there was no sign of Liberius's forces there.

The helicopter touched down in the station forecourt and Jessica briefly hugged Ackerman before she and Sam jumped out.

"What weapons do you have?" Ackerman asked the pilot.

"Only my revolver and a few clips of ammunition."

"Would you mind giving it to Sam? I don't fancy his chances without it."

"Of course." The pilot gave Sam the gun, which he tucked into his trousers at the small of his back.

As the helicopter took off, Ackerman called after Jessica. "Remember each of the Guardian's traps, one mistake could cost you your life!"

"I'll be careful," she said.

"What traps?" Sam asked as they quickly covered the short distance to the stairway and began their descent into the Underground station.

"The Guardian's tunnels and the tomb itself have been rigged with various booby traps to keep out unwanted guests. Some are very crude and date back to the Iron Age, others have been added more recently and include laser technology, trip wires and IEDs."

"You're kidding me! So not only do we have to worry about mercenaries and flesh-eating Romans but we also have to face our own Temple of Doom! If only Indiana Jones was with us right now."

"Who needs Indie when I have James Bond!" Jessica quipped.

"What has the professor been telling you?"

"Not much, only that you drive a James Bond car, can quote every line he ever spoke and I think he caught you posing in front of a mirror one morning!"

"Damn, I didn't think he noticed," said Sam rather embarrassed.

They jumped over the turnstiles and followed the signs to the Victoria and Northern lines, both of which led through to Kings Cross Station. They ran down a long escalator, through the pedestrian walkways and onto the platform. Sam was the first to jump onto the tracks and then he helped Jessica down from the platform. They walked along the track to the start of the tunnel careful not to step on the live rail. They had walked just 100 yards into the tunnel when they heard a slight rumble that quickly changed to a roar, then, up ahead, the tunnel began to brighten. Seconds later they saw the headlights of an oncoming train.

"What the hell!" shouted Sam. He had not expected any trains to be running after the morning's events. He grabbed

Jessica's arm and started pulling her back towards the station.

They ran as fast as they could but, just before they reached the platforms, Jessica stumbled and fell.

"Go without me," she shouted, as Sam bent to help her to her feet.

"No way!" he exclaimed. He reached for her and stared into the face of the oncoming train. Sam knew, at that very instant, that there was no time for either of them to get onto the platform and no time for the train to stop.

Chapter 53

4.20pm. The helicopter landed in the forecourt of the British Library. The first thing Ackerman noticed was a dead security guard wearing no trousers or shoes. He was puzzled and concerned.

The Dean would never shoot anyone and John would never kill a civilian - yes, Ackerman knew John too. Although he had never met John, Sir Gareth had bought the harbour master's unique skills to his attention some years ago and told him of some of the excellent work he had done for his country.

Ackerman concluded that hostiles must also be on the site, probably Liberius's mercenaries, but definitely not the Roman soldiers as there were no bite marks on the corpse.

He hoped he was not too late to save his friends or to prevent the summoning of angels, but he had to admit that he would rather his friends were dead, than the millions who might die at the hands of the angels if they had been unleashed.

He then looked up and saw the open window on the second floor. Well at least the Dean had safely entered the building, but now it was a race against time. He had to let the Dean know that he was alive and that there was still a chance they could use the trident and avoid the last resort.

Ackerman ran to the fire escape and entered the building.

4.20pm. John came out of his forward roll and took up a firing stance from the corner of the room. He moved his gun from left to right and checked under tables and in cupboards but the room was empty. He opened the door and beckoned to the Dean who tentatively joined him in the room.

Beside the vault door was a keypad and thumb scanner, beside which were three coloured lights: green, amber and red. Currently the red light was on. The Dean stepped forward and quickly typed in a 6-digit code. The light turned amber. He then placed his thumb on the scanner and it turned green. The door slowly began to open.

John was impressed, "How did you know the code?"

"As the Dean of St Paul's and a keen classical linguist, I am often asked to translate and interpret religious manuscripts. Sir Gareth arranged for me to be given my own access codes many years ago."

"Does the system track when the vault is opened?"

"It does," said the Dean.

"Then we have to assume that Sir Gareth has just been notified that you have entered the vault!"

"Crap!" said the Dean.

4.25pm. Right on cue Sir Gareth's phone began to ring. He answered it quickly. He had just returned from a chase through the tunnels and he was breathless.

"The vault at the British Library has just been opened," a voice said. "The code used belongs to the Dean of St Paul's."

Sir Gareth's supposition was correct - the Dean had gone to summon the angels and by now there was probably no time to stop him. He hastily dialed a number.

"Radford, I need you to send a team to the British Library"

"Again?"

"What do you mean?"

"I have just been informed that one of our teams has just escorted the Dean of St Paul's there."

"Well, send them back again, but this time get them to arrest him and, if he resists, tell them to kill him!"

Sir Gareth sat down and glared back at the other committee members who were all staring at him.

"We've had to seal off the tunnels," he told them. "They have been infiltrated by the Romans. There's now no way out of here!"

Chapter 54

4.25pm. Sam scoured the area around the tracks looking for a way out. The train would impact with them at any second.

Then he remembered an article he had read about the increase in suicides on the London Underground. They had combated the problem by digging pits beside the tracks. They were known as "suicide pits" or "dead man's trenches." Their purpose was to allow anyone who fell, jumped or were pushed onto the tracks to jump in and avoid being splattered by an oncoming train.

He quickly looked around and, although he couldn't see clearly due the glare of the headlights, he saw what looked like a pit about five yards to their left.

Without hesitation, he dived towards it, dragging Jessica behind him. The two of them fell into the trench just as the train passed over them. They clung tightly to one another expecting at some point to be struck by a cable or other protrusion from the bottom of the train. Thankfully, however, it passed without incident.

"Thanks," said Jessica, "you saved my life."

"We aim to please."

"Isn't that a quote from *Goldeneye*?"

"You're a Bond fan too?"

"I was, but now I think I'm a bit of a Sam fan."

"Only a bit?" responded Sam.

He was about to try for a kiss when he heard another sound coming from the tunnel. This time he was pretty sure it was footsteps.

4.25pm. Ackerman made his way quietly down into the basement and heard male voices coming from the archive room. He took a quick look into the room and he saw John and the Dean looking at manuscripts in the vault, but there was also a man dressed in black who stood just to the right of the vault door. He was observing them using a fibre optic cable which extended from his position round into the vault doorway. John and the Dean were oblivious to the man's presence.

Ackerman took another quick look and saw that the man was armed he had a SIG Mosquito with sound suppressor. Ackerman considered his best move; his only weapon was his sword and he would need to get within about three metres of the target undetected in order to strike him before he got shot. It was certainly possible, especially for a man with his skills, but the odds were too slim for his liking. He could shout out a warning, but that may just encourage the hostile to shoot his friends. He decided his best option was to create a diversion and get the mercenary out in the hallway.

Ackerman went into the adjacent office where there were several computers. He found one with speakers and turned them to the highest volume. He then searched on the internet for sound effects and when he found what he was looking for, he clicked the 'loop' button and then 'play'.

The speakers burst into life with such ferocity that it even made Ackerman jump. The sound of a pack of snarling, growling dogs shocked everyone.

John drew his pistol at lightning speed and saw the mercenary run for the hallway. Just as the man made it to the doorway John shot him in the back.

Ackerman saw the man fall into the corridor, less than a body length away. He shouted out to John, but his voice was drowned by the dogs. John ran into the hallway, saw a figure with a sword in the corner of his eye, spun round and fired at point-blank range.

Chapter 55

4.30pm. Sam and Jessica waited, listening intently, but the sounds of footsteps seemed to have stopped. There was a good chance, however, that whoever it was, was waiting for them in the tunnel, but they had no choice, they had to move on.

They emerged slowly from the 'suicide-pit' and headed back along the tracks. After about 200 yards they found a service walkway to the right about a metre above the height of the tracks.

They joined it via a metal staircase and proceeded along the walkway at a slight jog. They made good progress for almost a kilometre when the dim lights on the tunnel ceilings suddenly went out, leaving them in complete darkness. Sam stopped and Jessica ran into the back of him. She ran her hands down his arms and took his hands.

"This isn't good," said Sam, who was not a fan of the dark. "Take out your mobile phone and turn on the torch."

She did as Sam suggested and Sam did the same with his. The lights from the phones helped a little but in that great space they could barely see more that a few metres ahead of them.

They continued their journey at walking pace. After a while Jessica told Sam that she recognised that part of the tunnel. They were only yards from the entranceway to Boudicca's tomb.

It was then that they heard the sounds, faint at first but it was unmistakingly footfall, and it was increasing in volume. The walkway began to shake - someone or something was coming, and it was directly in front of them, moving in their direction.

At first they were unsure whether to turn off their phones, leaving them to face whatever was coming in complete darkness, or keep the phone lights on and make it easy for them to be detected.

They decided on a compromise. They left Sam's phone on the walkway, shining forward, and they took Jessica's phone with them as they quietly climbed over the railings onto the tracks. They then turned her phone off and hid in the darkness on the far side of the tunnel, waiting to see what or who would appear.

Seconds later a short, slight man, walked into view. He was dressed in workman's overalls with steel toecap boots and a reflective jacket that seemed several sizes too big. On his head was a yellow safety helmet with a bright LED torch attached to the front.

He was sauntering along the walkway eating a sandwich with his right hand and carrying a toolbox in his left. Evidently he had just finished his shift undertaking maintenance work in the tunnels and was unaware of what was going on above ground.

He stopped when he saw the phone lying on the walkway in front of him. He looked around and seeing no-one, he threw the remains of his sandwich onto the track and then reached down and picked up the phone.

As he stared at the screen it lit up his face. He seemed to be in his mid-twenties with short, curly dark hair, large curious eyes and an impish nose.

Sam thought he looked remarkably like Frodo in the *Lord of the Rings* films. He was about to say *"my precious"* in his best Gollum voice when Jessica's hand suddenly covered his mouth. Sam made an almost imperceptable muffled sound but the workman looked over in their direction, picking them up in the light from his helmet.

"Oose there?" he shouted nervously in a strong East London accent. "You ain't meant to be down 'ere ya know. It's a very dangerous place!"

Jessica was the first to speak. She thought her voice would be far less threatening than Sam's. "Sorry to startle you. We came down here to escape the mayhem above. We thought we'd be safer in the tunnels than in the streets."

"What may'em?" he asked, seemingly relieved that the intruder was a woman. "Not anuvver one of them riots?"

"It's worse than a riot I'm afraid. What's your name?"

"Me name's George, I work down 'ere. Been tryin' to fix these stupid lights all day. Just got 'em sortid and they went out again! Whole bloody place needs a complete over'al in me 'umble opinion. Is this ya phone?"

"It's his," said Jessica gesturing to Sam.

"Is 'e ya boyfriend?."

"No he's not!" she said, a little too firmly for Sam's liking.

"Come 'n' get it then," he said offering them the phone. He watched admiringly as Jessica climbed back onto the walkway, her long legs making easy work of the railings. Sam climbed up too and took his phone. "So where you 'eadin' then?" George asked.

"We're just on our way to Kings Cross Station," said Jessica.

"Why there?" he asked

"Why so many questons?" Sam demanded. He was beginning to suspect that George was not the maintenance engineer that he claimed to be.

"Just makin' conversation," George said looking a little offended. "But look 'ere, if you don't wannabe social, that's fine by me. I'll leave ya to it. But if yer gonna be walking through these tunnels you'll need a proper torch, a phone is bloody useless with the lights all out. I've got one 'ere you can 'ave."

He opened his toolbox and reached inside, but instead of producing a torch he pulled out a .38 calibre snub-nosed revolver and pointed it at Sam's chest.

"I told ya these tunnels were a dangerous place!"

Chapter 56

4.30pm. The bullet from John's gun deflected off of Ackerman's sword and ricocheted upward, bouncing off the side of his skull. His legs buckled and he fell to the ground. The Dean ran out to join John and saw the Professor lying on the ground.

"John, what the hell have you done? You've killed Ackerman!" The Dean couldn't believe what had just transpired. John felt for a pulse and thankfully found one.

"He's not dead he's just unconcious. He's an extremely lucky man at point-blank range that bullet should have killed him!"

"What are you doing shooting Ackerman anyway?" the Dean wanted to know.

"Just sort of happened. I saw someone standing there with a sword and my first reaction was to shoot."

"Well now, at least, we know what we have to do. If Ackerman is here and doesn't have the trident, he'd obviously decided to summon the angels himself so we'd better get to it, for better or for worse."

"OK, I'll wait here in case we have any more visitors. You go and do what you have to do."

The Dean returned to the vault to find the manuscript. Within a few minutes he'd got what he was looking for.

4.35pm. Sergeant Briggs was extremely apprehensive as they returned to the British Library. He felt very uneasy about killing John and the Dean. He actually really liked them, and felt that they were sincere when they said they had a solution to the crisis. What's more the Dean was a man of the cloth. But orders were orders and they had come from General Radford himself. He would do all he could to apprehend them, but if they resisted he would have no choice.

The Sergeant was now accompanied by four SAS men as well as Privates Wiggins and Bradbury.

As they exited the vehicle, a helicopter lifted off from the library courtyard and headed east. It looked like one used by the intelligence community but Briggs could not be certain as it was unmarked. But what was it doing here and who else was now in the building?

"I am not sure how they'll react when they see us," said Briggs as they started to gather at the entrance way. "They may just assume that we're here to check that they're safe. On the other hand, if they really are up to no good they may start shooting. I must say I still find it hard to believe they are now our enemies."

"I think it's best if they don't see us coming." said the SAS commander. "Let us go in first as we've practiced this a thousand times over. We'll take them down before they even know we are in the building."

"Over here sir!" It was one of the SAS team. "I've found a body."

They all went over and inspected the dead security officer.

"Well that confirms one thing," said Briggs, furious with himself for doubting his orders. "The guys we're after are definitely hostile. The man who called himself the Dean asked me for some dry clothes earlier, but all I had to give him was my commando jacket. Seems he killed this poor guy just for a pair of trousers and some shoes. I think you're right commander, enter by stealth and when you see them, shoot to kill!"

4.37pm. John had returned upstairs to shut the window and make sure there were no other mercenaries in the building. When he got there he saw Briggs and the SAS team in the courtyard below. He couldn't hear what they were saying, but when he saw them quietly cutting large circular holes in the windows each side of the main entranceway he knew they were in trouble.

He left the window and ran down the stairs. He had to find a way to cut the troops off before they reached the basement, or Ackerman and the Dean would be trapped.

Liberius had received word that the MI5 helicopter that took off from Oxford University had dropped off Callaghan and a female student at Euston Station and then delivered Ackerman at the British Library.

He called his mercenary there and was not surprised when he got no answer. The last report this incompetent had texted him, was that the Dean and the harbour master had entered the building. Judging by their resourcefulness that day, Liberius was sure that they had probably killed his mercenary. He chastised himself for making two major errors.

Firstly, he should have posted more men at the Library, but he had been certain that they would never make it there and, even if they did, he hadn't anticipated that they would consider calling on Destroying Angels without first bringing out the trident.

His second mistake was to assume they would access Boudicca's tomb via Kings Cross Station. Obviously his idiot commander there had left his army in full view, forcing them to go via Euston. If he had just hidden his men inside the station, Callaghan and the girl would be dead by now, probably Ackerman too. Later that day his commander would be executed for his stupidity.

Still, he had placed mercenaries throughout the tunnels, who he was sure would kill them anyway. Soon he would be in possession of the trident and his enemies would all be dead.

Liberius called his commander at Kings Cross Station and ordered him to take his forces immediately over to the British Library.

In a matter of minutes, hundreds of Roman soldiers were leaving Kings Cross Station and marching briskly down Euston Road, followed by two armoured personnel carriers, each containing eight mercenaries.

Liberius's orders were very clear: surround the library, storm into every concievable window and entranceway, kill everyone they find there and bring him the bodies or what was left of them.

Chapter 57

4.37pm. "I'd been waitin' patiently for you two to arrive," said George, the Frodo look-alike, still pointing his gun at Sam. "I'm afraid I'm gonna 'ave to kill you both. But first ya need to get me into Boudicca's tomb. I presume that's where you're heading?"

"No, we're actually on our way to Mount Doom," said Sam. Jessica elbowed him in the ribs but managed a faint smile.

"Mount what?" said George, clearly not a *Lord of the Rings* fan and completely unaware of his resemblance to Mr. Baggins.

Sam wondered if he could draw the revolver from the back of his belt before Frodo fired but he came to the conclusion that it was better to bide his time. There would probably be a better opportunity later when they entered the tomb, especially with all those booby traps about.

Jessica had the same thought. "Sam's being an idiot. You're right, we *are* on our way to Boudicca's tomb. But why would we take you there, if you're going to kill us anyway?"

"Simple really. If you don't cooperate I'll kill ya right now, using 12 hollow-point bullets. The first bullet will incapacitate you. The next eleven will be strategically placed to cause you maximum pain. In fact, I can guarantee you that by bullet four or five, you will be in such agony you'll be begging me to end it. Even after the final bullet it will take you about 15 minutes to die and, if by some miracle you are found alive, the damage'll be irreversible.

"It was a little trick I learned from the Taliban while I was working with 'em in Afghanistan.

"On the other 'and, if you get me into the tomb I'll just give ya a little tap at the back of the head. You won't suffer, in fact, you probably won't even know it's coming. So, my friends, do we 'ave a deal?"

"Well if you put it like that," said Sam. "How can we refuse!"

"Good, let's go. But first Mr. Callaghan, you will turn around so I can remove your gun. Oh yes, we've been watching you ever since your helicopter arrived."

Sam swore but did what he was told. Liberius was a little smarter than he had given him credit for. Maybe his brain was not as damaged as it had looked on the television broadcast that morning!

They continued walking into the tunnel. Jessica led, with Sam in the middle, and George taking up the rear. After about 200 yards Jessica stopped. "We're here."

She placed the palm of her hand on what seemed to be an innocuous metal plate on the tunnel wall. Suddenly there was a whirring sound and a narrow section of the wall began to rise towards the roof revealing a dark passageway with roughly cut walls of clay and stone.

Jessica knew that the first trap was just four metres into the tunnel. It was a simple tripwire, eleven inches above the passage floor, which when triggered, would release a bed of very long and very sharp nails that was hinged to the roof directly above. In a split second the bed would swing down towards the victim impaling them all over their body, from their knees up to the top of their heads.

"After you!" said Jessica to George, trying to usher him through the door.

"No, I don't think so. Sam, you go in first." With that he roughly pushed Sam into the passageway where he stumbled forward into the darkness.

"Sam!" shouted Jesssica in despair.

Chapter 58

4.40pm. John figured that the SAS would probably split up when they entered the Library. It was a huge building with multiple galleries, exhibitions, conference centres and reading rooms, all spread over five levels. As there were only four soldiers, it could take them some time to complete the search.

He knew they would all have communication links and the commander would be checking their movements by GPS as well as taking camera feeds from each of their helmets. If any of them came across their targets, the others would arrive in support in under a minute.

John's plan was to engage one of the soldiers and lead them all as far away from the basement as possible to give the Dean the time he needed. Once the angels were released the chances were that this elite team of government killers would end up on the angelic hit list anyway.

John crouched in the shadows by the main staircase as the SAS stormed the building. Two took the stairs to the upper levels, one took the ground floor but the fourth, which seemed to be the commander, headed straight for the basement. John estimated that the commander could find Ackerman and the Dean in less than 30 seconds, so he had to act fast.

He followed the soldier who was searching the ground floor, being careful not to make a sound, block light from a window, cast a shadow or do anything that would catch the eyes or ears of this highly trained operative.

He didn't want to kill the SAS man, even though that would be quick and simple, as strictly, they were on the same team. John just wanted to keep him occupied and use him to bring the rest of his unit on a wild-goose chase.

As the soldier entered the main reading room John followed and hid behind a row of filing cabinets and screwed the silencer onto his pistol. He then popped up for a fraction of a second, during which time, he took aim and fired a single shot into a glass wall, that partitioned off an office, at the far end of the room. The glass shattered and fell to the ground.

The soldier span round but saw no one. John was grateful that the silencer was so effective it had not given away his position. The soldier then took cover and got straight onto the radio. "I've encountered hostiles on the ground floor reading room, just to the right of the reception desk. I need immediate backup, but I am not sure of their exact location, so be careful!"

John heard the sound of Gore-Tex boots on the staircases. They were on their way. He'd bought the Dean more time but now he had four of them to contend with.

He dived under the tables as they entered the room and managed to stay hidden as they spread out and combed the area. As soon as they passed his position he fired another shot into the adjacent glass panel and as the soldiers turned toward the falling glass, he ran out the door, slamming it behind him. He then sprinted past the reception up a flight of stairs and on to the escalator, taking three steps at a time.

They heard the door slam, as he intended, and chased after him. John ducked as a hail of bullets hit the metal sheeting on the side of the conveyor. He just managed to hit the first floor and get out of the line of fire as they reached the bottom of the stairs and started firing upward. He tore round to the next escalator and continued up to the second floor. He then rushed into the room with the open window and climbed out onto the fire escape, closing the window carefully behind him.

He knew the soldiers were now spreading out covering each staircase, escalator and lift to prevent his escape. Hopefully they would be unaware of the external fire escape.

He used the handrail to slide down without making a sound. As soon as his feet hit the ground, he ran towards the main entrance intending to get to the basement and help his friends. However, as he passed the armoured vehicle in the courtyard Sergeant Briggs emerged from behind it with his two privates, all pointing their guns in his direction.

The game was up.

He raised his hands and was about to drop his gun when he saw, to his horror, an army of Roman soldiers clambering over the walls, railing and gates all around them. Briggs saw them too and alerted the privates, who ignored John and ran into the building for cover. It was then that the whole complex began to shake violently and they heard the sound of rushing winds coming from the basement. John knew what was happening.

"They're coming," he told Sergeant Briggs, "I hope you and your men are ready. It's judgment day!"

Chapter 59

4.50pm. As Sam stumbled forward the ground began to shake. Momentarily, the thin trip wire glistened in the light from the torch on Frodo's head. Sam recognized what it was, and immediately dug his leading foot into the ground, just centimetres from the wire. He then pushed upward, using his forward momentum to propel him into a forward roll. He just cleared the wire and landed safely on the other side.

"It's OK Jessica, I made it!" shouted Sam.

The ground tremors suddenly increased in intensity just as Frodo pushed Jessica through the door. As he reached for the wall to steady himself, Jessica grabbed his gun arm and swung him round in front of her, then kicked him forward into the wire. There was a rush of air as the board of nails swung down from the ceiling and impacted directly with Frodo's body lifting him high into the air. As the board swung back, his body was firmly attached, impaled by a hundred nails. He let out a weak moan and died.

The narrow corridor continued to shake and pieces of rock were falling from the ceiling. "Let me take the lead," said Jessica removing Frodo's safety helmet and moving carefully past Sam. "We'll have to avoid a few more traps before we reach the tomb - that is, if this passageway doesn't collapse on us first."

Ackerman was awakened as the floor began to shake wildly beneath him. A strong wind rushed through the corridor and ceiling tiles began falling all around him. A water machine fell over and rushed towards him, forcing him to quickly roll over to avoid its path. He then clawed his way to the archive door and peered inside. The Dean was on his knees reading the prayer from the ancient manuscript in pure Aramaic. Winds rushed around him throwing furniture and fittings, computers and peripherals against the walls in a wild maelstrom of destruction. An office chair flew out of the door, narrowly missing Ackerman's head.

The professor shouted as loud as he was able "Dean you have to stop this now. Jessica will retrieve the trident very soon. We don't need to summon the angels! If you proceed, you may kill millions of people unnecessarily. Is that what you want to be remembered for?"

The Dean paused momentarily and looked into Ackerman's eyes. "Don't you see Alexander, I have to do this. This city has become one of wickedest places on earth. What is happening today is just one manifestation of the sickness that lies dormant here. The trident may rid us of this evil today, but tomorrow another will rise. We have to tear out the infection once and for all."

Before Ackerman could answer him the Dean continued with the prayer loud enough to drown out Ackerman's protestations. The winds started to increase in strength and the building began to disintegrate around them.

The SAS team fled from the building just as John was entering. They ignored him and ran for the protection of the armoured vehicle, but before they could reach it they were overcome by ravenous Roman soldiers and killed in seconds.

Then, there was a burst of light that temporarily blinded them and anyone looking in the direction of the building. John stumbled into the room just as the angels began to manifest themselves.

"What have you done!" screamed Ackerman.

The angels appeared simultaneously. Both were about nine feet in height, extremely broad-shouldered and majestic in appearance. They wore long, white robes, which came down to their ankles and they were almost identical in appearance, with white shoulder-length hair, strong, square jaws, piercing blue eyes and a startling brightness that made it difficult to look at them for any length of time.

In their right hands were magnificent swords, about five feet in length, which were exquisitely fashioned from white gold and ablaze with white flames that flickered and danced from hilt to point.

They looked around the room and eventually their eye settled on the Dean.

"Why have you summoned us?" one asked, his voice deep and loud and reverberating throughout the building.

"We need you to destroy the evil that has risen in our streets," said the Dean surprisingly forcibly.

"If that is your will Dean, we will start with him!" shouted the angel pointing towards John.

"No!" shouted Ackerman as both angels extended their swords. The flames grew in intensity and then flew from the swords with a deafening roar reducing their victim to a pile of dust.

Chapter 60

5.00pm. The shaking stopped abruptly and the passageway went silent except for the slight creak of George's swinging deathbed. Sam searched his pockets and retrieved his pistol. He also took George's gun, which he handed to Jessica.

"So what's next?" asked Sam as they journeyed deeper into the passageway.

"Poison darts released by pressure plates in the floor. If you stand in the wrong place, they'll fly out of the walls on both sides of you. Just one small scratch and you'll die in a matter of seconds. In extreme pain I might add!

"Thankfully all of the electronic deterrents were deactivated by my palm scan at the entranceway, but these mechanical booby traps are all still active and we have to avoid them. Okay, we are approaching the danger area now."

Jessica slowed down and looked carefully at the markings on the floor. "You have two choices here. The first is the 'leap of faith'. If you are good at the long jump you can try to leap over this area completely. You have to clear six feet and then come to an abrupt stop because, if you travel just two metres further on, you will fall into a pit of snakes, all carefully chosen because of the toxicity of their venom."

"And the second option?" asked Sam, clearly not impressed by the first.

"It's called the 'walk of death'. You carefully step over those octagonal tiles avoiding any with the trident emblem carved into them. The problem as you can see is that the tiles are only four inches at the widest point leaving no room for error. One stumble and you're dead. So what is it to be?"

"I'll wait for you here!" Sam answered with a smile, but he secretly hoped she'd go for it.

"You're kidding me right?" She looked annoyed. It was time to back down.

"Of course I'm kidding," he said as convincingly as possible. "I'm going for the leap."

"In that case I'm going first. I'll do the 'walk of death' and then I'll wait for you on the other side to try and stop you if you overshoot. Does that sound like a plan?"

"Sounds good to me," said Sam relieved that Jessica would be there to stop him falling into the snake pit.

Jessica took a deep breath and took the first tentative step. "I've done this before so I can do it again," she told herself. She took another step and then another, and as she gained in confidence, she slightly increased the pace. Then she stopped dead. The ground was beginning to shake violently again.

"Sam!" she screamed as she started to lose her balance, "I'm not going to make it!"

Isabella was not going to her Mum's house. In fact, she didn't have a mother as her's died long ago. She was in London for a completely different reason and she had time to kill, quite literally. She had walked down towards Angel Islington and spotted a pub called *The York*.

The door was wide open and it was heaving with drunks who had decided that an alcoholic stupor was better than facing the realities of today's horrific events. She walked through the door and pushed through the crowds to the bar.

There was no one there to serve her so she helped herself to a bottle of whisky and a glass.

She then walked over to a table where there were two old men in their seventies, clearly the worst for wear. She pulled the stool from under the frailest of them, who fell immediately to the floor. She looked around to make sure that no one was watching, except for his companion, and then she stamped on his head with her stiletto heel. She smiled with pleasure as she heard the satisfying cracking of his skull.

She then took his seat and offered her hand to his terrified friend.

"Hi," she said, "my name's Jessica."

Chapter 61

5.00pm. Thankfully, the aim of both angels was perfect. The flames had flown over John's shoulder and disintegrated the Roman soldier who was about to take a chunk out of the harbour master's neck.

The Destroying Angels walked past him into the corridor where a host of the monsters were gathering. Then the battle began. Roman after Roman advanced, but they were instantly incinerated by the angels' flaming swords. John, the Dean and Ackerman stayed closely behind them as they worked their way to the staircase.

As they advanced, the Dean sensed something behind him. He turned to see one of the Romans emerge from a storage cupboard behind them. The frenzied creature leaped at the Dean desperate to bite into his neck and gorge on his blood. There was no way to escape. He closed his eyes waiting to feel its claws tearing into his flesh, but in that instant one of the angels turned and pointed his sword over the Dean's shoulder. The Roman exploded in mid air and fell as dust to the floor.

The group proceeded to the top of the staircase but the onslaught continued relentlessly. Romans clambered in windows at every level and either came down the stairs and escalators or just jumped down from the upper balconies.

White flames began to fly in every direction, filling the reception area with blinding flashes of light and the constant crash of thunder. The angels' fury grew and they rose from the ground growing in size and majesty. They roared like mighty lions as they destroyed everything that moved, but the Romans still kept coming oblivious to the futility of their attack.

The Dean, John and Ackerman stood back to back directly below flinching as wave after wave of Romans approached. They expected one of the creatures would break through at any moment. But the Angels were guarding them, and no matter how close the Romans got, they would explode before making contact with teeth or claw.

Eventually the numbers began to dwindle until there was only one. As it rushed toward the three men, the angels blocked its path and one of them grabbed the Roman's skull in his huge hand. The fury immediately left it, and it stood still and docile.

"We have cleansed the evil from this beast," said the angel, "and restored his soul. He is the strongest of them all and he was a just man in his lifetime. He will be invaluable to you as you strive to complete this quest. Farewell my friends, our work is done here."

"What do you mean your work is done? We still have to defeat Liberius and the hundreds of thousands of creatures he commands!" said Ackerman.

"You do not need us - you were given the tools to defend this island many years ago. Use them!"

"But I summoned you to help us!" said the Dean.

"And we came, but only to protect you and your friends from imminent danger, so that you can complete this task. We answer to only one, and it is not you, Dean." The Dean felt suitably reprimanded.

"By the way, there are a dozen or so mercenaries outside with rifles aimed at all the exits, but don't worry we will do you one last favour and destroy them on our way home."

John, Ackerman and the Dean covered their eyes as the blinding light returned and the building once more began to shake.

When everything had settled they emerged into the courtyard. The angles had been true to their word, it was littered with the corpses of mercenaries, whose skins had turned to black parchment and their terribly burnt faces were frozen in horror.

They then heard a noise behind them and spun round to see Sergeant Briggs and his privates leave the building with a look of immense relief across their faces.

"I guess you are the good guys after all!" said Briggs.

"And I suppose you must be too," said the Dean marveling that they were still in one piece.

"Any chance of a lift?" asked Ackerman.

"Sure, where to?" asked Briggs.

"First stop, Kings Cross Station," said Ackerman.

"And we're bringing this guy with us," said John reaching out to take the Roman's arm. "I'll take care of him. I think I'll call him Rover."

The Roman pulled his hand away and gave John a very disapproving look. "How about Caesar?" John said. The Roman nodded his approval and climbed into the vehicle.

Little did John know, Caesar had been the Roman's actual name. His mother had named him, two millennia ago, after the great Roman general, statesman and consul.

As they drove away Briggs cranked up the music. It wasn't long before Caesar was nodding his head to the beat of '*Jumping Jack Flash*'.

Chapter 62

5.20pm. As the ground shook, Jessica was trying hard to balance on one leg. It was clear to her and Sam that she would not last much longer. As soon as she put down her other foot, unless it was placed precisely, the darts would be released and she would be dead.

Sam took a few steps backward and then ran at speed towards Jessica. Years of playing rugby at private school had prepared him to make the perfect tackle. He launched into the air and hit Jessica hard lifting her into the air as he wrapped his arms around her thighs. The two of them travelled for a couple of metres, hitting the ground just on the far edge of the pressure pads. Jessica's trailing foot, however, hit the final pad and poisonous darts flew out from both sides of the wall. Luckily, they were out of the danger area and the darts hit the opposite walls and fell harmlessly to the floor.

Sam pushed Jessica to the ground but his momentum carried him forward. His body rolled across the stone floor and he fell over the edge, into the snake pit.

Jessica pulled herself up onto her feet. The corridor was in darkness. She called out for Sam but got no reply. She was too frightened to fumble around for the safety helmet in case she touched the tip of one of the poisoned darts, so instead she retrieved her mobile from her trouser pocket and turned on the torch. She pointed it up and down the corridor but Sam was nowhere to be seen.

She then heard a disembodied cry and immediately realized where it was coming from. Then she saw four fingers clutching desperately to the edge of the pit. She ran over and fell on her knees, then, she leant over the pit and grabbed Sam's wrist. He looked up at her in desperation - less than two or three metres below him was a mass of coiling snakes taking it in turns to try striking at his feet.

"Get me out of here!" Sam pleaded. Jessica pulled as hard as she could and Sam managed to take hold of the edge with his other hand. He was just pulling himself out of the pit when he felt a snake's fangs bite deep into his ankle, and it's deadly venom flow into his flesh.

As Jessica helped him to clear the pit she saw a snake release its grip and fall back into the writhing mass. The expression on Sam's face told her all she needed to know. He was dying.

5.20pm. Isabella was standing in the queue to use a NatWest cash machine. She didn't have a valid card but that didn't matter, the person in front of her did. She waited patiently, often letting people in front of her until there was no one behind and only one in front, then she stepped up directly behind them. The victim was a woman in her sixties who was clearly unnerved by Isabella's close proximity.

As soon as she withdrew the cash Isabella reached forward with both hands and, with more efficiency than a hangman's noose, twisted her head and broke her neck. She lowered the woman gently to the ground, then picked up the money and smiled broadly at the ATM's security camera.

A boy in his twenties had stopped his bike on the opposite side of the road and was filming her on his mobile phone. It was obvious by his expression that he had seen everything. As she walked towards him he stopped videoing and cycled away as fast as he could. Isabella smiled, certain that the video would be all over YouTube within the hour along with all the Roman zombie videos that were already getting incredible hit rates. '*Roman zombie rips off man's head*': 1,765,455 views. '*Roman zombies eat woman in her wheelchair*': 4,786,765 views. '*Roman Zombies tear apart screaming fat teacher*': 9,675,899.

"What a sick, sick world we live in," Isabella mused; oblivious to the fact that she was the sickest of them all.

Many who were on the verge of mental illness had been tipped over the edge by the terrifying events of this day, but Isabella did not have that excuse. She was born a little crazy and over the years her behaviour had become increasingly obsessive, compulsive and homicidal.

She started walking towards Kings Cross. It was almost time to meet up with the woman she was trying her hardest to destroy.

Chapter 63

5.30pm. Alexander Ackerman was telling John about Boudicca's trident and its amazing powers when the radio in the armoured vehicle burst into life. Briggs turned down the music just in case it was his colonel.

When they heard the voice everyone immediately recognized that it was Sir Gareth. *This is going to be awkward,* thought Sergeant Briggs, *but these men deserve to know why he and his men had returned to the British Library."*

"Well Briggs, did you kill them?" Sir Gareth asked testily.

"Not exactly," said Briggs

"What do mean 'not exactly'? Our satellite feed shows you have pretty much destroyed the British Library, a building that we recently spent £12,000,000 constructing. I would have thought that in the process you could have killed Ackerman and his renegades."

John, the Dean and Ackerman remained silent and slowly shook their heads in disgust. All of them had known Sir Gareth many years and never suspected that he would one day order their execution. They signalled to Briggs to keep him talking.

"Well, it wasn't us that did the damage to the library. It was the angels."

There was a moment of silence while Sir Gareth thought over the implications of this revelation.

"What angels?" he asked, feebly trying to pretend that he didn't know what Briggs was talking about.

"It seems that the Dean and his friends had gone to The British Library to summon the Angels of Death, hoping that they would destroy Liberius and his armies. The angels actually came and immediately wiped out a few hundred Roman soldiers. It was absolutely incredible. I was never a man of faith, but I am now. In my opinion you and the general made a huge mistake when you sent us to kill them. They are good men who have had more success in this battle than you, and that committee of yours."

"That is insubordination!" shouted Sir Gareth.

"It's the truth," retorted the sergeant.

"Where are they now?" he asked deciding to ignore the sergeant's attitude, he would have the man dishonourably discharged when this was all over.

"Where are who?"

"The angels, of course." He needed to know if they were coming for him, although there was probably nothing he could do if they were. He was pretty sure that no one could hide from them.

"I think they said they were on their way to Westminster!" said Briggs with a huge smile on his face. John gave him a thumbs up.

"Why would they want to come here?" said Sir Gareth rather flustered.

"Well you know what they say about politicians!" said Briggs.

"But I'm not a politician."

"Then I'm sure you have nothing to worry about!"

John and the Dean started to laugh loudly and Sir Gareth realized he was being played.

"Are they with you now?" asked Sir Gareth.

"Who? The angels?" asked Briggs trying to annoy Sir Gareth further.

"You know who I'm bloody talking about, I can hear them laughing in the background," said Sir Gareth getting extremely agitated.

"Then why ask me. Why don't you speak to them directly and explain why you wanted them killed." He offered the radio to his passengers and Ackerman took it.

"Hello Gareth, Alexander here."

"Alexander? What the hell are you doing there?"

"I came to tell the Dean that he didn't need to summon the angels as Callaghan's on his way to get the trident. But I needn't have come at all. The angels were not the merciless destroyers of the wicked that we envisioned them to be. It seems that you, Gareth, have more homicidal tendencies than they do!"

"Now listen here, Alexander, I did what I had to do. I couldn't risk the angels killing millions of our people, and you know how bloody-minded the Dean is - when he believes he's right, no one can change his mind."

"Well that's because I normally am right!" shouted the Dean.

"Well what good has come of your little escapade?"

"A few hundred Romans have been destroyed, I received a valuable lesson in humility, our faith has been strengthened and we now have a new secret weapon!" answered the Dean.

Sir Gareth's ears pricked up. "What secret weapon?" he asked.

"The angels exorcised one of the Romans and he's with us now. He's still immortal and unbelievably strong and he's now one of the good guys."

"Great bring him in and we can start experimenting on him immediately."

Caesar looked horrified.

"No chance," said John defensively. Caesar smiled and patted him on the back.

"What do you mean '*no chance*'?" said Sir Gareth, "It wasn't a request, it was an order."

"Order or not, we're not bringing him in. We need his help to make sure we get the trident, so he's staying with us!"

"Listen here John Brody, you work for military intelligence and you *will* obey my orders!"

"Cut him off Alexander" said the Dean resolutely.

"If you cut me off..." he barked, "I will hunt you down and---" Ackerman cut him off.

"Well I guess that makes us outlaws," said John.

"Doesn't matter," said the Dean. "By nine o'clock tonight we'll either be dead or bloody heroes!"

"Now what's happening about this trident, Alexander?" John asked.

"Sam and Jessica should be in Boudicca's tomb by now. We need to make sure they can get out again."

"Turn the music up!" said the Dean. Caesar nodded in agreement.

5.40pm. Sir Gareth was furious. He called General Radford who had been unable to return to the COBRA briefing room since he had been told that the tunnels were now sealed.

"That Sergeant Briggs whom you sent to apprehend the Dean, has turned rogue. I want you to track down his vehicle and destroy it now!"

"I think you must be mistaken Gareth, Briggs has served in the Queen's regiment for over twenty years, with an impeccable record. He could have risen much higher in the ranks but he has always chosen to lead his men into combat. He's highly decorated, brave and extremely loyal. There's no way he'd have turned rogue."

"Well I'm afraid he has. He refused to follow our orders and instead of capturing or killing the Dean and his accomplice, he's now aiding and abetting them! Look, I know you're not comfortable with this, but I one hundred percent assure you he's been turned." He then started to think how he could persuade the General to launch the attack. "Maybe Dan, he's a clone of the real Sergeant. I just tried to reason with him, but he completely refused to bring the Dean in. He even hung up on me! Talk to him yourself if you don't believe me. He's tainted, Dan. He's not the man you think he is. The more I think about his recent actions, the more I'm certain we are dealing with a clone. We have to destroy this vehicle Dan. It is a matter of national security."

"I don't need to call him. I trust you Gareth. We'll get onto it right away. We still have an armed drone in the area now so we'll pinpoint the location of his vehicle and destroy it. If you are certain."

"I'm certain, Dan!" Sir Gareth put down the phone with a huge smile on his face. Mission accomplished!

Chapter 64

5.40pm. Sam was already having trouble breathing. His chest felt tight and there was a growing numbness in his left leg.

"You must try to relax," said Jessica as she examined the wound. "The faster your heart beats the quicker the poison will spread throughout your body."

"Can't you just cut the wound open and suck the venom out? I am sure I saw it on a survival program once."

"No I can't Sam, it's not like an insect bite. The fangs sank deep into your skin and the venom is already in the blood stream".

"A tourniquet?"

"No, it will cut off your blood supply and concentrate the venom. You will quickly lose your leg."

"What then?"

"I have to administer anti-venom in the next few minutes or you'll be dead."

"Great! Is there going to be some good news anywhere?"

"Well the good news is that the Guardian left some anti-venom in the tomb in case of accidents, but the further bad news is that there are two strains, and we don't know what snake bit you. If I give you the wrong one, it will definitely be fatal."

"So I have odds of 50-50 then?"

"I wish I could say you did. But first I have to find the anti-venoms, then, administer the right one. Even if I get lucky and choose correctly, we have to hope you will not have an allergic reaction to it, which, I'm afraid to say, is pretty common!"

"So my odds of surviving this are…"

"Significantly better if you let me go and find the vials of anti-venom rather that staying here chatting. See you soon and remember, stay calm!"

Before he could reply, Jessica ran off towards the tomb leaving him in pain, in fear and in total darkness. He pulled out his phone and turned it on. There was no signal and only 10% battery life left.

He was about to play some music to keep his mind off the pain when he heard a sound coming from the entranceway. Someone was coming. If it was a mercenary he had a chance, if it was an invincible Roman soldier, his odds of survival had now dropped to zero.

Just when he thought things couldn't get any worse, he heard Jessica scream.

Chapter 65

5.40pm. London has several notorious prisons, most of which date back to the 19th century such as Holloway, Pentonville, Brixton and Wormwood Scrubs. One of the newest prisons is based in Woolwich in South East London. It's called Belmarsh, and it was opened in 1991 to house over 900 prisoners, mostly Category A, which means the inmates are really dangerous to the public or to national security. They have included serial killers, murderers, bank robbers, rapists, terrorists and a novelist politician!

The prison guards were too focused on their prisoners to notice the real danger until it began to smash through the doors and climb over the walls. Liberius had sent his legions to most of the prisons to increase disorder and to gain some new recruits.

It took less than fifteen minutes to eat the warden and the guards and to open up the cells. The prisoners were lined up and given the opportunity to step forward and join with Liberius or to go their own way. Those that chose Liberius were armed and added to their ranks. Those that didn't were quickly torn apart.

The same happened at the other high-security London prisons, except for Holloway. Liberius was sick of strong willed, loud mouthed, murderous women. As far as he was concerned they could be left there to rot.

As the surviving prisoners were driven in open-top vehicles back to Hyde Park, he made sure that everything was filmed, uploaded to every conceivable social media site and drawn to the attention of government leaders all over the world. He especially focused on the terrorists, the recognizable faces that would send a chill down the US President's spine.

The message was clear: Britain was falling apart and the lunatics had most certainly left the asylums. Something had to be done quickly before they left Britain's shores.

Chapter 66

5.40pm. The London Resistance was gathering at Blackheath in South East London. Thousands upon thousands of everyday Londoners who were determined not to allow an undead Roman army drive them from their homes and deprive them of their freedom.

They were armed with every weapon you could imagine. Many men had improvised with lengths of timber, power tools such as chain saws or nail guns and gardening implements such as forks, spades and hedge cutters. Women carried kitchen knives, pokers, barbeque forks and bottles of powerful bleach or acids used to unblock drains. And the teenagers - they brought the guns!

Ministers from across the capital gathered together with vials of holy water, taken from their baptism fonts, bibles and crucifixes. Word had clearly not reached them of the fate of their Pentecostal brothers.

There were many opportunists selling hot dogs, and cans of drink to the assembled masses and twelve ice cream vans were doing a roaring trade. A large number of missionaries were distributing religious pamphlets, and an even greater number of dealers were distributing Class A drugs.

There were even a few firearms dealers offloading pistols, rifles and grenades to those that looked like they had militant tendencies. Police were out in force but they were actually some of the best customers. After all, it seemed that the Romans had been targeting police officers in order to increase disorder. Those officers that still survived in London were now more interested in staying alive than keeping law and order.

Sections of the crowd were being whipped into a near frenzy by a number of very vocal activists who saw this as a great opportunity to get support for their extremist groups, unions and political parties.

The general idea was that they were going to take the fight to Liberius and his army rather than awaiting the 9pm deadline.

No one seemed to have any real idea how they were going to overthrow his immortal army but they figured that there were safety in numbers and maybe, just maybe, they would find a chink in the Romans' armour, where the army had failed.

The ministers assured them that God was on their side and all that was needed was a manifestation of faith. The activists assured them that it was all a stage show so the Government could gain the control of a desperate population and they had to show them that they were quite capable of standing up for themselves. The conspiracy theorists said that the Romans soldiers were simply the result of military bio-weapon experimentation and they would be withdrawn as soon as the testing was over and there were even some deluded souls who believed it was just a massive experiential marketing campaign for the latest Italian pizza!

Ninety percent of the crowd, however, realized that this was simply a fight for survival against something incomprehensively terrifying. At 7pm they were probably going to be marching to their deaths but it was better than waiting in fear for the monsters to arrive at their doorstep.

Little did they know that they probably wouldn't even make it to Hyde Park, as there were others on a different continent already planning a far more immediate threat.

Chapter 67

5.40pm. (12.40pm ET) The Americans had all of their satellites focused on Britain. For now, the Taliban terror camps were of secondary importance.

They were seeing more and more dead Romans rising from graves all across the British Isles and they were fully aware that the might of the British military had proven toothless against them. To make matters worse, hundreds of Category A criminals, including many ruthless terrorists, had been released from Britain's jails. In the last hour the FBI's most wanted terrorist list had doubled in size. This situation had to be contained and quickly.

President Miles Cluney called together his Cabinet to decide on the best course of action. They considered patrolling the entire British coastline and turning the country into a giant Alcatraz but it was deemed to be too impractical.

If things got completely out of control, there was clearly only one option, but it was unthinkable, unless, of course, they could get sufficient support from the other world leaders.

In the meantime US battleships were ordered to fire on any vessel that left Britain's shores and refused to turn back, and the air force were told, similarly, to intercept and, if necessary, shoot down any departing planes.

Their Armed Forces were sent within striking distance of every British military base around the world to control their troops should the 'unthinkable' happen and for similar reasons the CIA were instructed to shadow any British leaders, diplomats, civil servants and dignitaries who were currently abroad.

Their strategists looked carefully at UK assets around the world that could be seized by America before anyone else could make a legitimate claim to them. They had always been interested in the potential of the Falkland's oil fields, even if it meant a difficult negotiation with Argentina.

It was 'regretful', of course, that such extreme measures had to be considered, but it was undeniably a great opportunity for the United States to get its hands on some valuable footholds around the world and some much needed assets and financial resources.

Most, in fairness, suggested that, if a nuclear attack on Britain was the only option left, they should, at least, try to airlift out the senior politicians, businessmen, scientists, academics and royalty. However, it was deemed to be too dangerous, especially as the creatures were able to take on the appearance of those they digested. Who knows what they might be bringing back with them if a rescue was attempted!

No, there would be no rescue plan.

Britain was to be quarantined immediately and if NATO, the UN and their allies could be persuaded to tow the line, their rich history would come to a devastating end.

Liberius had several men planted, in very senior positions, within the White house, as he did in key governments all over the world. It took just a few minutes for the President's plan to be relayed to him and he was ecstatic. He was pretty certain that a nuclear bomb would probably kill him despite the witch's curse, but he didn't care. He had grown tired of life, and of the constant pain that racked his body and his soul.

Most importantly, he would have the deep satisfaction of knowing that the entire country, that he desperately despised, would die with him.

He looked to the heavens. "This is all for you Helena!" he screamed to his dead wife.

Chapter 68

5.45pm. As the battle-taxi approached King's Cross, Ackerman saw someone he recognized crossing Euston Road towards the Station.

'That's Jessica, what the hell is she doing out here on the street and where on earth is Sam? Pull up next to her Briggs."

As they approached her she started to walk away from the vehicle. Then she stopped and turned towards them. Ackerman did another take; he had been mistaken. It wasn't Jessica, but another of his students, Isabella.

"Isabella, what are you doing here?" he asked.

"I came to London to visit my mother," she said looking and sounding rather distraught.

"I know that, but your mother lives in Highbury, what are you doing down here at Kings Cross Station? It's a very dangerous place right now."

"I came to see if I could get a train out of London," she said. "I'm so frightened!"

"There will be no trains out of London today I'm afraid Isabella. And what about your mother, how is she?"

"She's dead Professor! After I spoke to Jessica I ran back to the flat and I was too late, I should never have left her!" She started to sob. "The flat was empty and there was blood everywhere!"

Ackerman climbed out of the vehicle and embraced her. "Now, now Isabella, you've suffered a terrible loss. Get in the vehicle with us and you'll be safe. I promise"

"Thank you Professor." She wiped her eyes with her hand and started to climb into the battle taxi. Then she saw Caesar and let out a scream. Caesar looked offended. She backed out and pushed away the professor, looking at him accusingly. She then ran off back in the direction of Islington.

"Shall we go after her?" Briggs asked the professor.

"No," he said sadly. "Let her go. We don't have time to chase her and frankly in the state she's in, she'll be a liability. Let's take a look inside the station."

They drove through the station doors, onto the main concourse. It seemed empty.

But it wasn't.

Chapter 69

5.45pm. Jessica was furious with herself. In her haste to get the anti-venom for Sam, she had forgotten about the 'dragon's breath' and it had nearly ended her life.

Just below the final entranceway to the tomb was a furnace with a stone cover. When the tomb door is pushed open, the cover is dislodged, and the flames from the furnace shoot up through a grill in the floor, incinerating any intruder.

Luckily for Jessica, or possible by fate, the mechanism that pushed aside the cover must have been damaged when the ground had shaken and it had only partially opened, scorching her trailing leg but doing no serious damage. The pain, however, was sufficient to make her scream. She hoped that she hadn't alarmed Sam in his already fragile state.

She ran around Boudicca's sarcophagus and opened a small door in its base revealing the two vials. She quickly grabbed them and put them into her trouser pocket. She then pushed aside the heavy sarcophagus lid and reverently retrieved the trident, helmet and shield from their resting place on top of the queen's now skeletal frame.

She then raced from the tomb back to her dying friend.

When she reached the snake pit she leaped across it without breaking stride and when she landed on the other side she searched for Sam, but he was gone. Then she heard a gunshot.

Sam could barely walk or breathe, but he was determined that whoever or whatever was lurking at the doorway, would not get to Jessica. He held his gun out in front of him, trying desperately to keep it from shaking as he slowly advanced, dragging his wounded, and now paralysed, leg behind him. He heard voices a few yards ahead.

"It's George, they've killed 'im. Looks like some kind of booby trap!"

"I'll bet there'll be more of 'em inside. I reckon we'd better wait here until they come out, then we'll shoot 'em, cut off their 'eads and take 'em back to Liberius in a bucket. What d'ya say mate?"

"Sound good to me. I certainly don't wanna end up like George 'ere."

"You wait in the tunnel just to the right of the entrance. I'll hide in the shadows opposite."

Sam's relief that they were leaving was short-lived. His leg spasmed, he lost his balance, and fell to the ground. The gun slipped from his hand and clattered to the ground. It went off with a deafening roar that echoed throughout the chamber. The bullet ricocheted off the wall and caught one of the retreating mercenaries in the back of his leg. He cried out and also fell to the ground. His companion swivelled around and started firing in the direction of the muzzle flash. Fortunately, the gun was a good two metres from where Sam was now lying. He painfully pulled himself up to hide behind George's swinging corpse.

"I know you're in there somewhere, come out where I can see ya!" yelled the mercenary as he moved tentatively forward with his gun pointing ahead of him. When he reached his fallen companion, he knelt to check on him."

Sam remained silent.

"Are you OK, Jenkins?" the mercenary asked.

"Yeah, just got nicked in the back of the leg. Can you see the shooter?"

"No 'is either 'iding or 'is gone back into the tunnel. Can ya walk mate?"

"I'll try!" Jenkins got to his feet sweating and swearing profusely.

"I'm gonna kill him" he said. Then he put his hand on his mate's shoulder and the two of them cautiously moved forward towards Sam. There was nowhere for him to go. He certainly wouldn't be able to outrun them and his vision was starting to blur. As they got to within a couple of feet of George's body and the bed of nails, he did the only thing he could think of and used all of his remaining strength to push it towards them.

The bed swung forward but only just enough for one of the lower nails, that hadn't pierced George, to catch the leading mercenary's thigh.

He shouted in agony but held his footing. Sam on the other hand collapsed helplessly at their feet.

"I'm gonna blow 'is brains out!" shouted Jenkins.

"Go ahead mate," said the other mercenary as he attended to his wounded thigh.

Jenkins knelt over Sam and stuck the gun against his head.

"Any last words?" he asked Sam, who was now shaking uncontrollably. Before he had time to answer the tunnel filled with the sound of gunfire and the head exploded.

Chapter 70

5.50pm. Ackerman, John and the Dean had descended into the Kings Cross underground station with Caesar.

Briggs and the privates had stayed on the concourse above continually surveying the area for Romans or mercenaries. They had deliberately driven the battle-taxi through the station doors, as they were certain Sir Gareth would have ordered it's destruction. At least, while it was hidden in the station, the drones wouldn't spot it.

Ackerman had called the helicopter pilot and told him to hover over Kings Cross Station until they emerged.

As Ackerman guided them toward the entranceway to Boudicca's tomb he heard a shot. They quickened their pace and then they heard another and the desperate cries of a woman. Ackerman sprinted towards the sound, recognising the voice to be Jessica's but before he reached the entranceway he heard a third shot and then there was silence.

5.50pm. Liberius had sent reinforcements from Hyde Park to Kings Cross. They were arriving in three stolen army vehicles that they had taken from the failed attack earlier in the day. Each truck was driven by a mercenary, and in the back they both had eight Romans. As they arrived at the station entranceway they radioed ahead.

"What's the situation?"

"There's just one armed vehicle on the concourse with three soldiers. The rest have gone down into the Underground. Jenkins and Harris are already down there, so they should be covered. What's your ETA?"

"We're outside now. I'm sending in the Romans and they're gagging for blood. Shoot one of the British soldiers if you can, that will make the buggers wild."

"No problem, I have a clear shot!"

Private Wiggins heard the shot but before he could react the bullet passed through his arm, catching his brachial artery. Blood immediately poured from his wound, just as the Romans poured into the building.

Wiggins looked wide-eyed and terrified as the zombies approached. He knew exactly where they were heading and why. Briggs and Bradbury also saw them coming and jumped in the vehicle. "Get inside!" the sergeant yelled to Wiggins.

"No sarge. You'd do this for me. I know you would!" He started to sprint away from the vehicle and onto the platform. All of the Romans followed him, ignoring the battle taxi completely due to their primordial desire for blood.

Wiggins opened the door of a deserted train and ran inside closing it firmly behind him. The Romans had obviously had no experience opening train doors and chose instead to dive through the windows. The corridor was wet with Wiggin's blood and some stopped to lick it from the floor. The others, however, continued the chase.

It took them only a few seconds to catch up with him but that was plenty of time for the battle taxi to get out of the station. The mercenaries saw it fly out of the entrance and they immediately drove in pursuit down Grays Inn Road, which was completely deserted except for some abandoned cars.

Briggs accelerated to 120 mph but the mercenaries matched his speed and then even began to catch up. He radioed ahead to the blockade on Waterloo Bridge.

"This is Sergeant Briggs, I am driving towards you right now followed by two hostile vehicles. When you see them, take them out!"

He swung right into Theobald's Road and then left into Southampton Row. The first of the mercenaries pulled level and tried to force him off the road. The battle-taxi, however, was surprisingly powerful and Briggs turned abruptly toward his adversary, pushing him towards the central reservation and into a large metal lamppost. The truck stopped abruptly buckling around the street lamp's base and the driver shot through the windscreen at 130mph. His shoulder connected with the lamppost shattering his collarbone and removing his left arm completely. The remains of his shattered corpse rolled across the pavement floor settling some 100 yards from his truck.

The second vehicle continued the chase, accelerating rapidly, its driver angered by the loss of his friend. The mercenary steered with one arm and fired his AK45 machine gun with the other, aiming for the tyres of the battle-taxi, but unable to fire accurately.

"Just one hostile now. I repeat, just one hostile." Briggs was back on the radio, also driving with only one hand. Both vehicles were forced to turn sharply as they hit the Aldwych. All traffic would normally turn left into the one-way system, so Briggs suddenly turned right. This momentarily confused the pursuing mercenary and as he tried to quickly readjust his steering he lost complete control of the vehicle and ploughed headlong into a traditional red London phone box and then onward into the huge concrete columns guarding the entranceway to the BBC's Bush House. He too exited through the windscreen and crashed into the large wooden door.

Private Bradbury cheered loudly and patted his sergeant on the back just as the drone locked onto their vehicle.

Chapter 71

5.50pm. Jessica saw that a mercenary was about to shoot Sam in the head so she pulled out the gun that Sam had given her, and fired. Ackerman's training paid off - her aim was perfect. The mercenary's head exploded and he fell immediately on top of Sam's, now convulsing, body. When she saw the state that Sam was in, she cried out.

The other mercenary fired at Jessica but she had raised Boudicca's shield and the bullet bounced off harmlessly, creating bright sparks as it ricocheted around the passageway wall. Jessica fired again, another precision shot that tore apart the mercenary's heart.

She put the relics aside and ran to Sam's aid. He was still shaking, his eyes were glazed and he was barely breathing. She reached into her pocket and extracted the vials. She really had no idea, which was the correct one. She leaned back and reached for the Helmet of Solomon, if she needed wisdom now was the time!

There was a red vial and a green vial. She has no idea which anti-venom to use, but as she associated red with danger, she decided to try the green one. She prayed she'd made the right choice. If she was wrong, Sam was dead. She broke it open and then poured it, without hesitation, into Sam's mouth. Immediately his face flushed and began to swell, he turned his head to vomit and as he choked his throat constricted completely blocking his airway. He gasped desperately for air, reaching out to her in desperation. Then his eyes rolled upwards and his breathing suddenly stopped. Jessica's heartbroken cry of absolute despair echoed through the chamber. She had made the wrong choice: Sam was dead.

5.50pm. The drone came down low behind the battle taxi and fired. Sergeant Briggs saw the missile streaming toward him in his rear view mirror, there was no way to outmaneouvre it. He could either save himself or Bradbury. The choice was a simple one for a battle-hardened veteran. He leaned over the private, opened the passenger door and pushed him out. As Bradbury fell onto the tarmac he looked at his sergeant in complete shock. What the hell was he doing?

The battle-taxi travelled forward just three more metres before the missile hit its rear and it exploded in a ball of flames. Then Bradbury understood. The sarge had just saved his life at the expense of his own. He was a bloody hero!

Chapter 72

5.55pm. The Helmet of Solomon had shown Jessica a vision of the future, so she would understand the consequences of making the wrong choice. The green vial would kill him; she had to use the red one.

She immediately broke it open and poured it into Sam's mouth. For a number of seconds, which seemed to Jessica like hours, nothing happened - the convulsions continued. Then slowly they started to subside. Sam's body relaxed and his breathing became deeper. Eventually, he opened his eyes and smiled faintly.

"You did it Jess, you beat the odds for me." Sam said weakly.

She leaned over and kissed him slowly and tenderly.

Ackerman and his comrades had just arrived at the doorway. Caesar was standing guard outside. It was time to let their presence be known.

"What are you doing to him?" Ackerman shouted as he walked toward them.

"Get a room," said John. The Dean covered his eyes.

Jessica looked up and smiled at them. She was so pleased to see that the professor was still in one piece and the Dean also. Jessica had met the Dean several times when he had visited Ackerman at the university and she had grown to love and respect him despite his odd ways.

"Whose your friend professor?" Jessica asked, looking at John.

"My name's John Brody, some call me Birdseye. I'm a harbour master, among other things. Please call me John." He offered his hand, which she shook.

"Nice to meet you John," she said.

"Come on Jessica, we have to go," said Ackerman. "We have a nation to save."

"I'm on to it," she said, "But what about Sam? He's too weak to travel. One of your snakes bit him."

"I figured that," said Ackerman. "We'll just have to carry him between us."

"I'll take the first shift," said John, lifting Sam effortlessly and carrying him to the door.

"By the way Jessica," said John, "There's someone outside we'd like you to meet. Please don't be alarmed. His name's Caesar and he's a friend."

Chapter 73

6.00pm. Andrew Smith watched Sir Gareth as he received the news that the battle-taxi has been destroyed along with all of its occupants, except for a Private Bradbury who had managed to jump clear. He was extremely surprised by the man's reaction. He had ordered the execution of three of his former friends and had showed no remorse or regret whatsoever, now that they were dead. In fact, since he had returned from the tunnels he seemed to be suddenly devoid of any morality at all!

There was something very wrong: Sir Gareth was not himself. Something had happened in those tunnels and he needed to find out what.

He excused himself, saying he had to make a few private phone calls to check on his wife and kids, and left the briefing room. As soon as he was out of sight he hurriedly descended the stairs into the tunnel that lead to Q-Whitehall. Andrew had seen Sir Gareth leave that way. He had been watching him carefully, something you do when you are head of MI5.

As he reached the bottom of the stairs, the first thing he noticed was that Sir Gareth had lied. The tunnels were not sealed. In fact, the door had been left slightly ajar. He walked for about 200 yards through the dimly lit corridor until he reached the door that led to the communications bunker. He reached for the keypad and typed in 0-5-1-1-1-6-0-5 then completed the retina scan. His face appeared on the LED screen and he took a moment to admire it as the lock clicked open.

He pushed aside the heavy steel door and was immediately hit by the smell of blood. As the door opened wider he saw bodies strewn all over the floors and desks. Each had been torn apart and most of their flesh and internal organs were missing. He walked through the huge control room with his hand over his mouth, trying hard not to vomit.

When he reached the far side, he came to the door that led through to the GUTN, the Governments' Underground Train Network. It was unusually ajar. He walked through and onto the platform where he saw a shuttle waiting. As he walked toward it he saw that the windows had been broken and the door was hanging from its hinges. He looked around the platform and saw nothing, then, he looked over onto the tracks.

The contents of his stomach, which he had tried so hard to keep down, rose immediately to his throat and landed on the track beside the naked corpse. Its head was twisted at an unnatural angle and most of its flesh had been torn away. There was even signs of bite marks in the bones. The face was mostly missing. There was no nose, ears or cheeks but it was still recognizable, especially as Andrew had seen it almost every week for the last twelve years. He knelt down, took off his jacket and threw it over Sir Gareth's bloody head.

Andrew stood and assessed the scene quickly, as he had been trained to do. Gareth had been lured down here by the text he received in the briefing room - obviously he had been instructed to go to a location that could only be reached, in the present situation, by the shuttle. As soon as he had taken his seat, and before he could move out of the station, he had been ambushed, pulled from the train and his neck had been broken.

They had then removed his clothes and his body had been fed to one of the creatures. When it had cloned his cell structure and taken his form, it had been dressed in Sir Gareth's own clothes. As the hair would not have had time to grow to the exact length they must have placed a wig on his head and sent him back to the briefing room to take the real Sir Gareth's place.

The reality of the situation suddenly seized him. The creature was under Liberius's control and it was now in a room with the most powerful people in Britain whom it could kill at any time.

For now, Liberius was using Sir Gareth's power and influence to track down and kill each of his enemies. He had to be stopped.

Andrew ran out of the terminal to the security door that led back into Q-Whitehall. He typed in his code and let the retina scanner scan his eye. The screen buzzed and turned red, the word "Unauthorised" flashed several times before it reset. He assumed that in the panic he must had entered the wrong numbers so he tried again, this time more carefully, 0-5-1-1-1-6-0-5. Again, the word "Unauthorised" appeared. It was definitely the right number - it was not something he could forget, after all, it was the date of the Gunpowder Plot of 1605 and he was standing close to where Guy Fawkes had been arrested.

He was locked in, and the only way out was the shuttle. As he ran back towards it, the mercenaries appeared with another Roman soldier.

One of the mercenaries was speaking on his radio. "We have the target, Emperor, what shall we do: Kill him or clone him?"

"Both," was the terse reply.

Chapter 74

6.10pm. Andrew Smith returned to the briefing room and gave a knowing nod to Sir Gareth who nodded back. Everyone was seated around the long teak table discussing their options. General Radford was now on one of the video conferencing monitors, as were other members of the cabinet and the Secretary General of NATO, who was currently addressing them.

Sir Gareth pulled out the seat next to him and ushered Andrew Smith over. As Andrew sat down, he whispered to Sir Gareth. "When do we kill them?"

"Patience," whispered Sir Gareth, "we have to seal the fate of this country first."

"...the President of the United States is rapidly building up the support of the other world leaders to take drastic action" said the NATO leader. "They do not want your zombies or your terrorists to leave your country, and I have to say I agree with him, though his proposed methods are rather extreme!"

"What are his proposed methods?" asked Karen Shaw.

"I would rather not say," said the NATO leader sheepishly.

Shaw rose and shouted at the Secretary General. "I don't want to have to ask you again. What are the proposed methods?"

He was now ruffled and prepared to speak his mind, after all this was the Presidents plan not his. "He wants to shoot down all of your departing planes, sink your ships, and if you cannot stop those monsters quickly, he wants to launch a nuclear strike to ensure they're incinerated."

"A nuclear strike!" she said incredulously. "You would condone the destruction on an entire nation!" Everyone in the room, except for Sir Gareth and Andrew Smith, were rightly horrified - they could not believe what they were hearing.

"I am not condoning this action but you must admit the situation there is completely out of hand, and you don't seem to have any idea how to control it. And frankly, neither do we!"

"But if a nuclear attack goes ahead you will be killing over 60 million innocent people, not to mention those in Western Europe that will be caught in the fallout!" she screamed.

"That is why I'm certain that President Cluney will not get the unilateral support he needs. There are many fighting your corner Karen, but sadly I think that over the next few days you'll all be dead anyway, unless you can hide from those creatures or destroy them!"

"Then get our key people out of here and take them to mainland Europe."

"Can't do it I'm afraid Karen. After the fiasco with the Prime Minister at your press conference, we have no way of knowing who's real and who's been cloned. Who knows, there may be zombies sitting round that table with you right now!"

"That's preposterous!" she yelled.

Gareth and Andrew shared a smile.

Sir Gareth rose to his feet. "With all due respect sir, you are nothing but Cluney's lap dog. Just admit it, you are all so terrified of these creatures that you've already decided to take us out. Well thank you for not sticking up for us!

Thanks for not coming to our aid and thanks for giving us no opportunity whatsoever to get out of here. I think I speak on behalf of all of us when I say, do your worst and we hope you rot in hell!" He leaned forward and cut off the communications link.

Karen Shaw stared at him in absolute disbelief. "What have you done Sir Gareth? He was our only hope. Given time I could have possibly reasoned with him. Now you've condemned us all!"

Gareth just stared at her with an eerie, unsettling smile. She held his eyes and was sure at that moment that he had gone quite mad! The pressure had clearly broken him. She would have to keep a very close eye on him from now on.

"General Radford, where are our nuclear submarines?" she asked.

"The Trafalgar is in the Gulf, the Vanguard is just off the coast of Afghanistan and the Astute is undergoing repairs in the Firth of Clyde."

"How soon can we get it in the Atlantic?"

"In a matter of hours."

"You have one hour, and I want all sixteen Trident II missiles locked onto Washington DC as soon as it is feasible. If that ass of a President thinks he can walk all over us, I'll teach him a thing or two. Get him on the line, now!"

One of her aids dialled the secure direct line and passed her the phone.

"Hello Karen," said the President innocently, "how *are* you?"

"I'm fine thank you, Miles. I just wanted you to know that the minute you shoot down one of my planes, sink one of my ships or launch a single missile towards our soil, sixteen nuclear warheads will be heading right up your backside. Have I made myself clear!" She slammed down the phone.

The men around the room shared admiring glances. Maybe this woman wasn't the pushover they'd imagined her to be.

"Andrew and Sir Gareth, I need an immediate progress report of Agent Callaghan's efforts to track down the trident, and I want him to be given all of the support we can muster to obtain it. Am I understood?"

Sir Gareth nodded. "I am truly sorry for my unforgivable outburst. We will get onto it right away Karen."

He then leaned over to Andrew Smith and whispered, "Nearly dinner time, I think."

"Good" said Smith, "I'm starving!"

Sir Gareth's phone received a text: *Ackerman and crew were not in vehicle. Spotted at Kings Cross Station heading for tomb. Make sure you destroy the place, right now!* He immediately stood to address the committee.

"Some good news at last. We've managed to locate the base where Liberius is keeping his mercenaries and communication systems. They are in the tunnels under Kings Cross Station. Karen, may I instruct General Radford to take it out immediately?"

"General," said the Deputy PM, "please do as he says. You never know, with his communication centre destroyed, Liberius may lose control of these creatures."

"Pass the salt," Sir Gareth asked Andrew with a smile.

Chapter 75

6.10pm. John carried Sam to the foot of the stairs and then set him onto his feet. "How are you feeling son?"

"Not too clever," said Sam taking a couple of tentative steps on his own, "but I think I can walk, just."

Ackerman's phone rang. It was Private Bradbury who told him about the courageous death of Sergeant Briggs, and warned him that there was, at least, one more sniper on the station concourse, and at least eight Roman soldiers.

Ackerman addressed his team. "I'm afraid to inform you that Briggs is dead. He was taken out by a government drone just moments ago. Wiggins was also killed, shot by a sniper and eaten by zombies. Bradbury survived and is back with his unit."

John and the Dean bowed their heads. They had admired Briggs and genuinely mourned the fallen soldier. They all believed that this was the work of Sir Gareth, and they found it quite incomprehensible that he would do such a terrible thing.

"We also have snipers in the station concourse, and several of those monsters are lurking around too." Caesar looked offended.

"Can we not call them monsters, Alexander. It's rather offensive to Caesar here."

"I'm sorry Caesar, I didn't mean to cause offense. Frankly we really need your help right now. There are several exits out of here but I suspect Liberius's men have them all covered. If we return to the tunnels they will have us trapped. Our best bet is through the station concourse and straight out the main entrance to the waiting helicopter. The chances are, however, that in that 100-metre dash most of us will either be picked off by the snipers or killed by the Roman soldiers. I need you, Caesar, to create a distraction. You have to kill one of the mercenaries and invite the other Romans to join you for dinner. Do you think you can do that?"

Caesar nodded enthusiastically and sprinted up the stairs.

"It's not a fool-proof plan," Alexander told the others. "There may well be more than one sniper up there, but it's our best shot."

They waited for about three minutes and then they heard a scream and the running of feet.

They climbed up the stairs and looked across the concourse. Caesar and eight other zombies were busy tearing a mercenary apart.

With Ackerman taking the lead they ran across the concourse as quickly as they could. John and the Dean, however, had to drag Sam along, as he was drifting in and out of consciousness. In the end Sam blacked out altogether and his legs completely gave way. John immediately caught him, threw him back over his shoulders and sprinted for the door.

Just as they were about to reach the entranceway, Jessica, who was at the rear of the party, saw a bead of red light appear between the shoulder blades of one of her companions. Before she could shout a warning, a shot rang out, echoing around the vast station concourse, and the bead of light turned into a bullet hole. Her comrade fell instantly to the ground. There had indeed been more than one sniper!

Chapter 76

6.15pm. The London Resistance were on the move and proudly walking in their thousands up the Old Kent Road into Central London. As they progressed, more and more Londoners joined their ranks, including several of the local gangsters who had been involved in the Hackney bloodbath.

Word had gotten out that the Roman army had now been bolstered by Category A convicts, who had been sprung from the local prisons. It didn't faze anyone; at least there was now someone they could actually kill!

Liberius heard that they were coming. There would be over 400,000 men and women with very little combat experience, against his 100,000 Roman soldiers, 47 mercenaries and just over 4,000 convicted murderers.

Despite the overwhelming numbers of the resistance, he had no concerns. He knew that he could defeat them with just 1,000 of his Romans, maybe even a hundred, but it would take some time and tie up a lot of his resources.

He was still certain though, that the Americans would save him the effort. They wouldn't back down after the hollow threats from the Deputy Prime Minister.

6.15pm. (1.15pm ET) The President of the United States sat behind his desk in the Oval Office. His secretaries of State, Defence and Treasury were all present along with the Attorney General.

"Right, this is the current state of affairs," said the President, "we can't get the approval of France, Germany, Belgium, Canada, Russia or the Netherlands and thanks to NATO the Brits now know of our plans. So the big question is: how do we nuke Britain without them knowing it's coming, and whom can we blame? I need deniability here."

"Deniability will be difficult, as everyone knows that a nuclear attack was your idea Mr. President," said Bill Albright, the Secretary of Defence. "However, once the dust clears I don't think there will be any retaliation or accusations, especially with China on our side. The other nations will back down immediately if we can give them reasonable grounds to believe the bomb could *possibly* have come from another source."

"That's just what I thought, Bill. Let's blame it all on the Taliban again. Start spreading disinformation that it was them who destroyed the Tower of London and Downing Street, that they released biologically engineered monsters to terrify the public and then wiped out the entire nation with a massive nuclear explosion."

"I like it!" said the Attorney General.

"The problem is," continued the President as he stood and walked over to his colleagues, "how do we get a nuke into Britain undetected, in the next couple of hours?"

"The quickest way," said Albright, "is to fly a commercial airliner into Heathrow airport, and detonate the bomb just as it touches down. Of course, we can't bring it in from the States, it would be too obvious and there isn't time, but we can fly it in from Germany. That way we can deliver the payload within your timescales and deny all knowledge."

"Do we have any nukes in Germany?" asked the President.

"Yes we do, unofficially, of course," said Albright.

"And how do we get the bomb on a German airliner?" asked the Secretary of State.

"No problem, we have the connections, which we will permanently break when the job's done," said Albright.

"No trail back to us then?" asked the President.

"None."

"Then make it so. I want that plane in Heathrow by 8.30pm latest. That gives you just over two hours."

"Consider it done," said Albright, a little hesitantly.

"What's up?" asked the President picking up on his tone.

"It's just that my wife has family there; her sister and three young children."

"I'm sorry Bill, I really am, but we have no option. You understand that, don't you?"

"I do Sir. We had family in the World Trade Centre too."

"Well, you have sacrificed much for your country," he said putting his hand on his Defense Secretary's shoulder. "Any other concerns?" he asked his Cabinet.

Everyone shook their heads. They all had friends, relatives or colleagues in Britain but they weren't going to let that stand in the way of their country and, of course, their careers.

"Then let's get on with it," ordered the President, "and don't breathe a word of this to anyone! Same rules apply as with 9/11, do you understand?"

They nodded in the affirmative. They valued their lives and those of their families.

Chapter 77

6.15pm. As soon as Caesar heard the shot, he ran in the direction of the sniper. The other zombies who knew that he was the source of a good meal followed him. The sniper saw them coming. There would be no time to take any more shots at his assigned targets and it would be totally ineffective shooting the zombies so he decided it was time to check out and turned the gun on himself. A single shot to the roof of his mouth ensured he was dead long before the Romans began devouring him.

The Dean lifted Ackerman's prone body onto his shoulder and ran out of the station's main entrance. Jessica stood behind John and Sam protecting them with her shield, but no more bullets came.

The helicopter pilot saw them coming and landed just outside the station in Euston Road. The Dean placed Ackerman's lifeless body inside and John unloaded Sam. Jessica stood covering the helicopter door with her shield and aiming her trident at the station entrance, expecting the Romans to come after them at any moment.

"Get in Jessica. We have to go," said the Dean.

"Not yet," said John, "we have to wait for Caesar."

"What makes you think he'll come?"

"He'll come! Give him a couple of minutes. He's probably just dealing with the sniper that nailed Alexander."

"I hope he tears him apart," said Sam, who had regained consciousness and was looking down mournfully at the professor's still body.

"We have incoming," said the pilot looking at his radar.

Before anyone could react, a missile passed over the helicopter and slammed into the station, which exploded, in a huge ball of flames. Concrete, glass, timber and steel flew through the air at speed towards the helicopter.

Jessica stood her ground and raised her trident. Instantly a huge wall of white light appeared in front of them, shielding them from the oncoming debris. She held her position until the danger had passed, then she lowered the trident revealing hundreds of tons of rubble that would have otherwise torn them and their helicopter to pieces.

The Dean had been tending to Ackerman, who was barely alive. More blood oozed from his back with every breath, which were becoming increasingly shallow.

John looked at what was left of the station and saw no movement. He wondered if Caesar could have survived the blast, after all, the Romans were meant to be indestructible. The trouble was they wouldn't have time to dig him out of there. He was going to miss Caesar, ugly though he was.

Jessica jumped onto the helicopter and they were about to slam the door when two things happened simultaneously. The rubble in front on them began to stir and up popped the smiling face of Caesar, who had obviously been one of the objects that had hit the energy wall, and secondly, they heard a woman's voice crying out desperately for help.

Caesar scanned the area around him and spotted a blonde-haired woman in her thirties lying on the pavement close to the Euston Road about 300 metres to the right of the helicopter. She had obviously been too far away from the energy wall to be afforded protection and had been caught up in the blast. Her head was bleeding profusely into her tangled hair and her left leg seemed to be trapped under a collapsed concession stand.

Caesar's first instinct was to run over and eat her but thanks to his new conscience, he knew that would be wrong. Besides he was full after the two-course mercenary lunch.

The woman saw him lumbering towards her and began to scream hysterically. John jumped out the helicopter and walked beside Caesar, putting a hand on the Romans shoulder in an attempt to reassure the woman. It didn't work. The screaming continued as they lifted the newspaper kiosk from her leg and Caesar carried her back to the helicopter. She only stopped when she saw Jessica.

"Are you okay?" Jessica asked.

"Are you friends with this thing?" she said pointing to Caesar and ignoring Jessica's question.

"I am. He's quite harmless," said Jessica as Caesar wiped away the remains of his last mercenary meal from around his mouth. The woman did not look convinced.

The helicopter began to rise from the ground. "Where to?" asked the pilot.

"Hyde Park," said Jessica with a deep inhalation of breath. She was about to meet her destiny, one way or another.

"Why the hell are we going to Hyde Park?" the woman asked. "Isn't that where all the zombies are?"

"Don't worry we'll drop you off somewhere first," Jessica lied. There was absolutely no time to waste. "Now how are you feeling?" she said looking into the woman's eyes to see if there was any sign of concussion.

"Well apart from a gash to the head, a possibly broken leg, very little prospect of living through the day and a creature from hell leaning over me, yes, I'm dandy!" said the woman with more than a little sarcasm.

Caesar went to throw her out of the helicopter again, but John stopped him with a faint touch of his arm and a shake of the head.

"I'm sorry," the woman said, "it's been one hell of a day! My name is Alison." She shook each of their hands except for Caesar's.

"What's wrong with him?" she said looking down at the professor's body.

"He's been shot in the back," said the Dean, forced to state the obvious.

"Is he dead?" she asked. "Only he's bleeding all over my shoes!"

Caesar looked at John as if to say, "Please can I eat this woman?" John reluctantly shook his head.

The Dean had also had enough. "If you don't want to get my friend's blood on your clothes, I would suggest that you get out of this helicopter and go back to wherever you have come from. You are possibly the most irritating person I have met today and that includes, snipers, mercenaries and monsters! No offense, Caesar."

The woman was taken aback by the Dean's frankness and realized just how extremely insensitive she had been. She apologized for her inappropriate comment and then started to sob. There was no way she was getting off the helicopter with all of those hideous creatures running loose.

No one showed her the slightest bit of sympathy, except for Jessica, who put some butterfly stitches on her head from the helicopters first aid kit, and took a good look at her injured leg. She had no medical training, but it was obvious it wasn't broken.

"Which hospital are you taking me to?" asked Alison.

"We're not going to any hospital just yet," said The Dean. "There is something very important we have to do first."

"What can be more important than fixing my leg?" asked Alison.

The Dean felt a swear word coming on and counted to five before he spoke. "Alison, we have to discuss some important matters. Would you mind sitting up front and putting these headphones on."

"Actually, I would!"

"Caesar, dump her in the seat next to the pilot!" said the Dean.

"It's OK, I'm on my way!" she said quickly.

Sam helped her up and guided her to the seat next to the pilot. Then he placed the headphones over her ears. Jessica noticed the way she had smiled at Sam and let her hand run down his arm as he moved away. Jessica hoped that she would get the opportunity to kick Alison's ass. She was not to be disappointed.

Suddenly, Ackerman began to cough. Then, he pushed himself up with his arms. The Dean helped him to sit and as he did a bullet fell from his back.

"That's better," the professor said. "Did I miss anything?"

Chapter 78

6.30pm. The catering truck travelled slowly alongside the SkyLine monorail at Terminal One of Frankfurt Airport. It was being driven by two CIA agents who both wore blue overalls and peaked caps bearing the logo of an airline catering company.

They kept their heads down and tried their best to be as inconspicuous as possible. They came to a halt at Gate B42, and strolled over to Flight LH933, where they showed the manifest to the steward; a twenty-something male, with eyeliner and a blonde buzz cut, who spoke and acted like a twenty-something woman.

The agents disliked him immediately but nevertheless handed him an envelope containing the extremely rare 1928 $500 bill that he had been promised in exchange for his cooperation.

The steward smiled broadly, revealing recently enamelled teeth. He put the envelope in his pocket and then minced over to the van. He helped them remove two thermal trolleys, which were loaded carefully onto the plane. One was marked 'Outward Flight' the other 'Return Flight'.

The first contained the passenger's evening meal; the second contained a nuclear bomb. When both trolleys were safely on board the agents thanked the steward while ignoring his outstretched hand. They quickly returned to the van and drove off.

The steward fixed the containers in place in the flight kitchen and then asked to see the Flight service manager. He explained that his partner had been taken seriously ill and asked if he could be replaced, apologizing for the late notice. Seeing his obvious distress she reluctantly agreed.

The steward headed back into the airport and made his way to the car park. As promised there was a brand new Mercedes A-class in bay R56 with a navigation system pre-programmed to his required destination. He climbed in behind the wheel and in fifty minutes he had travelled 64km south on the A5 to Heppenheim. It was here where he was to meet with a bank note collector, who had agreed to give him $427,000 in cash for his rare $550 bill.

The address that he had been given took him to an alleyway just off the marketplace in Heppenheim's Old Town. He found the door he was looking for and rung the bell. An old bespeckled man answered and ushered him inside. Having closed the door behind them, he showed the steward into a back room and asked him to wait. The steward sat there excitedly, working out in his mind how he was going to spend his windfall. He wasn't sure exactly, but it would involve plenty of drugs, booze and men.

A moment later his excitement turned to shock as the same CIA agents whom he had met at the airport entered the room. Before he could speak, they shot him between the eyes and retrieved the bank note. One of the agents then drove the A-Class Mercedes, which they'd hired with a forged credit card and driving license, up to the back door and threw the body into the boot. The car was then driven, just below the speed limit, to some wasteland. After transferring the steward's body to the driver's seat, it was set ablaze.

The main problem had been finding a flight to London that hadn't been cancelled. Flight LH933 had been the exception, as it was chartered to transport 82 journalists and TV crew desperate to become part of the world's greatest ever story. The Romans had now left London's airports, so it was clear to fly.

When the plane reached 20,000 feet a red light illuminated on the nuclear device beside a digital altimeter - it was now armed. When the plane next descended below 20,000 feet, the light would turn green and the device would explode taking the jet, the passengers and most of the British Isles with it. It was due to land at exactly 8pm. Britain had just ninety minutes left of its illustrious history.

Chapter 79

6.30pm. "Welcome back" said the Dean.

"Thank you" said the professor flexing his shoulders, "It's a good job they targeted me and not one of you mortals," he mused.

The Dean and Jessica smiled. John and Sam looked more than a little confused.

Ackerman saw the expressions on their faces and said, "I think I'd better come clean."

"I think you had!" said Sam.

"I'm two thousand years old and immortal!" said Ackerman as if it was perfectly reasonable.

It suddenly all made sense to Sam. Those feelings he had gotten during Ackerman's lectures that he had actually seen the events he spoke about, the reverence shown to the trident, his knowledge of the Boudicca's tomb and when they were down there, hadn't Jessica referred to the snake that bit him as one of Ackerman's? "You're the Guardian!" said Sam.

"That's right," said Ackerman. "I am."

"Then why haven't you told me before?" said Sam accusingly.

"I didn't need to."

"Then why now?"

"Hard to hide it when you come back from the dead!"

"Hang on a minute," said Sam, "I've seen photographs of your ancestors in the halls of Balliol College."

"They're not my ancestors – they're all photographs of me. Different hairstyles and colours, a moustache here, a beard there, changing fashions and a reasonable distance of time between each appointment, no one suspected a thing, why would they?

"I'd work at the college for many years, sometimes a decade or two, and then a war would start or an emergency would arise and I'd have to go and sort it out with the help of a trident bearer."

"So the women that you ran off with, they weren't your lovers?"

"Of course not! They were all carefully chosen to carry the relics and defend their country. They were my Britannias."

"And Lucinda?"

"She was the daughter of one, an amazing woman called Emily, and yes, after Emily's death she became a Britannia herself."

"But if your Britannias carry a shield of immortality, why aren't they all still around today?" asked Sam.

"It's because of the trident. You see Sam; it's a curse as well as a blessing. Remember the story of Boudicca, how she gave her life to save her daughter? Well that's what happens to every Britannia eventually." His voice began to break. "They find someone who is fatally ill or injured, whose life, they believe, is more important than their own, and they make the ultimate sacrifice.

"I choose them because of their courage and compassion, but it is these very qualities that cause them to give up their lives for another."

"That's what happened to Lucinda's mother, isn't it?" Sam asked rhetorically. "Emily didn't commit suicide, did she?"

"No. Not strictly anyway. When it became clear that Lucinda was about to die, she used the trident to cure her daughter's leukemia at the expense of her life. I begged her not to do it and she promised she wouldn't, but there is nothing that can stand in the way of a mother's love. When she heard that her daughter was about to die, she removed the trident from Boudicca's tomb and went straight to the hospital to save Lucinda's life. She knew I'd be notified as soon as she entered the tomb. She also knew I'd follow her. I saw her standing by the window of her daughter's ward looking down at me as I arrived at the hospital. By the time I got up there Emily was dead and she'd left a will giving me custody of her baby. I immediately hid the trident under my coat and notified the doctors."

"What about Lucinda then, why did she die if she had the shield to protect her?"

"The shield only protects a Britannia while they're holding it. Lucinda was unarmed that night - she knew that agents from the intelligence service were watching her, and she did not want to reveal the relics or her alter ego."

"Why did you let her do it?"

"I didn't, she was working for MI5 at the time, not for me. I expressly asked her not to get involved but she was strong willed, just like her mother."

"So Jessica. I guess you're the latest Britannia."

"I am," she admitted.

"So I was right in thinking that in this mission I was just the transport and the muscle."

"No Sam, you were my Guardian too, you saved my life remember, on more than one occasion. I wouldn't be here if it wasn't for you." She learned forward and kissed him.

"Not again!" said John and the Dean simultaneously.

"So, what do you make of all this John?" Ackerman asked.

"I have many questions of my own, of course, but there is only one I need to ask right now. Did Sir Gareth know about the Britannias?"

"Of course he did. It's the Government who calls upon us in times of crisis. My Britannias have fought against Viking invaders on our eastern shores, the Spanish in the Armada and the Germans in the Somme, the Battle of Britain and at Dunkirk. They have also accompanied Nelson and

Wellington fighting in many campaigns on foreign seas or soil.

"Whenever our country has been under threat my Britannias have been there to offer protection. Their presence has always been a closely guarded secret but, nevertheless, they've been honoured throughout the ages by a grateful government. You've seen monuments to their courage in the form of statues all across the country, especially around London. In Plymouth, for example, is a huge monument paying tribute to the role that one Britannia, Elizabeth Fleming, and her fleets played in defeating the Spanish Armada.

"They are also memorialized on our currency and also on our gold and silver. They have been immortalised on our stamps, in our hymns, on medals, and in classic paintings by some of our greatest artists. Their images have been used on posters for decades to rally troops and civilians at times of war and they have also had several warships and military colleges named after them.

"The Britannias are this country's greatest asset and also its greatest secret."

"OK," said John, "if, as you say, Sir Gareth was aware of the Britannias and knew you to be their Guardian, the only hope in protecting us from Liberius and his army, why did he try to have you killed on more than one occasion?"

"I'm certain he wasn't aware that I was at the British Library when he sent in the SAS. He was just trying to stop the Dean," answered Ackerman.

"Maybe so, but I'm sure he thought you were in the battle-taxi when he had it blown to pieces; after all, he'd just spoken to us, while we were on board, minutes earlier. I also bet he thought you were at Kings Cross station when he blew that to pieces, possibly destroying Boudicca's tomb in the process! I am sorry to tell you this Alexander, but either Sir Gareth is a traitor or he's no longer Sir Gareth, he's a clone. Let's face it; when he spoke to us in the battle-taxi, did you not think he was extremely aggressive, blatantly hostile in fact. Is that the Sir Gareth you have known for years?"

Ackerman realized that John was making perfect sense, the Sir Gareth he knew would never have tried to kill any of them, even if they had been summoning the Angels of Death.

"If you are right John, and I am beginning to believe you are," said Ackerman, "we have a serious problem. He's at the COBRA meeting right now with the Deputy Prime Minister and most of this country's leadership. If he's under Liberius's control, they're all in mortal danger. We have to find a way to flush him out before he strikes, and the only way we can do that is to rely on the fact that Liberius wants us dead. Dean, John, we will have to use you as bait!"

Chapter 80

7.00pm. (2.00pm ET) Bill Albright was having a late lunch with his wife at Café du Parc, a French restaurant just a stone's throw away from the White House. Usually by now he would have been heartily tucking into a plate of Coquilles Saint-Jacques (seared sea scallops), his absolute favourite meal, but today he was just moving food around his plate rather absently.

"What's wrong with you Bill? You've hardly said a word to me since you arrived, and what's wrong with the food? You haven't touched a thing."

"I'm sorry, Mary, I've got a lot on my mind at the moment, especially with everything that's going on in England. Have you seen the newsfeeds?"

"What do *you* think? I've been glued to the TV all morning! It's scary stuff, absolutely unbelievable! I called Melissa, of course, she's holding up OK. You know what she's like, always optimistic. She says it's just God's way of helping everyone get things back into perspective. Help them realize they actually need him. I wish I had her faith Bill, I really do. Do *you* think it's going to be OK? Honestly? Her daughters are only eight and four; they haven't had any kind of life yet."

Bill broke down. "Oh God, Mary, what have I done?" he said remorsefully as he put down the cutlery and pushed away his plate.

"What do you mean Bill? What *are* you talking about?" Mary asked, clearly concerned.

He leaned forward and whispered, "It's the President, he's done something terrible and I actually went along with it!" He looked at her and then looked away, fear and guilt evident in his face.

Mary took both his hands and looked directly at him until he eventually met her gaze. "Are you going to tell me, or am I going to have to beat it out of you?" she said with a faint, worried smile.

He cleared his throat and then began, she would know in a few hours anyway, and it was better if he told her himself and helped her to understand. "The President was concerned that those creatures might find their way over here, that whoever or whatever caused them to rise from the dead might do the same on American soil," he paused, "so he decided that the situation had to be contained."

"How?"

"He's going to destroy them."

"How can he do that? The Brits threw everything they had at them with no success."

"He's going to do something that the Brits couldn't do."

"What's that, Bill?" she asked.

"He's going to detonate a nuclear device in London, powerful enough to destroy everything and everyone in England and probably the rest of the United Kingdom!"

Mary took a deep intake of breath and withdrew her hands to cover her mouth. Her eyes were wide with horror. She looked around the restaurant to make sure no one was looking or listening, and then looked back at Bill.

"You've got to be kidding me! He's going to cold-bloodedly murder over sixty million people. Is he insane?" she whispered. Then she realized how complicit her husband must have been. "Are *you* insane too?" She stood up pointing at him accusingly, this time not caring if others were looking or not.

"You put this right, Bill, you stop this happening, because if you don't... if Melissa, her daughters and all those people die, you will no longer be my husband, you will no longer be welcome in our home, in fact, you may as well be dead yourself because I... we, will have nothing more to do with you!" She picked up her handbag and stormed out of the restaurant. Everyone was staring at him. He immediately called over the waiter.

"Can I have the check please, and make it quick!"

As soon as Bill had paid for the meals he put on his coat and exited, but instead of heading back to the White House he walked over to Memorial Park. There he found a bench, and after looking around to make sure there was no one close by, he took out his mobile phone and dialled an international number.

"I need to speak to General Daniel Radford. Tell him it's the US Secretary of Defence and it's a matter of utmost importance!"

Chapter 81

7.30pm. The Dean had just called Sir Gareth to arrange a meeting. He'd readily accepted, especially when he was told that the Dean had the trident in his possession. They agreed to rendezvous in the safety of the Whitehall tunnels and Sir Gareth instructed him to take the entranceway in the Admiralty Citadel on the junction between The Mall and Horse Guards Road.

The Citadel had been constructed in 1941 as a bombproof bunker for the Admiralty, with foundations thirty feet deep and a concrete roof twenty feet thick. Sir Winston Churchill had once referred to it as "a vast monstrosity" and every Londoner agreed.

The helicopter landed at Horse Guards Parade, right next door, and Ackerman, John, the Dean and Caesar all jumped out.

"Now remember," said Ackerman, "Sir Gareth has agreed to meet with you for one purpose, and one purpose only, and that's to kill you and take the trident, which he believes you are bringing to him. He may come alone, but he may have help, so be on your guard. The important thing is that you do not allow him, under any circumstances, to return to the COBRA briefing room. If he is one of those creatures, as we suspect, the only way you're going to do that is with the help of Caesar here. May God be with you!"

He hugged each of them, including Caesar, and climbed back on board. The helicopter then took off heading northwest to Hyde Park while the Dean and his team headed for the tunnel entranceway.

The door was, as Sir Gareth had said it would be, hidden in plain sight. All they had to do was push aside some of the Russian Vine that completely covered the bunker and pass through a metal gate that had been left unlocked.

This entranceway led to a large steel door and beside it was a keypad. They typed in the code that they had been given and looked up at the security cameras. At a previous stop on The Strand, they had broken into a tailor's and dressed Caesar in a tweed suit. Luckily for him, the snipers he'd eaten were reasonably handsome and his face had now completely regenerated. He no longer resembled the other Romans, and looked almost alive!

They heard the bolts withdraw and they pushed the door open. In front of them was an elevator door. As soon as they stepped inside, the doors closed and it began to descend deep into the earth. When the doors eventually opened, to their surprise, it was not Sir Gareth but Andrew Smith that was waiting for them and he was holding a pistol.

"Give me the trident!" he demanded.

7.30pm. "There's a call for you General" said one of his lieutenants.

"Tell them to call back tomorrow, can't you see I'm up to my neck in this crisis."

"He claims to be the US Secretary of Defense and says it's urgent."

"What the hell does he want!" he said, grabbing the phone from the lieutenant's hand. "Bill. Wonderful to hear from you, how can I help?"

When the call was finished and he had put down the phone, the general's face was ashen. He looked at his watch there was barely thirty minutes before Flight LH933 was due to land, and unless he could stop it, he possibly had less than half an hour to live."

"I need to speak to the control tower at Heathrow Airport. Now!" he barked. When they had put him through, he spoke as calmly and clearly as he could.

"There is a Lufthansa plane due to land at the airport at around twenty hundred hours. I need you to patch me through to the pilot immediately."

"And you are?" said the controller.

"I'm General Daniel Radford. Please put me through now."

"How do I know that you are who you say you are?"

"For God's sake man if you do not put me through to that pilot right now, this whole bloody country will be vaporized. Now do it!" he yelled.

The line went dead and for a moment the General thought that he'd been cut off, then he heard another voice. It was the captain of Flight LH933.

"Hallo, this is Kapitan Franz Saltzmann, can I help you?"

"Captain Saltzmann, this is General Radford from British Military Intelligence, I am also the highest ranking member of the British Army. We seem to have bit of a problem that you may be able to help us with!"

"What is the problem, General?"

"We have reason to believe that there is a nuclear device hidden in a catering trolley on board your plane. This is probably a false alarm but I need you to check for me."

"One moment General." The line again went dead for a minute or two, then, the captain returned, this time his voice had markedly changed. He was clearly frightened.

"Yes, unfortunately you are correct, there is a device right here in one of the catering trolleys which has a digital display on it. It currently says 25347 but it is dropping quickly. I guess I'm looking at an altimeter?"

"You're right Captain, you are. It's linked to the bombs trigger mechanism. You must not let your plane descend below 20,000 feet or the device will explode. Please climb again immediately and head for open water. How much fuel do you have?"

"As always on commercial flights we have enough in reserve for another forty-five minutes' flight but that is all. What are you proposing General?"

"We need to get your plane as far away from the mainland as possible, just in case it detonates, and then we will help you disarm it or dispose of it."

"We cannot dispose of the bomb General."

"Why not?"

"Because we cannot open the doors while the cabins are pressurized. That would result in an 'explosive decompression', a catastrophic loss of airframe integrity, that will cause the plane to disintegrate. Controlled depressurization can only take place when we are flying below 14,000 feet. That's probably why they set their altitude trigger at 20,000 feet; it's high enough to prevent us from dumping the bomb out of one of the exit doors, but low enough to wipe out everything beneath us."

"I see," said the general, "then we'll just have to disarm it. We'll find out exactly how and then get back to you. I think it best that you do not alert your passengers of the potential danger for now, just tell them that you have to divert to Dublin airport, then take the plane as far away from land as you can."

"I understand General, but please get back to me quickly."

"I will captain. I promise."

The General disconnected the phone. "Get the US Secretary of Defence back on the phone now, we need to find out exactly how to disarm this thing or those guys will be blown to kingdom come!"

7.50pm. Bill Albright saw the agents walking toward him from every direction. As he suspected his phone was bugged, there was no escape and there would be no justice or mercy.

He had committed treason and the penalty would be death. Under the circumstances there would be no trial to embarrass the current administration. He doubted that he would last the day and he was right.

He quickly sent a text to Mary: *I did the right thing. Love you so much xxx*. Within seconds of pressing 'send' Bill was dead.

7.52pm. "I'm afraid he's not answering his phone," said the lieutenant. The general was not surprised. Bill has signed his own death warrant the moment he made the call. Chances are, he wouldn't have known how to disarm the device anyway.

In less than forty minutes the plane's fuel would run out. It would glide for a while without its engines but it would descend to 20,000 feet within minutes. He knew the flight was probably doomed but he owed it to everyone on board to try disarming the bomb.

He would have one of his bomb disposal team try to talk the captain through the procedure, but the reality was that the device would have a failsafe. As soon as the cabinet was opened the bomb would most certainly detonate. The general's main concern was to make sure that the plane was far enough away to do as little damage as possible. He wished, however, that there had been enough fuel to direct it to Washington DC.

Chapter 82

7.52pm. As the Dean reached inside his new combat jacket, pretending to extract the trident, John kicked the gun from Andrew Smith's hand. The cloned intelligence officer dived forward in an attempt to grab the harbour master's throat but Caesar reacted quickly. He pushed his friend aside and punched Smith right in the face.

The clone fell to the ground and Caesar immediately pounced on him, grabbing his head and tearing it from his body. He then threw it in the elevator and pressed a button on the tunnel wall, which sent the disembodied head up to the ground floor.

John and the Dean looked at Caesar with new admiration. It seemed the angels had given him some of their *own* DNA!

"We have to get to the briefing room," said the Dean. "Sir Gareth is probably still there and we have to stop him before he kills the Deputy Prime Minister and the rest of COBRA." They ran into the tunnel just as Sir Gareth's clone emerged from the shadows and took out his mobile phone.

"They don't have the trident, sir, it's probably still on the helicopter."

"I hope you killed them!" Liberius was furious. He had heard that the plane carrying the nuclear device had been diverted and now the trident was still not in his possession.

"I'm sorry Emperor, they're all still alive, and they have someone with them who had the strength and power to tear off Andrew's head."

"That could only be the work of the angels!" he said under his breath.

"But don't worry," said Sir Gareth's clone. "There are more than thirty of your legionaries waiting for them in these tunnels. They'll never make it out alive and when we've killed them, we'll slaughter everyone in the briefing room, just as soon as your deadline expires."

"I am tired of waiting. Forget the deadline. The killing begins now!"

Chapter 83

7.55pm. Flight LH933 was now 300 miles off the south coast and Captain Saltzmann, was beginning to realize that his fate was probably sealed. The fuel had just run out and the plane had begun to glide. No one had called him back. He had told his co-pilots of their situation ten minutes earlier and they had agreed to keep their eyes on the instruments in the flight deck while they called their wives and had, what could realistically be, their last conversations.

He had just told the cabin crew that the fuel injection system had failed and they were going to have to bring the plane down on the ocean. It was something they had trained for many times, but thought would never happen. While they tried to calm and prepare the passengers, Captain Saltzmann knelt in front of the catering trolley waiting for the call.

When the phone eventually rung, it was Corporal Justin Cloverfield, who assured him that together, they would disarm the nuclear device. The Captain told him that they had just five minutes before the plane reached 20,000 feet. He'd managed to unscrew the front panel without incident, and was now facing a mass of wires and circuitry. Cloverfield asked him to describe what he saw. Given more time he might have found a way to transmit the images using satellite links but time was something he had preciously little of.

"OK," said Cloverfield, "I think we now have a good idea of what we're dealing with, so you need to follow my instructions carefully. You have identified the four wires coming out of the altimeter display and you have said there was one black, one yellow, one brown and one red, it that correct?"

"Yes, that's correct." He wiped the sweat from his eyes and looked at the altimeter: it now read 23675. When they dropped another three and a half thousand feet, or so, the bomb would explode. At their current rate of decent, he estimated they now had about four minutes left.

"And it is the black cable that leads to the battery pack, is that correct?"

"Yes!" he shouted. He was understandably starting to panic.

"Cut it," said Cloverfield.

"Are you sure?"

"I'm sure Captain. The altimeter will be disabled and the bomb will definitely not go off. Cut the black wire now!"

With a shaking hand Saltzmann did as he was asked.

The flash of white light could be seen all across the south of England, as could the large mushroom cloud that followed.

8.00pm. Liberius cursed. He was still alive and so were the millions of Britons that were infesting this island. He would now have to begin the laborious task of wiping them out one by one until they surrendered to his rule. It might take months, possibly years, but it would be eventually accomplished. He would have his revenge and succeed in conquering Britain where Nero and Caesar had failed. That is if the Americans, or even possibly the Chinese, didn't succeed in nuking them first, especially when his legionnaires started appearing on the other side of the Eurotunnel, as they would anytime now.

He had discovered that the British Government was as stubborn as Boudicca had been two thousand year earlier. Like her, they would never surrender, but he was not about to repeat the mistakes he made back then. Ironically, letting Boudicca live had resulted in the death of his family and it had taught him an important lesson that had shaped the rest of his life: *No mercy, never, under any circumstances!*

"Begin the slaughter!" he shouted.

Immediately his immortal army began to awaken from their passive state. They began to stare at the servicemen and police that were surrounding the park, choosing targets for their preliminary attack. Then they all began to sprint towards their hapless victims who were unanimously caught off guard.

Swords and spears were held aloft as they charged. Their roars struck their intended victims with a paralyzing terror. They barely had a chance to raise their guns when the Romans fell upon them hacking and stabbing in a wild frenzy, then feeding on the fresh meat.

The Romans then looked up at the guests, cameramen and reporters who were still observing them from the windows of the surrounding hotels. They charged across Park Lane and dived through the doors and large plate glass windows into the lobbies, slaughtering the staff and guests who were unfortunate enough to be there, and in the adjacent bars. Then the Romans charged up the staircases and began ripping open hotel room doors and devouring the occupants. They found their victims under beds, behind shower curtains, in baths and even cowering in the corners of wardrobes. It became a massive game of hide-and-seek, where the losers died a horrendous death.

When they ran out of food they dived from the windows, falling as much as twenty-eight floors - in the case of the London Hilton - onto the street below. Then, they immediately got to their feet looking for more sources of nourishment.

Liberius received word that the Resistance were now streaming up the Mall, past Buckingham Palace, heading towards Hyde Park Corner. He therefore directed his army to cut them off and cut them down.

More army trucks began to roll towards the park in an attempt to contain the Romans, but even with steel plating strong enough to withstand roadside bombs and heavy ordnance they could not keep out the marauding zombies who made short work of the drivers and their companions. It seemed that the British Army was the only organization still delivering 'meals on wheels'!

Liberius had to admit that things were going remarkably well, and resistance was almost non-existent. His men would enter Westminster in a matter of minutes and slaughter all of the politicians, including the COBRA committee, then, they would attack Buckingham Palace and kill the Royal family. This would effectively make him the unchallenged Emperor and supreme ruler of Britain, whether the people liked it or not, at least until the bombs began to drop.

There was just one hurdle he still had to overcome, and it was hovering above him. Fortunately, his mercenaries had brought along a rocket launcher and were now aiming it directly at the helicopter. "Fire!" he shouted. At this range, he knew the pilot would not be able to outmanoeuvre the missile.

Chapter 84

8.05pm. John and the Dean were making good progress through the tunnels with Caesar watching their backs. He had pointed back into the darkness many times; making it plain they were being followed. He had clearly wanted to go back and kill whoever or whatever it was but they did not want him to leave their side.

They had travelled about five hundred yards when the tunnel divided into two and there were no signs to give them any indication which way led to the Briefing Room, not surprising for a top secret location! They pondered for a minute or two, which tunnel to choose or whether they should, in fact, split up and take them both.

The Dean decided they should take the left tunnel. John, however, argued that if the left tunnel was the wrong one they would probably never get to the briefing room in time. He suggested that they split up.

The Dean shrugged, "I'll go left and you two go right."

"No way," said John, "I'm SBS-trained. Caesar goes with you."

Caesar nodded his agreement, put his arm round the Dean's shoulder and led him into the left tunnel. They then started to run, though the Dean found it hard to keep up, with his back and head still extremely painful from his fall from the dome earlier that day. John took off down the right tunnel, followed shortly after by Sir Gareth's clone who was determined to tear the harbour master apart.

8.10pm. "How much longer do you expect me to wear these ridiculous headphones?" shouted Alison, extremely annoyed that she had been excluded from their private conversations. No one acknowledged her, not even the pilot by her side and she was exasperated.

Sam's attention was riveted on Jessica who was removing her blouse and trousers revealing a black, skin tight, one-piece costume with the head of a silver trident pointing to the left, moulded just below her breasts. He could see that it resembled a 'B', for Britannia no doubt.

"Whose idea was the superhero costume?" Sam asked, unable to take his gaze from her. Jessica smiled at him, enjoying the attention.

"It is purely practical," said Ackerman, almost defensively. "Not only does it give her complete flexibility of movement, it is also temperature-controlled and, bullet or laser proof. It was developed by our former friends at MI5."

Jessica placed the helmet on her head and took up the shield and trident, just as the helicopter began to hover above Hyde Park. She slid open the fuselage door just as the pilot yelled "Incoming!"

Sure enough a surface-to-air missile was heading straight for them.

Without hesitation she pointed her trident in its direction. A fork of whitish blue lightning leapt from her weapon and struck the missile, which immediately exploded. For a moment the pilot wrestled with the helicopter to steady her against the resulting shockwave. Jessica lost her balance and was about to fall through the open door when Sam, who was still strapped into his seat, just managed to grab her shield arm and hold it firmly.

"There you go Sam, saving my life all over again!"

"No I didn't, if you'd have kept hold of the shield you would have survived the fall."

"And if I hadn't? Sam, when are you going to realize that you're as crucial to this mission as any of us?"

"There he is!" shouted Ackerman, pointing to a large man dressed as a centurion and wearing the robes of an emperor. He was riding a huge, black stallion and pointing directly at them. He was surrounded by mercenaries, convicts and Roman soldiers.

Jessica aimed her trident at him and released another firebolt. Liberius saw it coming and raised his shield. The bolt hit the shield and threw him from the horse but he quickly got back to his feet and started shouting and cursing.

"It's no good," said Jessica. "I have to get down there and battle him face to face. It's the only way I can locate the amulet and destroy it. Liberius obviously has some powerful relics of his own to use in his defence."

"How's the leg, Sam?" Ackerman asked.

He unbuckled his restraints and tentatively put his weight on the damaged ankle. "It hurts like hell but I'll be able to walk. I'll take on the mercenaries as best I can, though I doubt I'd be much use against the Romans."

"Sounds like a plan," said Ackerman. "I'll fight beside you and give you as much protection as I can."

"Let's get down there," Ackerman instructed the pilot.

The helicopter started to descend.

"What the hell are you doing?" Alison asked the pilot. "Surely you're not thinking of landing down there, the place is swarming with those monsters. We'll all be killed!"

"I'm sorry, I have my orders."

"Don't worry Alison," said Jessica. "He'll touch down just long enough to drop us off and then he'll take off again, you'll be fine."

"Thank God for that!" she said thinking only of herself.

As soon as the helicopter was within a few feet of the ground Sam, Ackerman and Jessica disembarked. The Romans and mercenaries, that were still in the park, swarmed towards them.

As the helicopter rose back into the air Sam and Ackerman stood to the right and left of Jessica, who had raised her shield and trident in preparation for the attack. It was time to make, what would undoubtedly be, the last stand.

Chapter 85

8.10pm. Whatever fear the Dean had felt on the dome of St Paul's Cathedral that morning, paled into insignificance compared with the fear he felt now.

Marching towards him, two abreast, were at least ten Roman soldiers. Their helmets and long swords kept glinting as they passed below each of the overhead tunnel lights. Their pace was brisk and the Dean was certain he would be unable to outrun them. He would certainly have tried, however, had he not spotted a similar number coming up from behind.

Caesar was looking in both directions trying to assess which group might be the easiest to overcome. He knew, however, that whichever band he chose to face, he would be leaving the Dean exposed to the other.

They both looked up at the tunnel roof to see if there were any ventilation shafts or ducts of any kind that they could escape through, but there was nothing.

"Let's carry on forward," said the Dean. "If this *is* the way to the briefing room we must try and get past them."

Immediately Caesar charged forward at an unexpected speed that caught the advancing Romans off guard. As he reached the first two soldiers he tore their swords from their grip and used them to remove their heads. He then continued forward beheading the next two rows before they could even raise their swords. By the time Caesar reached the fourth and fifth rows they were ready for him but no match for his superior angel-enhanced strength and with a matter of seconds he had disposed of them as well. He turned to see that the Dean had remained close behind but the pursuing solders were now just a few metres away.

He stepped between them and the Dean, who immediately clambered over the fallen Romans and ran on down the tunnel. As the first of their pursuers caught up with Caesar, he leant forward and roared. They stopped immediately, surprised to be confronted by one of their own. That moment of hesitation was all Caesar needed to disarm and decapitate them all. He then sprinted after the Dean hoping he would find his friend alive.

8.10pm. John knew he was being followed. Sir Gareth's clone was not particularly light on his feet. He scanned the walls and roof for somewhere to hide so that he could discover who was pursuing him and noticed an air vent high on the right-hand wall.

He carefully removed the grate with his penknife, pulled himself up inside and waited.

As soon as his footsteps stopped, those of his pursuer began to slow. It was several minutes before John saw who had been behind him. His first instinct was to jump down and confront his once friend, but he realized that, if Sir Gareth had been cloned, it would result in certain death. So, he let Sir Gareth pass below him, then, he lowered himself back in the tunnel, removed his shoes and followed him.

After a few minutes Sir Gareth reached a door with a keypad and thumbprint scanner. John was close enough to see the code being typed in, as Sir Gareth was slow and deliberate, but he knew that getting past the thumbprint scanner would be a challenge. As soon as the door began to close John ran over to it, hoping to prevent it from re-locking, but it clicked back into place just as he reached it.

He was just about to run back down the tunnel to grab one of Andrew Smith's thumbs when he began to realize how strange Sir Gareth's behaviour had been. He must have known that he was still in the tunnel so why hadn't he searched for him? He concluded that the clone must have been aware of others in the tunnel who'd been ordered to kill him. He turned abruptly and, sure enough, there behind him, were two mercenaries, and both had guns pointing at his chest.

8.15pm. The Romans had also been systematically searching Buckingham Palace and the Houses of Parliament in an attempt to assassinate the remaining leadership. The Royal family, however, had long since left and the politicians had never arrived that morning. Having seen the events unfold on the news, they had decided against travelling to Central London and cowered away in their London homes, constituencies or their lover's hotel rooms.

The only exception was Debra Cardy MP who, uncharacteristically for a member of parliament, had been working in Parliament throughout the night, answering letters from her constituents. The Romans found her in her small office on the second floor of Westminster Palace. Her letters would never be sent or read, as they were soaked in her blood but she gave a good account of herself battling to keep her attackers at bay until her heart ceased to beat.

The only other victims in these historic buildings were the administrative, security and domestic staff who were unfortunate enough to be working that day.

8.15pm. The London Resistance walked side by side, and, in some cases, hand in hand. Determined. Resolute.

Courageous. Liberius had indeed underestimated the British people. They marched on, fully aware that they were no match for the approaching Roman army, but willing to lay down their lives, if necessary, to try and protect their country and their people. They firmly believed that, given time, a solution would be found and their actions that day might buy those extra hours needed to give their families, their loved ones and their fellow countrymen, a chance to survive.

Even when they realized that they were being attacked from every direction their bravery and tenacity did not fail. These Britons' hearts had been forged in a crucible of courage over thousands of years, as generation after generation had fought to protect their small island against all those who would try to invade and conquer.

Slavery was never an option, death was always preferable, and because of that stoutheartedness and determination their nation has always remained free.

The Romans were descending upon them now on their right flank, across Green Park, and on their left, from across St James's Park. They were also flooding out of Buckingham Palace and climbing over the entire length of its garden wall, jumping on those Resistance members who were walking below, and tearing them apart.

The Romans were also charging up the Mall behind the Resistance cutting down those who were at the rear, and ensuring there was no possibility of retreat. The undead also met them head on as they reached Hyde Park Corner. The weapons the Resistance had brought with them were totally useless against these immortal soldiers, but still they fought on.

The Romans had effectively hemmed them in and now they began to slaughter them mercilessly, yet as one fell another stepped forward to take their place.

8.15pm. When the Dean and Caesar reached the end of the tunnel they came across a large steel door. They did not know the key codes and had no way of getting past the scanner but it proved to be of no consequence as Caesar broke through the door in seconds. When they entered the room to their dismay everyone was dead. The Dean searched the bodies but could not find the Deputy Prime Minister or any of the COBRA committee members.

"This can't be the COBRA briefing room," the Dean observed.

He searched further and found another exit that took them through to Trafalgar Square Station. There, they found the bodies of Sir Gareth and Andrew Smith.

The Dean knelt beside his friend and offered a short prayer. The body was very cold and rigor mortis had already set in. "He's been dead for some time. The Sir Gareth who ordered our deaths was definitely a clone." He told Caesar.

Caesar looked at him quizzically. The Dean felt he should explain.

"There seems to be two different types of Roman soldier," said the Dean, "well three if you count yourself, but you are clearly a one off. The first type regenerates its organs and body tissue from the DNA of those it kills, but it has no consciousness of its own. It is purely controlled by Liberius using some ancient relic that he obtained this morning. I guess that was what you were this morning, before you met the angels.

"The second type, also seem to be able to absorb the memories and consciousness of their victims. They are still under the direction of Liberius, but they have the ability to function independently as well. You met one of these when we entered these tunnels: the man whose head you tore off was the clone of Andrew Smith, former head of our secret service.

"Another clone has taken the place of my friend here, Sir Gareth Fraser, who was the Director of GCHQ, another of our intelligence organisations. He is now, most probably, in a meeting with our country's leaders, either killing them or preparing to.

"We need to go back and meet up with John, he must have taken the correct tunnel. Stay close to me Caesar!"

They ran back past the carnage in the Q-Whitehall control room and into the tunnels, returning to the junction were they had separated from John minutes earlier.

They had only just begun running down the tunnel John had taken, when they heard two gunshots.

8.15pm. Sir Gareth's clone looked, with hatred burning in his eyes, at the COBRA committee members. The first to notice his strange demeanour was Vince Jones, the Metropolitan Police commissioner. He felt an irrational fear when he looked at his colleague and immediately understood what must have happened. He placed himself between Sir Gareth and the Deputy PM but he was uncertain that he could do anything to protect her from the clone if and when it chose to attack.

"Is everything OK?" he asked Sir Gareth.

"You know it's not," the clone said menacingly as it moved towards the commissioner. The other members of the committee, who were sitting around the briefing room, now sensed the same fear that the commissioner had. They all rose, and edged slowly towards the exit.

"No point in any of you trying to escape!" said the clone. "There are more of us outside that door. I am afraid it is time for you all to die."

Karen Shaw was frightened, but unwilling to let her colleagues die on her watch. She wondered if the clone had absorbed more than Sir Gareth's memories - perhaps it had absorbed a little of his humanity too.

"Gareth, do you remember the time you and your wife spent with Steve and me last summer?"

The clone's expression softened a little. For a moment the thought of his wife had confused him and he felt less of a compulsion to kill. Karen realized she was getting through.

"Grace and yourself were so happy together that Steve remarked that you were acting like newlyweds," she said with a smile.

Sir Gareth looked troubled. His eyes darted about and his hand rose to his forehead. For a few seconds Karen actually believed that she could stop the clone from attacking, but she was wrong. Sir Gareth suddenly screamed and his face once more hardened. Liberius was back in control.

"As I said, it's time to die!"

He reached for the nearest committee member and grabbed them by the arm. With hardly any effort he tore it off and threw it across the briefing room table.

8.15pm. There was no way that John with all his SBS training could disarm both mercenaries without being shot. So he decided to bank on the fact that they were probably almost as scared of the Romans as he was. He pointed behind the mercenaries and shouted, "Zombies!"

Both of the mercenaries momentarily glanced behind them. That was all the time John needed. He grabbed one of the mercenary's guns and used it to shoot the other. Then he elbowed the man he'd disarmed in the face and as he stumbled backward he shot him in the chest. He checked their pulses - both were dead. As he picked up the other mercenary's gun he heard more footsteps running towards him. He spun round and simultaneously fired both guns back into the blackness of the tunnel.

Chapter 86

8.15pm. Jessica wielded her trident with the speed and grace that Ackerman had instilled in her. As row upon row of Romans attacked, she cut them down with the deadly lightning bolts emanating from her unique weapon. Every creature it struck exploded instantly leaving nothing but dust.

Sam and Ackerman were now crouching back-to-back firing at the mercenaries and convicts who were attacking from the flanks. The hours that Sam had practiced with his air pistol in his back garden as a child were paying dividends and almost every shot he fired was fatal. Ackerman's aim was also true and between them, they managed to eliminate Liberius's remaining mercenaries and many of the convicts in a matter of minutes, without either taking a bullet themselves.

Sam then spotted Liberius bearing down on him at speed on his black stallion. He stood while reloading his pistol then planted perfect shots into the tribune's face and chest, but they had no effect - the head shot passed straight through leaving a gaping hole, but not a drop of blood was shed. The chest shot just bounced off his breastplate, another of the occult relics no doubt.

Recognising that Liberius was indeed immortal, Sam aimed his third shot between the stallion's eyes. The beast instantly collapsed throwing its rider to the ground. Liberius rolled over and stood, in one movement, and then strode towards Sam with his sword pointing toward his throat. Sam tried to run from his path but his damaged ankle gave way and he fell on one knee. He looked up helplessly as Liberius raised his sword for a fatal blow. The sword, however, never made contact. Ackerman pushed Sam aside and took the blow on his own back. It cut open the Guardian's jacket and shirt but the blade did not pierce his flesh, he was now wearing similar body armour to Jessica. Sam guessed he must have put it on when they stopped to get Caesar's suit, it must have been in the rucksack he'd bought onto the helicopter when they had left Oxford. Ackerman spun round and faced his age-old enemy face to face.

"So the Guardian arrives once more to save the day!" sneered Liberius. "But I am afraid this time you and your Britannia are far too late. Your country has been discredited, your leaders are dead or dying, your people now understand the reality of evil and will live out the rest of their short lives in fear, and your little band of heroes are now trapped in the tunnels beneath us."

"You continue to underestimate the British people and their fighting spirit," said Ackerman. "Now give me the amulet, Liberius."

"What amulet?" the tribune asked.

"The one you have around your neck, the one you are using to resurrect and control your Roman army. Hand it over now!"

Liberius closed his eyes as if in deep thought, then suddenly two huge Roman soldiers appeared clawing their way out of the ground just below Ackerman. They instantly grabbed his legs and no matter how hard he tried, he could not break free.

"I know I can't kill you, just as you can't kill me but my centurions here will keep you captive while I dispose of this

Britannia and her pathetic boyfriend. You'll have a front row seat from which to watch their deaths!"

Liberius looked around for Sam but he was nowhere to be seen. Jessica, however, could not be missed; she was wiping out his army with ease. Liberius ran at her from behind. Ackerman screamed a warning, but she was already aware of his approach. As his sword fell upon her she glanced away the blow with her shield, which she had raised to cover the back of her neck. She then turned to face him and attempted to thrust her trident underneath his breastplate. He blocked her with his own shield and pushed her away.

There were still over a hundred Romans in the park and they were all coming to their master's aid. As Jessica stepped backward she saw the Guardian's predicament and was about to blast his captives with her trident when Liberius attacked her again. She blocked his sword again with her shield and released another lightning bolt that hit him full in the chest and threw him back several metres, but he immediately got back on his feet. Jessica realized, as Sam had done, that the breastplate Liberius was wearing was giving him supernatural protection. He advanced on her again and behind her the remaining Romans were only seconds away.

"Destroy the amulet Jessica, quickly!" shouted Ackerman. "It's around his neck!"

Unfortunately, as she raised the trident to strike, one of the Romans, who was now at her back, grabbed her arm with a vice-like grip that caused her so much pain that she dropped the weapon to the floor. The other Romans menacingly advanced toward the, now unprotected woman, and Liberius stepped forward to make the kill.

8.18pm. John was still crouching beside the two dead mercenaries and he was greatly concerned that despite his shots, the approaching footfalls continued to grow louder. He went to reload but found he was out of ammunition. Suddenly, two figures appeared from the darkness. John was about to run when he recognized the large frame of Caesar, and the much smaller figure of the Dean, who was trying hard to keep up with the Roman's pace.

"I 'm so glad to see you two!" said John.

"Is that why you were shooting at us?" said the Dean, rather put out.

"Sorry about that. I thought you were more of those mercenaries," he said, pointing to the bodies beside him. Caesar pulled him back to his feet and gave him a welcoming hug, which almost broke his ribs.

"Thanks Caesar" said John rather breathlessly. "Now, can you get us through this door?"

Caesar nodded and pulled it open with ease tearing apart the two-inch diameter bolts that had kept it locked. There were stairs leading up to the floor above; the problem was that a host of Roman soldiers were descending them, too many for even Caesar to deal with. He put himself immediately in front of his companions, but he knew that even if he could take down the first dozen, the rest would swarm around him and make short work of John and the Dean. So he did what he had to do. He entered the stairwell, closed the door behind him and leaned against it, hoping to give his friends, who were now alone in the tunnel, time to escape. What he didn't now was that more Roman Soldiers were now approaching from the opposite direction. They were surrounded and death was imminent.

Chapter 87

8.25pm. Jessica no longer had her trident and was about to be overcome by the rest of the Romans who were now almost upon her. She smashed the zombie that held her arm in the face with her shield but he held firm and wrenched it from her hand with his free hand. He then opened his mouth to bite deep into her neck.

Suddenly, the ground began to shake and she heard the sound of a large vehicle approaching. Sam had jumped into an abandoned Chieftain tank while Liberius was confronting Ackerman, and now he drove it into the Roman soldiers who were attacking Jessica. They were so focused on their victim, that they were caught off guard.

The soldier holding Jessica's arm released its grip and failed to take the fatal bite because its body had been caught under the tank's metal tracks. Liberius was also momentarily distracted by the advancing vehicle, which gave Jessica just enough time to dive to the floor and retrieve her trident. She aimed it immediately at the tribune's throat. The lightning bolt struck the amulet and it immediately disintegrated.

The Roman soldiers, who were now trying to tear the tank apart, also turned immediately to dust, as did those that were attacking Jessica. The two mighty centurions that were holding Ackerman captive, suffered the same fate, and their armour clattered to the floor.

In the tunnels below Whitehall, the soldiers who were beginning to overcome Caesar and about to tear John and the Dean apart also perished, much to the heroes' surprise and relief.

In the briefing room, Sir Gareth, who had already killed six of the committee members, was about to set upon Karen Shaw and the Police Commissioner when he too was vaporized, leaving nothing behind except for a wig and Sir Gareth's clothes and shoes.

Karen wept with joy and relief as she saw the Romans falling in their thousands on the video monitors all around her.

The London Resistance had fought resolutely and courageously, and only three quarters of their number remained alive. When their executioners started to collapse and disintegrate all around them some leapt with joy, punching at the air, but most fell to their knees and wept, thanking a God that they had really only just got to know, for delivering them. As they stood, they began to embrace one another and cheer loudly. An unbreakable bond had unified these incredible, ordinary people, in a matter of hours, as they had fought against this great evil.

Ackerman and Jessica fell upon Liberius, who was stunned by the blast to his throat, and they relieved him of his sword, shield and breastplate as well as the pentangle ring on his finger. Jessica immediately used the trident to destroy the relics, fully aware of their evil powers.

They then securely tied him and escorted him to their helicopter, which had just landed in the park to collect them. Jessica surveyed the battleground for Sam, and was not just relieved, but also overjoyed when she saw him emerge from the Chieftain tank that had mowed down her attackers. He took just a few steps before his ankle gave way again and he fell to the ground. Jessica ran over to him and helped him back to his feet.

"So you saved my life again!" she said, almost in wonder. Then she kissed him longer, harder and with more emotion than she had ever kissed another man before. Ackerman looked on from the helicopter with an approving smile. Alison was too busy staring at the restrained Liberius to even notice.

"Why on earth have you brought that disgusting creature on board? Throw him off now!" Alison demanded.

"We are taking him with us whether you like it or not Alison. If anyone should leave the helicopter right now it should be you!" responded Ackerman angrily. This woman was really getting on his nerves and there was something vaguely familiar about her that was extremely disconcerting.

"You would seriously consider leaving me on a battlefield full of dead, broken bodies and bomb craters? Are you mad? Besides which, I hear that there are still hundreds of escaped convicts on the loose! I am staying here in this helicopter and if you're going back to Kings Cross you can drop me off there. I suppose I can put up with this creature for a while, as long as you keep him under control."

Ackerman sighed, she had a point - it would probably be dangerous to leave her in Hyde Park and he knew that, if he did, he would never hear the last of it.

As soon as Jessica and Sam were on board the helicopter took off and headed back to what was left of King's Cross Station.

8.45pm. As the helicopter flew over London's West End, Ackerman called John's mobile phone. Being the Guardian had at times been a lonely task, but now he felt he had a true brotherhood to share his mission with. The Dean, John, Sam and yes, even Caesar, had proved by their actions that day, that they were all worthy Guardians, so he was extremely relieved when John answered his phone after just two rings.

"It's over John," said Ackerman. "We have Liberius. The amulet is destroyed and all of the Romans are gone. We're now on our way to Kings Cross to lock this mad man away forever. Are the Dean, Karen and the rest of COBRA ok?"

John began to answer but he was out of breath, "Hang on Alexander," he said. Then after taking some deep breaths he continued, "The Dean's fine, he's with me now. Not sure yet about the COBRA committee, we were attacked before we got there. We'll head there now and report back."

He then had a very disturbing thought that created an instant knot in his stomach. He ended the call and began to sprint back towards the door where they had left Caesar. The Dean ran after him - he'd heard the conversation and was pretty sure he knew what was going through John's mind.

If all the Romans had been destroyed, did that include their newest friend? Caesar had saved their lives on more than one occasion that evening and the thought that he was now, most likely gone forever, was a crushing one.

They reached the door and pushed it open. The floor and staircase was littered with Roman helmets, shields, swords, daggers and leather shoes all covered in a thick layer of dust. Nothing else was left, but there was also no sign of a tweed suit. Hope sprung in their chests as they ran up the steps.

When they got to the top of the staircase a corridor went off in both directions. One seemed to head west, presumably towards Downing Street and the Cabinet Office. This was presumably where the Roman soldiers had just come from. The other corridor headed east. John was sure that this would lead under the Ministry of Defence building and, therefore, to the COBRA briefing room. They ran in that direction and sure enough they came to another secure door. As they approached it opened.

Karen Shaw stood in the doorway extending a hand of greeting. "So you are two of the heroes who have saved our nation today. I and the rest of this country owe you an incalculable debt of gratitude."

"What have you been told and by whom?" asked the Dean.

"I just got a call from General Radford who has just arrived at Hyde Park. He told me that you two, with the help of a young MI5 agent called Sam Callaghan, had managed to defeat Liberius and destroy the relic that had brought those Roman soldiers back from the dead.

"There is no need to be so humble, gentlemen. You are national heroes. You have, in my opinion achieved as much, if not more than Nelson or Wellington whose tombs lie beneath your cathedral, Dean. Oh and I understand that you had a little help from your handsome friend here."

She opened the door fully to reveal Caesar shaking hands with the remaining members of the COBRA committee. As soon as he saw John and the Dean, he ran towards them, and hugged them both. This time, to their relief, he was a little gentler.

"Doesn't say much does he?" remarked Karen.

"Just one more thing," asked the Dean, "how does General Radford know what happened?"

"Someone called anonymously and told him. They said you would want to keep your role confidential because of your positions at the cathedral and in military intelligence, and I respect that. Only the members of this committee will ever know, and in the interests of national security and the reputation of the British Empire, my government and I will, of course, take all of the credit. Is that alright with you?"

"Yes of course," said the Dean, rather bemused. He knew full well that the anonymous caller was Ackerman. He fully understood that the role of the professor and Jessica in the day's events would have to be kept absolutely secret at all costs.

"In fact," continued the Deputy Prime Minister, "I am about to call the President of the United States right now. I think you might find our conversation extremely interesting, maybe even a little enjoyable. Excuse the bodies by the way!"

For the first time they noticed the ravaged remains of the six committee members who had been too close to the rampant clone.

"I have the President on the line, Karen," announced her secretary.

"Thank you Rose," she said taking the phone.

"Mr. President, so nice of you to take my call. I suppose you weren't expecting to hear from me again?"

"Of course I was Karen," said the President feigning a cheery disposition, "I had no doubt that you and your Cabinet would find a speedy and effective solution to the challenges you were facing there on your little island!"

"Look you patronizing, condescending son of a bitch. Before I make a series of heavy demands, which you will comply with in full, you need to know that we have tape recordings of conversations between our General Radford and your Defense Secretary, Bill Albright, who I understand has recently died from "natural" causes. These recordings have been verified as genuine and I am assured would hold up in any international court of law should those involved ever be charged with attempted genocide. Do I make myself clear?"

As the conversation continued, John and the Dean were dumbfounded by the events that had transpired without their knowledge, that could easily have resulted in the total annihilation of their country, and made all of their efforts that day of no consequence.

They listened intently as Karen Shaw laid down a series of demands, which expertly brought Britain from international pariah to its strongest position on the world stage since the end of World War II. In fact, she just came just short of forcing him to abolish Independence Day! They were absolutely certain that they were looking at the next Prime Minister.

The Dean left the room alone and said a silent prayer of thanks. *There are some things that are so evil only God can put them down,* he thought to himself, *but he gives us the tools we need to fight these battles ourselves, so that we can become stronger, braver and wiser.*

He looked over at Caesar who was undoubtedly one of those tools. "What are we going to do with him now?" he wondered. "Maybe Ackerman would know?"

Chapter 88

8.50pm. As the helicopter headed back to King's Cross Station, Liberius lay sedated and bound on the cabin floor. Ackerman sat over him staring intently at his prisoner, uncertain whether to hate him or pity him. Alison was made to sit once more in the cockpit with the headphones blocking out all external sound. She was not happy with any of them, even though they had probably saved her life.

Sam sat close to Jessica on the opposite side of the cabin to Ackerman and Liberius. "Why are we taking Liberius back to King's Cross with us?" Sam asked Jessica in a soft whisper. "Shouldn't we be handing him over to the police or the military, or something?"

"There are two reasons why we can't do that Sam. Firstly, we need to give the people a chance to heal. They need to start believing that this nightmare can be rationally explained, so that they will be able to sleep at night, and get on with their lives. The Government will come up with some cover story to explain the unexplained, probably along the lines of terrorism and biological weapons but while Liberius is on display that just won't wash.

"Secondly, although he deserves to die for his crimes, no one can kill him. So they will just put him in an institution or military prison, and one day he will escape and the nightmare will begin all over again. We know this for certain as it has happened before. You see, Liberius has friends in very high places, all over the world, and he also has unlimited financial resources. That's what comes of being around for two thousand years! So there are plenty of people he can call on to get him out of any facility. For example, we are pretty sure that he funded President Cluney's entire presidential campaign two years ago. That may explain the President's extreme actions today, though we can never prove it."

"So you're going to make him disappear somehow?" asked Sam rhetorically.

"That's about it. Under Boudicca's tomb there are other rooms and tunnels that the Guardian has created over the last millennia. One of those rooms is a secure facility where he can be locked away and never found. No one will know he's there except for us, so none will ever be able to come to his aid."

"So how are you going to explain away his disappearance?"

"We already have," said Jessica, "Ackerman just texted General Radford and told him that Liberius was destroyed along with the amulet. No one will be looking for him."

The helicopter touched down once more in the forecourt of what remained of King's Cross Station. Ackerman and Jessica said goodbye to Alison and the pilot and bundled Liberius out of the door.

Sam struggled to get to his feet.

"Wait here Sam until we get back," said Jessica, "and then we'll take you to St. Thomas's Hospital and get that snake bite properly looked at. I'd get the pilot to take you now but I'd really like to be there with you. We shouldn't be more than half an hour. Are you OK to wait here for me here?"

Sam sat down on the edge of the cabin floor and let his legs dangle over the side. It seemed to help the pain. "I'll be fine, just go and do what has to be done and be careful, there may still me more mercenaries or convicts out there."

"Don't worry, we'll be careful." She kissed him and ran to catch up with Ackerman, who was already forcing Liberius down the badly damaged staircase into the Underground below.

Sam desperately wanted to go with them, not wanting to let Jessica out of his sight for a moment, but his ankle was now swollen and the flesh around the wound was showing signs of decay. When he had put his weight on that leg, it caused him severe pain, so he knew he had to wait this one out.

He suddenly felt the need to call after her to tell her that he had fallen in love with her, but she was already disappearing from sight down the stairs to the underground. He felt he'd missed the opportunity and had a very uneasy thought that he might never have that opportunity again.

The pilot went off in search of a place to relieve himself and Sam was left alone with Alison, who had emerged from the cockpit and stood behind him.

"Don't turn round, I'm changing!" said Alison sharply.

"No temptation there," he said under his breath. "I'll guess you'll be off now Alison. Where are you heading?"

"That's none of your damn business!" she said with her usual charm.

"Sorry I was just concerned about your safety."

"I don't think so. I think your concern right now begins and ends with that whore of yours?'

Sam was taken aback - he knew Alison was rude, but that was way beyond the mark.

"How dare you talk about Jessica like that!" said Sam angrily.

"So you know the bitch I'm talking about then."

"Get out of this helicopter now and get on your way, you have most definitely outstayed your welcome!"

He turned around to face her and discovered with horror that she had indeed been changing. Another woman, wearing the same clothes, stood in her place.

She was tall and dark, exotically beautiful yet her large dark-brown eyes burned with an orange glow, as if a fire burned beneath them.

She brought her left hand from behind her back and revealed a dagger with a shaft of bone. He immediately recognized her and her weapon from Ackerman's story. "Rionna!" he exclaimed.

She pounced on him with the speed and grace of a panther. He threw himself from the helicopter but when his feet hit the floor, he immediately collapsed and fell on his face.

Before he could turn to face his attacker she had jumped on his back and, with one thrust of her knife, buried its blade deep into Sam's already fragile heart. She then ran toward the station in pursuit of Ackerman and Jessica.

Chapter 89

8.50pm. "Do you know this woman?" Vince Jones, the Police Commissioner, asked John and the Dean as he showed them a series of photographs and videos on his tablet. "She was seen in the vicinity of Kings Cross Station, where I believe you have spent much of the day."

"Yes, of course we recognize her," said John, "that's Jessica Pickering. She's one of Professor Ackerman's students."

"Why do you ask?" said the Dean suspiciously, keen to ensure that her role in today's events was never discovered."

"Well in short, this young woman is a cold blooded killer! While the Roman soldiers were running amok she was having her own killing spree in Islington. This shot is of her emerging from a pub where she had put her stiletto heel through an old man's skull. This is her walking away from breaking the neck of an Eastern European with an extensive criminal record, and finally this shocking video shows her breaking the neck of an elderly woman at an ATM. This girl is seriously twisted."

"She is not twisted at all, she is a hero and she was with us all of the time!" blurted out John before the Dean could stop him.

"Then how do you explain this evidence?"

"We can't," said the Dean immediately. "But we will contact Ackerman immediately and help you get to the bottom of this."

"You're not trying to protect this woman are you?" asked the Commissioner suspiciously.

"No. I can assure you we are not. Now if you will excuse us, we will speak to Ackerman and report back to you as soon as we have some answers." The Dean grabbed John by the arm and pulled him out of the briefing room. Caesar ran after them

"We have to get hold of Ackerman, Sam and Jessica immediately, their lives are in danger!"

"There is only one way that someone exactly resembling Jessica could have done those crimes, and that is, if that someone was Rionna?"

"Who the hell is Rionna?" asked John.

"An evil, shape-shifting witch, who has probably orchestrated much of today's nightmare. I think that we took her on board the helicopter unwittingly when she was pretending to be injured at Kings Cross Station."

"So Alison was a witch! I've got to say she certainly acted like one!" said John.

The Dean borrowed his phone again and called Ackerman as soon as they were back out on the streets of Whitehall but it immediately went to voicemail. They then tried Sam's phone and although it rang, it was not answered.

"We need to get to Kings Cross immediately," said the Dean. They looked up and down the streets but the only traffic were police and military vehicles. They tried to wave them down but they were completely ignored.

"Can you help us Caesar?" John asked.

Caesar nodded and stood in the middle of the road. The next car to pass was a BMW police car. As it approached Caesar, it slowed and started its sirens. When it was clear he wasn't going to move they pulled up in front of him and both officers got out of the car pulling out their extendable batons as they advanced on Caesar. They had had one terrible day and they were in the mood for a fight.

John and the Dean quickly ran to Caesar's side. Not that he needed rescuing, but they were afraid of what he might do to the police officers.

"What on earth are you guys playing at?" asked one of the policemen. "Don't you think we have enough problems to deal with right now?"

"We need your car," said the Dean getting right to the point.

"Not a chance," said the other police officer.

"OK then, just give the three of us a lift to Kings Cross Station, lives depend of it!"

"Look, I don't know who you think you are, but there are lives still in danger all over this city. The streets are full of the injured and dying. Why should you get any priority?"

"Because we have Caesar," said John nodding to his Roman friend. Caesar reached out and grabbed both officers simultaneously by their baton arms. They did their best to get free of his iron grip, they kicked and punched, tried nerve holds and one even managed to pull out a taser gun, which he was about to fire when he realized that it would just incapacitate all three of them. By the time they finally calmed down, the Dean and John were behind the wheel of their BMW and heading north up Whitehall, toward Trafalgar Square, with sirens blaring and blue lights flashing. Before they were completely out of sight Caesar let go of the officers, patted them on their heads and ran after the BMW. It took him just three minutes to catch up with them. When John saw him striding effortlessly beside the car he stopped to let him in. Five minutes later they pulled up beside the helicopter and found the pilot leaning over Sam's body.

"It's bad, I'm afraid!" said the pilot as they approached him.

"What happened?" said the Dean.

"I don't know, I just walked off for a pee and when I came back I found him like this. He's been stabbed in the back and judging by the position of the puncture wound and the amount of blood, I'd say it entered his heart. I've closed and sealed the wound using supplies in our survival kit, but he's barely breathing and his pulse is getting weaker by the minute."

"Did he say anything?" asked the Dean.

"He kept whispering a name and pointing towards the station."

"What was the name?" demanded the Dean

"Rhianna, Rionna. Something like that."

"I was right, Alison was the witch, Rionna. We need to get to Ackerman and Jessica before she does and stop her, and only one of us can do that." He turned to the Roman. "Caesar, the woman who did this to Sam is down in the underground trying to kill Jessica and the professor. You must get there as soon as you can and prevent her from doing so, but be careful, she can take on any female form; human or beast."

Caesar gave them a thumbs up and ran at incredible speed towards the staircase, jumping down the stairs in one single bound.

John immediately rang 999 but the line was constantly engaged. He tried two or three of his highest-level contacts in military intelligence, but no one was available. He couldn't even speak to anyone at MI5. "I can't get any help, everyone is too busy and he needs surgery now. Let's get him back in the helicopter and take him to the nearest hospital."

The three men carefully lifted him up and placed him on the cabin floor. The pilot then climbed through to the cockpit to start the engine, but there was no response. He tried again, still nothing.

"I think we've been sabotaged!" exclaimed the pilot.

"It's probably too late anyway," said John, "He's stopped breathing!"

John immediately began artificial respiration, "I'd say we have minutes before we lose him. Any ideas? Anybody?"

Chapter 90

9.00pm. Rionna's plan was coming together beautifully. In less than an hour Liberius would be free, Ackerman would be entombed in his own prison, Jessica and her boyfriend would both be dead and the trident would be destroyed forever.

Even if Jessica somehow managed to get away she was now wanted for multiple counts of first-degree murder, so she would have to remain in hiding for the rest of her life, or risk getting jailed for a very long time. After all who was going to believe her defence? *"I know it looks like me, but actually is was a shape-shifting witch who was trying to set me up!"*

She would also probably blame herself for leaving her boyfriend to an untimely death. How marvellous!

Rionna had watched Liberius's many attempts to overthrow the British Government over the years and each time the Guardian and his Britannias had gotten in his way. This time, she had decided to intervene, but she had done so without his knowledge, as she knew he would never agree to work with her.

Rionna had always known of the existence of the Amulet of Ankhef, in fact, it was her people, the evil Heka, who had created it in Egypt, over 5,000 years ago.

She had visited Liberius, in the form of a bitter old woman, a decade earlier and told him of the amulet's existence and where it was located, and together they had hatched the plan. He had been completely unaware that he'd been scheming with the woman responsible for the death of his family, and when she mysteriously disappeared he'd quite missed her. Rionna had spent a great deal of time with Liberius over the centuries, in various forms, but she needed him to love her in her true form, as she really was not as the women she had become. Besides which, shape-shifting was painful and tiring, and could not be maintained for more than a few hours at a time. She needed to convince Liberius of her loyalty, that way he would grow to love her, and the best way to do that was give him the two three things he wanted above all; the trident, Ackerman and the nation he despised even more than her.

She had no trouble passing the Oxford entrance examinations; after all, she had more knowledge than any other woman on the planet. As Isabella, she had quickly identified the Guardian's current Britannia and gone out of her way to become her best friend. She'd put up with Jessica for over a year and had patiently waited for Liberius's plan to come together. Now, she was in the perfect position to end this once and for all, in exactly the way she had planned. She would come to the rescue of a desperate, defeated Liberius, present him with the trident and the body of its bearer and offer him the Guardian to take his place in the underground prison. Liberius would be overcome with gratitude, see how much she loved him, and would agree to her terms. She would lift his curse and they would rule this island together.

A warmth passed through her body as she anticipated the fruition of a dream that had grown inside her since she first met the tribune almost two thousand years ago. A Heka witch will only ever love one man, and long ago she had chosen Liberius.

9.00pm. Jessica and Ackerman had secured Liberius in their underground prison. He was strapped and cuffed to a chair in a room that had been fitted with the very latest security systems. Unlike the "impenetrable vault" that had housed the relics below the Tower, this room had been designed, and in most part constructed, by the Guardian himself. Once the door was sealed no one would be getting in or out, ever. It would be Liberius's grave, although he would not be dead!

"This is inhumane!" shouted Liberius. "You can't just leave me here to rot!"

"Liberius, you cannot lecture us on inhumanity! You were prepared to kill over 60 million, mostly innocent, people today. Most people would agree that you deserve a slow and painful death, yet we cannot kill you. Instead we will just ensure you can't kill anyone else."

"You promised me you would save my family Guardian. You owe me!" shouted Liberius in desperation, straining against his bonds and contemplating an eternity in a metal box. Tears of anger and frustration flowed down his face. Jessica looked away.

"I owe you nothing," said Ackerman solemnly, although deep down he wondered if things could have been different. He had played that fateful day over and over in his mind to see if there had been anyway that he could have kept his promise and saved Liberius's wife or child, and the possibilities had plagued him.

Jessica picked up the relics and they were about to leave the detention unit and seal the door when they heard frantic shouts emanating from the tunnels.

"Jessica, Jessica, it's Isabella. Where are you?"

Jessica ran out to meet her. "Isabella, what are you doing here?"

"I came back to the train station trying to find a way home when I saw a helicopter outside. The pilot called me over and asked for my help."

"Why, what has happened?"

"He told me to tell you that Sam had been stabbed and it looks pretty bad for him." Jessica didn't waste time with any further questions and she ran from the room, eyes filling with tears.

"Be very vigilant" shouted Ackerman, "something is very wrong here!"

"So Isabella, how did you find the tomb and make your way through these tunnels?"

"You left the front door open and you clearly forgot to reset your little booby traps. Shoddy work for the Guardian!"

"What do *you* know of the Guardian?" he asked, suspicions rising.

"A great deal, we met many years ago, if you remember. When you, and Liberius here, were tied to posts just outside St Albans. I thought then that I'd saved your life, I've since learned that you are another immortal."

As Isabella changed to Rionna before his eyes the memories of that fateful day came flooding back. He remembered the witch's visit after the execution of Helena and Flavius and how she had tried to excuse the role she'd played in framing Helena for Alvena's death. He had never once suspected that she had any involvement in today's events; now, he suspected that her role might prove to have been the most crucial of all.

Rionna dived at Ackerman and grabbed him by the throat. Her strength was incredible and Ackerman's head began to spin as the supply of blood and air to his brain were cut off. As he drifted into unconsciousness, Rionna whispered in his ear, "When you recover, you will find yourself incarcerated in this cell. Jessica and Sam will be dead and your so-called 'holy' relics will be lost forever. Sleep on that Guardian!"

Chapter 91

9.10pm. Jessica raced through the tunnels, climbed the stairs to the tomb level and then leapt over the snake pit. As she arrived on the other side she had barely taken a few strides when her path was suddenly blocked by a huge, imposing figure.

"Caesar, why are you here?"

He did his best interpretation of an evil witch, but charades was not his strong point.

"I'm sorry, I don't understand. Have you seen Sam?"

He nodded and looked very sad. He stabbed himself in the back with an imaginary knife and when he saw her horror he hugged her and felt her body tremble in his arms.

"I must go to him," she said gently pushing Caesar away. "If you are looking for Ackerman take the stairs at the rear of the tomb. When you get to the bottom, turn left and keep going, you'll find him in a room on the left with a large steel door. He's with a friend of mine called Isabella"

Caesar's face showed panic and he started to shake his head frantically.

"What's wrong Caesar?" He again tried his witch impression.

"Is there something bad in the tunnels?"

He nodded.

"And it has to do with Isabella?"

He nodded again and repeated his impression.

"Isabella's in danger?"

He shook his head.

"Isabella is the danger?"

He nodded frantically.

"Are you saying that it was her that stabbed Sam?" she asked incredulously.

He nodded somberly.

Jessica was stunned and torn. Did she run to Sam or return to rescue Ackerman?

"Are John and the Dean with Sam?"

He nodded and pulled her towards the tomb. It seemed that Caesar had made the decision for her. She prayed it was the right one.

9.15pm. "After two thousand years you come back to rescue me?"

"I have never been far away," Rionna told the Liberius.

"How did you know I was here?"

"Like I said, I've never been far away."

"Get me out of here!" Liberius demanded straining at the bands on his wrists and ankles.

"And in return?" she asked.

"What do you want?"

"You know what I want, it's what I've always wanted."

Liberius recognized an opportunity. He would give her what she wanted for a while anyway. Then he would find a way to kill her. He didn't care that she was here to save him; she had caused the death of the only woman he had ever truly loved, and he hated her for it, just as much now as on the day Helena had died.

"You still want me?"

"Why else would I be here?"

"Then release me from these bonds and from this curse and I will be yours. I promise!" Promises meant nothing to him.

Rionna was overjoyed; it was all she had hoped for. She kissed him gently on the lips and immediately his wounds began to heal and the pains he had endured continuously for two thousand years instantly left him. Liberius felt a euphoria, unlike anything he had experienced in his long life, a moment of joy that he had not felt once since the death of his family. Rionna believed that it was her kiss alone that had caused the happiness that was now clearly evident in the tribune's eyes and she hurried to release him, tearing away the bonds with her bare hands.

Liberius stood and looked at his reflection in the large window of ballistic glass that made up one of the cell walls. He saw himself exactly as he was before he had the misfortune of meeting the witch.

"Am I still immortal?" he asked

"Of course, how else will you live with me for eternity?"

He smiled knowingly - maybe today would not turn out to be a complete disaster after all.

"Let's bind up Ackerman and seal him in his own tomb," said the witch. "Then together, we'll kill Jessica and take their relics once and for all."

Caesar and Jessica arrived at the cell just as Liberius and Rionna left the cell room. Jessica's first instinct was to let loose with the trident, but the likelihood was that her actions would bring hundreds of tons of rock and dirt down upon their heads. In this enclosed space she had to be careful. Rionna reacted without a moment of hesitation. She kept her burning red eyes on her quarry as she instantly transformed into the great black she-wolf, almost filling the entire width of the tunnel. Jessica had barely raised the trident when it pounced upon her.

Caesar immediately threw himself between Jessica and the beast encircled its neck with his long muscular arms, trying desperately to keep his head away from its powerful, snapping jaws. Its claws tore at his flesh but still he held on, trying to crush her throat and break her neck. As they fought Jessica raised the trident, it howled with fury and then, by pushing forward with its hind legs, it managed to grab the trident's shaft in its teeth and tear it from Jessica's hand. It then shook its head from side to side trying to impale Caesar.

The Roman, however, would not let go; even though the flesh on his back had been torn to shreds by the beast's claws, and his left shoulder was being constantly pierced by the trident. He finally felt his way through the creature's thick coat of fur and managed to grab hold her windpipe with his left hand. He then crushed it with all the strength he could muster until he heard it crack.

As the beast weakened, he pulled the trident from the beast's mouth and handed it to Jessica. He then leaned backwards pulling the creature off of the ground and exposing its chest. Jessica thrust the trident between its ribs. The entire chest cavity took on a blue light, which momentarily exposed its entire ribcage, like some kind of monstrous X-ray. Then the she-wolf exploded into dust. Rionna was dead. but echoes of her destruction were sensed by the Heka in every corner of the earth and their evil eyes were all immediately turned to London.

Caesar fell onto his back and as he rolled over onto his hands and knees, Jessica saw the terrible wounds on his back, but still he would not rest. He got immediately to his feet and surveyed the tunnel in both directions. Liberius had gone. They ran into the detention cell but he wasn't there either. Caesar tore the restraints from Ackerman who was rapidly regaining consciousness.

"What happened?" the professor asked.

"The witch is dead," said Jessica, "but I'm afraid Liberius has gotten away. Are you OK?"

"Of course, I'm fine, just a little embarrassed that I let Rionna get the better of me. Where's Sam?"

"My God, Sam!" Jessica ran from the room taking her trident with her. Ackerman and Caesar followed.

As she emerged from the station she saw the Dean and the pilot standing by the helicopter, with heads bowed. John was leaning over Sam, alternatively breathing into his mouth and pounding his chest. Blood was everywhere. John was crying unashamedly. He knew his actions were futile, but he wanted to keep him alive until Jessica got there. Those that could, looked up as Jessica arrived, with Ackerman and Caesar close behind.

"I'm sorry Jessica," said John tearfully. "We did all we could!"

Jessica jumped onto the helicopter and laid down the trident carefully while she leaned over Sam. John stepped down to join the others and they all stood around mournfully watching Jessica's heartbreak.

She cried openly as she kissed him softly on the lips. She then ran her fingers though his hair and down the side of his face. When she reached his neck she placed her finger on his carotid artery.

"There's a slight pulse. He's still alive!" she shouted.

"A slight pulse yes, but in a minute or two it will be gone," said John. "There is nothing that can be done Jessica. He's lost too much blood."

"But there is something that can be done," she said excitedly. "Alexander, you know there is!"

"Don't even consider it!" Ackerman demanded.

"I have to. He saved my life so many times today. Now I have to save his!"

"What's she talking about Ackerman?" asked John.

The Dean spoke for him. "It's the trident, it can be used to save Sam's life, but at a very high price."

"What price?" asked John.

"If Jessica uses the trident to save Sam's life it will take her life in return. It will transfer her life-force over to Sam," Ackerman explained mournfully.

The full realization of Jessica's dilemma hit each of the men hard. Sam or Jessica had to die that evening and the decision was in her hands. The Dean prayed for her. John considered taking the trident and the decision from her. Ackerman waited and watched, wondering if he could bear to let this happen all over again.

Most people would just let nature take its course, after all, Sam was practically dead anyway, but Jessica felt wholly responsible for his predicament. She had led him into the tomb where he sustained the snakebite and she had left him in the hands of Rionna to be stabbed in the heart. In contrast, Sam had repeatedly saved her life. Now she felt she had to do the same for him.

But she did not want to die. She desperately wanted to live, to graduate, to marry, and to have children and grandchildren. But could she live knowing she had let Sam die? The decision had to be made immediately, once Sam's heart ceased to beat for any length of time and the brain was starved of oxygen it would be too late.

If only she could just have time to say goodbye to her parents and sisters, but she didn't. Would they understand? Would they feel she had done the right thing, or would they feel that she had deserted them? Would they hate Sam and hold him responsible for her death?

Ackerman knew Jessica all too well. He understood what she was thinking and he was pretty sure what conclusion she would eventually reach. "You can't do this my child! You're only twenty years old, you have your whole life ahead of you!"

"So should Sam!" She started crying uncontrollably as she reached for the trident. "I'm sorry everyone but I can't live without him and I just can't let him die!"

With tears pouring from her eyes, she raised the trident high above Sam's chest and as she brought it downward everyone reached forward to stop her.

- THE END –

The sequel 'The Britannia Contagion'

will be published in December 2014

The Britannias

July 1588. Ramon Almeida Sanchez spent the last few hours of his life, cooped up in a crow's nest on the foremast of The São Martinho. This magnificent galleon had just valiantly defended the Spanish Armada against the English fleet in Northern France, and was now limping back towards Spain having sustained significant damage from canon fire.

When arriving at Cadiz, the São Martinho would get vital repairs and load much needed supplies, before returning to battle. With 48 heavy guns on two enclosed gun decks, this was undoubtedly one of the most impressive vessels in the Spanish fleet and essential for the campaign's success.

The sea was relatively calm and morale was high, after all, they'd received a blessing from the Pope, so victory was assured. The Spanish believed that this was not a war but a Holy Crusade and God was undoubtedly on their side.

Ramon didn't believe a word of it. He was born a Catholic but had taken a different path many years earlier. Tired of constant hunger, he had taken to theft, then murder, several murders in fact. 'Razor' Ramon was being sought all over Lisbon, so he had decided one night to stowaway on the São Martinho, which had recently arrived from Spain and was on its way to England.

When the crew found him, their first instinct was to throw

him overboard, as they did with most stowaways. But when they saw the speed at which he clambered up the rigging to make his escape, they decided they could make good use of him.

The sun had just set over the horizon and as the sky darkened it started to rain. Suddenly, Ramon spotted the silhouette of a ship bearing down on them at speed on their stern. He could just make out the flag which bore the reviled cross of St. George, so he shouted a warning to the helmsman. Moments later he heard the galleon's captain order his men to load the canons in anticipation of an attack.

As the enemy vessel approached, the lookout's eyes were drawn to the ship's figurehead, which was in the shape of a beautiful, young woman, with a full figure and long, raven black hair. She was carrying what looked like Neptune's trident in one hand and a shield in the other.

A streak of lightning tore through the sky, illuminating the ship in an unearthly blue glow. In that brief moment it seemed to Ramon that the figurehead was moving, her dress flowing around her legs and her wet hair blowing in the wind.

He was sure it was just a trick of the light, but as he strained his eyes against the darkness, he saw the woman rise from the prow and point her trident toward his ship.

The scene was illuminated by another lightning bolt. But this one didn't descend from the heavens, but travelled horizontally from the trident to the foremast in which he sat. The wood splintered and the mast broke in two, falling to the deck with sails ablaze. As Ramon fell to his death he realized that, despite the Pope's blessing, the Spanish Armada was doomed to fail. The Gods had chosen the other side.

November 1888. Mabel stood on the streets of Whitechapel in the early hours of the morning, in an area infamous for prostitution and all kinds of nefarious behaviour. She was dressed perfectly for the part in a blue linsey frock, which showed ample cleavage and a long, red, coarse twill cloak. Her smooth, brown, unblemished skin made her stand out significantly from the other women plying their trade there in the dead of night.

The thick London fog rolled through the narrow, cobbled streets and the gas lamps were proving to be totally inadequate. Someone could get within a few yards of these women totally undetected.

Everyone was understandably on edge due to the barbaric murders of East End prostitutes that had plagued the Spitalfields area over the last few weeks.

The latest victim, Mary Kelly had been brutally mutilated sending shock waves throughout the profession. The girls who still worked the streets now kept each other in sight at all times, but many had made the decision that life in the work house was now more preferable than life on the game.

At 2.23am, Mabel was approached by a tall, skinny, well-dressed man with a large, beak-like nose, a small handlebar moustache and dark, cruel eyes. Mabel knew instantly that he was the one they called 'Jack'.

He asked her if she would like to take a walk with him and she readily agreed. The girl beside her gave her a concerned look but Mabel assured her with a smile that she would be OK.

The man led her into a narrow alleyway and immediately pushed her up against the cold, damp brick. He looked menacingly into her eyes as he held her by the throat with one hand and with the other removed a long serrated knife from his belt. He expected to see the look of fear across the woman's face but instead she smiled.

"Is that all you've got sonny?" she said mockingly as she withdrew a trident from under her cloak and thrust it into his abdomen. The cruel eyes misted over, blood ran from the corner of his mouth and he collapsed to the floor. With another thrust of the trident the body burst into flames and within seconds there was nothing left, other than a pile of dust, which tumbled away in the wind across the cobblestones.

It served her purposes that no one knew of his death. For a while, at least, the fear of the Ripper would keep many vulnerable girls off the street. She wrapped her cloak around her once more and disappeared into the night.

August 1918. Private James Farnell of the British Fourth Army was hurriedly writing home from a waterlogged trench on the Western Front, near Amiens. At any moment they would be told to stand by the ladders, and when the whistle blew they would climb out into no man's land and certain death.

German ordinance had been flying over their heads since 4 am and without exception the men were terrified. James told his mother how much he loved her and missed her. He told her that although he wouldn't be coming home, she should be brave, and he assured her that he would always be watching over her and his little sister Peggy.

As the order came, he hastily signed his name, put the letter in an envelope and tucked it away in his trench coat pocket. He held onto the ladder, shaking visibly as he imagined himself being caught up in barbed wire, repeatedly shot and left to die. Over a million young men like him had already fallen in this conflict and he knew he would shortly be part of that horrific statistic.

He closed his eyes and started uttering a final prayer, when the sound of gunfire suddenly decreased. To his immense surprise, it was replaced with a cheer, faint at first but quickly becoming a loud roar.

He opened his eyes to see the other men had left the ladders and had run to the back of the trench looking at the battlefield behind them. They were jumping up and down and shouting excitedly, and many were even wolf whistling. As he turned he expected to see a huge army of reinforcements supported by the Mark V tanks that were rumoured to be on their way.

Instead, all he saw was a lone woman wearing the khaki

uniform of the Women's Army Corp, charging towards them with a main of red hair flowing behind her. She held a circular shield in one hand, which deflected the odd bullet that flew her way. In the other hand she held nothing but an ornate, silver trident.

Her legs were long. Her stockings were torn in several places and covered in mud. Her face was also dirty, but it was stunning, and carried a look of sheer determination.

She raced at speed, and when she reached their trench she leaped over their heads, easily carrying herself over the ten-foot gap.

On she ran until she was just yards from the enemy line, then, she slowed and thrust her trident into the ground. The earth was torn apart and flames rushed through the crevice into the German trenches. The enemy screamed as they burned. Many got out of their trenches and ran. James and his men didn't wait for the whistle they climbed their ladders and chased after the fleeing Germans.

Tomorrow he would write to his mum again and tell her that the war had taken a dramatic turn. He was coming home after all.

September 1940. Flight Lieutenant Ian Swaffield of the 72nd Squadron ran across the airfield at Biggin Hill towards his Spitfire T MK VIII. He had just received a briefing that over 200 bombers with fighter cover had been spotted flying over Dunkirk en route to England, in the biggest air attack that the Luftwaffe had ever undertaken.

His squadron had orders to intercept the German formation near Maidstone, in South East England, and keep the Messerschmitt fighters from providing cover for their bombers.

As he approached his plane he was shocked to see that there was someone already seated in the cockpit. As a trainer, he was the only pilot with a two-seater Spitfire, but surely air command would not expect him to carry a trainee on a day like today!

He opened the cockpit, fully intending to tell his unexpected passenger to clear off, but he didn't. His passenger was a woman, an extremely beautiful blonde with a killer smile. He was immediately disarmed.

"Hi. I'm Lieutenant Swaffield," he said with a killer smile of his own.

"I know who you are," the woman responded. Then, making it clear that there was no time for small talk she said, "We'd better get going Lieutenant." She put on her helmet and oxygen mask before he could ask any questions.

"I thought you girls were banned from combat," he observed, but received no reply.

It took them just 20 minutes to meet up with the German bombers. At first there was no sign of their fighter cover, then suddenly hundreds of planes emerged from the clouds above. The Luftwaffe pilots wanted to take advantage of their superior numbers before further British squadrons arrived. Before Ian knew it, he had three Messerschmitt Bf109s on his tail.

He tried every technique he knew to shake them off but to no avail, and their gunfire came perilously close to his tail. Suddenly his passenger leaned over from behind him and started to pull back the cockpit covering.

"What the hell are you doing?" the Lieutenant screamed above the roaring wind.

"Mind your language," was the only response he got. Then to his horror she started to lean out of the window and look behind her.

"Get back in the plane you idiot, you'll get us both killed!" shouted the pilot.

"That is no way to talk to a lady!" she said in a rich, educated voice.

She then reached down between her legs and pulled out a trident, which she lifted out of the cockpit and pointed at one of the pursuing Bf109s. Immediately a fork of lightning flew from the weapon and the German fighter exploded, burning wreckage falling from the sky and spiralling to the earth below.

Seconds later the other two pursuers had suffered a similar fate. The Lieutenant couldn't believe what he was seeing as one by one the Messerschmitts burst into flames, giving their pilots no opportunity to bail out.

"Do we all get one of those?" he asked.

Meet the Britannias

The Britannias were used in propaganda posters during both World Wars to encourage men to enlist. The poster *(top left)* shows Britannia Catherine Huxley leading reprisal attacks on the German Navy in 1915 and *(top right)* supporting troops on the Western Front in 1917. The poster *(bottom left)* shows Britannia Nancy Crawford, who fought in the Battle of Britain and later in Dunkirk. Only those who fought beside them knew of the significant roles they played, and the relics they carried.

Monuments to the Britannias can be found throughout the British Isles. The impressive statue *(top)* can be seen outside St.Paul's Cathedral. The memorials *(bottom)* commemorate some of the Britannias' greatest victories and stand in remembrance of those heroes who tragically died fighting by their side, while defeating the Spanish Armada in 1588 *(left)*, and during World War One *(right)*.

The Britannias sit or stand proudly on many of Britain's most historic buildings. This impressive sculpture (bottom) of the first Britannia, Boudicca, riding her chariot with her daughters, stands right opposite the Houses of Parliament of the north side of Westminster Bridge.

From Roman times to the present day the Britannias have been honoured and memorialised on British coins, bank notes, gold and silver, in recognition of their courage & leadership during Britain's darkest hours.

Image Credits

Book Cover *(front)*	BFM/fotolia Pisaphotography/shutterstock YorkBerlin/shutterstock
Posters (Page 349) *(Top left to bottom right)*	© Imperial War Museums (PST 5109) © Imperial War Museums (PST 13959) © The National Archives UK (INF 3/129) © Imperial War Museums (PST 13276)
Statues (Page 350) *(Top left to bottom right)*	Tony Baggett/iStock BFM/fotolia RFStock/iStock
Statues (Page 351) *(Top left to bottom right)*	Honeybee_Photographic/iStock Steve Geer/iStock Chris Mansfield/iStock
Coins (Page 352)	PM/BritanniaPublications

About the Author

Peter C. Middleton was born in Lewisham, London in 1959 and at the age of twelve he went to a traditional English boarding school called Christ's Hospital in Horsham, Sussex.

He married his wife Debra in 1988, and now has four children, Gareth, Samuel, Emily and Lucinda and two grandchildren.

Peter still lives in South East London where he runs a successful video production company (OnlineTVGroup.com) and a publishing company (MyLifeBiographies.com) that produces wonderful biographies to ensure that the lives, loves, memories and achievements of our loved ones are never forgotten.

Peter is an avid Arsenal supporter (Come on you Gunners!), who loves writing, travelling, music and movies. He and his wife are also foster parents.

The Britannia Conspiracy is his first novel and he is greatly looking forward to writing several more books in this series featuring these same characters. This novel is primarily based in London and he hopes that the story may inspire more people to visit this incredible city.

To find out more about Peter and the Britannia books visit BritanniaConspiracy.com. You can follow Peter on Twitter at @petercmiddleton.

Acknowledgements

A lot of the history in the novel is based on fact. Boudicca, was indeed the courageous and inspirational warrior-queen of the Iceni tribe who, in AD61, defeated the Romans at St.Albans, London and Colchester. It is also true that she was defeated in the battle of Watling Street, thought her exact fate is disputed. There are legends that point to her burial at the site of Kings Cross Station, though they are highly disputed. This remarkable woman was the inspiration for this book.

I'd like to thank my daughter, Lucinda Middleton, who has faithfully read and edited every revision of this novel, making some wonderful suggestions to enrich the story. Thanks also to Anthony King, Haestella, Josie Briggs, and Kevin McKenna who have taken the time to read and edit the first full draft of this novel. Thanks to Antony Thorne for his advice on youth slang. Thanks to Ilian Georgiev who designed the dust jacket and Nural Akmal Markani who has drawn the maps and illustrations.

I am grateful to my wife and family who have put up with my inability to concentrate on little else but the plot over the last few months.

The next Britannia novel by Peter C. Middleton will be published in December 2014

THE BRITANNIA CONTAGION

Sam has miraculously made a full recovery from his terrible injuries, but emotionally he is a complete wreck. Having loved and lost twice in his short life, he spends every waking hour immersed in his work at MI5, especially in his attempts to locate professor Ackerman and his last love, Jessica Pickering, who have both mysteriously disappeared.

To make matters worse, the evil and powerful Heka are gathering in London to seek a terrible and devastating revenge for the murder of the witch Rionna. They have bought with them a seemingly incurable strain of the bubonic plague that causes death, in extreme agony, in a matter of hours.

With millions of Londoners dead or dying, Sam must rally together the same maverick heroes who defeated Liberius and his undead Roman army. Together they have to embark on another race against time to find out how to destroy the evil Heka, and stop the deadly disease from wiping out Britain's entire population.

To fulfill this seemingly impossible mission, they must find out how London survived the Great Plague of 1665 and discover the clues left behind by Sir Christopher Wren, Samuel Pepys and Sir Isaac Newton in the literature and architecture of this period.

Meanwhile Britain's enemies believe that another Great Fire, like that of 1666, is the only way to stop the Plague from leaving Britain's shores and spreading throughout the civilized world.

32181595R00208

Made in the USA
Charleston, SC
11 August 2014